Collected Stories, Volume II

By Mark Van Doren

POETRY

The Narrative Poems of Mark Van Doren—Collected and New Poems: 1924–1963—Collected Poems—Jonathan Gentry—A Winter Diary—Mortal Summer—The Mayfield Deer—The Seven Sleepers and Other Poems—New Poems—Spring Birth and Other Poems—Morning Worship and Other Poems—Selected Poems

FICTION

Collected Stories, Volume I—Collected Stories, Volume II—The Short Stories of Mark Van Doren—The Witch of Ramoth and Other Tales—Nobody Say a Word and Other Stories—Home with Hazel and Other Stories—The Transients—Windless Cabins—Tilda

NONFICTION

The Happy Critic and Other Essays—Henry David Thoreau—John Dryden—The Private Reader—Shakespeare—Liberal Education—The Noble Voice—Nathaniel Hawthorne—Introduction to Poetry —An Anthology of World Poetry—Don Quixote's Profession—The Autobiography of Mark Van Doren

DRAMA

The Last Days of Lincoln

Collected Stories
Volume II

by MARK VAN DOREN

 HILL AND WANG • NEW YORK

With the exception of twelve published here for the first time, the stories in this volume appeared in *The Short Stories of Mark Van Doren, Nobody Say a Word and Other Stories,* and *Home With Hazel and Other Stories.*

Manufactured in the United States of America by
American Book–Stratford Press, Inc.

Contents

v

Collected Stories, Volume II

Tregaskis Horror

THE SUDDEN DEATH of Harry Tregaskis had been the sensation of the town. Everybody said he was too young—only forty—to go like that, by heart failure in his sleep. Too young, too happy, and too handsome. In the old house, too, where it was assumed that he would some day have a wife to share its quaintness. His father's house, that he had never changed. He entertained his friends there with such cleverness, such grace, such wry amusement as they wandered, drinks in hand, from room to incredible room, poking into this mystery, asking about that.

But there was even greater excitement over the news, announced on posters and in the columns of the *Bee*, that the Tregaskis place was to be auctioned with all of its contents. Harry had left it to Helicon College, where he was never a distinguished student, but he amply remembered it in his will. Everything he owned was Helicon's now, and the trustees were advised that an auction would be the best way to profit from their gift.

Everybody would be there this morning: everybody, said Lennie Harbaugh to his wife at breakfast, everybody but her. Why wouldn't she go? It was just down the street. It was a fine day. It might be fun.

"Fun!" Laura didn't look up from the letters she was reading. "Ghoulish, I would say. And of course we couldn't buy anything; I mean, we wouldn't."

"No? Well, I understand that. I hadn't even thought of it. But it will be our last chance to see his place as it was. Tomorrow, or the next day—"

Laura folded her last letter and slipped it slowly into the envelope. "You go," she said, "and tell me about it."

"But what will people say if"—he hesitated.

"If what?" she asked, a little sharply, trying to sound dull.

"If both of us don't go. All of his friends are, and we were nearly the best." He watched her with a care he took pains to conceal.

"We *were* the best. That's why—don't you see?"

"Actually, I don't." He knew it was dangerous to press her. He knew what she was thinking: her lover was dead, and she could not bear to be where he had been, where they had been, so many afternoons, so many nights. Lennie knew all about that, and nobody knew he knew. Certainly not Laura. Or he thought she didn't. Otherwise, would she always have been so frank about her feeling for this one man in her life? That man was not himself; it had been obvious for years, and to him alone among their many acquaintances. In public she could seem very fond of her husband and of his good friend Harry; she could even make it appear that Harry was her good friend just because he was Lennie's. When all the time—but it was dangerous to press her now. She might suddenly break down and tell the truth. The truth was the last thing Lennie wanted to hear.

He had lived so long with his lie: that he didn't suspect. He had worked at deceiving her, and worked well—oh, all those times when he contrived that she and Harry should be together, without either of them guessing how much he wished it, how much he luxuriated in the thought—of what? Of their being together? No, he had always told himself, not quite that; though there was nothing he didn't imagine. No, it was rather in the thought that neither of them knew he knew. He had worked at deceiving Harry, too, and that was even harder. But he was sure he succeeded.

Then these weeks since Harry died. What had happened to make his own life so pointless, so empty? Laura could say of him, and almost every day she did: "Lennie misses his old friend terribly; he's not himself at all; he doesn't seem to get over it." Perhaps she believed this, and was glad to, since it left *her* secret safe. Whereas it wasn't anything like what she said. He missed his old friend for the same reason she did. They couldn't be together any more, she and Harry, with him pretending that he didn't know. The pleasure he took in that pretense had grown, he now knew, into something more delicious than food, than drink, than love itself. It was a career, an occupation. And now, suddenly, he was deprived of it, he was nobody, he was dead.

Going to the sale might help, though he couldn't quite say how. At least he would be *there*. And if Laura could be persuaded to go with him, better yet; though again he was unclear as to why he so much desired it.

"Actually," he said, "I don't feel your scruple. I respect it, but is it necessary? I mean, does it do anything for him?"

"Do anything? Why should it have to?" She got up wearily and started out of the kitchen; then stopped. "I only thought, it would be better—for us, not him—to keep the house in mind as it looked when he was in it. All those people today, and the auctioneers"—she shuddered. "Things being taken off the walls, things being described as if they never had belonged to anybody in particular. I only thought, you wouldn't like that either."

"I won't, of course. But if we got there early we could take one last look—"

"Oh, Lennie!"

Be careful now, don't make her say too much.

"All right, then, I won't go either." He would try that. He didn't in fact intend to go if she didn't. The only point was, to be there with her.

She went aimlessly into the hall, then into the living room where he could see her at the window, watching the cars as they slowed down before they reached Tregaskis Horror, as Harry sometimes called the huge brown house with its numberless gables, its unbelievable gingerbread. Harry called it that but no one else did, at least in his presence. He was the only critic of his father's and grandfather's mansion, the one surviving monument of its kind. They all knew he loved it too, and would have stayed in it forever if he could.

So people were already arriving. There was no such thing as getting there early enough for the last look he had suggested:

mistakenly, he supposed, for Laura's gaze as she stood at the window was, yes, positively stricken.

Then suddenly she came back to where he was. "I think I'll go after all."

Now why was that?

"Are you sure?" He was almost ready to argue that she shouldn't.

"Yes. I don't want to keep you from—from—"

"What, dear?" He almost never dared to call her that.

"Oh, anything. I'll get dressed now. There will be a crowd; I wonder if we'll know them. Or will they be strangers?"

"Both, probably."

And it was true. As they walked through the tall door with the griffins carved on its panels they were waved at by the Morrisons, the Hochschilds, the Bevanses, the Browns; but also there were dozens if not hundreds of idle, of curious, of predatory persons—all kinds of the unknown and undesirable.

Beth Brown came through the door from the dining room and said to both of them: "Isn't it awful? Especially for you people. I was just saying to Hugh: 'The Harbaughs won't come.' But here you are, and I'm glad to be with somebody I know."

"Did you think we shouldn't?" Laura was looking up the great spiral staircase. There were fewer people on the next floor; it could be an escape, Lennie thought she was deciding.

"Oh, no, but you *were* such friends, the three of you."

"Yes," said Laura, "we were. But then we realized, or Lennie did, that this would be the last"—she didn't go on.

"Just what *we* thought," said Beth. "Well, is there any sense in our staying together? Hugh's already out in the carriage shed—he has his eye on that old rickety coach—and I think I'll rummage among the dishes. Sets and sets of them. Harry could tell you where each pattern came from."

"I never heard him do that," said Laura. She was still occupied with the stairs; she was even moving toward them, like a woman in her sleep.

"Oh, there isn't much up there." Beth noticed too.

But Laura went on up, her hand light on the walnut banis-

ter, her face flushed by the stained-glass windows that overlooked the first landing. She never looked back to see if Lennie
was coming, or if anybody was.

"There you are," said Beth. "Laura's all woman, and so she
wants to see the bed where Harry slept. I saw it once myself,
when he was showing Hugh and me the house. It's big enough
for six, and as high as the town hall." She giggled, then suddenly was serious. "But he died in it—Mrs. Flannery found
him—so I couldn't bear to see. Do you want to fight your way
out to Hugh and tell him for me not to bid on that coach?
Whatever would we do—"

"No, I'll just look around."

He knew now why Laura had gone up there, and it was all
he could do not to follow her, with Beth watching. Yet there
were the back stairs, the ones that creaked when you mounted
them—talked, said Harry once, making out that he had ghosts.
He would go that way, and be at Harry's door almost as soon
as Laura was.

But it took longer than he had calculated, what with the
crowd in the laundry room and the heaps of furniture, pulled
out of place and waiting to be sold, that got in his way before
he even reached the stair door, the door not everybody knew
about. Of course Laura did. There wasn't anything about this
house she didn't know. But she had chosen to ascend as any
stranger would. If "chosen" was the word. It was rather as if
she hadn't quite known what she was doing. She was *being*
chosen—to go up. He still saw the deep red flush on her cheeks
and hair she made her slow turn on the landing. It could
have been more than the windows that did this, the windows
with Saint George in his ruby coat, and bleeding dragons all
around him. It could have been something within her, something deep and secret. Not too deep for Lennie, though. She
had no secrets from Lennie. The night Harry died—didn't he
know where Laura was that night? He had even made it easy
for them to be up here together. Up here; in there. For now
he was at Harry's door, and it was delicious not to look in at
once. It was like love itself, filling him, filling him, then flow-

ing out. He wasn't empty any more, he had his occupation back, he was alive.

When he did look in, there was Laura with her back to him, standing like a dead woman propped up so she couldn't fall. Utterly motionless she was, her head bent like a mannikin's, seeing yet not seeing the vast four-poster which of course had no mattress or linen on it now: just the cold spring, a little rusty, which would be up for sale in perhaps another hour along with the massive frame and the fluted posts that soared almost to the ceiling.

He knew what had happened here. It was why he wanted to come, and it was why she didn't—at first, before she got to thinking—and here his knowledge stopped. There were some things he couldn't imagine after all. To have a man die in your arms, to know that you had killed him. Or *it* had.

Laura was very late that night. He had provided her with an excellent excuse—Aunt May—but of course he must seem to be asleep when he heard her steps, deathly still, on the stairs at half-past four. Sometimes he let her see he was awake, for he enjoyed the breathless stories she had ready for him: a different one every night. At half-past four, though, he didn't trust himself to seem indifferent enough; to sound convinced. And the next day, when Mrs. Flannery came screaming over with her news, he was glad he had kept still. For this at least was something Laura couldn't have handled. And he preferred that her stories should be good ones, easy on the surface to accept. But *this* time—ah! How could she have had the composure to tell him even the feeblest tale? Shattered, she must have been; and so she might have come right out with it, gasping with terror, guilt, disgust—oh, yes, disgust as well as guilt, though the guilt would certainly be unspeakable, something never to be forgotten, even if confessed. He rejoiced that there had been no confession, or that none had come when Mrs. Flannery brought word of finding Harry dead in bed. Lennie, watching Laura then, was so absorbed in the spectacle of her response that he nearly forgot to register grief himself. Grief, or shock; for by that time, having put two and two together, he was well past the point of feeling Harry's death as anybody else would feel it. Laura's behavior, once Mrs. Flannery had stopped screaming and said what she came to say, was perfect, Lennie thought. Shock, yes, and a stunned grief; but no observable disgust or guilt. Nor when the two of them, left together, looked at each other and spoke at last, did she betray anything that he would have had to show he was aware of. Then they set about doing the things that needed to be done. There was the funeral, there was the talking with friends about the terrible suddenness of it all, and afterwards there were certain long silences that Lennie thought it better not to break. On the whole, however, Laura had been perfect. For him, anyway.

And now she stood here like a dead woman who couldn't fall. Thinking what? For once, he was shaken to realize, he didn't know. Before this he had believed he did know. Certainly that day he did, that first day when his mind raced back to Harry's house, to Harry's room, and saw Laura, once it was clear that the impossible thing had happened, doing desperate things to remove all traces of her presence; thinking she had done so, and starting home; then doubting that she had, and stumbling back; then being sure—because she *had* to be sure, or else she would go mad—being sure at last and running home; yes, running home, though she should have walked; running, and at the top of the stairs, outside their room, finding herself unable to control her breathing, and wondering perhaps why Lennie didn't hear it. As of course he did; and supposed there had been a quarrel or something. A quarrel! Instead of this hideous queerness, this death in the midst of life, this unthinkable end to everything.

Could that be what she was thinking as she stood there so stiff, so unconscious of his own eyes behind her, his own eyes that couldn't look away?

If they had done so they would have seen that Beth had come up too and was standing by him, as silent as he was, staring. When she touched his arm he jumped, then looked sidewise at her in a kind of fright, for he hadn't had time to compose his face, and he wondered what she saw in it. But she was interested only in Laura, whom she watched a long time before she made any sound.

"Dear!" she cried. And Laura, stiffening even further, let out all her breath as it were at once. A moan, a whine—what was it? Then she turned and saw these two in the door. And they saw her: inconsolable, transformed. It wasn't Laura any more, thought Lennie. She's not my wife, the one that—

"Dear!" cried Beth again. "What is it? I came up after all—I thought—dear!—can I do anything?"

"No," said Laura, and she didn't look at Lennie. "No, nothing can be done." Her voice was strangely calm; it was almost matter-of-fact. "I'm his widow, you see, and nothing can be done for widows."

Such a silence as there was. The auctioneer downstairs kept up his singsong, and the buzz of voices grew loud, then soft, then loud. But here there was such a silence as only death can generate.

"What, dear?" Beth was barely audible. "What did you say?"

"You heard me," said Laura. "Now I'm going home."

Lennie, his features fallen quite apart, stepped forward, uncertainly, but Laura passed him as if no one were there.

"I don't live in this town," she said. "I don't know anybody here."

"Laura!" Beth was scared. "You know me, and Hugh—and him." She looked at Lennie.

"I don't know a single living person," Laura said.

Without either of them stopping her she went swiftly out and started down the stairs.

The Man Who Had Died a Lot

"THOU FOOL, that which thou sowest is not quickened except it die."

Young Dr. Beals went on from there, but the little boy in the black coat was lost at once, and didn't hear any more words. They were about the resurrection and the new body, the better body that was incorruptible, but he was thinking about the tight black coat he wore, and about his father who had stayed at home.

His father seldom came here on Sunday mornings with him and Mother. She wore black, too, with buttons that matched his own. She liked to come and sit quietly while the new preacher talked of death that was yet not death. For it was his favorite topic, and the text this morning was repeated from a month ago, when Oliver paid less attention to it than he did today. Today he got lost in it, thinking how much he hated his black coat with its narrow lapels, and how glad he was that Dad had never died.

The last thing Oliver had seen as he walked with Mother down the brick path to the street was Dad in his blue workshirt, the faded one whose neck he never buttoned, leaving by the side door with a hoe in his hand. It was the only hoe they had, in fact; it was older than Oliver, and its corners were worn smooth with many filings. Dad had filed it again before breakfast. Its bright edges flashed in the sun as he disappeared between their house and Holdens', on the way to the May garden where he was going to plant peas. He had turned and waved at them. Mother hadn't looked around, but Oliver did, and the smile that came with the wave was like the hot sun playing on the hoe.

Dad was happy, for he had never died. Oliver wanted to be that way too, and would when he was old enough to stop wearing black on Sunday. He wondered if his father had had to do it when he was little. Probably not. Certainly not. It was unimaginable. But Oliver had to admit that he knew nothing about this. Perhaps he had, and then had got too old to do it any more.

"Except it die." Maybe that meant nothing more than being small and hard for a while, like one of those dry peas he knew Dad had in his pocket when he left by the side door. They were all in the ground now, the black ground out of which in a week or two they would send up green leaves that the wind would blow. But for a while, ever since last summer when they were shelled for seed, they had lain in their box down

cellar as if they were dead. Now they would live again, as his
father had begun to do whenever it was that he got old enough
to stop wearing the black coat with grey cloth buttons which
his mother, Grandma Hendricks, may have made him wear on
Sundays. Oliver thought of himself, sitting straight up in the
hard seat while Dr. Beals talked, as encased in a dry shell,
faintly wrinkled with darkness and time, which would some
day burst and let him out of it. Then he would be free like
Dad, having never to die again as long as he lived, having
never, like Mother, to want to die, to like to die, every seventh
day in this high room with purple windows through which the
sun came with such effort that it had lost all of its sparkle
when it came. Was that it? Was he dead now? Was he only
waiting for time to crack the shell and set him free?

The sermon ended abruptly. They were singing the last
hymn before Oliver was ready for it. He liked hymns and the
moment's hush before the congregation rose to go.

It rose, and he went quickly beside his mother to the wide
door where Dr. Beals already stood, shaking hands.

"Very fine this morning," she murmured. He thanked her,
patting as he did so Oliver's small shoulder, warm under its
wool.

"And your husband—how is he?"

She nodded, bowed, and pulled Oliver on.

Had there been a hint of criticism in the question as it was
asked? If so, thought Oliver, Dr. Beals was wrong. He didn't
understand Mother. He didn't know she never criticized her
husband, at least for not coming to church.

Oliver wondered why this was.

She held her boy's hand tightly at her side as they walked
home under the maples that had begun since last Sunday to put
out delicate, pointed leaves.

It would be wonderful to see Wolf again. Silly to say this,
for she and Oliver had only been gone an hour. But that was
the way it was. She had never got over wanting to see Wolf
again.

She didn't tell him this, but it was true. And the reason she didn't tell him was not what many wives would think it was: that it would spoil him. Nothing could spoil him, for he didn't care. He didn't need compliments to make him happy. He didn't even care about being happy. The way he lived, that didn't matter.

He had lived so much more than she had. When he had done it she didn't know, but it was the first thing that made her fall in love with him, back in those country days when all the neighbors said he was such a sad-faced boy. She thought so too, in the beginning, when his family moved next to hers, with only a hundred and sixty acres between them. She said to herself—fighting, she supposed, against the charm of his dark hair and eyes and his hollow cheeks—he would never have any fun.

She remembered when she changed her mind. Commencement Day at the Academy. The girls sat on one side of the stage, the boys on the other. She had been proud of her long white dress because it made her feel at once so grown-up and so innocent. It was the way she imagined a bride must feel; and then she blushed. Across the stage, when she looked up, Wolf was staring at her without exactly seeing her. Like the other boys, he had on a black suit which was expected to make him look older than he was. It hadn't changed him at all. The other boys were so changed it was ridiculous; most of them, terribly uncomfortable in their stiff collars, looked younger rather than older, as if their clothes had set them back a year, two years. With Wolf it was different. He didn't seem to know what he had on, or where he was. He wasn't *trying* to be serious, for he already was. Serious, and yet not sad. It was as if black were natural for him, and only by accident had he never worn it before. Now it suited him; in a sense it made him happy. So far as she knew he had never worn it again, but that was because he didn't need to. The colored garments he preferred, the blue shirts, the brown shirts, still had the black in them somehow, just as his smile did. The smile he gave her and Oliver when they left the house this morning—Oliver thought she hadn't seen it, but she did—that had the black in it too, like a deep shadow, a shadow you wouldn't know was there unless you lived with Wolf, and understood how simple his happiness was.

It was simple because he didn't care. He wasn't ambitious for one thing. And this had caused some words between them; it always had, and she guessed it always would. But that wasn't the main thing. The main thing was that he had been some-where she hadn't, and nobody else had that she knew. Some-thing had happened to Wolf, a long time of course before she ever knew him. Yet that was early in his life: so early that she couldn't puzzle it out. It oughtn't by rights to happen to chil-dren. He must have been a child when he—Wolf must have been a child in Wyoming, for that was where the family had moved from, when he—

But she couldn't say the word. She had thought it every day since Oliver was so sick that time when he was two—just two, and Wolf hadn't been afraid. He had cared, but he wasn't afraid. Her own panic was something she never stopped being ashamed of. It made her say all sorts of crazy things, such as that Dr. McCune, the one person they both thought could save Oliver, wouldn't even come because they were poor. He came when Wolf went for him, of course. They were already good friends by the time they reached the porch steps, which they walked up slowly, still talking about whatever they had been talking about in the doctor's buggy, and not hurrying at all. Wolf cared about Oliver's pain, and about her panic; he also cared about Dr. McCune, and the way his team should be tied. Wolf cared about everything. But he wasn't afraid. And Oliver got well.

Of course, Wolf was glad of that. But the way he was glad had been what she noticed. It threw a lot of light backwards, on him and her and everything. It explained the way he looked on the stage at Commencement, when she caught him staring at her. Commencement was important to him, and she was going to be important to him. He seemed to know both things, the thing that was ending and the thing that was beginning; yet he wasn't in a flutter, like all of the girls that day and most of the boys. It was as if he were used to passing through important moments, and these were only two more. They represented change, but there was something about Wolf that didn't change. So with Oliver when he was sick. It wasn't that Wolf wanted him to die. But he didn't act as if the only thing he wanted in the world was for Oliver to live, either, *in the world*. Whatever happened to him, he would still be Oliver, and Wolf wouldn't have lost him. He never lost anything, just as he never found anything. Nothing surprised Wolf. Even others noticed that.

Dr. Beals had been good this morning. *Except it die.* They were her favorite words, and perhaps Dr. Beals knew it from the way she always praised his sermons on this text. For he regularly came back to it, and she was sure he would have been disappointed if she hadn't said what she said after church.

Now she could say what Wolf had done. It was what she wanted to do, in life, in the world, while all three of them were still young. Oliver of course was, and Wolf was no age at all. But she was growing older. She felt it, and wished she could die so that time would stop for her, too. Die as Wolf had died, when he was a child in Wyoming. Die so that she could live with him as he deserved.

Jim Patchen, who was Wolf's best friend, if he had a best friend, once said Wolf had lived a lot. He didn't mean he had been in lots of places, or done lots of things, or—oh, no—made lots of money. He meant what she meant now when she could say to herself, after five years of not being able to: Wolf has died a lot. She could never say this to Jim, for even Jim wouldn't understand. Nobody would among all of Wolf's friends. Perhaps Jim wasn't the best one; there wasn't any best one, though each one of them thought he was. Wolf cared for them all, as he cared for all things and places, equally. Including her and Oliver. Equally. And she didn't mind. She would rather be one of the million things he cared for than be the only thing if he was different, if he was like other men and other people.

Except it die. She wished she could. But the black dress she wore, and the little black suit she had made for Oliver, never seemed to do either of them any good. Wolf didn't need to go to church because the black was in him everywhere, like a shadow that brings out all the colors. He was in church all the time, Sundays and weekdays, sleeping and waking. But that was because of what he had been through once. Was it in church? Did he go through it there, whatever it was? Perhaps it wasn't in church at all. Lincoln didn't go to church and it happened to Lincoln. He was sadder, and smiled more, than most men in the world. Lincoln didn't care either. Or he cared about everything, equally. He was famous and Wolf was not. But that didn't matter in the place where both of them had been. Lincoln was dead and Wolf was not. That didn't matter either, that kind of death. It wasn't the kind she meant.

The day he asked her to marry him, when they were still neighbors north of town and he walked over through the swampy field his father was always promising to drain, she said no because she was mad. He was wet to the knees, and didn't seem to care that he was. He didn't care *too* much, she thought, what her answer would be. It was almost as if he expected her to say no. She said no. Then she was sorry. But she kept it up a whole year, till he stopped asking. Then she had to ask *him*. For by that time she knew she would never meet any other man like Wolf. There wasn't any in the world, if Wolf was in the world.

She wondered about Oliver. Should she let him stop wearing that suit to church? He didn't like it, and Wolf probably didn't either, though he said nothing. What if next Sunday she simply got out the blue cotton coat and pants and put them on Oliver's bed without saying a word? It might be the best thing to do.

Yet she did want Oliver to—she couldn't say it, and she was almost glad. She shouldn't want this thing for other people, even her own boy. Who was she to say what Oliver should go through? She could feed him and dress him and see to it that he had manners, and help him with his reading. But he was such a little boy for her to be thinking these big things about. One thing she knew she didn't need to do. She didn't need to tell him his father was a great man. He understood it in the right way, and always had. Perhaps—but lightning doesn't strike twice in the same family. She had no right to expect it as a natural thing. That was why she had done everything she could to make it happen to him in church. Maybe she was wrong in this. She had seen people looking at him, and feeling sorry for him because his suit wasn't comfortable. She should have made those arm-holes bigger, and the top button hadn't been necessary; when it was buttoned too, the coat looked as if it were choking him. But if it made him listen to Dr. Beals she didn't mind. She wondered if he did, and what the words meant to one so small and sweet. For Oliver was a sweet boy, even if he was regular too. He could do plenty of things, and plenty of other boys liked him. There was Bud Holden now, waiting for him on his porch.

But Oliver, who had taken his hand out of hers and was already running far ahead, was on his way down to the hot garden where Wolf stooped, planting peas.

Wolf must be about through, she thought, for he was only going to put in two rows today. He was still there on his haunches, though, when Oliver arrived beside him. What were they saying?

When she looked at them again out of the kitchen window they were where they had been before, except that Wolf was sitting down now, in the warm dirt at the end of the second row. He was leaning back, his hands over his knees, and they were talking. With Oliver standing, they were exactly the same height.

Oliver took off his coat and hung it on the nearest stake. He picked up a clod and threw it, and then another, and then another. He was trying to hit the corner post, the white one there by Holdens'.

He had known he would get the coat dirty, and so he had taken it off. Also, he couldn't have aimed well with it on. Those arm-holes. But she wouldn't have cared if they had ripped. She knew what she was going to do with the coat. She needed just that much wool for the quilt she would make next winter.

Help for the Senator

THE SENATOR with the silver hair—no paper ever failed to mention that—stood without moving as the young man behind him said over and over: "You must let me do it, sir. I can go to him and say—"

"No." The Senator, staring through the great window of his apartment that overlooked half the city—the better half—still did not move a muscle, except that the fingers of his right hand, held so rigidly beside him, tightened and loosened, tightened and loosened, around a letter they had crushed out of shape an hour ago.

"But, sir—"

"No. I have too much pride. I won't go begging. I'll weather it out in my own way. Leave me alone now, Huddleston—please."

But his private secretary disobeyed him for once. Whatever the risk, he had more to propose.

"I wouldn't call it begging, sir."

A silence. Then: "Why not? When a man has lied in public it is asking a great deal of him to take it back in public. Morgan wouldn't have done this thing in the first place if he hadn't hated me so bitterly that—well, nothing can change him now. Particularly, the news that I am hurt. He will like that, and only think of further ways to hurt me. He never forgave me, you understand, for my refusal even to consider recommending his contract. It was crooked; I told him so; he had already invested more money in the scheme than he could recover without my support; and when I withheld that support, in my opinion he went mad. Only a madman would accuse himself of bribery—not merely of the attempt, but of success with the attempt. His story, which every editor knows by now"—he crushed even more completely the white envelope in his hand—"is that he brought a briefcase full of hundred-dollar bills, and that I accepted them. How can I disprove it? He and I were alone in this room."

"Sir, I think I should relieve you of the letter. It's only a carbon of what he broadcast, but we have no other copy, and—"

"And what?" The Senator spoke sharply; but then he turned and tossed the document onto a small round table near him, a table with nothing on it save a slender vase of flowers. "It isn't evidence. Or if so, the newspapers share it with me."

"Nevertheless I'm glad you didn't destroy it." Huddleston picked it up and smoothed it out as well as he could. "May I read it again, sir?"

"Of course. You might even memorize it, as I have. I thought I had lost the power to do that. I hadn't."

Huddleston studied the contents with a care that was out of proportion to their length. He was thinking rather than reading.

"Well?" The Senator watched him curiously. "What can you say to a man like that?"

"I can ask him whether he really sent duplicates of this to the press."

"What? You can be sure he did."

"But no paper has called about it."

"They will, as soon as they have caught their breath. I imagine they will sound embarrassed, but they'll call."

Huddleston was scarcely listening. "First, sir, I would ask him whether the copies have actually been mailed."

"Why do you think he will tell you?"

"If they haven't, he will know I can discover it. A ring here, a ring there—"

"A hazard here, a hazard there!"

"Oh, sir, I'd be ever so careful. They would hardly know what I was asking about."

"Yes, yes, you're good at that. But of course he did send it. I know Morgan."

"Probably he did, sir. And satisfied of this, I would go on

then to make at least two things clear: he ruins himself by this, assuming it is believed."

"*You* don't believe it?"

"No, sir." He looked startled.

"Thank you, Huddleston."

"You know I don't."

"Such things cannot be known. I take your word for it, however, and am grateful."

"But you *must* know." He was terribly earnest.

"Well then, I do." The Senator smiled for the first time. "The second thing to be made clear—what is that?"

"Oh, yes. If it is not believed, or if it is disproved, then he is in danger. Great danger. Perjury, I mean. Or slander."

"Hm. He hasn't sworn. And I'm a public man—fair game, it seems."

"Nevertheless—"

"No, Huddleston, I can't permit you to do this. I must ride it out myself. I must see what *they* believe; and I mean everybody. If I don't merit their faith, what have I been doing all my life? I am trusting my career to speak for itself." It took no effort for him to say "my career." He thought of it that way. The words went somehow with his straight back, his high forehead, his not very intense blue eyes. "If my wife were alive, I am sure she would agree. Mrs. Glenn was proud too. No, Huddleston, you will say nothing to anybody. Nor will I."

"The papers, sir?"

"No comment."

"Beyond, I take it, a firm denial."

"As firm as brief. And then, no comment." He made a sign of dismissal. "You have those books to get from the Library. Why not go now?"

"But the telephone, sir."

"Leave that to me."

Huddleston, hesitating, went out of the room at last, and the Senator listened until he heard the door of the apartment close. Then he pulled his favorite chair, deeply upholstered in dark green, with high wings at its back, to a position directly in front of the window. But instead of sitting down he walked over to his desk and turned off the telephone; there was a small switch for the purpose, and the click it made gave him so sudden a satisfaction that he sighed, standing there, like one who has received unexpectedly good news.

Why had the bell not rung? What were they thinking in the offices where the letter had been read—yes, and reread, and passed around by men whose faces—

He closed his eyes for a moment. Perhaps he was foolish to postpone the denial. He could even call *them*, and give it to them now.

No, no. He must compose the sentence he would speak when the time came: the same sentence for everybody, with no fear in it, no argument or explanation, and certainly no hint that he was asking favors of any man. Faith is not a favor. It must be there instantly, or never be.

As for Morgan, the rabid fox who had bitten him—ah, he must not call him that. He would call him nothing; he would, if possible, avoid using his very name. "Morgan? Who is Morgan?" No, not even this. Let Morgan lie; let the truth bury Morgan a mile deep, a thousand miles, a million.

As soon as he was in his chair he knew how tired this thing had made him. He could sit here forever, merely staring out. Yet he must compose the sentence. "Senator Glenn indignantly denies"—no, not indignantly. There must be no feeling in it. "Senator Harlow Glenn"—and he trembled. The words had been music to him for so long, a rich, deep music, that he could not bear the thought of its being threatened, being ended. The orphan who had risen to fame and wealth and power, who had come all the way in the world entirely through his own efforts—that story, so familiar and so true, so widely known, so reverently told by others with the same words that he had used in his original rendering of it years ago when fame such as he had now was only dreamed of, that epic of success was even more in danger; for there might be those who in sheer, unmotivated malice would delight in turning it sour as they retold it. Ada could never have endured that. He couldn't be glad that Ada was dead; at least, however, she was spared this possibility of woe.

The slightest of noises behind him made him twist about and glance at the telephone. But it couldn't have come from there,

with the switch off. Probably he had imagined it. And then he
thought of the other telephones, the extensions. They should
be turned off too, or Sadie would be answering one of them
and calling him. He got up again, went to the desk, and pressed
the housekeeper's button.

The door opened at once, and there was Sadie in her black
apron.

"I was just going by, and heard you buzz." In a way it was a
relief, not having her call him "sir." She never had since the
day she came, six months after Ada's death. She had no style;
sometimes he felt like apologizing for her to company, to
callers; but Sadie, poor stringy woman, was faithful; she did
two women's work. She was almost as old as he was, and
possibly looked older. Not that he looked at her much.

"Just going by," he said."You weren't out there, were you,
when Huddleston—"

"Yes, I was. I heard you two."

"What!" Now he did look at her, frowning.

"Huddleston went right by me, absent-like. I'm glad he's
gone. I want to tell you something."

"When I want you to tell me something, I'll say so."

"You'll want me to say this. I heard you tell him you were
proud. Well, I know that. But not too proud, I hope; not crazy
proud."

"Sadie, what is this?" She had taken a new tone with him, as
if he were more than her employer; or less. "What are you
trying to suggest?"

"I'm not *suggesting any*thing. I heard you say you wouldn't
take help from any man. But what about a woman? I can help
you plenty. I can save you. I can take care of this mess you're
in. I can make it go away—like that." She raised both hands,
rather gaily, and snapped her fingers.

He leaned hard against the desk, as if he needed it there,
then pulled himself upright again. He looked intently at her,
his own face pale with astonishment. She had high cheekbones,
and her dark eyes never left his.

"Sadie—"

"Why don't you ask me what it is? Go on, ask me. At least you could do that."

"Well—"

"Oh, don't bother. Proud! Listen. I heard you tell him you and that Morgan were by yourselves in this room. You weren't. You've got a witness. Me. Sadie Harris—only, that's not my name. What do you think my real name is?"

"Good God!" He could hardly keep his voice down. "How could I have any thoughts about that? But now—you say you were in this room? You weren't, you know. You must not make things up so irresponsibly."

"I was, though, just as much as I was here with you and little Huddleston. I heard every word. And when the time comes I'm going to tell it."

"No, no. You couldn't have understood even if you did hear. It was business."

"What's business? Only money, and who doesn't understand about that? I didn't see the inside of his satchel, but I know how many hundred-dollar bills he tried to give you."

"How many?" He held his breath.

"Five hundred. That's fifty thousand dollars. After he left I went to my room and did some multiplying. But you wouldn't take it. You called him—don't ask me to say what, it wasn't nice."

"Say what." It was an order.

"A filthy stinking pimp and sonofabitch. Do I say it right?"

The Senator turned away from her and groped for his chair; but she followed and looked down at him as he sat there, bewildered, breathing hard. "You were to tell the Committee it was a fine contract for a fine gun that shoots backward, I believe. But you threw the satchel at him—I heard it hit the door—and that was the last of Morgan. Lord, if he had only noticed me out there in the hall! But he was blind, like Huddleston just now. No wonder, seeing how much he invested in his plant."

"How much, Sadie?"

"More than ten million, six-and-a-half of it his own. The rest—"

"Stop it, stop it!"

"Why, what's the matter?"

But he had grown strangely quiet; he wasn't seeing her at all. His gaze went past her, out of the window and then on into the dusk that was forming over the high towers across the park.

At last he said: "You were there, Sadie. It couldn't be otherwise. I had no idea you were a chronic eavesdropper—I don't approve of that, but let it pass. You ask me what the matter is. I know now, and I'll tell you. I don't *want* a witness. I insist on managing this mess, as you call it, entirely by myself. I have to find out what people think of me: how much they trust me after all these years. I want it to be his word or mine, and the devil take the one of us they don't believe." He paused. "You understand me, Sadie?"

"No, I don't." But her voice had lost its harshness; she was thinking only of him, he somehow knew. She was a good woman, a good friend. He had never thought of Sadie as a friend. Now, suddenly, she seemed to be someone he had always known. Perhaps that was the definition of a friend.

The extension phones rang like firebells down the long hall; in his bedroom; in the kitchen. They both jumped.

"There," he said. "That was what I called you for, then I forgot. Will you go and turn them off? Every last one of them?"

"All right. This is something I do understand. You're not ready to talk yet." She went out, then in no time returned, facing him again with her back to the window.

"Thank you, Sadie."

"If that was anybody, I could have told them—you know what. I even thought—"

"Please, Sadie!"

"Don't worry, I won't if you say not to. But how can I understand the main thing? How could any sensible person? People, you say. Well, don't you know about people? You're supposed to. They like to believe the worst about the best. Or half of them do. You can't count on anybody; some will, some won't. And that's as bad as if they all did. If you want my opinion, you're committing suicide. What a pity."

He was silent awhile before he said: "Have you considered how much weight my housekeeper's word would carry? I'm not arguing the principle with you, Sadie, I'm trying to be as practical as you think you are."

"I *know* I'm practical." Yet she looked a little disturbed.

"Have you considered, too—I hesitate to mention this—how they would come at you about your other name, supposing they found out, as sooner or later they would? A witness must be reliable. Sadie Harris—isn't that your name? And if it isn't, why did you change it? I'm putting the question to you as a lawyer would, or an investigator. Or merely a reporter; those fellows can be keen. Perhaps you had in mind your maiden name. But you didn't come to me as *Mrs.* Harris. Are you married? *Were* you married? Forgive all this; I'm trying to protect you."

"Protect *me?*" There was the faintest trace of a smile in her eyes. "So you try to change the subject. Let's get back to what would happen if I told. You say they'd come at me. Now why would they? Wouldn't they want to believe my story? You like to think they would—or do you? Don't you trust them after all?"

He was silent again. Then he straightened himself in the chair and said: "No, Sadie. I can't use your help. Thank you, but that's all."

Why, the woman had tears in her eyes. Only for a second, but he saw them.

"You mean," she said, "you don't *want* my help. You don't want *me*. You never did." She put a hand to her mouth, appalled by what had come out of it. "My God, Captain, why did I say that?"

He stood up so suddenly that he felt unsteady, felt weak. "Captain!" He repeated it barely aloud.

"Why did I say *that!*" Now *she* was weak. She stumbled to a small chair to the left of the wide window and dropped on to it, covering her face with both her hands, her shoulders shaking. "*Your* other name. I was never going to say it. I was never going to let you know. And now I have. Oh, my!"

Captain. He hadn't been called that for fifty years. Fifty-one, because he left Mrs. Brown's Home for Orphans when he was twenty-two; and now he was seventy-three. Seventy-three. Senator Glenn. Harlow Glenn: from orphan to national leader.

He saw the long tables again, heard the scuffling in the corridors, smelled—yes, smelled it all, that place where he had spent too many of his youthful years. The family that took him lost their money and brought him back, and he became a helper while he waited to be taken a second time; but so capable a helper, Mrs. Brown said, that she couldn't let him go. She kept him out of sight when people came, in the kitchen, the store room, the office; and finally he was head of what she referred to as her staff, with maids and janitors under him. They called him Captain.

Maids.

A shiver ran over him, and he looked at Sadie's shoulders, still shaking as she held her face too low for him to see it. But the high cheekbones, the dark eyes—

Milly Harper.

He sat a long time, trying not to remember what for years he had thought was put away for good. Milly Harper. The one thing he couldn't be proud of, now that it was back with him—back *in* him, where it would never be rooted out. It worked there like a sudden drug, stealing his strength.

Milly Harper. Helper to the cook, fat Mrs. Francis. And pretty then. So pretty, with her eyes always following him—he knew it, he felt them at his back—but always down when he addressed her, as if she were afraid. It wasn't Milly's fault, what happened that day; unless her always keeping her eyes down was what started him thinking, thinking. But he was twenty, and already ambitious; it wouldn't do to fall in *love* with Milly. And he never did, though he thought of her constantly, waking and sleeping. Then on his twenty-first birthday, when Mrs. Brown had planned a special noontime dinner for him, with roast beef and a cake with candles, his thought of Milly took a turn that terrified him. He did his best to conquer it, but he couldn't. So far in his life there had been no girls; then here was Milly, whom he had dreamed of last night; it seemed to him that she stood at his bedside, her eyes looking straight down into his. He woke, and an image of her hung for a moment in the room. Come closer, closer, he heard himself whispering. But nobody was there; and that was when he planned it. Appearing for breakfast, he said he wasn't well; had a dizzy headache; would have to stay in bed all day. Mrs. Brown of course was disappointed. "Oh, dear," she said, "my dinner; but you go back and lie down, and I'll bring it to you when it's ready." He protested. She would be busy with those people from Bloomington. Milly could bring it. He insisted that it be Milly. And so it was.

Did she suspect? When she came in with the tray, and set it down on the small table by his pillow, she was nervous, and didn't look directly at him. Which was why—perhaps—he seized her hands as soon as they were free and pulled her to him, shaking her to make her look. She never did, even when he had her down with him, even when she was letting him do the utmost that he pleased; she didn't resist, yet all the time her eyes were elsewhere, or were closed. Then his were. And when he opened them she was standing by his side, as in the dream. She was looking straight down at him, uncertain, unbelieving, and afraid—yes, afraid. Which was why—perhaps—he couldn't bear the thought of her coming closer to him now. He couldn't bear *her*. It was finished; *he* was afraid. "Get out," he said to her. And when she didn't move, but stared at him with hot tears in her eyes, he said again: "Go on. Get out." He couldn't comprehend this now, any more than then. She didn't want to leave like that; she wanted him to say something about the two of them. It was important to her, what they had done. She belonged to him, she seemed to think. She wasn't sorry if he wasn't. But he was more than sorry. He was outraged, by himself, by her. "Go on! Get out!"

He shut his eyes now, unable to endure the memory.

When he opened them she was looking at him. "I never meant to let you know," she said.

But he scarcely heard this, so carefully he was studying her face. Yes, Milly's face. How could he have been so blind to it? Worn as it was, and dismally altered, it was Milly's; and day after day he had failed to recognize it.

"Then why did you come here, if you didn't mean to"—he hesitated—"make me remember?"

"To be with you after she died. And help you if I ever could."

"Help me." He pondered this, his eyes half closed again. "I shouldn't have thought—"

"Who would, Captain?" She managed the least possible smile. "But that's the way it is, and let's not talk about it. Did you miss me when I left the Home? I skipped out."

He remembered Mrs. Brown saying, when she found Milly gone: "I could murder that girl." Mrs. Brown never knew; nobody knew. "I could murder that girl, with me so short-handed." From that day to this he had never seen Milly, or known he did.

He decided to let her question pass. "All this time"—he put one of his own—"where were you?"

"Places. Working. Forty jobs, I guess; I never counted. This one I finagled at the agency—I thought I was so smart. Now *it's* over."

He shook his head. "No, Milly. Stay here."

"And make you remember? No. So you forgot?"

"Yes. In a way."

"In a way I didn't. You've been my only man—now don't have fits."

He shook his head, seriously, slowly.

"Don't think I meant anything by that, though it's true—for me it's true. So tonight I'm off. Will you give me a reference? But don't say I listen at doors. I never did before. It wasn't necessary."

"Reference?" He looked at her a long time before he said: "I'll give you a pension. You won't have to work."

"Pay me to go away and stay away—that it? Oh, Captain, I'm sorry!" For he had turned red, then pale. "I didn't mean what I just said; I guess I don't mean anything. But you know I oughtn't to stay here. I don't even want to, now that—now that—"

"Now that I haven't said, 'Get out'?" He flushed again.

"That's right, you didn't." She was silent, thinking. "And

then there's this. My story would hold more water if I was working somewhere else when I told it. Right?" He nodded before he thought. "My name, too. I changed it only to come here. I'd change it back, and who would know or care? Right?"

He didn't nod. Instead, he brushed a speck of dust from his sleeve and said to her without looking up: "But Milly, you're not testifying."

Now it was her turn to keep him waiting. She took her time.

"Listen, Captain."

He listened.

"Are you still proud?"

Slowly: "Yes—of everything since then."

"But not of then?"

"Milly, I'd give anything if—"

"You'd give *me* something?"

"Anything, if—"

"All right, give me this one thing: let me tell my story. Let me *help* you, Captain. All my life I haven't been able to—the one man I was meant to, and I wasn't where I could; *he* wasn't where. Now don't have fits. I'm not trying to make you feel sorry. I never felt sorry."

The apartment door opened and closed.

"Mercy! Huddleston's back!"

The Senator did not stir.

"You hear? He's back, that busybody. Now he'll ask how many calls there've been. What are you going to say to him and his precious notebook?"

The lines in the Senator's face had deepened. "The first thing—your reference. I'll dictate it. The second thing—"

But Huddleston was already in the room, saying: "Sir, there were three reporters in the lobby. I told them you were not at home."

"But I *am* at home, Huddleston. Call the doorman and have him send them up in five minutes."

"Then you intend—"

"Yes, I intend. There have been some new developments.

But first, will you take this reference for Sadie? She is leaving us."

"Oh! I'm sorry."

Was he, she wondered? Didn't he know how jealous of him she had always been? He was so much help to the Senator in his little way.

God Has No Wife

"THAT REMINDS ME," said Sunderson, though nothing had, "of a thing that happened to me when I was very small. My brother Reed was in it, too. We still lived on the farm."

He was going to tell the story now, and he must watch Angus while he did so. He made sure before he began that the lampshade in their booth was tilted exactly right. He must watch that face every minute; it was younger than his, and less able to hide a guilty thought.

"We put a lump of coal in our wagon and pulled it up and down the yard all day. It was a red wagon, with a picture of three black horses on either side—three strong horses, neck to neck, and each of them had a white star in the middle of his forehead.

"I don't know where my mother had gone, but Reed and I were alone on the place except for Otie, our grown cousin, who had been asked to come over and keep an eye on things till evening: on us, chiefly, though I don't remember anything about her being there until she leaned out of the window and let us know she had been listening.

"Reed was six, I think, and I was four: too young almost for the memory to last, but it has lasted. I couldn't talk plain yet—I was slow about that—which is why, maybe, I can still hear myself saying the four words she heard. 'By Dod, Dod damn'—those were the words, and as we went under the window I was uttering them, I suppose, with all my might; for Otie suddenly appeared there, frowning down on us with a shocked face, and said: 'Boys, boys! I'm going to tell your mother how you talk. Just you wait. I'll tell her when she gets home tonight.'

"I have seldom felt such terror since—nor Reed, I imagine, though we haven't spoken of this day for years. The big trees in the yard became a dark wood in which I was lost forever. There was no escape from it, or from the punishment we deserved—I more than Reed, for it was worse to swear in baby talk than any other way. We were imitating the hired men, whom naturally we admired. We had pretended the wagon had got stuck, and the painted horses were too lazy to pull it free. We were swearing at the horses. And it seemed a great thing to do. We felt important, we felt strong. For a moment there were no women in the world; no bad, no good; nothing but men and horses, and black coal to be moved. Then there was Otie, leaning out and frowning and threatening to tell.

"How the day passed I don't recall. This was in the middle of the afternoon, probably, but time in such cases doesn't matter. We had to spend it somehow, and of course we did. I don't remember Otie again; perhaps we kept out of her sight in the dim hope she would forget. My guess now is that she did.

"But no such guess was possible then. It was dark when we were eating supper; Mother was late, and Otie had waited as long as she could. Otie hadn't mentioned our sin again, but it filled all the mind I had. I was still in the terrible wood, watching for a way out that I knew would never open and show itself.

"One thing, however, I had resolved, and so had Reed. Just as soon as we heard Mother's buggy in the barnyard we would rush out and help her unhitch. This might not save us, but then again it might. If we were good enough, and Mother noticed, Otie's revelation when it came might lose a little of its force, might be received, we even hoped, with some faint touch of mercy. If we could manage to be *perfectly* good, or to seem so, then Mother might forgive us altogether. I'm not sure I believed she could or should forgive us. Nevertheless I hoped; and doubtless ate very little of my supper; and listened for the sound of hooves and wheels.

"Both of us heard it before Otie did. Mother was home.

"We jumped up from the table and raced like ponies to the barn, where Mother already was, undoing one of Prince's traces. Then our good works began. We hardly had time to kiss her, or be kissed, or answer any of her absent-minded questions about how things had been all day. I remember being struck by Mother's absent air, as if she didn't know where she was. She must have been surprised by so much zeal, she must have been searching her thoughts for an explanation. Or was she happy because we loved her and were showing it? We did love her, even though we feared her. Anyhow, our good works went on. I trotted back to the house for a lantern; Reed, who was bigger and knew better how to do it, helped put the harness away; and all the time we talked—demanded that Mother tell us where she had been, what she had done, and whether she was tired.

"When I say we feared her I don't mean that she was more fearful than mothers ought to be; or fathers, either, but my father didn't count in this case, since he was gone on a long trip west, buying cattle, or maybe mules; and anyway, he was the more indulgent of the two. She was the punisher, she was the one who could grow tall and red with wrath, and make us feel that mercy might be the sweetest thing on earth. Or in heaven; for with her straight back and her handsome fair head and her grey eyes that flashed, she sometimes seemed a goddess who had us in her power. This evening, especially, she struck me so; her straw hat with the wide black band and the knot of blue flowers standing stiffly up in front, nodding when she nodded—she had style, you must understand, she had authority. Also, she had the farm on her mind while Father was away; doubtless she had been off this day on important business; and it was more than usually important that she shouldn't be distracted by reports of our wrongdoing. Swearing was a serious crime, we knew; and knew that she would have to attend to it in whatever way she considered best.

"We ran at her side to the kitchen door and stood waiting, half paralyzed, while she and Otie greeted each other. Would Otie say it now? She didn't. She was too busy, it appeared, bringing food out of the oven where it had been keeping warm; and straightening up the table while Mother went upstairs to take off her short, tight coat with the many buttons down its front. When she came down again she looked softer than she had, and freer of the preoccupied air we had noted at the barn. We had made her happy and she showed it. We were good boys, and loved her. So she moved gaily about the kitchen, in the red apron she had put on to help Otie with the remains of supper; and insisted as she ate that Reed and I sit by her, listening to some tale of how Prince had shied when a rabbit ran across the road: shied, and almost turned the buggy over.

"So far we had nothing to worry about. And as it turned out we never did have anything to worry about—in the way of punishment, I mean. For Otie never told, either that night or the next morning before Uncle Morton, her father, drove down to take her home. Or if she did tell, Mother kept the secret. We never heard a word about the bad thing we had done. We never had to pay.

"Except that I did, in a strange fashion. I have not forgotten. Of course I couldn't talk about it then, and I haven't talked about it till now. I believe I comprehend it at last. Say Mother was a goddess; say she was God. I had learned about good works. I had learned how little they have to do with whether or not we are saved. For it may not have been our being good that decided things in our favor. To begin with, we weren't *being* good. We were only trying not to get scolded or switched. We helped Mother for our sakes, not hers. And it seemed to me that she knew this. It would explain her abstraction, her almost puzzled mood as we helped her unhitch; and later, too, when we went with her to hold the lantern while she milked. Otie would have done this, but we couldn't leave them together. We scarcely did, all evening, though once or twice it happened that they were alone for a minute. Why was she absent-minded? Of course I didn't know; but if it was because she suspected we were trying to save ourselves, then she must

be wondering what we had done, and assuming that it was
worse than any good thing we did now could ever make up
for. So there was nothing in the theory of good works: they
didn't cancel anything out, they didn't balance badness—real
badness, anyway, like taking a certain name in vain. But suppose she didn't suspect. Then she was merely musing, merely
whispering to herself: 'The boys love me even though I am
strict with them sometimes; they are glad I've come home, and
they are showing it this way.' That would be the worst possible
thing, for it meant we were deceiving her in affection's name,
we were taking advantage of the one soft side she had. I
suffered, thinking of this. But then the thought would go away
and I would be left with another one, colder and less com-
forting: we weren't in her mind at all. She was still going over
the business of the day, or planning what should be done tomorrow; or simply, in the way grown people had, revolving in her
head a world of matters with respect to which we couldn't be
consulted because they were quite beyond our understanding.
What we had done was of trifling importance in comparison
with all that. It might be attended to some time—it was even
now being added to the sum total of our misdeeds—but for the
present it would be ignored. It might even be ignored forever.
Maybe no total was kept. Maybe it didn't matter what anybody did. Maybe there was no justice, no mercy. This staggered me, and I preferred the warmer thoughts of punishment
and wrath, and tears, and being finally forgiven.

"The point is that nothing happened, nothing at all. It is
possible, as I have said, that Otie never told. The look on our
faces as she threatened us out of the window may have satisfied her; we were punished already. Or she may not have taken
the whole thing as gravely as we thought. She may have forgotten it by sunset. Who can say? The point is that nothing
happened. Except that I kept on thinking. Not, I grant you,
quite in the terms I have been using tonight; but I went
through all this, I really did. And it wasn't fun. What do you
make of it, Angus? Did such a thing ever happen to you?"

"No—no, I think not," said the younger man, and signaled
the waiter that he wanted his bill. He was looking everywhere

except into the eyes that watched his across the table. "No, it never did," he said; and stood up suddenly. "Shall we go now? I'll pay at the desk unless—oh, here he is."

Out on the street, Sunderson, walking away alone, said to himself: He does want my wife. His confusion showed it; he understood me perfectly. He knows I know why he has been so nice to me—his oldest friend, and he has been treating me like God. He's afraid. He wants her, and he's trying not to get hurt. As if I could hurt him for that. As if anything I thought would be worse than what he did. Or may do. Or has done.

Sunderson walked faster, wondering how Marian would look at him when he got home. She knew Angus had taken him to dinner after another long day at the office. It had happened three times in the past month. Also, Angus was so attentive to him when the three of them were together, as if it were he, not Marian, that anyone would want to be with. And Angus bought him that set of chess men he had seen in Barclay's window. He had spoken of it night before last, and last night it was waiting for him at home—with no card, but no card was required. Marian knew as well as he—

Knew what?

And how much did *he* know?

Only that Angus had understood why he told the story, and why he talked about it as he did, making himself out a theologian at four. The story was true, but of course he didn't have those ideas then. He never *had* had them till this winter, when Angus began acting kind; began doing things for him as if he couldn't do them himself; began proving that they were friends in spite of the difference in their ages.

But no proof was needed. Or at least he had thought so till Angus seemed to doubt it. You prove the things you doubt.

Not that he felt like God, toward Angus or anybody. God has no wife, he said; and was shocked that he had said it.

All he knew for certain was that he felt very old. He was sure he looked older already—old enough for Marian to notice the minute he came in—old enough for Angus, tomorrow at work, to notice without even glancing up. Angus wouldn't be surprised.

The Birds

THE LINER was losing time. Long Island, invisible on the left but tangible there to one who knew this part of the sea, should have been passed long ago. The incessant horn, which never seemed able to clear its throat, hooted through the slow, mournful afternoon, hoarsening each hour, Sylvester thought, into thicker despair, into more raucous, more raven gloom.

Sylvester was old enough to be making the voyage alone, but he was young enough to love the forlornness of this first day out of New York. He had explored the ship's interior—the cabin passages, the writing alcoves, the lounges, the barred windows of the purser's office, the long main cabin, the great central stairs with their ever so imperceptible creak, the dining room of course, and the mysterious approaches to the hold—he had explored these breathlessly, until it seemed to him that there was nothing left to smell or see. Then he had gone out on deck.

It was a smooth ocean they were feeling their way through. Sylvester, even though the deck heaved under him now and then, so that he always had to be aware of his feet and knees, was certain that the only bad weather there would be today was fog and more fog—for the swirls of it that drifted in from off the Atlantic were ever more numerous and purposeful, as if the sea had an object in view, and that object was the slowing up, even the stopping in midwave, of the *Arcadia*, mistress now of everything except the speed at which her eighteen thousand tons could move.

Not that for Sylvester the fog was bad. As he paced the deck in a solitude he found delicious because the very breath of it was so cool, so melancholy, and so salt, he congratulated himself upon the greyness of the world. He was going where

34

all things were different from what he had thus far known. He was going where his father was, and where his mother, whose sweetness he barely remembered, once had been. So it was proper that the ship he went on should so soon have plunged into mist and chaos.

But even had this not been true for Sylvester, he would have adored the dismal moment he lived through. For he was young enough to like the taste of misery in his mouth. He was in love with being alone, and with this fog that felt like tears. In his explorations of an hour ago he had pretended he was the only passenger, indeed the only person, on the white-and-green *Arcadia*. He and she were abandoned together on a nameless sea; and if others seemed to pass him in the cabins or on the stairs, they were but ghosts from an older voyage with which he had nothing to do.

His steward, a monkey-faced little man of fifty, had become aware of the spirit in which the lean, brown-eyed boy roamed over the ship, and in so far as he could do so had assisted. Whenever, that is, he encountered Sylvester along a passage he had respected the trance in which he walked; had gone by without seeming to know that anybody was there, his own face pulled suddenly long, his own head down about the business of luggage or towels. This in spite of the familiarity they had already established between themselves in Sylvester's stateroom. Sylvester, to whom the steward was more than a servant, was indeed his only friend on board, would have liked to stop and speak, if only to say "Hello." But Leo always darted past and disappeared.

Later, knocking at the stateroom door, he would become talkative again, advising Sylvester about the life preserver, the porthole, and his meals; or confiding the details of his own family life, long ago in Scotland. But here in neutral territory, in the public walks, he had been a perfect stranger; had even seemed to be one of those ghosts from former crossings. He had a mobile countenance; he winked and grinned—or suddenly straightened the wrinkles around his eyes—as if there were a deep secret between Sylvester and himself. And there did seem to be. The secret was that Sylvester voyaged alone,

with thoughts in his head which nobody else was to understand.

For this reason—a reason Sylvester could never have stated
to himself—Leo had his complete confidence; so that now
when the little man appeared on deck, grimacing in the mist
and touching his blue cap, he was welcome as no one else
would have been.

Two birds had just alighted on the rail by Sylvester's hand.
He had seen them spiralling down, their wings performing
equal miracles in the air, and then he had watched them as
they settled into possession of the perch where they now sat,
facing inward from the sea and looking without fear at his
wrists and eyes.

They were grey-brown birds, and their own eyes—sharp,
unclosing little circles of clear yellow—fascinated Sylvester so
that he found it hard to look away from them. He did so now
only because Leo had appeared.

"Look!" he said. "Those birds—they've just come. What do
you suppose—they're not gulls, are they? They haven't flown
over from the land."

Leo screwed up his face to inspect them carefully before he
ventured a reply. He had not been interested in the birds until
Sylvester spoke. Now, between critical glances at their backs
and beaks, he shot a special glance of another kind at the rapt
face from which the question came.

"Ay," he said thoughtfully, as if the question were not for
him.

"I mean," said Sylvester, "they seem to be birds of the sea—
entirely of the sea. Or am I wrong, Leo? I've heard of birds
that build their nests on waves—petrels, and the like. Is that it?
They seem to be at home, you know. I can't think they are
land birds that have been lost. They don't look tired or anything. See how they sit there and stare at us—or at one another. They're a pair all right. Male and female, do you
suppose? Mates, maybe?"

"Ay," was all that came from Leo.

Sylvester turned to him almost impatiently. "You don't
know, then."

"Don't *you?*" Leo looked at him with the intensest concentration. "Hasn't anyone on the ship told you?"

"What?" said Sylvester. "What?" The birds meanwhile sat eyeing each other with something that could have been affection. But as Sylvester repeated his "What?", a touch of irritation coming into his voice as he did so, they sprang up a foot or two in the air, fluttered and turned, then settled down the other way, facing out to sea, their tails dipping and rising toward Leo and Sylvester as they managed the new equilibrium that now was necessary.

And next, from the security of their perch, they did what Leo seemed to have been expecting them to do. They stretched their necks forward and looked down. As the sea slipped slowly by, they stared steadily down, as if the thing were visible at last which they had come out of the far world to see.

"There!" said Leo. "That's it! We're passing over the place. I didn't know where it was exactly, but they do."

Sylvester moved closer to the rail, placed his hands on it, to the right and to the left of them who sat there so strangely indifferent to the fact that he did this, and studied the water below. Seeing nothing on its surface but a little foam, a little weed, he stood upright again and gazed at Leo.

"You said 'the place.' What place? And how would they know?"

The ship's horn hooted again.

"Why wouldn't they?" Leo came closer to him and whispered. "It's where they died."

Sylvester continued to gaze at him, more soberly now, like one who is lost and listens to directions.

"They're not birds, you know," said Leo in a low clear tone, looking solemnly over their tails and backs. "Not really. Or they weren't once. You haven't heard the story?"

Sylvester said No with his lips, silently.

"They were people," said Leo. "A lighthouse-keeper and his young wife. Notice here—the one on the left is smaller than her mate. That's the wife—or was. She was sitting with her man in a small boat that was taking them back at the end of their first year off yonder." He pointed through the impenetrable mist and Sylvester thought he heard a horn there, answering the ship's horn that had sounded again. "There was going to be a bairn. That was one reason. But another reason was she hadn't stood the monotony as well as he hoped she would. There had been fits of crying. And so they were coming in. He didn't mind too much, for he would have gone anywhere she said. Well, she had said dry land, and so they were coming in. Their relief at the lighthouse, two brothers named Larsson, that talked to them a good deal before they shoved away, testified later how they left in high glee, laughing—or the woman was laughing—at a certain danger that was mentioned. There was fog that day, like this. And this ship, homeward bound, was expected within the hour."

He paused, and Sylvester opened his dark eyes wider. "You mean the *Arcadia?*"

"Yes, sir, it was this ship. But I wasn't on it then. I've only heard the tale. She ran them down—right here, or rather back there where the birds were watching. They're not interested any more. I think they're getting ready to leave us again. They only come for this."

It was true. The visitors from the sky—or water—were treading the oak rail and uttering small cries.

And now they sprang away, holding their height at the level of the deck for only a few seconds before they dropped in a slow, slanting dive toward the stern of the vessel, where they disappeared in the fog that obscured the wake.

Were they returning, to wheel awhile above the scene of their death, before they went—but where would they go? Perhaps they would enter the water as once they had, or as the others had, the man and woman whose places in the cold world they had taken. Sylvester, leaning over and looking back, wondered if Leo could answer these questions too.

He turned, and Leo was eyeing him guiltily. He must explain to Leo that he had done right to tell him. It was not a depressing story. It was beautiful, really. It went with everything else today. He would never be unhappy because he had heard it.

Yet there were some questions left.

"They come here every voyage? Just like this—whenever the *Arcadia* passes?"

Leo still looked guilty. "Oh, I don't know," he said. "I think they only come in fog, and on the anniversary of that day, or as near it as they can—the schedule, mind you, and the weather."

"And they just come? Does the captain hear about it? Was he with the ship then? How long ago was it? Wouldn't Captain Scott like to know they had been here today?"

"No," said Leo sharply, with apprehension in his eyes, "no, he wouldn't."

"You mean he doesn't like to be reminded? He *was* here then!"

"That's not it. You see, son—"

"I'll tell him tonight at dinner. He's an old friend of my father's, and I have a letter to him. I wasn't going to use it, because I thought I had nothing to talk about. But now I have, of course. I'll tell him tonight."

"No! No you won't!"

Sylvester was incredulous for the first time since their conversation began.

"But why! If he doesn't object to hearing about the birds— Oh! I see! You think he would be angry at you for telling me—for scaring me, or something."

Leo merely said: "But you won't tell him."

"Or it isn't true. The story isn't true."

Leo merely repeated: "You won't tell him. Promise me, son. Promise you won't say anything at all."

"But why?"

Leo started off as a bell sounded somewhere inside the ship. "Why? Because I might lose my living. That's the why."

"Oh! But I still don't see—wait a minute, Leo."

Leo was halfway through the white door he had opened. "Duty," he called back. "I can't wait. You do what you please. But remember, governor—I asked you."

Sylvester hesitated. "All right. I won't say anything."

"Not at all?"

"No, not at all."

"Thanks, governor." And he was gone.

The horn cleared its throat again, or tried to. The deck heaved gently, and Sylvester resumed his walk.

It was growing dark. The fog would last all night. He would have dinner, and then after another walk out here he would go to bed and lie listening to the horn, the cleaved water, and perhaps the birds. He would not hear them actually, but he was sure he would never forget their little cries as they sprang off the rail.

Where were they now? Where were the man and woman the *Arcadia* had drowned? Where was his mother whom he so meagerly remembered? He remembered her sweetness, and a certain something in her voice when it sang French songs, but not herself, he sighed and said. Where for that matter was his father? Where, through all this ocean straight ahead, this ocean without color or end, was he who had sent the nice letter to the captain?

Sylvester said, patting the rail: But I won't see the captain, I won't give him the letter.

Would Leo be near the stateroom after dinner tonight, when he went below to sleep? And would there be further talk of the birds—of the reason why Sylvester must not mention them? If Leo didn't begin it, he wouldn't. It was a sore subject now, it had better be avoided.

Yet why? Surely Leo wouldn't lose his job for telling a true story. Anything that is true, said Sylvester, I can take. And this was beautiful.

Or *was* it true?

But nobody could have made it up so quickly. Why, Leo no sooner saw the birds than he began to tell it. He couldn't have arranged their coming there. They had just arrived; and then he told the story. People don't tell lies that easily, Sylvester said.

The horn hooted and hooted, resigned now to the prospect of fog, fog all night long.

My Son, My Son

As long as the dry spell lasted, he told her, he would sit here every day. "That is, if you don't mind."

"Mind what?" said Emmy. She kept on stitching at the snow-white flannel shirt he was to wear back to Virginia, under his new blue jacket, when he had to leave her. "You know I don't care about anything except to get you well enough for *that* to bear your weight."

She pointed to what the General himself was looking at: his leg, huge in its bandages, that extended before him like an object not necessarily his and rested upon two stools with brocaded tops.

"I mean," he said, "the labor of lugging the old elephant out." He looked across the Hollow with exactly the same expression in his eyes that had been there each afternoon since the tenth of October. That was the day the Housatonic train brought him on the last lap of his journey as a convalescent from Antietam. Between thirty and forty neighbors had gone to meet him at the station, and had driven home behind the brother and sister as far as this high place where both of them were born. But after that he wanted to be alone with her, and the neighbors consented. For one thing they understood why he should wish it to be so; and for another they were short-handed on their farms, what with so many men and boys gone off to war, a few of them in the very Corps the General commanded.

The expression in his eyes was such as none of his soldiers had ever seen. With them he was humorous and kind, even if he was strict, and they called him Uncle John; but for none of them, nor for any person, any object in the world did he have the simple, pure affection that he had for this small hollow in

41

the golden hills: golden now at any rate, for the autumn trees
were only one week past their prime, and the dry weather—
every day of it just like another, with no wind, no rain, no
sudden cold to strip the branches—hung upon them like a
spell, delaying the end which sooner or later, of course, was
not to be avoided.

"But I have Heman to help," said Emmy, whose eyes, busy
with sewing, did not follow his: downhill by the cemetery,
then up again past the small white schoolhouse to the top of
Foxbrush Mountain where smoke from two or three houses
thickened the haze in which his vision came to rest. She knew
it had done so, and chose to leave it there if that was where its
pleasure was. Hers was in him alone. The landscape, familiar to
her in every season, was the one thing that kept his pleasure
from being in her alone; or so she might be thinking, anyone
would say who watched her at these times when so few words
passed between them. It was not like their letters, which
crossed each other incessantly as long as he was in the field; had
done so during his four years at West Point, and then while he
was down in Mexico; and now, certainly, would continue to
do so as far into the future as this terrible new war would last;
as long as *he* would last, she might be saying to herself, bending closer to her stitches. Whereas John never spoke of the
war, so far away now and so oddly smaller than himself; when
he spoke at all it was of the new house, handsome with its
peaks and gables, whose long porch lay behind them in the
shade of locust trees their father had planted the first month he
was married; or else it was of the neighbors who so consider-
ately left them to themselves.

"Heman," he said. And Emmy thought he strained his eyes
to see, off to the right, across the cemetery road, some sign of
life about the Harvesters' red barn. The house was invisible,
for trees; and so was most of the barn, except that an open
door, where the cows came and went, was framed at the far
end of a tunnel, stretching all the way from here to there, of
hectic maple leaves. But now there were no cows. Heman
would come over to help her take John in before he went for
them down the steep back slope they never ascended unless

they were driven. "Heman's not much help. He's aging fast. I can't tell you how shocked I was when I saw him at the station."

"He's only your age. He's not old."

The General looked at his leg. "No, not very old. But he's had to work hard all his life. I suppose that's it. There's nothing like farm work to—"

"Work! As if you didn't."

"When I do." He turned his leg a little, experimentally, and winced. "Otherwise, Heman would have plenty of right to say it wasn't work at all. Between wars, I mean."

"As if we had to keep on having them!"

The General did not respond. There was nothing he enjoyed more than an argument with Emmy, but he would have none with her on this subject. Unless she kept it going. Which she made as if to do.

"With the Old Country, twice. Then Mexico. And now ourselves. Who else is there to have one with? Who else?"

The General said nothing as he looked away again across the red and yellow wonder of his chosen world. It would not be his to look at as he now did; not, he thought, much longer. Maybe a month, if the last army surgeon who came to study his leg—Wednesday, it was—half knew what he was talking about. He probably did. He spoke of duty again by Thanksgiving.

The General glanced quickly over at the top of his sister's head, bent lower than ever above the flannel that filled her lap. Her head, seen thus, was all one glossy black; he could not discover a grey hair upon it. Beautiful hair, if fiercely straight—he preferred it that way, though nobody else did: no woman, he meant. Women were always for wavy hair, which just as often as not men had; he did, for instance, without valuing it a penny. He stroked his thick black beard, contemplating how much white the past two years had put there; and no wonder.

Would Emmy's hair have turned if she had married? If there were children? If she had found it hard to have them? If she had lost one, even, and almost died herself?

And why was she not married? He knew that people said he was the reason. She lived only for her brother, the General.

And was the General married? No. Why not? He knew that people said she was the reason. After the army, and after the place here, he lived only for his sister, Emmeline Sperry.

So he did; and had, as far back as he could remember. He confessed it freely, to himself at any rate, and then he could stop thinking about it.

Today, though, Emmy's black hair, which he knew he would remember in Virginia as he remembered those red and yellow mountains, did not let him stop thinking about her. Hence these questions. And there were more, many more, where they came from. For instance: what if either one of them *had* married? Many times it had been possible. Well, then, what if one of them had? Or if both had? Might there not be children—sons and daughters, and nephews and nieces—and wouldn't some of those be old enough to have been taken by the war? "Uncle John." He knew his men called him that, though he had never heard them do it. He was more than twice as old as some of them; almost three times as old—certainly three times as heavy—as one boy who lied himself into a uniform. Then he might have a son—two sons— four or five sons—who had been taken by this war which Emmy thought should be the last one.

"John," said Emmy.

"What, dear?" His massive head could multiply, as it did now, a certain tone in him of abstractedness, of suddenly not being there at all. She was used to this; and latterly she had suspected in it a device to protect himself from what he called her power to read his mind. She didn't think she had it; nor did she want it, ever. But he said she had it, and she had never been sure that this was one of his little jokes.

"When Heman comes, I hope you can make him feel better about Clyde. I don't know what you can say, but could it— well, could it at least be non-committal? Couldn't it encourage him the smallest bit to believe he will see that boy this year? It's what his mind is set on. You know that."

"Whose mind?"

She wouldn't answer this.

"Mine? There you go reading it again."

"John!" She didn't know how light to be.

"But you did, Emmy. You guessed what I was thinking. It wasn't precisely about Clyde, but it was about a son of Clyde's age who belonged to me." She looked at him. "Or you." She looked at him again, her blue eyes incredulous, intense. "But both of us are glad, aren't we, that we don't have children for this war to swallow up as Moloch used to swallow up his sacrificial victims?"

He had never said anything like this. They never talked about it; and they mustn't now, she told herself as she turned the top of the shirt and examined its shoulder seams.

"Of course," he went on, "I swallowed you before you were of age. So there was never any chance. I've been trying to remember how cold it can be up here in January. It's hard to do this in the middle of Indian summer, if that's what we are having now. But I don't have any trouble recalling the day I wouldn't let Frank Campbell pull you home from school on the sled I had made, I said, for you and me, just you and me. Every day when there was snow I pulled you down there and I pulled you up. This day I wanted to; and I wanted to kill him because *he* did." She shook her head, it might be at the discovery that one of her measurements was wrong. "I really wanted to kill him. Nobody must touch that sled, at any rate when you were on it. Not even Father could. I found it hard to understand, and I still do more or less, why other boys had so little use for their sisters, or seemed to. They wouldn't even walk with them, let alone put on a harness as I did and haul them like a horse to school. And there was when we hunted eggs. Mother wondered why you always found the most, and got the prize: the biggest egg, hard-boiled, with your initials on it in red and black, 'E.S.,' to put in your lunch box so you could show it to the rest of us at noon. You knew, and didn't tell her either, that I always put some of my eggs where you were sure to find them. Almost any other boy would have got there first and robbed the nest—anything to be ahead of his silly sister. The sled, I suppose, burned up with the old house."

Emmy nodded, still intent upon the shirt.

"Look at me," he said.

She never would until he changed the subject. But who was reading whose mind now? Suddenly she seemed to know why Clyde these days was in her thoughts so much. Naturally, of course, he would be; the Harvesters were her closest neighbors; she had known Heman all her life, and so had John. Poor Heman, poor Ruth. Of their three sons only this one left, and he had written that he couldn't come home. He was all right, he hadn't been hurt—he meant he hadn't been killed, like Harry and young Heman—he hadn't even been sick, he didn't so much as have a cold; but his captain, even though the company was idle, on detached duty guarding stores behind the lines, at Aquia Creek, wouldn't give him a furlough till next year. Next year! And Heman almost dying for a sight of him, not to speak of all the work he did alone; he even had to go for the cows, down that steep hill and up again, since Shep went off one day and died in the locust grove. Naturally enough she would be sorry for them, and she was. And she would comfort them if she could. But ever since John came she had felt Clyde's case almost as if it were her own; as if he were one of the family; as if she were one of *their* family; as if he were her—nephew?—no—and the needle pricked her finger, so that she started, like someone stung—no, her own—her—

She couldn't say "son," even to herself, silently. And she didn't know whether, supposing she *could* say it, she agreed with John about being glad that after all it was only something to say. To pretend. It wasn't pretending, exactly. It wasn't dreaming. Though she did dream of Clyde—of his coming home—almost every night she did; last night she had, and it wasn't something she could tell John. It was one of the few things she never would.

She dared to look up at last, and John was waving at someone on the road. It was Heman, come to help her take the General in. She hadn't thought it was time yet, but by the shadows she knew it was. No telling how long she had sat there: wit-wandering, her mother used to call it.

John ponderously saluted Heman as he came closer over the

brown lawn. But Heman, poor Heman, had nothing military
in him with which he could respond. His oldest friend, his
neighbor all his life, was Major-General Sperry, and the fact
had never ceased to confound him. Particularly now, when
boys were dying for such men—when two of his had—when
Clyde—Emmy supposed it was things like this that ate him out
somehow, so that he was the merest sallow shuck of his old
self. Never big, like John; but at least he once was merry-
minded, with color in his cheeks. His work clothes hung on
him like garments handed down from Harry or young Heman.
Perhaps they were. Perhaps he insisted on their being so.

"Well, Captain!" Should John say that?

Heman said nothing.

"You've come in time. Emmy has been telling me how important it is for this to get well"—he pointed to his leg—"so I
can go away again. I hardly blame her for wanting to get rid
of us." He pointed as he had done before.

Heman looked at Emmy, understood her by the way she
shook her head—ever so slightly—and stooped without a word
to pick up the crutches that were lying where he had left them
at three o'clock. But Emmy, having risen, was at his side to
reach them before he did.

"Here," she said, "here, Heman."

Heman didn't know how to acknowledge the dark, new
sweetness in her face except by saying: "Don't you think I can
pick up a pair of them things, Emmy?"

"Yes," and she laughed a little. "I know you can. Or else I
wouldn't trust you with *him.*"

They both looked around at the General. But he was staring
over both their heads as if he hadn't heard or seen them there.
He was even raised a few inches in his chair, his hands grip-
ping its arms, his own arms visibly trembling.

Suddenly he relaxed, sat back, and smiled. "Heman," he
said. "Heman. Did you get a letter from Clyde today?"

Emmy shivered. Should John ask such a thing? It wasn't
kind of him. And he was kind.

"You know I didn't." Heman's voice was but an imitation of
itself.

"How?"

"I'd have been over, or Ruth would, to show it off—let
Emmy read it. You know that, just like you know there's
never come a letter from him all the time since you *been* here.
You wouldn't have to ask. We'd bring it over."

The General appeared to have lost all interest in the matter.
"Whose cows?" he merely said. "Whose cows?"

Emmy, coming close to him, stared where he did, down
through the tunnel of russet and vermilion maple leaves—
stared, and screamed.

"Heman!" She was almost breathless. "Come here—come
over here and look! Whose *cows?*"

Heman hung back a minute, but then he came and looked.

Emmy held him lest he fall.

Down at the barn the last of the animals was going in, and
the thin blue soldier who brought them—up the back slope he
had come, not whistling, not singing, not making any noise
they might have heard—the thin blue stranger stood at the
driveway door, looking in to see if Heman might be there.

But Heman was here.

No, he was on his way. Not tottering, as Emmy had feared a
minute ago, but not hurrying either; not especially so, she
thought. He was holding on to himself. He was getting ready
to say the first thing he would say. He might even be hoping
he would get there before Clyde turned around.

"So!" said the General. It sounded like a barrel of breath let
out of him at once.

"So?" Emmy glanced down at the crutches, lying where
they fell from Heman's hands. "So? You knew it? You knew
Clyde was coming? All the time you knew!"

"So!" said the General. "Every day I've waited. Captain
Marcus took his time about letting him go. I said, at the Captain's convenience; then up here I regretted that. I did think
your boy would never come."

"My boy?"

"Might as well be. But then, mine too. I made the arrangements before I left; I had Clyde up from his company, and
together we contrived this little thing—he to come up with

the cows as Heman went down to fetch them. He was a shade early, but that doesn't matter. Does it, Emmy? It was even better this way. And ten times better than a letter!"

"Letter!" Emmy shook his arm. "You told him not to write?"

"Not exactly."

"But you hoped he wouldn't? It would be a bigger surprise then? You suggested that?"

The General groaned by way of answer.

"It may kill Ruth."

"Not it won't," he said quickly. "Or Heman either. You saw *him—he* didn't die. But I'll admit I didn't know three weeks ago how bad he looked, how bad he was. I haven't enjoyed thinking about that."

She looked down at the crutches. "Here! I can help you in myself."

"No," he said, settling into his chair. "They'll come."

"They'll see Ruth first. They should, and they will."

"So! And what's the hurry? They'll bring her too."

Emmy sat down and resumed her sewing.

My son, she said almost aloud, my son.

And what would John be saying to himself? She didn't know at all. It wasn't as if he were the father. But then do mothers ever know? Real mothers?

Real fathers.

Whatever John was, he was good, and she was grateful. She loved John.

Mr. Hasbrouck

THE LONGEST DAY of the year was going to be the shortest, thought Martin as he helped Lucinda over the stile. Afternoon was trying to be night. The silent thunderheads over North Mountain were no longer silent. They had grown during the

last hour into immense, muttering things that shut out the sun;
and now this powerful wind was swelling them till they
threatened to blacken the whole sky. The leaves of the excited
trees were turning pale, and out of the bent hay between here
and the house a rank odor blew, as if the green surface of the
summer earth itself felt fear—or it might be joy, thought
Martin, it might be a savage sort of joy because every visible
thing was about to change.

"We'll have to run, Lucy, if we don't want to get wet.
Come on," and he took her hand.

But Lucinda, instead of running, came to a stop. She had
been staring ahead of her at the big house whose distant gables
awaited their return across the meadow.

"Come on," said Martin. "Do *you* want to get wet? We
might even be struck by lightning." The sound of kettledrums
that had been coming to them out of the thunderheads grew
suddenly too loud to be thought of any more as music. The
skins of the drums seemed to be ripping and bursting, and
forked white lines made dazzling patterns in the firmament,
the new firmament that now had unrolled its full self above
and around them, so that to the last horizon the world they
walked under was purple and dun.

"There's just as much danger there," said Lucy, still looking
toward the house. Martin looked too, and saw that the white-
trimmed gables, more vivid now by contrast with the dark
clouds so close above them, were something like eyebrows,
like pointed eyebrows, in a face that frowned at them and
urged them to come on, though not as to a destination they
would find comfortable or kind. "Lightning strikes houses,
too," she added, as if that were an explanation. But Martin
knew it wasn't.

"You're thinking of him," he said. "You're afraid of him.
You have been, ever since we came."

"That's right. And so have you."

"But—"

"Yes you have. It was a mistake to come, Martin. I can see it
now, I can see it in the very way the roof-line scowls at me. It
looks exactly like Joel; that's the way *he* scowls. And all the

things he says—in a sense I do understand them. He doesn't want us there. He belongs there, and we don't. Even if Mr. Hasbrouck gave us the house, even if it is ours by law, we're strangers in it. That's what it's saying to us now; and Joel, I'm certain, is in some window of it this minute, seeing where we are and saying the same thing to himself."

The wind, doubling its force, struck them in a kind of fury, and brought with it drops of rain—the first few of many that would come—which startled their warm faces. Martin involuntarily ducked his head.

"All right," he shouted, "but come on!"

She let him take her at his own speed. Running with him, she let him pull her along the path that skirted the meadow beyond which the big house crouched on its eminence, among huge trees which now the storm was laboring to break. They were at the gate when rain really started to come down. The door was barely visible by the time they reached it, so thick were the sheets of water they went through. But there at the top of three steps it was at last. And it was opening for them.

Joel, standing inside and smiling, was not the same old man at all, thought Martin, who looked at Lucy and saw her staring, too. Even while she shook her hair and picked at her dripping dress she stared frankly into the deep wrinkles which only a few hours ago, indeed only a few minutes ago, she had found sinister and disturbing. Perhaps the ancient face was still disturbing; but it smiled, and that was the fact at which Lucinda stared.

"Come in, come in, my dears, so I can shut the door. We have to barricade ourselves against this weather. What weather!" He rubbed his hands and chuckled, shaking his long head with its shock of white hair. He was tall and thin, but he stooped now as if in gratitude to the inclemency of the hour.

And he had said "my dears."

Martin and Lucy, glancing quickly at each other, made no move to mount the stairs which would take them to their bedroom and dry clothes. Joel had started toward the kitchen whence he must have come, for the door to it stood open at the end of the hall; had started, and expected them to follow.

It was almost a command, the way his fingers clenched and unclenched themselves as he went along.

"See here," he said, turning back and beckoning to them as soon as he was through the door, "see what I've got going for you."

Fire blazed in the wood stove: a recently made fire, of paper and shingles, but already heat was coming from it in pleasant waves.

"I knew you would need to dry yourselves," he told them as they turned this way and that before the box of black iron whose inner music competed cheerfully with the din of the storm.

"We were going up to change our clothes," said Lucy, watching her two hands.

"Yes, yes, I know, but this is just as good. Here!" and he dragged two chairs from the table by the window. "You can sit down, too—you should, since you're out of breath."

Martin, starting for the third chair, was stopped by a rough hand on his arm. "No, no," said Joel, "I'd rather stand and look."

He was at the window now, studying intently the rain tracks on the glass, and stroking his long fingers whenever thunder broke over the house, whenever lightning hissed and crackled as if its aim were to burn up the world.

"Mr. Hasbrouck always came in here to wait out bad weather," he said over his shoulder. "Mr. Hasbrouck—his house, he said, was his fort. When the elements attacked it he came in here, no matter how wet he was, and dared them to do more. Thunder was cannon to him, and lightning was gunnery fire. Mr. Hasbrouck—ha! he knew where his strength lay. It was in these walls, this roof; which incidentally, my dears, he kept in excellent repair. Between storms he was busy with boards and nails. That was why he could be calm when hell broke loose. He had done his best. And the fortress held firm."

Martin stood up suddenly and faced away from the fire. Joel heard him, he thought, but nothing showed that he did.

"Joel," began Martin, "that's more than you ever told us before about Mr. Hasbrouck. Considering what he did for us, we ought to know him better than we do. Go on."

Joel turned at this, and a cunning grin revealed his teeth at the same instant that lightning, filling the window, made an unholy halo over his head.

"What's that, Martin?" Lucy shivered, for this was the tone she was accustomed to. "The two of you have been asking the same question, like parrots, ever since you came. It's not your fault if you don't know more about Mr. Hasbrouck. The truth is, my silly dears, I've told you all *I* know. What have I ever been but a servant on this place? Oh, he called me a companion once, and once he lied to an old fool of a woman who came to pry; he said I was his cousin, an orphan cousin he had taken in. But I was and am and will be nothing but a hired man in the house. If Mr. Hasbrouck had wanted to tell me more, he would have. He didn't talk to me much." The teeth showed themselves with new emphasis as the grin widened. Then he was serious again. "But you might help me. What do *you* know? What did the lawyer say? There must have been a lawyer. If you would tell me what you came here knowing, maybe I could go on from there—a little distance, anyway."

Martin sat down again, his eyes half on Lucinda, half on the stove door through whose holes fire flickered. "Why," he said, "I thought I told you." Did the old man like to hear it? "My grandfather was Mr. Hasbrouck's best friend when they were boys. But he went west when so many people did, and there was never anything between them after that except letters. Many of those, I believe, but they didn't meet again. My grandfather has been dead a good many years, and my father died last year, a week after Lucy and I were married. We were going to live with *him*, so then we decided to live in his house. That was when the telegram came; and afterwards the lawyer, Mr. Sturgis. It seems that Mr. Hasbrouck kept up with everything out our way. That is, he knew about me. He had never been able to get my grandfather back, so he settled on me. I was to be his sole heir, provided I accepted this house and land. If I did that I came into his money too. It wasn't much, but it was more than I was likely to have soon, and it was enough to keep the place going as he wanted it to be. There was one more condition, of course. You were to be

here, and you were to stay. The will described you as an
ancient and faithful friend. Well, there you are. Now what can
you add?"

"Nothing, nothing! That's all there is, that's all!" Joel had
turned to the window again, and Martin, looking over his
shoulder, saw the storm departing. The sky was lighter and the
thunder had thinned out. The rain, too, had suddenly stopped.
The trees dripped, and one of the horses had his head out of
the barn: out of the square hole that reminded Martin now of
the openings he used to look at in a big picture of the Ark
they had had at home when he was a boy.

"That's all!" Joel had turned again and was glowering at
both of them. It was as if the storm that brought his good
spirits had taken them away. He was dismissing the couple
from his kitchen. It was their kitchen too, Lucinda seemed to
be saying, for she didn't move. Yet it *was* his in a way, as all
the house was most of the time: as houses have a way of being
when servants run them. So they had better leave. Martin saw
this, and after a few seconds realized that Lucy did too, for she
got up from her chair and without so much as a glance at Joel
preceded her husband to the door.

"There's one thing I could add," Joel said to their two
backs, so that they paused, listening. "But I won't, because I
really can't. It's about Mr. Hasbrouck his own self. I knew
him as of course you never will, now that he's dead. But you
wouldn't have known him anyway. He was hard to know; for
these times he was a queer fellow. Yet he wasn't queer. He had
a good idea. His house was his—well, I told you what it was.
And he would defend it against anything. More things than
storms, mind you. For he knew what was coming, the big
thing that was coming. And still is. Do *you* know? Do *you*
know, my dears?"

The term was ironic now, and Lucy shivered again.

"Of course you don't."

Martin, closing the door on these words, put out an arm to
draw Lucinda nearer so that he could reassure her with a kiss.
But she ran on ahead of him to the front door, and escaping

through that was halfway across the sodden lawn before he
could catch up with her.

She accepted his kiss abstractedly. "You can't make him
out," she said, "any better than he is. He's horrible. Or else we
are. We are to him, I think. He doesn't like us. We're the
wrong kind of people, and we'll never hear the end of it. He
won't precisely say it, but it will growl at us between every
two words he does say. We were crazy to come—you know
it, Martin, we were crazy to come."

"But he says, 'my dears.' "

"Oh, Martin! So did the wolf to Little Red Riding Hood."

"He's not like that."

"No," agreed Lucinda slowly, "he isn't. He's worse. He—"

"Now who's crazy? Look, Lucy! The brook down there! It
was a cloudburst, and this is a flood. See? Under the bridge?
That water's still rising, too. It may take away the bridge.
Let's watch."

They went, but neither there nor in the house next day did
Lucy retreat from her position. Joel was their enemy, and
these rooms their prison. She said it over and over, so that
sometimes Martin was afraid Joel would hear. If he did hear,
he gave no sign of it as he came and went through the many
rooms of what to Lucy had been from the first an ugly, for-
bidding mansion. It had been built, she said, in another age,
and *for* that age. Generations had lived in it, and its cold
influence over them must have been a powerful thing, permit-
ting no deviation from the original rituals, the frosty reti-
cences which Mr. Hasbrouck, coming last, had been able to
understand as a command that he feel the entire dwelling to be
a fort, a blockhouse whose enemy was all the outer world. Mr.
Hasbrouck, the last of its owners before luck—bad luck—
bestowed it upon Martin and herself, had perhaps outdone the
first one, the one whose name she didn't know. But at least he
knew how to live here, as she and Martin never would. She
said this only in the privacy of their bedroom, to which as
often as possible she escaped, taking Martin with her when she
could. He went because he loved her, and he listened for the
same reason; though pride prevented his agreement with the

words she used. They had been fools to come? He still wasn't
sure of this, he said.

The farm, for one thing, was so beautiful. He would call
Lucy to their corner window and make her look at the little
valley they owned: a little valley, but all of it was theirs, for
the farm exactly filled its two irregular slopes and the fine
bottom land between. It coincided with all of the earth that
could be seen, except of course for the road that cut through
North Mountain and connected them with the level country
beyond; they could look through the pass and see that level
country lying in its own haze, its haze that hummed with
rumors, yet only rumors, of another universe. Lucy, listening
to him and in her intimate, sweet way letting his arm do what
it would along her slender back, her shoulders and her waist,
would nevertheless always shudder before he finished and say
that the farm too was a prison; they were shut out from mankind, and the beauty of it only made it the more horrible. The
farm was theirs and yet it wasn't theirs. It was still the property
of that Mr. Hasbrouck whom no one would describe. Even the
neighbor beyond the mountain who brought his horses over and
plowed or mowed the fields—even Charlie Regan was the
property, or at any rate the deputy, of a dead old man who
dominated everything here still. She would ask Martin when
he was going to take over and run the place as *he* saw fit. And
he would only smile, answering that there was plenty of time
for this. Or he would draw her from the window and lie with
her for a luxurious summer hour before they had to go downstairs and face him who Lucy even then insisted was the
master of the house. He was its hidden master, she said, an old
man who withdrew into his compact quarters beyond the
kitchen—the sitting room and the little bedroom which Mr.
Hasbrouck seemed to have built for him to live in like a
spider—but only waited there, listening and grinning, till it
was time to come forth again and torture them.

She was musing thus, aloud in Martin's ears, on the afternoon that followed the storm. She lay looking at the ceiling in
a trance that Martin, finding irresistible, was about to honor

with another kiss when both of them heard Joel clumping up
the stairs and knew that he had come to interrupt them.

The door, thank goodness, was locked, but he didn't try its
handle. He only called out that someone was driving up, and
that one of them must go see who it was. Then he descended
the stairs, and Lucy heard him slamming his own door beyond
the kitchen.

"I'm going with you," she said to Martin who had sprung
up, flushed, from the four-poster. "A visitor! And see? Joel
has scuttled into his den. He won't be seen by anybody, not if
he can help it. I wonder if he was always that way. But I'm
going with you," she repeated, giving her hair a quick toss.

The visitor was a lady with a parasol and a wide, wavy, grass-
green hat. She was Mrs. Lord, she said, and she was their
nearest neighbor—not that she was very near, she lived over
the mountain, or that she was an old inhabitant, for she hadn't
been here much longer than they had. But she did confess she
was curious about them and their wonderful big house. The
boy that drove her over would wait in the car.

"Please do come in," said Lucy. Her delight was real. "This
is my husband, Martin Miles. We haven't been off the place,
hardly. Perhaps we should have called on you."

"No, no, my dear. My dear, it *is* a wonderful house. My
husband will be jealous because I didn't bring him. We never
knew Mr. Hasbrouck, but we *have* heard about the marvellous
luck that brought you here. Tell me, is it strange? Are you
getting settled all right? Can I help?" Mrs. Lord beamed on
both of them.

"Thank you," said Lucy. "There was someone here, of
course. It wasn't like coming to an empty house."

"Someone?"

"Joel—Mr. Hasbrouck's old—well, companion. *He* was
here. And he still is, in the wing there at the west end. But he's
a fixture, he doesn't go out."

"I never heard of *him*. But there it is, the people here are *so*
close-mouthed. They don't tell you anything unless you ask
them to, and naturally in this case—what do you say his name

is, Joel?—I wouldn't have known to ask. My dear, it *is* a dark house, though. Isn't it? But handsome."

In due course they showed her every room—every room except Joel's, the lock in whose door they heard quietly turning as they inspected the kitchen.

But Mrs. Lord did not linger very long, and after she had gone Lucy said she knew why. The house, she told Martin, was nothing to be enjoyed. It hadn't been built for that, and the years had not changed its character. Even its furniture—the highboy, for instance, Mrs. Lord so much admired—well, that was it. Admiration, not enjoyment. Not pleasure. Not love. Mrs. Lord hadn't said she *loved* the house. Who could? For it didn't love you. It didn't know how to. Nobody in it had ever loved anybody, at least until they came. She went to busy herself with the teacups she had set out so hastily for Mrs. Lord.

She couldn't have known that Joel was listening as she talked, for he had made no sound as he came from his den, and the last thing she imagined was that even now he followed the two of them into the living room where the tea service stood in disarray, waiting upon her hands that would tidy it.

But there he was behind them, gaunt in the tall door, and suddenly he was saying: "Here! I want a cup of that."

Lucy almost dropped the red-and-white hot water pitcher.

"Why," she said, turning to him slowly, "I didn't hear—of course, Joel. You could have had a cup before, with Mrs. Lord, if you had wanted to."

"I didn't want it then," he said. "Mrs. Lord is a fool."

Lucy wondered, pouring tea into the fourth cup she had brought for good measure, whether he really wanted it now.

He pulled a chair to the table, the embroidered chair that no one ever sat on, and said to both of them: "Sit down. Sit down, I want to say something. I heard you out there, I know what you think, but now you listen to me!"

It was a servant's command, and they sat down. Lucy's eyes had fire in them; but she sat as quietly as Martin did, with Joel between them on the third side of the table, the side nearest the door that led into the front hall.

Joel, smacking his lips over the tea, set down his cup with an emphasis that said he would not lift it again.

"I heard you out there," he began once more. "I know what you think. You think Hasbrouck—that's what I call this house—is to be enjoyed. I just wanted to tell you what its old owner thought. He thought it was to be defended. Preserved, my dears, and defended. The world, he knew, was against it. The world of thunder and lightning, of overgrowth and decay, of time, of dry rot, of people. Yes, people. Like Mrs. Lord and all those other fools. The world was the enemy of this house. As long as he lived he thought so, and he would think so now if he could. Martin, you say you will be a good manager, and I guess you will. I've seen you looking at the barns and the fields, I've heard you talking to Charlie about his plans for next year, and the year after. Maybe you have some plans of your own; I hope you have. But that's not it; that's not all of it by any means. You'll have to see as Mr. Hasbrouck did the horns of devils hiding among those woods." His gaze sought the window over their heads and through that the distant fringe of forest bounding the farm. "The woods want to move in on us, and so they have to be fought. Really fought, like an enemy, like an evil, like Satan himself who has so many tricks. You'll have to hate the woods."

Martin, remembering the pleasure he and Lucy had taken yesterday in the red oaks and tulip trees beyond the stile, was about to protest. But he waited for more.

"You'll have to hate them, I tell you, as you hate too much rain, as you hate thistles and moss, and brush. Brush! You've got to think of it, Martin, as something that would break you if it could, break you slowly and diabolically, as the constrictor cracks the bones of what it wraps."

If Lucy shuddered in her chair he did not know it.

"Then the people. That's the main thing. The few people and the many. The few are not so serious; they are simpletons, and easily discouraged. I mean the brainless ones who wander out of cities in midsummer. The ones who drive up and ask for a drink of spring water, the ones who want to picnic in the lane, the ones who wear such—well, I don't call them clothes!

Those can be shooed away. They are the gnats of creation and don't need to trouble you much. It's the many Mr. Hasbrouck feared. They're not here yet, they've never been seen at all, but they are coming. The cities—the whole world, Martin, but especially the cities—they're sick to death. The cities of the world are set to overrun us. Creatures such as you never saw are dreaming even now of the day when they will pour up out of their cellar holes and overwhelm us if they can. First, of course, they'll overwhelm each other. Wars will multiply. Laws will wither. Courtesy will stink in the gutter like the corpse of an abused woman. All that will happen first. Then the battle moves here. Mr. Hasbrouck knew that; he knew what was coming. He saw the roving bands of starved men that some day, even if not in his day, would be climbing these fences to see what they could trample and steal. The very house you sit in, dears, drinking tea and smelling Mrs. Lord's perfume, will be the haunt of wild children who have armed themselves against the long-haired guerrillas, the wall-climbers, the mad souls from the dying cities, the refuse of rack and ruin. All that, my pretty couple, is what Mr. Hasbrouck wanted you to think about. He wanted you here, but he told me to make sure you understood. You've inherited a war. You have to fight. You have to get ready for the nightmare of that latter day. It didn't come in his time, but it will in yours. This house is your fortress, remember. Keep it firm, he told me. *Tell them to keep it firm!*"

If Joel, risen to his feet now, had been unaware of Lucy's shudder a moment ago, he was no less unaware of what Martin, noticing a shadow fall in the room, had turned his head and seen at the window with its twelve small panes.

Joel saw nothing, and neither did Lucy, whose head hung in helpless loathing of what she had heard.

But Martin saw a boy there, staring in, his mouth open and his face white. He saw him, and in his astonishment could barely listen when Lucy looked up at last and delivered her mind to Joel.

"You're horrible!" she said. "Whoever you are, you're horrible! And so was Mr. Hasbrouck, if you haven't made him up.

The way you think and talk—that *is* the way to kill the world.
But you're mad. Living here has made you mad. It made both
of you mad. You haven't anything to do with us, I tell you.
You can't make *us* mad. We're leaving. The will said you were
to stay; and that's all right, because of course you want to, you
want to be where you can think these terrible thoughts. But it
can't keep us here. You can have all of it, every bit of it, do
you understand? Martin! Are you listening? Why don't *you*
speak?"

It was then the boy yelled.

"Mr. Hasbrouck!" That was what he was saying. The words
came through the glass as if no glass were there. "Mr. Hasbrouck!" And now the boy was running across the lawn and
leaping the far wall beyond which Mrs. Lord's car still waited.

Then Joel was at the window, his breath coming with
difficulty, his tall figure stooped as he watched the car move
headlong away.

"He'll tell her, he'll tell her, and then *she'll* talk. It's over,
my dears." But he didn't seem to be addressing anybody. "It's
over. I couldn't make it last."

He staggered, and Martin, who thus far had not moved,
went quickly to him.

Lucy watched the two of them, her pale face twitching.

Suddenly she said to Martin: "Be careful with him. He's not
well."

"I know," Martin answered quietly. Joel was in his chair
again.

"You're talking about me as if you thought I couldn't hear."
The old man leaned forward a little, smiling painfully. "I'm
not that bad. I won't live long, but it won't be today I go out
of this house, or any day soon. That was young Herman
French. I guess he drives the Lord woman around. She must
have sent him back for something. Well, he found more than he
was looking for. He found the ghost of yours truly. I'm Joel
Hasbrouck. I didn't lie about the first name, anyway, did I?
That death of mine—when the doctor in Boston told me I
wouldn't last through the year—it was then I got the idea. I
didn't die here, you know. It was quite mysterious, I suppose

the neighbors thought. Don't ask me about those lawyers. They mustn't get into trouble. I'm the only one that knows everything about it, and *I* won't tell."

"Martin," said Lucy, "he ought to be in bed. I'll go ahead and get his room ready."

"Wait a minute," said Mr. Hasbrouck. "There's one thing I've got to know right now. You're not leaving me, you two. You can't leave me."

They looked at each other.

"That will keep till later," Lucy said.

"No, it won't!" The voice was losing its oddness; the old acerbity was coming back. "No, no, it won't. I've got to know, I won't take a step till I do. You said you were leaving me, Lucy. But you thought you were talking to another Joel. He told the truth, you know; in his way, that I made up for him, he told the truth. But you won't have to hear it again. Let it go. It's all true, though, I won't go back on that."

"If it's all true," said Lucy, "then Martin and I don't belong here. We can't live that way—nobody could. I'd rather be free and starving than stay and think such things. So would Martin."

"No!"

"Yes, Mr. Hasbrouck." Martin knew that his words were punishment to hear. "I agree. Besides, it isn't ours any more, this place."

"Oh, but it is!" The whole figure trembled now in its effort to rise. "The deeds and all—it's yours, Martin, as it should be. Don't leave me. Don't let her go, and don't *you* leave me. Lucy, you said there was no love in this house. There is. Please don't think it will be hard to stay. I'll keep to myself, I promise."

"Poor Joel," said Lucy, coming to his side suddenly. "Poor Mr. Hasbrouck. Now you *must* get into bed. Tomorrow we can—"

"No we can't!" He was querulous again. "We must settle it now."

"Besides," said Lucy, "you must move back into our room. That little one—you were only pretending it was yours."

"It always *was* mine; it's where I've lived most of my life. I like it—please don't make me move."

But he returned to the question they must answer. "You won't leave me, will you—you two?"

They looked at each other again.

"No, Mr. Hasbrouck, we won't leave," Martin said and reached to help him up.

"That's good, that's good!" He needed no help; he was on his feet instantly; he was shuffling toward the door.

Arriving there, he turned and grinned at them in the old way, his hair wild and his teeth showing. He was still a terrible old man, Lucy thought.

"A bad joke, I'm afraid, a bad joke. Yet there were some good things about it. It brought you here, my children. And now you'll stay till *you* have children. You will, won't you?"

There was no answer to this, but he seemed satisfied. "That's right. There must be many of us, Martin, to defend this place. It's war, you know. We must have numbers."

"There!" cried Lucy. "You said—"

"I know, I know. You won't hear *that* again. Did you say you were coming to my room?"

"Oh!" Lucy went ahead of him, down the hall and through the kitchen.

Joel looked after her, squinting. "Many boys, Martin, many girls!"

"We'll see about that," said Martin, taking one elbow in charge.

"Well, don't forget. Boys and girls."

Feebleness had grown on him by the time he reached his bed, which Lucy was straightening as best she could.

"Tomorrow I'll fix things up here right," she told him as she folded the sheet under his chin. "I'll make a lot of changes."

"Don't touch him, though." He pointed to an ancient photograph in a cherry frame. It stood alone on the low bureau, and it might have been a picture of him, so downward the mouthline ran. "That's my father. That's Henry Hasbrouck."

"Of course." Lucy smiled. "I won't do anything you don't like. Goodbye now, goodbye till I bring your supper."

"Goodbye." He put out a veined hand and stroked hers. "Thank you, my dear."

She had never imagined she would feel like this.

"Well!" said Martin in the kitchen.

But she was already busy at the stove.

A Wild Wet Place

THE NOVEMBER sun had set, but for a long time light would be coming across the fields, and the old man made no move to start the lamp that stood on the oval table by his chair in the warm living room.

"What are you looking at, Grandpa?" The boy on the rug listened for any sound of his sister upstairs, heard none, and asked again: "What are you looking at?"

"Well, son, come here, come closer." He always said "son," to Sally's amusement. But Sally was up in the sewing room with Grandmother Sims, and there was no one here to wink with Forrest about that word. Forrest himself never found it funny. He got up and stood by the old man, studying the white beard that had grown so still.

"You see, son, what a clear view we have of the orchard?"

Forrest, following the faded blue eyes down the dim length of the room, stared through the far window with its twelve little panes. The apple trees, climbing the familiar slope to the woods that went all the rest of the distance up the mountain, leaned east, away from the light, as if that, and not their extreme age, were what bent them into such odd shapes and queer positions.

"But you may not see one thing I do." Forrest looked at him quickly. "You may not—no, I am sure you don't. Nobody ever did but me."

"What, Grandpa? What?"

"Now be patient, son." The voice, as if resting before a longer effort it was about to make, lingered nevertheless in the boy's ears. It had lost its old dry sound. There was now a ring of sweetness in it, a coming closer to the thing of which it spoke. Already, the boy felt, the thing was there.

"At the far end of the orchard, where the pines begin— stand behind me, son, and look through the second pane from the left, just above the lock—there is a dark opening, like a cave. A low cave, wide and low. Do you see?"

Forrest, staring over the silent white head, did see such an opening. Everywhere else the branches swept well down across the line where stones used to make a wall, but for a space there was nothing but darkness: a wide, low arch of it such as he could imagine crawling through on his hands and knees. Except that it was cold and dark, and he wondered what animal, hidden in complete shade, lay and looked out of it, waiting for the last light to die. He shivered, and his grandfather seemed to be aware that he did, for he folded his hands with satisfaction and went on.

"That's right, son. It's something big. But don't be scared. It's something big and fine. I've seen it all my life—ever since I was your size, and right here in this chair. It's big and fine, and always coming. They're coming, son, as every, every evening they have come since I was your size; since I was something like you—oh, I was. Your father wasn't like me, but you are. And now they're coming for both of us to see."

The old head did not turn the least part of a degree as it said these things. The boy, in spite of what he had been told, grew frightened and thought of running upstairs where his grandmother was. But he stayed, and with an effort said: "What things! What things are coming!"

"Horses," said the old man.

"Horses!"

"And riders. That's the main thing, riders. When I was just your size I saw them. Sitting in this chair—where I shouldn't have sat, for it was your great-grandfather's—one evening like this, a few minutes after sunset, I looked up and saw them. There were three of them ahead of all the rest, and these three

had halted suddenly—I could tell that—to take breath before
they came on. Perhaps it was to view the world before them,
the open world that lay this side of the woods. Anyhow, there
they waited, and the horses' heads, shining with the gold on
their bridles and the white linen masks in which their eyes
were set, shook up and down and sideways. But the riders
were still as statues. How high and splendid they sat there, the
three of them; and the middle one was king. I could see that,
even though he had no crown. I could tell by the white hair,
though he wasn't old, that shone on him where a helmet might
have been; but there was no helmet. The other two wore
helmets, and were broad-shouldered in their bright, heavy
armor. His majesty needed no armor. He was broader than
they were in his simple linen gown, open at the neck and
hemmed around with silver braid."

The boy, clearing his throat, interrupted with a question
that sounded, as soon as he had asked it, unimportant even to
himself. "Could you see such things as silver braid, so far
away?"

"I could see everything. They were neither far away nor
close. They were clear. And they were waiting. Do you know,
son, what they were waiting for?"

"For the rest of the riders to come up?" The boy, staring at
the cave which by this time had begun to lose its identity in
the darkness that flooded every part of the world, wished he
could see anything but that darkness.

"No. The rest were in their places, you can be sure of that.
There was authority in these three. No, they were waiting for
someone to join them."

"Someone. Who?"

"Me."

The silence in the long room lasted a full minute.

"They were waiting for me. Their eyes looked straight
ahead of them, well over this house, as if they had no thought
of me. But I knew they were thinking of me, and waiting. And
I didn't go."

"No, Grandpa, for here you are now, with *me*." Forrest was
sure of this.

"I would be here, son, if I had gone. But then I'd be a different fellow. I didn't go. And pretty soon they started. The column moved all at once, like waves around an island, down in two streams, past me here in this house. One of the three kings—for they were all kings of a kind—swept by on the right and another on the left. The middle one, the great one, thundered right on through, right through this room, and he did not look at me, nor did he hurt the walls. The windows rattled and tinkled a bit, as if an earthquake were happening ten thousand miles away, but that was all. He passed right through, solid and yet not solid; and in a minute the whole company was gone like a wave that has passed, and the island of this house, this room, this chair, was dry and quiet again."

The boy looked about him at the familiar objects under the low ceiling: the unlighted lamp, the Boston fern in its big pot by the west window, the rocking chair on the other side of the fireplace, the brown clock on the mantel with its fancy edges of carved wood, the portraits that hung in their walnut frames, dark ovals of dusk against the wallpaper. "Dry and quiet," he repeated as if to himself. "And safe. Safe, Grandpa, like an island in the sea." The brown clock ticked, giving tune to his words.

"Safe!" The old man's voice rose to a thin, high note; and a sweet one, Forrest thought again. "But I didn't go, son. They came down around me, and rode by on beautiful horses. I listened behind me and heard them a long time. But finally they were gone, and I was here, unchanged. I wanted to go with them. But I never have." He waited, as if listening to an echo of the words, then said again: "I never have."

"You mean they came again?"

"They always came. Every night they came, and stopped like that, and looked over my head. They have come all my life, son, and I have never gone with them. Now, though, they don't think I will. That's the only difference now. They have given me up. But they go by on their own business just the same. Their business is like the business of the sea that long ago forgot the islands. Here and there an island may say to itself: I am an eternal thing, I sit here unchanged and watch the waves go back and forth. But the waves, son, are the eternal thing. They are always, always going; but they are always coming too. The island dries and dies, and time forgets it. Eternity, my son, is a wild wet place that seems to be all change; and yet it never changes. I missed eternity."

"But Grandpa." The boy scarcely knew how to go on. "If you had left we wouldn't have you now. Sally and I—this is our favorite place in the world, with you and Grandma always here."

"A dry island, son. You would still have me, I tell you, if I had left; but I would be something to have. Here, all right, right here, but wild and working; and never really changing. Do you see anything up there, son? Tell me honestly, do you see anything at all?"

Forrest did his best, and failed. "No, Grandpa. I don't see what you see."

"Then it isn't time yet, for you will. You will, son. And you must let them take you with them. Don't be afraid; just go along. It isn't safe to stay, it isn't safe. I'm the one that's afraid now. I wouldn't have been, out there, where I might have learned everything. All I know now is that I'm a chip of time, a dry, dry chip of nothing but time."

The voice thinned to grasshopper fineness, sad in its soliloquy, and Forrest, oppressed by its monotone, tiptoed out to the foot of the stair that would take him, if he wanted to go, where his grandmother sat with Sally in another room.

He set one foot on the bottom step, then hesitated. How would he answer if he were asked, as well he might be, what he and the old man had been talking about downstairs in the dark? He could see a crack of yellow brightness under the door of the sewing room, and knew the lamp up there was lit. Doubtless Sally and Grandma were telling each other stories, and good ones, too. He wanted to be there and hear. But he waited, his left foot on the bottom tread, listening and hearing nothing; or looking back now and then through the doorway at the almost invisible figure of his grandfather, a dry old man who sat and saw horses coming, horses with gold on their bridles, horses, horses, horses, coming and coming; and on one of them, the one in the middle, sat a bareheaded king who could ride right through a room and leave it the same as it was. No, less than it was; emptier, drier. The rocking chair might rock by itself, fanned by his coming through; but pretty soon it would be quiet again. No great waves here, rocking wet and wild and never stopping. No great constant waves whose wild face never changed. The boy, fixed there with one foot lifted, waited and waited.

The girl, stepping out of the skirt she had just tried on, handed it to the old woman who sat by the hot lamp and looked over her glasses, not so much at the garment as at the portion of her granddaughter it had covered.

"Child," she said as she took the cloth in her bony hands, for she was big and gaunt all over, this old woman who sat where the bright brass lamp revealed dozens of deep wrinkles in her face, "you're growing up. I'll declare, you have a figure. I measured you well enough," touching the tape that hung about her neck, "but I didn't quite notice. You've stopped being a little girl. That makes all the difference. Now I know how to cut it. Here!" And she proceeded with determination, pins in mouth and scissors in hand, to alter everything.

The girl stood, pleased and erect, her hands self-conscious at her sides, saying nothing.

"Yes, child. Soon you will be a woman." She lifted the garment until it was a veil between them and pulled one edge of it firmly. "*Then* what?"

Sally knew she didn't have to answer, but something in the way her grandmother waited told her to try.

"Then—oh, Grandma, if I could only grow up and be like you!"

"Now, now! You didn't need to say that. You're my good girl; you understand more than most children do; but you shouldn't understand being old, being old like me."

She said this with so little rebuke in her voice that Sally bent suddenly down, half kneeling by the chair, and seized her grandmother's hand to kiss it. "But I do, I think, I do under-

stand. To be like you is what I want most in the world.
Mother knows I do."

"Did you stick yourself with that needle?" For Sally had
withdrawn her right hand, and was rubbing it with her left.
"Be careful!"

"It wasn't anything."

"But it was something like what happens, child," and the
eyes were quiet behind their lenses, "to anyone who hurries to
be old. Who jumps over too much time."

The girl answered slowly, walking away across the room.
"If I could be sure how it would come out, I wouldn't care
how long it took. But if I weren't sure, Grandma, and I don't
care what you say, I'd want to be you now—if I could."

"But you can't. You can't go faster than time does, dear.
Come now, don't be too good a girl. Don't care too much what
old ones think of you. It may not matter what they think; and
anyway, you can't imagine it. You can't know what it means
to take things as they come—so many, many things—and one
at a time, dear, just one at a time. Is there a boy anywhere that
you like better than the others? There wasn't last Thanksgiving, but I think there might be now."

Sally reached for her old skirt, the one she had thrown over
the stool by the window when she tried the new one on, and
let it down over her head.

"There is, I suppose," said her grandmother, watching.
"Well, I won't ask his name. In time I'll hear it, or in time I
shan't. But I'll never live long enough to know all the things
you're going to remember. And you haven't lived long
enough to guess the things I remember. You want to be older,
dear. I don't."

Sally, her fingers at her waist, looked up in time to catch the
smile, half bitter and half sweet, that had not been intended for
her alone.

"No, no," the old woman went on, "I'm not anxious to be
bones and dust. You want to be all bones, like me—you, with
that pretty softness I've been fitting. But there's the dust.
Some day I'll be a boxful of it, some day when you are like me
now—all bones and spectacles. Oh, I'm not hurrying that
day."

The girl, showing her horror, stared through the warm rays of the lamp.

"There's a skeleton in you, my soft thing, that's waiting to be noticeable; and waiting after that to be nothing at all, nothing at all anywhere. Just let it wait. Don't force it to do antics, jumping time. Let it be, dear."

"Grandma, Grandma! I didn't mean that." The girl came closer.

"Yes, you did, dear. You didn't know it, but you did. You were wanting to be old. But you can't be old, you can't be old right, till things have happened to you. There'll be that boy. Maybe there'll be another. There'll be a man. For me there's been your grandfather; you don't know what it's been like—"

Sally's mind slipped downstairs to the other figure in its chair, to the white beard and the small bones that were so different from these; and she wondered what Forrest was doing.

"You've always loved Grandpa, haven't you?" Why did she ask this?

"Of course I have. But like most men, he's had to be comforted. He thinks he missed things—missed everything. No man, hardly, is a satisfied soul. You'll find that out."

"He didn't miss you."

Was it a chuckle Sally heard? "He couldn't. I was there. The woman, dear, always has to be there. She can't waste time regretting time. She must know how to be satisfied—with being young, with being old. But each thing in its order, dear, each thing as if it were the only thing. And it *is* the only thing. Life is a long list, a long, long list, of the only things. But you don't understand, do you? I'm a bigger fool than I thought I would be. I'm trying to make you see what I see now. I didn't once myself. I was just like you. I cried, too, dear. Don't cry. There now, run down and see what those two are doing. I'll be along in a minute and get supper. Your mother and father are coming tomorrow, and I want you children to look fed. Run on now."

But Sally did not go till she had thrown both arms about the neck that was so badly fitted by its woollen yoke and kissed it over and over.

"Run on now," said her grandmother, lifting the garment again.

At the foot of the stairs, starting apparently to come up, Sally saw Forrest. How little he looked, she thought, how little and young and far away.

As she descended to him he whispered: "Grandpa said funny things to me. He said—"

"Grandpa's not satisfied?" she whispered back, preparing to descend and pass.

Forrest withdrew his foot from the tread and stared. "Smart one!" he said aloud.

"Is that you, Sally? Come here."

She went in to look down at her grandfather, sitting in his dark chair, needing first of all the comfort of lit kerosene.

No Thunder, No Lightning

JIM AND JEFFER met at the club—the Argus—where they used to meet before Jeffer moved to the country.

"Uncle Ned's house," said Jim while he examined a second cigar, "was just the thing, I gather. I'm still glad you bought it from the estate. I was glad at the time, you know, because it simplified my problem as executor. I don't think I realized how much good it would do you, not to speak of Harriet and June. You say June likes the view."

"She lives on it. The first day she came, after we had made things comfortable for her, she appropriated the northeast window—you remember, the one that looks out over Canaan Mountain where it bends and runs due north—and that has been her domain ever since. I thought she would prefer the bay window on the south side, where your uncle kept his flowers, and I planned accordingly. But June said at once, as she has said many times since, that she would see more weather the other way. She gets most of her excitement out of north winds: the wet ones from the east, the dry ones from the west. It didn't matter. We wanted her to choose. She'll never walk, you know."

"I'm coming up some time to see those ladies, if not you."

"You've been asked."

"I know, thanks." He appeared to meditate before he went on. "You wouldn't have any ideas about this, would you? They used to say in the valley—I heard it as a boy—that every house over a hundred years old is haunted. Uncle Ned's—I mean yours—is a lot older than that now. So I consult you as an authority. Do you see anything? Hear anything?" Jeffer bent down to pour fresh coffee in his cup. "Do you walk through cold places in a room? Do you feel the timbers trembling without cause: no wind, no wagons going by? Excuse me, I mean trucks."

Jeffer still stared down into his coffee.

"Well then, I guess you don't. I wasn't serious, by the way. It just came back to me, what I heard them saying when I was a boy. Uncle Ned never said it. He got mad, in fact, if anybody asked him what I've asked you. He must have known. He was dead, though, eight years before you went there, and the place was empty all that time. I was playing with the notion that if there *was* anything in it—well?"

For it appeared that Jeffer wanted to interrupt.

"The house is not haunted," he said. "The *house* isn't."

Jim looked at him curiously. "Some other building then? How serious are *you?* The barn? The pig pen?"

Jeffer shook his head slowly.

Jim pretended to shiver. "Outdoors, you mean? Pity the poor spirits in a winter such as we have had! Even these spring nights—"

"I do pity them," said Jeffer. "Or him. There is only one."

The startled look on Jim's heavy features had perhaps a trace of guilt in it.

"He stands and looks at me," said Jeffer in a tone that settled the question of his seriousness. "But I don't pity him because

he's cold. It never occurred to me that he was. Besides, I have
seen him in all weathers; or he has seen me. Almost from the
beginning he has been there, in summer and fall as well as
winter and spring."

"Been where, been where?"

"Oh," said Jeffer, "don't let it alarm you, for me or for the
ladies. I've never spoken of it to them, or to anyone for that
matter. I haven't been in the least alarmed—in itself a curious
thing. He is standing there whenever I go out of the house at
dusk, to get something from the tool shed, to shut the wood-
house door, to run the lawn mower in, or whatever it may be.
And he is always in the same place: back from the house a
little way, between it and the woodhouse door, or between it
and the gap, you know, that leads down into the big northwest meadow. Sometimes he seems a little closer, sometimes a
little farther off. But there he's sure to be, standing quietly and
looking at me. Not threatening, not advancing, not moving
even. Simply there."

"Who, Jeffer?" Jim tried to sound detached. "Who is
there?"

"I don't know, of course. How could I know? You must
understand he never worries me. I don't walk faster or anything like that. Some evenings I don't even look to see; I know
he's there, and that's enough. Besides, his figure isn't what you
would call defined. If I saw him in broad daylight I wouldn't
recognize him. He wears a wide hat that darkens his face even
more than the dusk does. He is tall, I should say, and loosely
hung together. Sometimes it seems to me that he hangs rather
than stands, as if he had no weight for the ground to feel. His
clothes are loose too—a sort of ample, old-fashioned country
clothes that belong to him without exactly fitting; they flow
down from his shoulders, and droop like his hat. He is a droop-
ing person altogether, if he is a person. Rather sad, very
thoughtful. But I wouldn't say he was thinking of me. Maybe
he is, though—I confess I sometimes wonder if he isn't simply
the old people personified as one; as one man who concentrates
in his gaze all the concern they have felt for the place. This
would include some concern about me: whether I was doing

well by it, and whether I knew what I had. I do love it, you know. I suppose I'm merely inventing a fellow who measures for me whether I love it enough. The place has a life of its own for which I can't help feeling responsible; and that may be all there is to this. I'm glad he's there, on the whole. He's company out of the past, he's the history I took on when I signed the deed—and eased your problem as executor. But it's getting late, Jim. I've made my last night here too long for you."

The next afternoon, sitting in the train that slowly climbed from sea level to the region of mild mountains where New York would sound and look so far away, Jeffer said to the window at his side: I could hardly have explained to Jim about the wheelbarrow. I might have got a contractor or someone to dig out under the back wing so we could put the new burner there, but aside from the expense of that I wanted to do the job myself. It's slow work, but it's good to do. As for the fellow who stands and stares at me, I think it was a mistake to speak of him at all. I made too much of him—or too little, if I suggested he wasn't real. He is real all right. I think I described him a bit more clearly than I have ever seen him. To improve the story, I suppose. I'll have a better look at him tonight, unless talking about him has made him go away.

After supper Jeffer strolled out and rounded the rear corner of the wing, the corner where the stranger had always been visible.

He hadn't been visible, of course, when Jeffer drove up the hill with Harriet from the station; the sun was still shining then. The big hole in the dining-room foundation was just as it had been; the planks sloped up to the level of the yard as he had left them, and down through the hole he could see that the wheelbarrow was where it should be tomorrow morning when he began his work again. The long-handled shovel leaned against it, and the brown clay stains on its sideboards showed a nice pattern in the last light from upper day. The dining-room part of the excavation was half done; then there would be the woodshed; then the cement work could start—Lester Wofford was to do that—and by early summer the burner could be delivered. Harriet wondered why he didn't wait till summer to begin the whole business, since they wouldn't need heat between June and September. But he didn't trust the burner to come on time. This way, too, he would have all summer to make his terrace out of the dirt he was bringing up. The dirt and the stones, for there were many stones, and some of them were big. Tomorrow he would have to tackle the biggest one yet, the one he so far had only picked around. If he couldn't get it out by himself, there was always Lester. He thought it wasn't too high to bury in the terrace.

The darkening lawn was bare of the tall shoulders, the sagging hat. He looked hard, but there was nothing, no one there. Perhaps his foolish words *had* laid the ghost, if ghost it was. He was going in again when something decided him to wander down the planks and size up that stone.

As he stooped to go under the sill he started back at the current of icy air that all at once set itself in motion around him. It *was* cold down there; Harriet had been right. But it wasn't merely that. The current had set *itself* in motion, had come as it were to meet him. Then it enveloped his chest. Then it chilled his legs. And now it was gone again, as if it had passed him, or as if he had passed it—passed through it, maybe. Anyhow it was gone. The new cellar, now that he stood upright in it, was not so much colder than the lawn outside. And this couldn't be because he was adjusted to its temperature, for he had just come. But there was the stone, the irregular round boulder that he had isolated on its base. That wasn't any different. He was imagining things. He had no business here at night. He heard steps over his head—Harriet, clearing the table. Up there was where he should be, helping her.

As he stooped and went up the planks again he felt his heart do a sudden, odd thing. It jumped. For there, only a few feet beyond the top of the slope, the drooper stood. But with his back to him. And he wasn't exactly standing there. He was moving away—drifting, rather, as if on feet that didn't need to press the ground. Then he turned and looked at Jeffer. Did he have eyes? Was there a face under the hat? Jeffer only knew he was being looked at, mournfully, by someone who had passed him under the sill, by someone who had been down *there*. By someone whose garments made a difference in the air through which they flowed. But they *were* air. They were the current he had felt.

He lowered his eyes and shivered, for there was that coldness once more about his legs, which he tried to move and could not. Then he could, for they were natural again. He lifted his eyes to where the stranger's feet had been. There were no feet. There was no stranger. The gap in the stone wall and the meadow beyond it were empty of everything save the darkness, now nearing its completion. If the man were there he would still be visible—just visible. He was not there. Had he—the question stated itself reluctantly, against Jeffer's almost spoken desire—had he gone under the house again?

"Jefferson!" cried Harriet at the sideboard as her husband came stumbling in. "Whatever have you seen? I could think there was a ghost!"

"There is."

She turned and put the last of the silver away in its shallow drawer, counting it carefully. "What's that?"—over her shoulder.

But he had composed himself, so that he could smile and say:

"I'm it. I got cold out there. Just feel."

But she held on tightly to his hand. "You're sure you are well, Jeffer? Don't work tomorrow."

"Oh, I'm all right. Let's make some extra coffee; then I'll go to bed. Of course I'll work in the morning. That stone—you know, dear, it won't wait. I was down just now, looking at it. It's exposed on three sides. Tomorrow I'll be entirely around it, and then if it won't budge I'll go for Lester."

It was exactly twenty-four hours later that Jeffer put in his call for Jim, who was out for dinner, the maid said, but would be home by ten; when he did come he would call—yes, at once, the maid promised.

"What is it you want of him, dear?" asked Harriet, but he didn't stop walking the floor to answer.

Harriet, who should have gone to bed an hour ago, was still unwilling to do so. She watched her husband as she pretended to read at her end of the sofa. She had never seen him quite like this: so intent, so solemnly excited. She wondered whether June had noticed too. But June was in her alcove and was not to be disturbed.

At half-past ten the phone rang, and Jeffer, with no preliminaries, began to insist that Jim come up on the morning train tomorrow. When there was argument he insisted again; and again; until it seemed that Jim consented, for Jeffer hung up with grim relief on his face, and drew a long breath like one who has waited a long time to do so.

Still, however, he didn't answer Harriet's question, though he refused gently now. And it was not until she was falling asleep that she remembered he had not explained to Jim either. But Jim was coming. He had been beaten into it. Well, she would know tomorrow.

Yet she learned nothing from the two men when they arrived from the station; for after the greetings were over, Jeffer took his stocky friend away at once to the barn. Harriet watched them descend the slope of brown lawn, past the piles of rock and clay that waited to become a terrace. The slighter figure of her husband was well in the lead, as if no time were to be lost. Then the grey door closed behind them.

It was of her they spoke as soon as they were in the shadows of the ancient building.

"Don't you think I was right not to tell Harriet? For a while, anyway?" Jeffer had moved to a feed box in the far corner and was about to lift the lid.

"Of course," said Jim. "Is that it there? . . . God!"

For the lid was up and he was looking down at a heap of bones. There were not as many of them, he found himself thinking, as one might have supposed.

But there was the skull to prove that this had been a human being. Its sockets and sinuses were crammed with clay; yet there it was—the proper study of mankind.

"God!" he said again.

Jeffer was less intense now, having parted with his secret. "Lester," he said, "still thinks they are calf bones, or an assortment of I don't know what. He never saw the skull. I got rid of Lester as soon as I could. I had asked him over to help me with a stone I thought I couldn't move myself. These were directly behind it, in the space I hadn't excavated yet. We came on a rib almost at once, and then another. A few more, and I pretended I was taking cold—he could come back another time. He was slow about it, as usual, but he went. You're the only other man who knows this was—a man."

Jim had pulled an empty nail keg across the floor and now sat on it near the one window in the wall, studying Jeffer's face.

"What do you think?" demanded Jeffer. "What shall I do? Shall I tell anybody—anybody else?"

"No," said Jim after a pause.

"Look here, Jeffer," he went on quietly. He had taken something from the inside pocket of his coat. It was a leather wallet with untarnished brass tips at the corners. "I'll do the telling, and to you. I know who that is. Or was. I've always known."

Jeffer stepped forward, then stepped back again.

"Wait," he said. "I knew him too, in a way. Didn't I? Don't you think I did? Were you listening the other night when I told you about the . . ."

"Was I *listening?* Couldn't you see I was? But then I never thought . . ."

"Before you open that thing, whatever it is, let me tell you about my sad friend. I think he's gone."

Jim looked at the box whose lid was safely closed again.

"In there?"

"No," said Jeffer, "the part of him I knew. That part could move, and very gracefully too. Most of the time he stood still, as I told you in town. But the night I came back I saw him turn around once. And I *felt* him"—he chafed his hands in reminiscence—"go by me, at least twice. Last evening—"

"You saw him *then?* After you found these?"

"Wait a minute. It's worth telling right. I found *them,* you know, about the middle of the afternoon. But it took most of the daylight that was left to get Lester away and carry them here—a few at a time, so Harriet wouldn't ask questions. I was coming up from the last trip when I realized the sun had set. So—and there he was. But a long way off.

"He was leaving us. He was going down the meadow—you know, the big one behind the house—he was swinging right along, down through the far gap where the lane starts that takes you to the highway. He was reduced by the distance—quite an insignificant citizen now—but his hat still looked enormous in proportion to the rest of him, and his gait was—I should call it, now that I think of it, liquid free. Free and liquid easy. As if he knew where he was going, and had no doubt he could get there. He was certainly going away. I won't see him again. You never will."

Jim opened the wallet. "I hope that's right," he said deliberately. "For his sake, and yours, and mine."

"You don't believe he left, do you? For that matter, I didn't think you believed he was here."

Jim squinted at him in the half-light of the dusty window.

"I believed it all right, after a certain point. And now—yes, Jeffer, I do believe he's gone. What business I've got believing such things at all is another matter I'll settle with myself some time. The hard thing to believe is that I believe. But today I do. And I agree with you: the poor sinner's gone for good. The poor hymn-singing devil."

There was a moment of shocked silence before Jeffer said: "That wallet."

"This wallet," said Jim with a kind of relief because he could be busy with it—he was removing from it several sheets of paper which had been folded and unfolded a perilous number of times—"is something I've had all along, and I should have told you about it when you bought the place. I didn't because it would have seemed silly then. It was Uncle Ned's. But he got it from his father, Jefferson Buell. I should have told you about it because—but then I don't know how much trouble it would have saved you. Maybe none. Maybe you wouldn't have believed it any more than I did. And whether you did or didn't—what difference would that have made? Uncle Ned himself was never sure old Jefferson hadn't made it up. He was a queer one too. He fished it out of his feather bed when he was dying and handed it to his only son—too late to say a single word about it, but Uncle Ned thought he called it a confession. Anyway, Jeffer, you've inherited—but I'll just read."

He smoothed the pages carefully on his knee and read:

I have talked with Him about this, but He has not heard. Or if He has, He has manifested no concern. Many and many a night I have done so, and there has been no sign—no thunder, no lightning, no whisper of wrath, no syllable of mercy, no searching of the joints in my body to paralyze them. I had thought it might be that, but so far it is not even that.

But even now I am hesitating to write the words that I should write. Let Him not deny me courage.

I have killed a man, and he lies buried under the room of this house in which I sit alone and write.

Once I was not alone. There was my wife Esta. I know that I loved her in the beginning more than she loved me, and I tell myself that I should have taken this into account when our families pressed the marriage on us both. But I could not, because the knowledge was not with me then. Or if it was, in the dim forms of doubt and hope against hope, I believed in the goodness of time, which I supposed would work for me.

Time made things no worse, but neither did it make them better. Esta never loved me in the simple way of Sarah and Naomi. She was dutiful, and her words were not cold or harsh; but neither did they pierce me, nor warm me where I myself was cold.

Eighteen years passed and the farm prospered. But in the summer of heavy rains I needed help. And help arrived. I can see him coming now, through the far gap by the pines, then up across the northwest meadow to the near gap by the wood-house, and then into our back door. He did not knock. He seemed to know we needed him. I did, of course. And so—as—

sist me, Lord, not to be angry now—did Esta. But she seemed
not to know this that first day.

He sang hymns. He was tall and melancholy: a good man in
the hayfield, for he wasted no strength in words. His words
were those he sang, after supper in the front room. He sang
hymns: unearthly, heathen hymns, for they were strange to
me, and they were not about the God of the old believers.
They were dark words about the sun and moon, not Him who
made the sun and moon. They were not holy words.

And they disturbed me. But they were what my dutiful
wife had waited all day to hear. I knew this once, a week after
he came, I watched her at the door, her lips open, listening to
his voice. It was a sad voice, not very deep, not very musical;
but it was musical to her because it came from him. I cannot
say whether she attended to the words as I did. There was no
sign that they offended her. Nothing about Luke offended my
good wife. She loved him. I knew this instantly, and considered what I should do.

I should have sent him off, but for two reasons I did not.
Both reasons shame me now. As husband of the farm I needed
him—every day I needed him, so that I could not bring myself
even to imagine him gone. And secondly, as Esta's husband I
needed him. To discipline my jealousy, I said, in the secret
places where I lived, an outcast from those two. But in reality
I meant to feed my jealousy with looking at him every day,
and with watching how they looked at one another. I pretended that it was noble to do this, and admired the moderation in me which never spoke, which never struck.

There was no moderation. Months passed and Esta con-
ceived. After eighteen barren years, in a cold February, she
told me she was going to bear a child. And then I knew what I
should do. I should acknowledge the child, and love it if I
could. I have loved my son, whom alone among men I trust
with this truth, to do with as he pleases. He is not my son, but
I desire him to know by what means he lived at all. It may not
matter to him as it did to me. To me it meant that the true
father should disappear from the sun and moon his heathen
hymns propitiated. I would remove him from the presence of

good men, and I would put his body in a dark place where neither sun nor moon could find it. The moon visits grave-yards, but it does not look through the floors of houses. I had my plan. He was to lie under the room where every day he broke my bread. When I said grace it was to be in gratitude because he lay there, safe.

Once I had my plan, it was easy to carry it out. I wish it had been harder. I pray—had it been impossible! For although I still believe he should have died, I have had no rest. I did it when Esta was away. I did it with the very axe I had ordered him to sharpen. I did it when his back was turned, when he was stooping at a stone to help me move it. I could not use the sharp edge of the axe as I had planned, but the blunt end was sufficient. He died without a word, to me or anyone, and I took up the floor boards with a cunning I had practiced in my thought. Esta found it difficult not to swoon when she came home and I told her I had quarrelled with Luke and he was gone. But she was equal to her need, and we never said his name again. The neighbors had no reason to doubt his leaving me as suddenly as he came. That was the way of help, they all agreed.

Neither they nor Esta—till she died, bearing my son—ever knew how many times in my mind I saw him coming back. He walked lightly for a man with such long bones. That first day, as he came up across the meadow, I said he had an easy way with grass. No living man will know how many times I have seen him. I am looking out of the window now, and once again I see him. He will not do me harm. Nothing has done me outward harm. But I have not been able to forget. That is my punishment. That, I believe, is why He does not heed my words. He has chosen in His wisdom not to keep Luke away. He knows I see him—as I see him now—and counts on me to understand how The Word is never wasted. I do. Have mercy on me, death, and do not wait too long.

Somewhere a beam creaked as Jim folded the pages again and laid them scrupulously back in the leather out of which they had come.

"God," he said, so quietly that it did not seem to be an oath. "To think I had this all the time, and didn't know how much of it to believe. Uncle Ned said he didn't know either, but I'm not sure about Uncle Ned. He never married, and we didn't see him much. He got mad when there was talk of ghosts, but that could have been because he saw them. Or saw *him*. I'm rattled—I shouldn't be taking any stock in this. I never did, in such things. But—well, Jeffer?" And he looked up for the first time since he had started reading.

"I don't think he saw him," said Jeffer slowly. "Your uncle, I mean. His name wasn't Jefferson. And he wasn't a mover of stones."

Jim stood up suddenly. "Come on now," he said, "that *is* getting fantastic."

"I'm not fantastic."

"What are you going to do with *them?*" Jim was standing by the box, which he made no move to open.

"The old cemetery—it isn't used any more, and most of the markers are gone. I think I'll put them there."

"That's good. That's right. I'll help you."

"Not now. We must go up to the house."

At the door they were called by June, who said she wanted Jim to see what she saw from her window.

But Jeffer was there first.

"What is it?" he asked with an odd urgency, bending down to look through at the level of June's eyes. "To the left there, at the bottom of the big meadow? A man with a broad hat?"

June's small features, always more attractive when she laughed, were very pretty now.

"A scarecrow? Oh, no! It was the wind. Have you ever seen the wind? Anybody can if he cuts his eyelashes. I can, without. Look there!"

"I don't see anything," said Jeffer.

"Oh, Dad, you never do."

"Yes he does," said Harriet.

The Miracle

No ONE had ever loved him, then she did.

"No one?" The man in the train, the stranger to whom he had said it over and over, smiled.

"Not even God."

The stranger, startled, stopped smiling. "How would you know that?"

"At least you would know when He didn't."

The stranger shook his head and looked out of the window. Curt watched him, not the flying landscape, every mile of which was familiar now because he was so near home.

"You would know, I mean, what you deserved. Whether you were worth noticing. I never thought I was."

"But that has nothing to do with it," said the stranger, who didn't see the lake either, or Connor's Woods that came next, or the Great Hollow they entered even as he spoke. "He doesn't take our measure. How much would that be in the very best of us? He loves us anyway; loves all of us; all things."

"All? Or each?"

A pause, reflecting. Then: "Is there a difference?"

"Oh, yes. All—that's easy. But each—how could He even know about so many, and no single one of them the same? How could He have time for that?"

"He has eternity."

Curt was silent.

"And He is not a man, a busy man with—what shall I say?—important matters on his mind. You're trying to think of Him as that. Remember, He is not a man."

"I know."

"Do you?"

"Yes. And so He has the whole world on His mind. Not people merely. Rocks, and winds, and chemicals, and stars. Mountains, and animals. Empty space. Gases."

"So He would have no leisure to notice you?"

"Me, or anybody. That was the way it felt. But then when she did, He did."

"What?" The stranger turned back to him abruptly.

"Why, of course. She was the one that changed it all. And there was no reason in her case either. Why should *she* have noticed me?"

"You made her. You did something, said something—"

"No. It was more wonderful than that. She simply did, that's all. And then He did."

"But how would you know He did?"

"I can't tell you. But I knew it. I still do."

He would never be able to tell anybody. Not this nice man, not even her. The Hollow closed behind them, and the train rumbled through the narrow cut this side of Lenfield where fallen oaks had caused a wreck after the hurricane of—what year? He didn't remember exactly.

"Then you're a lucky boy. Not everyone—"

"Oh, I appreciate that. It was a miracle. A miracle happened to *me*. I won't forget."

"Please don't." The train was slowing down, and Curt stood up. "Good luck to both of you."

"It can't be otherwise," said Curt, who now leaned over his companion to look out of the window. White houses moved by them, more and more slowly, and a crossing-bell began to count the seconds till they should stop.

"Is she meeting you?"

"Of course she is. Goodbye!" He said it from down the aisle, a small bag bouncing at his knees.

The stranger pressed his face to the glass, not to miss anything, and saw a girl running with all her strength toward the forward vestibule. A trainman descended first, then the boy, who looked into her eyes a full second, as she in his, before they rose into each other's arms—yes, said the stranger, rose, as if they were about to leave the ground together. But they didn't. They stood there, obstructing the traffic of other passengers, until the train started again and crept by them, almost holding its breath; or the stranger did, wondering if the boy would glance up at him and beam a last goodbye, as if to say, "You see?" But already he had ceased to exist for Curt, or of course for Lisa whose name he did not know. Or Curt's either. Strangers in a day coach, never to meet again.

"Oh!" said Curt, dropping his hands suddenly and gazing after the train.

"What's the matter? Did you leave something on it?" Lisa looked too as the last car disappeared around a curve.

"I left him—a man I was talking to—I meant to wave."

She was not interested. "Come on."

Curt picked up his bag. "I told him about you."

"You did?"

"I tell everybody; not by name. But he was someone particular, someone I'll remember. I hope he saw you."

"And what a sight." She laughed and pulled him into step with her. "I thought this day would never come."

"It never did. I'm still at school. You just think you see me, and I just think I see you. Every day and every night I saw you—"

"So did I!"

"So what's the difference where we are? Why did I come? Shall I go back?"

"You fool, there's this difference." She pinched his arm.

"That hurt. But so did it not to be here. No difference, then. I think I'll wait and take the next train east. About an hour, I seem to recall."

"You seem to make me sick."

"That's funny. You never looked better."

"I never was. Oh, Curt!" She hugged his arm where she had hurt it, and wept for joy. Without shame or explanation she looked up at him, her face working—so sweetly—and wept for anyone to see.

He pretended not to see; pretended that nothing was happening to him, no waves of warmness, one after another, flooding through and through him as an answer to her tears.

"You said 'Come on.' Where to?"

"Well," said Lisa, brisk again, "there are just two places. My house, your house. Which of them first? Sooner or later we're expected at both, but now—well, you decide."

"No third place? What about the world? We're in it, it's in us. Let's see the world."

"You mean, just walk?"

"Why not?" He considered something. "You know, Lisa, I should have waved at that man I met on the train." They had left the station and were going down Railroad Street, where nobody would know them. "He said one or two things—"

"And so did you. You told him about me. What did you say, Curt, I mean about me?"

"I simply told him, and he said"—he hesitated.

"What?"

"He said, 'Remember, He is not a man.' "

"Who isn't?"

"God."

They stepped over several cracks in the cement sidewalk before she said: "I should think not. It would be too hard. It would be impossible."

"What would?"

"To watch everything, and understand everything even before it happened. After, too, of course; and during."

"Also, he said—now listen, Lisa—love everything."

"Why, yes. How could a man do that?"

"You mean, there are so many things, so many people?"

"Just think how many."

"But it isn't the number. It's the kind—I guess I mean, the quality. Which of them is good enough? To be noticed, first, just noticed. Then loved."

"They're all bad. Or good. And only He knows which it is. Maybe, Curt, He doesn't care, maybe for Him there isn't any difference. We only think there is."

"You should have been on the train."

"It was more fun waiting. Or now it seems so. You did come."

"You should have been on the train and helped me say something. I started, then couldn't finish. I said God loved me because you did. But when he asked me how I knew this, I couldn't tell him. You could have helped. You're helping now. I think I know, though, I *think* I do."

"It's a lot to know."

"Isn't it, Lisa, isn't it? Listen. You can't imagine what it feels like to be loved when you never were before. Everybody's always loved you."

"And you. Why do you say such things?"

"Because they're true, that's all. At least this is. Being loved is like nothing else in the world. It *is* the world. Everything changes when it happens, everything becomes so beautiful—why, it's crazy."

"Now don't you be."

"You know I'm not. It's like being created. Not merely born, to parents who will love you because you're their son."

"Bad or good—that wouldn't matter. But you were good. Lucky parents."

"Listen. I say it's like being created, like joining all the other things that are glad to be just what they are."

"You're glad to be Curt?"

"Am I! And you did it. You had no reason, you simply did it. I said to him, it was a miracle. And then this other one happened: the *world* grew glad because I was in it. That's how it seems now. Am I crazy?"

"Yes. But where do we go? My house, your house. Everybody's waiting; they'll wonder."

"Let them."

"Now *you* listen. Don't you know, Curt, it's the same with me? Everything you say I might have said, but couldn't."

"You could. You have. You helped me."

"Did I? Well, I hope I always will. Come on, though." She squeezed his arm. "I almost died, Curt, thinking you might not come. I owe my life to you because you did. You say you owe me all the world. I owe you all I've got: my life. It's less, but it's my own."

"No, they're the same, and I have them both, each one

because of the other. I told him that, but couldn't explain. I wonder who he was."

"And now he's wondering who you were. Well, I could have told him. You're Curt."

"You're Lisa."

They had reached the end of Railroad Street. There was bare country beyond. They kissed each other, laughing and crying, then turned west into town.

Testimony After Death

EVEN THE INSPECTOR WAS MOVED. The dead boy's face was beautiful despite its wound: a great bruise that disfigured the left cheek and extended back into the dark hair which many examining fingers had tangled till it was wild. But the face itself had never been wild. It still wore an expression which the inspector kept turning about to consider. Again and again he went over it; and then, as if there were nothing in it after all, he shrugged his shoulders and gave the customary order:

"Take care of this till we get identification. Plenty of pictures, too, in case—but he must have lived in the neighborhood; somebody will claim him."

Nobody did; and when the burial notice was brought to the inspector he said a strange thing.

"Too bad. He almost told me who did it. I kept thinking I could find out from his face what happened. But of course I couldn't, there's nothing in that. It might have been accidental anyway—slipped or fell, or a truck chain swung and slugged him; he could have been near the curb; we had a case like that last year. But I don't think so. Somebody did this. And damned if I see why. There couldn't have been any money on him, with those clothes. And it was a good face, if you get what I mean; it almost told me what I wanted to know."

None of the officers did get what he meant. Some of them hadn't gone with him to Dominick Street, and those who had were busy with other things: ringing doorbells in the block, interviewing bystanders, and consulting their list of local gangs. None of them looked for evidence in the pale features on which peace sat as if it were a bird with no intention of flying away. As if it were the boy's soul, determined not to leave his body yet. It was more in fact than either of those; it was a rapturous contentment with what the boy had seen, was seeing when something or somebody killed him and he dropped in the dark street to lie until a dog barked, a woman screamed, and a patrolman came running from the corner. The woman knew nothing, and neither did anybody else who was questioned.

It was a closed case until the day next spring when Clancy came in and said to the inspector: "There's a man here, a painter, wants to see you about the Dominick Street boy—remember?—that we never identified. He's been looking at the photographs; says it was his son."

"I'll see him."

The man was half starved, and the inspector made him sit down.

"A painter? Where do you work?"

The man was nervous; he would rather have stood. "At home, sir, in my studio."

"Don't call me sir. You're not a house painter."

"Oh, no."

"Clancy, did you take his name and address?"

"Certainly. Philip Strong, 231 East Third."

"That's nowhere near. Strong, why didn't we hear from you before?"

"I don't read the newspapers, I don't go out."

"But you missed your boy—you had one, didn't you?"

"I had *him*." He still held one of the photographs in his hand, that shook as he looked down.

"I can believe it. There's a resemblance." But the inspector thought: The face I remember is only half there. "Your wife living?"

"No, sir, not since he was two years old."

"Don't call me sir. How old was he in October? What was his name?"

"Raphael."

"What?"

"Raphael. He was seventeen."

"Can you prove he was your son? I hope you can, frankly; I won't make it hard."

"Only"—he hesitated—"by my paintings. Most of them are of him; a hundred, nearly. If you would come and look—or send somebody—"

"I'll come." Clancy was astonished. "Call my car. Tell Jones I only want the car; I'll drive."

The studio was nothing but a north room over an empty store. The painter went in first, apologizing for the disorder; but it must have been years ago that he gave up caring how his habitation looked. In the two corners away from the window were two narrow beds, only one of which was made. "Where he slept," said Strong, following the inspector's glance. The rest of the space was cluttered with broken chairs, a stove, a sink, some unwashed dishes, rags, brushes, dirt. But an easel stood in the best place, and on it, in a gilt frame, was a portrait which the inspector went at once to examine. He stood close to it, then backed away; looked over at Strong; then grew absorbed again in the face before him. The open eyes—soft, beautiful, black—were what he studied most. He had never seen them open.

"That's him," he said, and when he saw tears in the father's eyes he did all he could to speak gently. He still had questions to put.

"You said there were others, nearly a hundred." The painter started toward a closet whose door would not shut on all it contained. "But this is enough, don't bother. Is it finished?"

"No, I keep working on it. Ever since he left I've been tormented by this memory of mine"—he rubbed his forehead—"it changes every hour of every day. But that is Raphael. Thank you for recognizing him."

"You say he left. When was that?"

"October 6th."

"The same day—"

"Yes, or the same night. He was on his way to the ferry; he was going west; I made him go." He struck his hands together. "I made him go. But I expected to hear from him—cards and letters. When they didn't come I got a certain satisfaction from this"—pointing to the easel—"I tried to see him as he must be then, wherever he was, whatever he was doing."

The inspector looked for the least untrustworthy chair and sat down in it, carefully.

"What do you mean, you made him go? If it's any of my business."

"He was too good."

"What?"

The painter, it appeared, hadn't expected to be understood. "You would have to know more about Raphael than you do. Or than I can tell you." Yet after a minute of looking out of the window, over the ramshackle roofs on which a cool clear sun was shining, he continued.

"Raphael didn't know about the world. I sent him off to find out what it was like in other places. Here in New York he didn't see what others see—what I do myself, what anybody does. He would pass a bar, would look in at the dingy lamps, the men there with glasses, the whole terrible, stupid scene, and the most wonderful expression would come over his face. I knew what it was, for sometimes he told me, though not very well; and never, mind you, proudly. He was thinking of the light inside those men; they sat in darkness, but their souls were bright within them—made so, of course, by rye and bourbon, and cold beer."

"We all see that," said the inspector. "We call it being lit. Of course we don't say anything about the soul."

"Oh, but he did, and went on then to think about his own. It was still brighter. It was drunk too in a way, but not from drinking. He had his natural light, that I've tried to paint and always failed. It was really a light, I think. He was going to beautify the world with it—not by preaching, or blaming

others because they were different from him, but simply by
existing to the full extent of what he was: by walking the
streets, or coming home here and sitting by the window, or
getting into bed there and letting his eyes go round and round
the ceiling—well, dozens of ways, but the point was that something burned like a diamond in him, and this was all he considered to be necessary. If it was true, it made a tremendous
difference in the world. And he made sure it was true. He did
nothing but think how things would be if they were purified
by fire: not real fire, but the kind he carried around with him
inside of his dark head. He walked in the world like a fine day.
He loved it, and he wanted it to love him. I tell you, it was a
kind of intoxication, the purest and sweetest kind. But now—
maybe I've made him sound insane. A pryomaniac or something."

The inspector, ignoring his gaze, said nothing.

"That would be a horrible mistake. Raphael was serene. Except, to be sure, during the past year, when he grew restless and
wouldn't tell me why. Then one day in June he did. He said
he had found out something by himself: something I never
have, or anybody else I know. I can't imagine how one could,
but Raphael did. It came to him as clear as glass, or ice. He
suddenly understood what it means to say that it makes all the
difference in the world what each of us does. Not merely is,
but does. Most of us couldn't bear to believe that; we'd be
watching every move we made, every breath and every
thought, and we'd be crushed at last by the responsibility. And
so he was, in a way; but with him there was no old guilt, no
habit of being disgusted with himself, to make the burden
intolerable. Raphael knew how to be pleased with his own
soul; it contented him, it soothed him, it was his best and most
beautiful friend. This was why he didn't have to think about it
any more than he did. It left him free, as our lungs do, when
the weather is sweet, to enjoy nothing but that sweetness.
Don't misunderstand me, Inspector. Raphael loved himself,
and therefore he could love the world. But now he had this
vision of the universe as a great curved mirror in which each
act, each utterance, each idea is magnified forever; and worse

than that—or it would have been worse for you and me—the mirror was a kind of mind, a kind of heart; it was indeed all mind, all heart, and both at once; it was a person, and it judged us; it was gratified, was grieved, according as we played our parts below; and it concealed in its depths the consequences of our lives—our whole lives, and each minute of them too. Even for Raphael this was hard, because there was a next step to take, and nothing showed him how. He had no sense of what he ought to do, of what the great person up there would be most pleased by if he did it. He was on the stage, and ready to act, but still there were no lines for him to speak. What should he do? What should he not do? To do nothing might be the worst thing; yet there he was, helpless to go or come. It was then I began to talk about his leaving me awhile. I couldn't answer his questions; but the big world west of the river, once he was moving through it, might teach him to forget them. Not that I thought them wrong—or mad, oh, no!—but I was at the end of my wits, and for all I knew he was just at the beginning of his; and if so, a change of some sort would be good. I was the mad one, Inspector. I made him go. Everything I had was in him, and I sent him off."

He felt his way to the window, found it, and turned about, the light behind him almost obliterating his thin figure.

"What will you do now?" The inspector blinked. "I'm sorry for you, Strong. What will you do—go on painting that?" He inclined his head toward the easel.

Strong threw up his hands, then let them fall of their own weight. "I don't know. Until today, when I thought of asking the police—the idea came to me before, but I fought it off—until I saw your photographs I wouldn't admit there was anything *to* do. He would come back, I said; over and over I said it; then suddenly, this morning, I had doubts; and as soon as doubts, fears. I just don't know, Inspector."

"Can you live? I mean, do you ever sell any of those?" He motioned toward the closet door.

"Oh, none of *those*." Strong was alarmed. "Occasionally another kind, that I can do to order. Also, my wife left me a little money—just a little. Yes, I can keep alive."

"Did you notice anything in particular about the photographs? I had them taken because the boy's face—well, it struck me. It seemed to be about to—" He searched for words, found none that wouldn't embarrass him, and gave up.

"About to—please, Inspector, what?"

"Well then, *say* something. It was what you would call a speaking face. Even with the eyes closed I thought if I waited long enough it would tell me—"

"What? What sort of thing?"

"Who killed him. Or what killed him. But then he couldn't have known it was going to happen."

"No, no! Of course not!" A singular agitation seized the man. "For one thing, he wouldn't have believed it possible that any object, any person—"

"You think it was one person?"

Strong stared at him. His face worked strangely.

"You're not trying to tell me, are you, that *you* did it?"

In the deep silence of the room the gasp that Strong made seemed to keep on echoing and coming back. It was a dreadful sound, and the inspector spoke now in a low, deliberate voice, as if he measured every word against that echo.

"Have you been telling me all the time you couldn't take him as he was? You couldn't live with anyone like that? You couldn't stand him being—perfect? Pity, perhaps? For him, more than you? I don't mean, Strong, I don't necessarily mean anything ugly, at least in the first stages. Is that what you've been—"

It was no noise that stopped him, but rather the absence of any noise at all, inside the room or out of it, over the roofs or anywhere, while the boy's father wept. Tears formed in his eyes and fell; and others formed, and slowly fell; and he wiped none of them away as he watched, incredulous, the face that had accused him. The inspector, watching him in return, saw nothing but tears, and behind them the wide-open eyes of one who had supposed he was his friend.

He was.

"I had to do that, Strong." The inspector got up suddenly. "It was one angle, and I had to—here! sit down!" For Strong was staggering away from the window. The inspector lowered him into the chair, and now his own back was toward the light. "One possibility, on paper at least, was that you went with him as far as Dominick Street and then—but stay where you are, I won't give you any more, sit still, Strong, sit still. The business you can't imagine—well, I can't either. It could have been more than one, you understand. A mob of them—wild boys—and they wouldn't have taken the trouble to look before they—"

"Oh!" It was a pure groan, not meant for ears to hear.

"Now then, there won't be any more." The inspector turned about. "I hate to leave you, Strong, but I'll be back—tomorrow, maybe. You stay here. I'll come again and see how you're doing."

"Inspector!" He wasn't trying to get up. "I wasn't there, of course I wasn't, but I know how he looked when—I know what you saw in his eyes, even if they were closed. I saw it in the photographs; I see it here in that picture; I see it everywhere, and always will. Raphael was happy when he died. It was all clear to him. The mirror, I mean, and the great mind. Do you know what I think, Inspector? He had just got the parts of it in place—he knew for the first time what to do, what not to do—he may even have turned around and started home to let me know I mustn't worry any more."

"Yes, yes, that may have been it." The inspector, hat on head, stood soberly at the door. "I wouldn't be surprised, Strong, if that was the way it was. But now don't think about it any oftener than you have to. I'll be here tomorrow, early in the afternoon. You wait. I'll come."

"Where would I go?"

The heavy steps continued down the stairs.

Back at his desk the inspector said: "Clancy, let me see that list of Dominick Street gangs. All of them, and those nearby, as far uptown as Houston. I want every name we've got there on those lists; I want each one checked over, and each kid brought in here by the end of this month."

"The kids themselves. One at a time?"

"Not necessarily; two or three together wouldn't hurt. But every last one—you get me?"

"What'll we do then? Chloroform 'em?"

"Maybe, but before they go under I've got something I want to beat into their heads so it will stay there, Clancy."

"Listen, Inspector. You won't find out a thing about that boy, if he's the one—"

"He is. We're going to have his father on our hands too; or the city will. But first, bring in the kids, the muggers; young or old, I want them all. This is serious. Understand?"

"No, Inspector."

"Thought you wouldn't. But it's nothing off my nose. Simply an order. Run on now and get it out."

"Yes, Inspector."

He sat there a long time wondering how he would put into words the thing he wanted them never to forget. The thing they did to someone they hadn't looked at twice. Or even once, in that dark block. There could be another light at the far end—there would be, he decided—but it wouldn't take the place of this one that could never burn again.

Sebastian

SHE WOULDN'T think about it any more tonight. Such a fine cat, so wild, so wayward—nothing could have happened to Sebastian. Those shoulders, those great orange eyes: he was strong enough to last, oh, longer than she would. And who but he was keeping her alive this fall? She lived to see him, didn't she? He almost seemed to know this, so regular he was: at nine, on the big flat stone outside the woodshed door, sitting there, looking up, waiting for the deep dish of leftovers she would bring. So regular. Yet this was the tenth night he hadn't come. She looked at the calendar over the range. Yes, a week ago Tuesday was when—but she wouldn't think about it any more tonight.

She did, though, as after another hour she climbed into the bed she had made up in the little room off the kitchen so that she could hear him if he came later than usual. Came from where? She wouldn't even try to guess. None of the neighbors knew anything about him: she had asked, and all of them had said, without much interest, No, we haven't seen a tiger cat with a long tail—stray, you think?—we can't think of anybody who has such a cat, he must be living in the woods, and maybe he's moved on from here, you never know about these strays. And Celia Hunt had said, laughing a little, "Florence, you have a friend. He's yours. But you say he won't come in? That's not so funny, wild as he is. It takes a long time for them to trust you. He will, though, if you're patient. He'll be a companion these cold nights—till Cal comes home."

She didn't explain to Celia that she had stopped expecting Sebastian to trust her. All she did was feed him her leftovers; and after he ate those she brought him the red bowl full of milk, slightly warmed on the stove. It had to be the red bowl, the one she had kept since she was a little girl, the one Cal used to have his oatmeal in. She thought Sebastian recognized it in her hands; anyway, he knew so well what was in it that he often started lapping from it before she set it all the way down. Sebastian wasn't afraid of her then, while she was feeding him. It was only when she first appeared at the door, and pushed it carefully open, that he backed away, spitting, and circled the steppingstone as if it were a place of terrible danger. But then he would suddenly stop, his eyes on hers, and lift one forefoot after the other from the frosty ground as he cried pitifully, like a small weak kitten, to be fed. He was always so hungry. And perhaps he was grateful afterward, for he folded his paws on the stone and stayed there—she could see him from the dining-room window—at least till she went to bed. Of course he wasn't there in the morning. Night was his time, and nine o'clock his hour. And Sebastian was his name, though nobody else knew this; she hadn't confided it to Celia.

Where was he now? A week ago Monday was the last time

he came, and she said to herself then: He's thin, he doesn't
look so well, he may have worms or something, he may have
eaten a sick animal that made *him* sick. The next night, she was
sure, he would be all right again. But there was no next night.
Oh, dear, ten of them now and no Sebastian.

It was worse, almost, than waiting for Cal to come. Sometimes, she thought with a little start of guilt, she had stopped
doing that. Her own son, of course, wherever he was, must be
more precious than any four-footed thing. But it had been so
long. He had written that he might come, and then he didn't.
Year after year, no Cal. His father would have been angry, as
he was too often while he lived; that was how Cal had got into
the habit of staying away. And doing what? She knew he
wasn't successful at anything. Not married: no, or certainly
she would have heard. Where *was* he? She didn't ask this so
often any more. From despair, perhaps from pride: she wondered which, and whenever she did so, felt guilty again.

She got up suddenly, went barefoot to the door she called
Sebastian's door, and opened it a little bit, not making any
noise. No Sebastian. But up the mountain—right there, over
the smokehouse roof, yet of course a long way off—she heard
a great horned owl; and she shuddered. They caught mice,
mostly; but rabbits, too, and skunks—things big as cats. And
they tore them into bloody strips to feed their young, or else
themselves.

She hadn't heard any owl that night he didn't come, that first
one. But they didn't always make this dreadful sound. They
were quiet killers, with big round eyes that some people said
were similar to cat's eyes, though she didn't. They were stupid
and ruthless, whereas Sebastian's eyes, for all the fear in them,
the needless fear—so needless—were perfectly familiar with
her own, and so as Celia said were the eyes of a friend. Even
that last night, when they had the gaunt look in them, they
were familiar at any rate to her. The gaunt look: *was* it
worms? If so, and one of the owls had got him, she hoped it
would be sick all night, she hoped it would feel great pain and
die.

The worst thing after all was that Sebastian had been thin,

had had something the matter with him. The shock of this was what she remembered now, returning wearily to bed and pulling the spread up tightly under her chin. Sebastian mustn't lose his strength, for then she would lose what was left of hers. Nobody seemed to notice how she was failing. She wouldn't tell the doctor yet, if she ever did. She had always been thin, but never poorly, or almost never. This summer, though, it was different. She never woke up rested, and her appetite was gone. That was why there were so many leftovers for Sebastian; she cooked as much as ever, then only picked at it. And it didn't seem to matter so long as Sebastian came. When she fed him she felt better. But there was more to it than that. When she merely saw him she grew stronger. Sebastian was good for her: so good, she decided, that he must have been *sent*. For it seemed like that. He was medicine, he was well-being, that came to her all by itself, on four feet, slyly and shyly, out of the cold night from nowhere.

She wouldn't go to sleep just yet. Something might have delayed him: a fight, maybe, with another tom, a wild one in the woods, or even a tame one that had gone off hunting as of course they all did. Or he had found a snug place to doze, and in doing so had lost track of the time. There—she was badly mixed up again. As if cats knew about clocks, as if for Sebastian there was any difference between nine and ten, or eleven, or twelve, or one, two, three, four, five. She was silly to have thought it. And she stared up into the darkness of the little room, saying aloud: "I must watch myself, I must keep things in their right places. Celia looks at me some days as if she believed I didn't."

Her mind wandered off to the kitchen, where the red bowl, with only a few nicks in it, was the last thing she had seen as she turned off the light. There was plenty of milk in the bottle, she always saw to that, and there were some really nice leftovers in the oiled paper beside it in the icebox. The best slices of last evening's lamb, all cut into pieces of the size Sebastian liked. The plate on which she would arrange them was where it belonged, on the middle shelf where she kept all of Mother's dishes. What would Mother think of its being put

on the cold stone out there for a cat, one that didn't belong
here either, or belong anywhere at all? She could hear Mother
asking why, and it took all of her resolution not to explain out
loud, not to say, "But Sebastian is different, he's wild and yet
he's mine, he's mine, he keeps me breathing, Mother, so that I
can be here when Cal comes if he ever does. You never had
much use for Cal and his father. I was the only one, as if
nothing mattered in the world but women. You can see,
though, can't you, that my only child must be *something* to
me? Well, so is Sebastian, and you don't need to think he
dirties your best dishes. He leaves them—there, like all the
others. A person would never know which one, he's that
famished, he's that thorough."

It must be after midnight, and she ought to turn over on her
right side and go to sleep. The window was that way. It woke
her in the morning better than any alarm clock; gradually,
without commotion, the light was there just when it should be,
and she was ready for another day. Not rested, but able at least
to slip out and start the stove.

She turned only her head, measuring the distance to where
the white panes, invisible now, waited to do their duty. There
were twenty-four of them, and she must wash them tomorrow: only the inside, but that would make plenty of difference. This room was one she hadn't used lately; not until she
needed it to hear Sabastian if he came. The lower sash was
open just a crack: enough so that she could hear the queer cry
he made when he was out there and she hadn't seen him yet;
sometimes he came a little early, sometimes a little late. Not
this late, though. It was silly not to get her rest, what there
would be of it.

A steady, soft wind was blowing into the room. It came
clear over to where she lay, and she made sure again that the
spread was well tucked-in around both shoulders. Yet it wasn't
a cold wind. It couldn't be, straight from the south like that.
Father used to call this "the little south room," saying it had
the warmest exposure. A south wind, she remembered, was a
rainy wind, or could be.

She felt moisture on her face, as if a cloud had drifted in.
And then she heard the rain—yes, suddenly, a real rain, that

made small thuds against the glass, like someone touching it helplessly, without much hope of being heard. Then they grew louder and more numerous, until the sound of them was single, steady, and somehow good in Florence's ears: old ears, she whispered, like everything else about me, but they haven't lost their sharpness, I can hear as well as the next one, I could even hear Sebastian if he cried. But he won't be there now. He may have known it was going to rain—animals do, they say— and kept to his hiding-place in some dry corner of the woods. Not that he hadn't come sometimes when the weather was bad. Snow last winter didn't bother him a bit—she remembered how the flakes stuck in his fur without his seeming to know or care if they did—and there had been spring drizzles when he had to shake himself all over before he settled on to the steppingstone for what she called his thank-you nap. This rain, however, was too much for anybody. She could imagine the waterfall it was making down the panes—washing them, in fact—and her mind went pleasantly back to girlhood days in this very room, for she had never lived in any other house. Mother used it for sewing. It was the only room that didn't have to be picked up; Mother simply shut the door when company came. It was Florence's favorite place to play and think. Nobody paid attention to her here—certainly not Mother when she was busy at the machine—so that she could play games with the rain and not have to account for what she did. She would pretend that she was small enough to open one of the panes and pass through it into the downpour; then she grew smaller still, and slipped between the drops so that none of them touched her. She was smaller than a bird, than a moth, than a fly, than anything that had a name. Then she would pass in through the pane again and resume being a little girl who nevertheless was big now, was enormous, compared with just a few seconds ago. How old was she when she did all this? Four? Five? She found she had no idea, and sighed as she turned her head again and looked straight up at the darkness.

The rain was making all sorts of noises around the house: on the walk, on the windows, on the roof. It was even beating at the doors, and rattling those that weren't a perfect fit. Or was it just the rain? Sebastian's door, by the steppingstone,

sounded as if it were being tried. Of course it was locked, but
rain wouldn't know that. Or *was* it rain? She held her breath
and listened. Sebastian never scratched the screen or threw
himself against the lower panels. For all his beautiful muscles,
his fierce eyes, he was polite. He simply stood or sat or lay
there and waited for her to come out; and though she had
studied every device by which he might be tempted over the
threshold, he never crossed it. He would stretch his neck and
peer through, and almost tremble with desire to enter the
woodshed, then the kitchen; but even the plate, the bowl,
wouldn't bring him. There was always the backing away, the
circling, the hissing and spitting; and then the pitiful cry, after
which he settled to his meal without any further worry about
who had provided it for him.

Yet this night, with so much rain, might be another story.
And his hunger might be desperate after ten days of hunting
without perhaps too much success. She would get up and see if
he was there; and if he was, she would ask him where he had
been. She wouldn't have told Celia this, but she talked to him,
and sometimes she could imagine that he wished he understood
her.

She was in her bathrobe and slippers before she knew it; was
turning on the woodshed light; was shuffling to the door; was
sliding back the bolt; was making herself taller so she could
look down through the pane of glass that Father had put there
the summer before he died. This was how she always saw Sebastian, who sometimes looked up to meet her eyes, the eyes he
should have trusted but didn't, the eyes that ought to have told
him how she felt.

There was still that thumping, that rattling at the catch. The
door moved as if a wind were at it, though there was no wind.
Only water, that prevented her from seeing anything clearly,
or seeing anything at all, for something broke the drops into a
fine mist that filled the night beyond the glass. Something? It
was those leaves and twigs in the gutter; tomorrow she must
reach up with a rake and get them out. Now, with her hand on
the knob, she saw nothing. And what would there be to see?
No cat could possibly be there, they hated water so.

Nevertheless she pulled the door open—and almost screamed because Sebastian was so big. There he was, stepping back and staring at her, his eyes level with hers. No, higher than hers, higher. How could that be? Things looked bigger in a fog, but not this big. There he was, though, fearful of her as ever. Yet he wasn't hissing at her, wasn't telling her to keep her distance. No sound from him whatever, except—oh, my God—

"Hello, Mother."

She must have tottered forward when she fainted, for her bathrobe and nightgown were still wet when she came to on the bed she had left to let him in. He had pulled the covers over her and now was standing there, himself drenched and miserable, fearing—what? Struggling back to life, she thought she knew. He wasn't sure she was glad to see him.

"Cal."

"Yes, Mother."

"You carried me in."

He was almost apologetic. "I had to, it was raining so hard, and you not—"

"Has the rain stopped?" She couldn't hear a thing. She could hardly hear him.

"No, but it's less now."

"You must change those clothes. You must get them off."

"Oh, I'm all right."

"You're not. Go in the front room and take down some of your father's things. They're still in the closet."

"I will in a minute." He didn't move, except that he shivered; he couldn't help that.

"Go on, Cal. I'm all right."

"You sure?"

"Yes, yes. Go on." She closed her eyes. It was delicious to do so. "I'll sleep a little, then we'll both have something hot to drink. And eat. You're hungry."

"Not very."

"Yes, you are, I can see you are." She didn't open her eyes.

"Mother."

She opened them. "Now what?"

"Was it all right for me to come home?"

She nodded, as in a dream.

"I want to stay."

Her eyelids hurt her, and she shut them tight. "Good, good. I want you to. I thought you would never come."

"I know." A long pause. "Then when I did, you thought I was somebody else. I could see this. You even said—"

"I thought you were Sebastian."

"That's it, that's what you said."

"I did?"

"Yes. Who's Sebastian?"

What could she say? "Go on now, Cal, go on."

"I will, but who is Sebastian? I never heard of any Sebastian. Is it someone you would rather—instead of me—"

"Someone very strong. Someone I depended on. But now you'll be here. You're strong; you carried me in. And I'm not so little, either."

"You don't weigh much."

"All I want to, all I should. Go on, Cal." She knew he hadn't moved, and wouldn't till she said more. Could she say it? Yes. "You're the one I want."

He tiptoed out, and she said to herself, Will I be alive when he comes back? I will, I must be. Have to keep him strong. But I shouldn't have cut up that lamb so small. Have to explain. Cat food, Cal, for this one time. Cat food. But the best. Now tell me where you've been. And don't you think of not staying. You're the one. Dear me, the only one.

The Dream

HE DREAMED that with great effort he opened his eyes at last and looked as far away as possible from what he had done; looked straight up, straight up, into such deep blue that it might have been night above him. It might be dark, he thought in his dream; and yet those two big clouds—he kept on looking, straight up between them and beyond, to where the stillness was. It was a good stillness, considering what he had done. There might have been the sound of dogs or guns or running feet. There might have been her family—her father—yelling in the pine woods. But there was only this blue stillness, up beyond the two soft clouds each one of which was like a round world by itself. A round white world, each one of them, hanging there on the under side of night. And yet it wasn't night. He knew this in his dream, and heard him call himself a fool to ever think so. Fool, he said, and laughed. But not out loud. They don't do that in dreams. A good thing too, with all the stillness. Who was he to break it up? If it was there like that, after what he had done, maybe nothing minded. Maybe it was all right, what he had done. He could even go home.

But she wouldn't be there.

And his dream ended—clank—as if an immense rusty chain had been let down—clank—to close some door between where he once was and where he was now.

Clank. Then a steam valve blowing off—whushhhhhhhhh—and pistons knocking. Clank, clank, all along the line. A freight coming in or going out.

He remembered where he was, so the dream must be over. More than a hundred miles from home, and not in any town he ever heard of. There was an elevator, and sheds along a siding, but as far as he was concerned he had gone to sleep in another world. Three railroads, crossing one another in open, flat country more than a hundred miles from home, cut off a triangle of weeds and grass that nobody had any use for. And in the middle of it, where the grass was softest and coolest, was where he had crawled for the rest he needed. He had lain down on his back and shut his eyes—when was it?—then had dreamed. A good dream, toward the end, for it seemed to him all at once that he wasn't in trouble any longer. That blue sky—it was the same as this one, clouds and all. The same silence, too, now that the freight was gone. He thought he still heard a humming in the C.&E.I. rails, but the freight was miles away by this time, going west. No, southwest.

But the sky shouldn't mean the same thing any more, now he was awake. He stared up and knew that the old fear was in him, good and strong. He was here, not there, and what he had done was still in his mind. Nothing could change that.

He groaned and rolled his head, as if to escape the sky.

Whose eyes, so close to him in the grass? How could they be there? How could they follow him so far? How could they follow him at all?

Nothing but her eyes, like blue flowers in the grass, close up to him, the lids wide open, wanting him to look. The same expression in them as—the same as just before—

"Godalmighty!"

He sat up, shaking all over, and looked back down to see if he hadn't been making a crazy mistake.

There they still were. Only they had turned up and were shining at him. So blue they were, just like *her* eyes the last time—just before—

"Honey! What's the matter?"

Then all of her was there: the whole head, the hair, the yellow dress, the bare brown legs crossed at the ankles, and the sneakers with one sole worn so that the canvas showed through.

"Honey! Don't look like that! Listen—you would think—"

"Godalmighty." He said it quietly, without strength, and covered the top half of his face with his left hand.

"You had a nightmare," she sat up and said. "Right here in daylight you had a nightmare. I thought *I* was tired, but you *must* have been. Look at me, Steve. Anyone would think you wasn't awake *yet*."

Her hands were pulling at him, trying to uncover his eyes.

"I wish I wasn't, almost."

She couldn't get his hand down.

"Say! Wake up. I really believe—"

"No, I'm awake." But instead of letting her see his face he turned away and lay down again, his back to her, his knees drawn up as far as they would come. He was a strange object there, at the far edge of the hole they had made in the tall grass. A light wind blew suddenly and waved the weed tops all around him; but he scarcely breathed.

"Steve." She patted his shoulder.

"Steve!" She pounded his back. "For God's *sake*, Steve, whatever did you see? Was it in your sleep?"

After a while he told her. "Yes."

"Well what *was* it? Did it scare you? I'm scared, too. You got to tell me."

They both seemed to be listening.

"I dreamed I killed you. We didn't just run away. I killed you."

They both still seemed to be listening.

Here came another freight train, and he was glad. From the south, on the Illinois Central. A long one, too, and he was glad of that. It would take a long time to go through. Rumble, clank—there would be a lot of noise, and it would last—well, maybe till she got over the worst of this. Then he would sit up and say something.

Say what?

But the seventy cars—he counted them as their trucks chugged over the B.&O. crossing—weren't enough to make much difference. The noise was fading out already, up toward Champaign, and here he lay like a dead log, wondering. Should he have told her? He had known right away he shouldn't have. Or was this true? Was he sure he shouldn't? What could he have made up that would satisfy her mind? Good enough—or bad enough—for Stella to believe?

The sound of the train was now a faint whine up the right of way, a whimpering of far wheels, complaining.

Or was it Stella crying?

There hadn't been a word from her since he said what he did, and he hadn't felt her hands on him either.

He turned over slowly. Her eyes were above his now: serious, startled, and without any tears in them.

"Did you hear what I said?" A foolish question, but he asked it and after a couple of seconds asked it again. "You hear me, Stella?"

She stared at him so hard he almost didn't know her.

"Funny thing. I thought I dreamed—"

"Funny thing!"

He hadn't meant it that way, but he was glad if it made her find her tongue.

"I mean," he said, "I only dreamed—there was nothing about *doing* it—I only dreamed I woke up a long time after, when it didn't matter any more. Nobody minded. That's all I remember, and that's the funny thing. I felt good because nobody minded. I felt *good*."

He laughed, but it didn't sound natural. She still stared.

"Understand, Stella? It was a damn *dream*. I wasn't awake yet, not by a long shot. Why, I don't believe I really woke up till I heard you asking what the matter was. Ever since then I've been trying to figure out—"

"Nothing to figure out."

He reached for her wrist, but she pulled away from him and stood up. "Nothing to figure out. You felt good, and you say it's funny."

"I mean crazy. You know I mean crazy."

"How did you do it?"

Now he stared.

"Tell me how."

He comprehended gradually. "That wasn't in it. I don't know. That's what I'm trying—"

"Tell me when."

"Stella! You talk as if I really—"

"Tell me why." She was walking off now, through the weeds. The same sky up there, and the same three road banks hemming them in.

"Listen," he said. "Stand still. It was all a damn *dream*—don't you get that? Where you going, Stella?"

"Home." Sure enough, she was headed west, toward the I.C. tracks.

He caught up with her, but he couldn't touch her yet, he couldn't stop her. They walked abreast, maybe ten steps, maybe twenty; then she halted of her own accord.

"You never did want to run away," she said. "It was my idea; *you* didn't want to. In the dream there wasn't anybody with you, was there? You felt good *because* there wasn't. Then here I am. You wake up, and here I am."

He guessed it would be easier now. "Nothing but your eyes—that's all I saw. A ghost, with shiny eyes. Never did see two such pretty eyes." He laughed again, and it still sounded unnatural; but she listened like somebody that knew why. She listened, anyway. "You're trying to explain a damn *dream*, Stella. *They* don't signify. What you mean, I didn't want to? Look here, you don't believe that. Looky here!"

Her refusal was a good sign. She simply stood there, refusing to lift her face. He did it for her, and saw she was crying.

"Now, Stella, don't do that." But he wasn't sorry. "Come on, let's go."

Their straw suitcase, with one strap broken, was under the water tank where he had left it. It felt so light in his hand that he swung it in easy circles, signaling cars to stop.

"When one does," he said, "will both of us get in? Most of these is hell-bent for Chicago."

She stopped the suitcase as it swung, took it out of his hand, and studied the broken strap. "We can get this fixed up there," she said, and looked straight at him for the first time since he found her crying.

A yellow car stopped, and they got in together.

Ten miles. Twenty miles. She hadn't looked at him again, she hadn't said a single word. The driver, a candy salesman bound for Kankakee, wasn't talking either. They had the back seat to themselves.

What was she thinking now, he wondered?

And yet he knew. The question really was, how long would he be wondering this way? Was Stella ever going to forget? Godalmighty. That damn *dream*.

All Us Three

OF THE Bertolocchi brothers who built the circus and made it as famous as a small circus can ever be, only Papa Bertolocchi was left, and even he had retired this afternoon from the ring where he used to turn somersaults over five elephants in a row. To celebrate his seventieth birthday he had added a sixth elephant and cleared it too; then, when the long applause died down, had lifted a megaphone to his mouth and announced to all the world that he would never jump again.

Only a few of the spectators appreciated what this moment meant to him, or understood, even, the difference between five elephants and six. But the people of the circus did: the girls who sat on the upcurving trunks and smiled even as they trembled—for he could have missed—and all the others, down to the waterboys and roustabouts, who crowded near the north exit to witness the old man's last public act.

But Papa Bertolocchi was not through with being boss. After the show he scolded them for doubting he could do it, and refused to believe they had assembled merely to demonstrate their faith. He clapped his hands and shooed them off; he grinned fiercely, exposing his white teeth, at the girls who trembled—he knew they had—before they stepped so daintily to the ground and made special bows in his direction; and back in his trailer he fumed at Angelina because he found her crying from relief; or so he thought.

"Girl, girl!" he said, "You thought your Papa was no good!"

He was her Papa only in a sense that he was father to all the circus. She was his youngest brother's child: Antonio's, who died ten years ago and left her without a mother either, for Anna his wife had been killed when she fell from a trapeze. Papa Bertolocchi—Cesare his name was, and no one doubted that it fitted him—took her in with him and his own wife, dead also now and perhaps content to be, since she had never forgiven herself for bearing him no children.

Angelina was his niece, his foster-daughter, and his darling all in one. He had trained her until she was known among circuses of this size as the best tight-rope walker in the business. Not only could she do more things up there than others could; the way she managed her silver parasol was in itself bewitching, and she descended the steps at last like some utterly weightless object falling, her hands and arms, and her black hair and eyes, paralyzing the audience so that it almost forgot to applaud; but then it did, tumultuously, as she skipped away to join Cesare at the foot of the bandstand. He always waited there, watching, with more love in his face than he seemed to be aware he showed.

"Didn't you, girl? You thought—"

"No, Papa," said Angelina, wiping the tears from her eyes with exquisite care, for she was still in costume, makeup and all, "it wasn't that I was crying about."

"So!" Illogically, he was disappointed; he was almost angry. "You didn't worry, you didn't care if I was killed."

"I knew you wouldn't miss, Papa."

"When I didn't know myself." He looked lugubrious, and suddenly old. "What was it, then and therefore?" He was fond of those two words, learned long ago when English was for him a language scarcely to be believed.

"You really want me to tell you?"

He knocked his head with both hands, so hard you would have thought it hurt. "What a question! All the saints! 'You really want' "—he tried to make his voice small and sweet like hers, to mock her, and of course he failed—" 'really want me to tell you?' When you tell me everything. Don't you, Angel, don't you? Tell Papa now. Good girl, tell Papa."

"I will," she said, turning without another word and pulling back the curtain that hid the other half of the trailer.

There stood Archie, so beautiful to her, so fair, so slender in his riding suit, so fearful of Cesare, whom nevertheless he

looked at steadily out of his blue eyes. The customary high
color was gone from his cheeks.

"All the devils!" shouted the old man. "Him! Didn't I say—
that boy—he's got to keep away!"

For Archie, who was not Italian, had dared two years ago to
ask if he might marry Angelina. He was not even a son of any
circus. Sitting in the crowd that summer day, he had fallen in
love with Angelina as she did her act, and he didn't go home
between shows, but sat through the evening performance too,
and insisted afterwards, following her to the trailer, that she
must be his wife—he, no son of any circus, a nobody who
wasn't even Italian, who was only good-looking and graceful:
yes, he was graceful, and Cesare, outraged though he had been,
let him stay with the trucks that took them to the next town,
Danbury it was, and ordered him to help the men as much as
he was able.

It was torture for Cesare to do this, and he did it only
because Angelina begged him not to beat Archie with both his
hands as the boy stood there, incredibly, and asked for Cesare's
most priceless possession. Just like that: I want this girl, I love
her, I want her. And worse yet—all the fiends—Angelina had
loved him from the moment she saved him from Cesare's
hands. Before that she thought him merely strange; then,
without knowing why, she felt him to be hers. And she had
never wavered in her devotion, just as he had never ceased to
find her somehow perfect.

Now Archie stood there, returning Cesare's stare, and
waited for Angelina to explain.

"I know," she said, "how mad you get when you see
Archie."

"I see him all the time. I watch him with the riders; yes, he
gets better, he can stand up bareback on Esmeralda some day
soon. But he can't sneak in here; not yet. A whole year, twelve
months complete, he will stay away till then, or—all the
bandits!" His hands worked at his sides. "And what about my
birthday?"

The circus people had wanted to celebrate it with him, but
he said No, only Angelina would. Maybe a cake, maybe a

candle—he had shrugged—maybe presents. He had in mind the locket Nella left with him when she died. He was going to give it to Angelina, whether she gave him anything or not. It had two pictures in it, of him and Nella when they were married in Milan. He thought of it now, in the tray of his black trunk with the gold laurel leaves stamped on it.

"Your birthday, Papa—that's why he's here. I asked him."

"No, no!" It was more than he could bear. The cake he supposed she had hidden: that must be for just him and her. Not for this terrible boy who wouldn't leave her alone, who wouldn't forget what he had been promised, who wouldn't disappear, who wouldn't die.

He started at the last word as if it had been really spoken: started, and himself grew pale.

"Please, Papa. I asked him."

"But why? A whole year yet. Sweet stars and moon, why did I ever promise? Three years, I said, then you could have him—if he worked and learned. I told myself, I said to old Cesare: 'Listen, he won't do it, he'll be gone before winter quarters, he's nobody, he's not Italian even, he won't stay.' Fool, I was. But maybe no—a whole year yet."

"But you did promise, Papa. And he won't change his mind. Will you, Archie?"

The young man adored her without a word. Then he looked back at Cesare, who for some reason—odd—turned his head away. His big nose, his close-cropped grizzled hair, made him look like an emperor of some ancient time.

He said, more quietly, as if without belief: "One complete year—who knows?"

"Papa," said Angelina, "I don't understand something. Why did you ever promise? Three years, you said, he must work for me, and then—oh, Papa, why did you let him stay if you couldn't stand the thought of it? You could have sent him home—called the police—something! All you did, Papa, was make us love each other more and more, till now"—she flushed, unable to go on, and seemed about to weep again.

"Till now—what?" His voice was husky with suspicion, even with fear.

"I mean, Papa, till I can't have your birthday with you if he doesn't. I asked him, and he came. I know. You promised because you thought he would get tired of us and go home, or else not be able to learn enough in three years to stay forever. But he did, you know he did. You say yourself he can ride Esmeralda in the big act—soon, you say. You even gave him dancing lessons so he could: yes, he can dance on Esmeralda, and you're just as sure as I am that the crowd will go crazy, he's so graceful, he's so good, and bows so beautifully before he steps off. I've watched him practicing, and when he waved I thought the people were all there, although they weren't; there wasn't even any tent."

"All right, all right, girl, but you said—"

"I said, Papa, you will have to have your birthday by yourself if Archie can't be here."

"No, no, no, girl! No!" He was more bewildered now than wrathful.

"Then, Papa, we're both going."

Cesare sat down suddenly on the small folding chair that nobody else used; he had broken it twice and had it mended, but this time it stood the shock. "Going! What's that? Going!"

"I mean, Papa, we're leaving you—the circus—everything. We're just going, that's all."

"Then and therefore! That's all, you say to me, that's all. Is it a joke, girl? You notice, maybe, I'm not laughing."

"Neither am I, Papa." But she wasn't crying either. Rather, she was looking at Archie, expecting him to speak. Archie, however, waited.

"Going!" groaned Cesare. "You can't go. You won't live. What can you two babies do out there in the world?" He waved, grandiosely. "Going! Going where? Cesare will certainly die, but you two won't—right away. All you will do— you'll starve."

"No, Papa, we won't starve. His father wants him home."

"Then let his father's son *go* home. Archie, I gave you dancing lessons—"

"Thank you, sir. And dying lessons, too. I learned from both."

Dying lessons. Cesare looked up at Angelina, who turned pale. But she hadn't been taken by surprise. She simply stood there, listening.

"What does he mean, girl? Dying! All the ghosts. I don't know what he means by that."

"I don't mean too much, sir. I can take care of myself. But they've all told me."

"Told you! Who told you? What?"

"Why, sir, that you hoped I would be killed. Then you wouldn't have to keep your promise. All the riders say this."

"All the witches!" Cesare was on his feet again. "I'll hang, I'll burn them. And you, boy, I'll break your back."

He raised both hands as if to do it, but was stopped by the very quietness with which Angelina said: "Listen, Papa."

Without turning, he dropped his hands and listened.

"If you hurt him, Papa, they will tell. They've told me too, so *I* could tell. They've told me how if there were dangerous things to do you made him do them. They noticed; it was always Archie. The truck that hit the bridge—you knew it would, they say, and you put Archie in it. When he wasn't even hurt you ground your teeth; they heard you in the dark, when word came that only Nicky was dead—poor Nicky! Then in the act—you pushed him too fast, you didn't seem to care what awful things might happen. You worried about the others, but you never worried about my sweetheart. One of them, I won't say which, but one of them thought you cut old Nero's shoulder-band that day when Archie fell. On his feet, though. And this one heard you swearing—'All the imps!'— because of that. And Esmeralda. They think it's too soon for him to try Esmeralda and the hoops. They say—"

"They say!" But he sat down again, this time weakly.

"Yes, and more—"

"I don't want to hear it." He looked at his knees, spread helplessly before him. "More? I want no more."

She kneeled at his feet, sobbing. "Then it's true? Oh, Papa!"

He had closed his eyes, but now he opened them on her. "And you don't hate me, girl? Why not?"

"I love you, Papa."

"When I wanted—"

"Oh, I don't think you really did. You were proud of him too. You bragged—I heard it—and you gave him dancing lessons."

"Dio, Dio! Dancing lessons. When all the time—"

"Sh-h-h."

"Let me say it. All the time I wanted—"

"Sh-h-h."

"But I didn't cut the strap."

"I know it. So does Archie."

Cesare looked up. "How does *he* know? What does *he* know about harnesses?"

"Archie knows everything. Don't you, sweet one?" She got up and kissed him lightly, over and over, missing no part of his face with her swift lips.

"Well, hardly." He was pleased.

"You do too. You know Papa loves you because I love you. Don't you, Papa?"—over her shoulder.

Cesare only groaned.

When she turned and came to him and kissed him too, he groaned again.

"Papa, you must say so even if—listen, do you love me? Do you love Angelina?"

"Oh, oh!"

"Then you love Archie, for he is me, and I am him. It has to be that way. So?" She knelt by him a second time, gently, as if she could wait forever.

"You and him," he said at last, hoarsely. "O.K. My girl, my boy, Cesare loves you both."

Angelina sprang up and danced. There was no room to do it, but even so she danced—rose on her toes, and whirled, and spun. The old man, the young man, watched her without a sound.

And then she clapped her hands. "The cake!" She had not baked it herself, but it was in the oven for safe-keeping. She drew out the red and green box that contained it and said to Cesare: "You open it, you be surprised."

For the baker had lavished all his art upon the icing. "Cesare

Bertolocchi—70—with love from Archie and Angelina," the letters said.

"Lightning and thunders! You did this—his name too."

"Wasn't I smart?" she said. "Wasn't I a fortune-teller? But that is only one present, Papa. There's a big one from the circus they're all giving you tonight. I won't tell you what it is, but remember, it's big, it's wonderful; you wouldn't dream. And now there are two more from us. Archie, you first."

It was a small box, heavy for its size, that rattled. Inside were seven miniature bronze elephants. "The seventh"—the boy smiled—"is for when you retire next. We know it's not too many. We'll be there."

"Good!" shouted Cesare. "Why not? Yes, you be there. Grazie, grazie!"

"It was Archie's idea," whispered Angelina proudly. "And this was mine." She unwrapped a velvet case, pressed open its catch, and lifted it for Cesare to see. Nella's locket was lying there, newly polished, neatly fitting into a white silk recess designed to receive it. "I took it out of the black trunk when you weren't looking, Papa, and had this done. It's better, isn't it, to have a case? Or don't you like it?" For he merely stared at what he now held in his hands.

"Don't you like it, Papa?"

"Cherubino, serafino!" Then, without warning, he laughed. "Girl, I was giving *you* the locket. For my birthday I was giving *you* a present. A surprise. Now who's surprised?"

"Oh, Papa, we both are! But you will keep it, won't you? It oughtn't to be mine. You're so good—thank you, thank you, Papa—but I couldn't bear—"

"Some day, some day. Then *you* will keep it."

She ignored this as she kissed him—thank you, thank you— and as he kissed her, murmuring "Nella, Nella! You should see."

Then, suddenly, there was the bell for supper in Alfredo the cook's tent; they had been invited, and must go. A few others were to be there too: not all the circus, Alfredo said, but those who were the closest. Cesare looked out of the little window by his chair and saw the Sicilian tumblers, his special friends, stepping nimbly over ropes and rubber cables as they obeyed the summons of the bell.

"Those there," he said, pointing, "did *they* tell you?"

"Tell me?" Angelina looked too, and was puzzled.

"Tell *him*."

Archie understood. He shook his head.

"Oh!" said Angelina. "That. Forget it, Papa. Nobody will say anything again. There won't be anything *to* say. Archie has forgotten. I've forgotten."

"Sure?" Cesare was serious. "You said—remember?—*you* would tell."

"You knew I wouldn't, and you know I won't. Don't you, Papa?"

He beamed at her and yet he shrugged his shoulders just a little. "Good girl. And so you got your way."

"We all did. But now you two shake hands."

Cesare even took Archie's head between his rough palms and kissed it loudly, several times.

"That's better," said Angelina. "Happy Birthday, all us three, and live forever."

The Imp of String

IT WAS not until all her children had gone away that Hannah Bascomb began to do what the imp told her.

He had been at her ever since she married Hiram, thirty-six years ago, but only now did he have any success. She and Hiram still lived in the low white house which hugged the lee side of North Mountain, and there was no difference for neighbors to see, outside or inside the place, for a long time after that first day.

It was the day of Betty's wedding. The youngest daughter was married and gone, and Hannah sat alone by the front

window where she had watched the buggy disappear with
Fred and Betty in it on their way to Sulkin Station. Hiram
must be feeling it too, but he showed it in his own way, by
pottering at the barn. He wouldn't be in for an hour, probably; so she sat right on, looking through the open window
and wondering why she didn't get up and tidy the room.
There hadn't been a big crowd, but they had left their litter
just the same: grains of rice on the carpet, flower petals under
the center table, and over in that corner the discarded wrappings of a wedding present—Hannah couldn't remember
whose.

"Burn the paper," he said, "but not the cord. It is strong
white cord, and if you make a little coil of it around two
fingers it will come in handy some day."

She nodded, as if of course the advice was good; then she sat
up and looked around. The voice had come from a long way
off, but she heard it all right; it was for her.

"Go on," he said, "it's good cord and you will be glad you
saved it."

"Who are you?" She could have been talking to herself.

"You know."

In a way she did, for he had been at her so long, trying to
get her attention.

But she said sharply: "Go away!" Then she went over to
pick up the wrappings from the corner where they had fallen.

Sure enough, inside the crumpled paper there were perhaps
two yards of strong white cord. She began at one end, coiling
it slowly around the first two fingers of her left hand.

"That's right." Then he was still there. "You'll be sending
your daughter things—a year from now, for her baby—and
you'll want string on hand. Especially strong string. You're a
saver, but I've never seen you admit it. This is soft string, too.
It will make a tight knot."

She nodded, and that was the beginning.

Hiram didn't know for several years. It went on from string
to buttons, and from there to wooden boxes—not big ones, but
the kind spectacles came in, or certain sorts of spices, and

indeed anything for which thin wood was a satisfactory container, thin wood with a top that slid back.

Hiram merely noticed that Hannah grew more and more secretive about closets and cupboards. He was always coming upon locked doors: at first the closet in her sewing room upstairs, which was natural enough perhaps, then everywhere else as well. He would try a door, and he couldn't open it. If she saw him she called out: "Hiram, keep away from there"—sharply, as if he were a thief or something.

It was funny, the way Hannah changed. She had business of her own that she never talked about. It took her all over the house, rummaging and mumbling to herself like one possessed.

Then one day he found the string. Hannah was out of the kitchen—he heard her walking upstairs—so he knew he was safe. He yanked hard at the narrow door of the broom closet, and when it opened suddenly, almost upsetting him, there was the string. Not coils of it any more, for she had stopped doing that, but lengths of it hung over the nails where dustclothes used to be. There were no cloths or brooms at all. Nothing but string, sorted as to size and quality, and hung over the square-headed nails he had driven in when he made the closet years ago.

"What in thunder?" said Hiram, and closed the door as suddenly as he had opened it, for Hannah was coming downstairs. He wasn't aware that the cardboard wedging she used to keep it tight shut had fallen out and was lying on the floor by his feet.

But she was, and she made for him at once, shaking her finger like—he hated to say it, like a witch.

She peered in suspiciously before she turned to him and said: "At least you didn't take any."

"Any what? You think I'd want—"

"My string. I save it."

"By the continental, I see you do!"

"That's all right, Hiram. Make fun of me if you want, but it's a good thing to do. I'm never out of string, the way you are sometimes with straps and bolts."

"I'm never out."

"Then you're a saver too, I can tell from the way you talk. I'll bet you've known him longer than I have."

"Who?"

"You know."

Hiram did, though he would have died rather than let on.

When was it he first heard him? The afternoon of Betty's wedding—yes, that was it, when everybody had gone off and Hannah was here at the house, sitting lonesome in the window. He would have liked to cheer her up, but instead he went to the barn and began fooling around his tool bench, the bench he had built in the driveway, opposite the hayloft. He didn't keep it very neat, but he knew where to find things.

He picked up a spare axle-nut he had once started to throw away, but hadn't because it fitted the buggy, and you never knew when one of those nuts would turn off and need to be replaced.

"It fits the buggy Betty's riding in now, to Sulkin Station. Better put it away and remember where you put it. They may be sending back for it, Hiram."

He jumped and looked around.

"Who are you?" demanded Hiram.

But he knew. He had never given in to him, no matter how many times he had heard this voice that came from far away, like something long discouraged and unused.

Now it was as if he had to. So he brushed the shavings from a narrow shelf above his bolts and cotter pins, and drove a thin nail there to hang the nut on.

"I'll bet," said Hannah.

"Don't know what you're talking about," blustered Hiram, turning away. "String! Before I'd save that I'd sew myself into a winding sheet. How you do save it! Ever use any? Talk of betting—I'd risk a dollar you never take an inch of it out of here. I don't notice you tying and sending. Why, you even pretend you can't find any; and all the time you're rich as Croesus, if you call these snippets anything."

Hannah was furious, or she wouldn't have shown him the wooden boxes.

She pulled him into the parlor with both hands, which then she lifted to open the cupboard over the mantel, the deep one that went back and turned a corner around the chimney. He thought it hadn't been used for years.

She twisted a contraption around the handle and jerked open the ill-fitting door; jerked it so violently in her anger and her pride that the boxes rattled in a shower down over the hearth-stone.

"Maybe you don't think *these* are something!" She was picking up the little containers with their sliding tops, and looking to see if any were broken.

"Playthings!" he said. "You'll never use that many in this mortal life. Anyway, you don't ever take one out, do you? You only add to the pile. I've been wondering where they went. I could have used one the other day, but of course, being misered like this—"

Hannah stood up. "What did you want it for?"

Now he was angry. "My business," he said, and started back to the barn.

"I'm coming too," said Hannah.

"No you don't!"

But she did. She followed him.

The top of the toolbench looked as it always had. That was only for show, she told herself. What about the oatbin? It was swept off, and it had a padlock on it.

"Ask him where the key is. He'll have to tell you."

Each one of them pretended not to hear.

"Go on," said a small voice, far away. "Ask Hiram. He knows."

Hannah and Hiram looked at each other. Neither of them felt easy.

"Key's there," said Hiram, pointing to the cigar box where he used to keep an assortment of washers. "But wait a minute. What does he sound like to you—the one that said something just now?"

"Why," said Hannah, opening the cigar box and finding it

empty except for the key, "I don't know. I suppose you mean—why, what does he sound like to *you?* I'd say a book-keeper."

"You would? I'd say a blacksmith."

There hadn't been any oats in the bin for winters and winters. Only these coils of thin wire, and these high piles of hinges—every size and shape of hinge you could think of, and all of them oiled. Some of them had been rusty when picked up, but their condition now was as good as it could be. And some were new. They looked as if they had just come out of a hardware store.

"What's the wire for?" asked Hannah unsympathetically.

"You know," said Hiram. "Never can tell when you won't need a bit of that to bind—"

"Before I'd save wire!"

"Well, string!"

"And what about the hinges? What about this pair?" She snatched at two that still had white paint on them, though Hiram had tried to scour it off.

"Why," said Hiram, "that—why, that pair I believe was on the cupboard door where you keep the boxes. They needed fixing, so I—"

"So, magpie, that's where! I had to patch the place with a piece of leather. And all the time you—Hiram! What about these new ones?"

"Well," and he scratched his head, "I didn't have that size of strap hinge, so I thought I'd do some filling out."

"And me without the money to—"

"Buy string and boxes. That's what you'd like to spend it for, isn't it? Come to think, you bought a big ball of brown cord the last time we went to Sulkin. What happened to that? Cut it up?"

She was busy shutting the lid of the bin.

"Look here, Hannah."

She looked at last, and Hiram didn't seem to be mad any more.

"We *are* a pair," he said.

"Are we crazy, Hiram?"

They laughed; and after this they had only each other, that day and every other day till Hiram died.

Hannah was an old woman then, and her children, as many of them as could, came for a month to stay with her in the quiet house, bringing the grandchildren so it wouldn't be too quiet.

There wasn't much for them to play with, though. Nothing but string and boxes, and a bin full of old iron that ought to have been left in the barn.

"How did you happen to have all this?" asked Betty once, leading her youngest daughter out of the living room. "These boxes and hinges—I don't remember ever—"

"No, you don't," said her mother. "It was after your time. I don't remember either. Very well, that is."

She missed Hiram so much.

Me and Mac

"LIKE I SAY, it's none of my business, but I couldn't stand a jealous man—jealous, I mean, the way he is."

Both women glanced toward the kitchen to make sure Mac wasn't listening. Each measured the distance, and felt safe. There was no other means of making sure; his face wouldn't show it; he always saw to that.

"What do you know about it, dear?" Belle, his wife, kept on wrapping sandwiches for the customers who would come in at noon. The Triangle Snack Bar was empty now except for a boy who had ridden up on his bicycle and was devouring doughnuts at the far end of the counter, near the cash register.

"You mean, he's not my husband and who is? Well, I never had one, but I've seen a thing or two, I guess I know as much as if—"

"Skip it, Sadie. We all know everything, and I never meant

to say you didn't. In general, that is. But Mac—what do you mean, 'the way he is'? How could anybody know that but me?" She must have thought she still sounded touchier than she was, for when Sadie said nothing by the coffee urn she added: "I'm just wondering, dear."

Just wondering. Sadie studied her reflection in the shiny metal of the urn and said to it: You shouldn't have started this. Now watch your step. She can't read your mind, but you can give it away. Open any page, and there it is.

But silence wouldn't do either. "Oh," she said, polishing the spot where her eyes and mouth had been, "I've noticed a few things. He hates every customer you feed—every *man* customer. This ought to be a tea shop, or a ladies' reducing parlor; then he wouldn't have to suffer."

"Suffer?" Belle, carrying another plate of doughnuts to the boy, came back as soon as she could.

"Sure. He's in the wrong business. His wife's a waitress, and that's more than he can take. Funny thing, waitresses. Why do men think so much of them? We all know they do, though. Every last one of them seems to believe she puts on her uniform just for him, and is a kind of—you know, wife. Well, Mac knows all about this, beginning maybe with himself; and he can't take it, though day in and day out he's got to as long as he runs a sandwich joint. The worst thing is when they talk to you. Man, that drives him crazy."

Belle placed the last sandwich on the pile, adjusting its position carefully, slowly, as if she were sorry she had nothing further to occupy her at the moment.

"Of course there's something in what you say—generally, I mean. But Mac, now—couldn't he be an exception? What sign does he ever give that he's like all the rest? You're imagining things, dear."

Why does she call me dear that way? I should have kept my mouth shut. "Signs? They're plain as day. Not in big letters, or any at all, but I can read them. You're just pretending you can't."

"Letters is all I can read. I don't go in for sealed envelopes or crystal balls."

"Sealed—you said it. He's stuck tight. But *that's* the sign. Of course he never says anything, or I judge he doesn't. But does he turn pale? I'll say. And his eyes don't know where to look, so they look everywhere except at you, and they get black as coal—they agonize, I tell you. Your customer passes the time of day; all right, Mac listens, and believe me he makes the most of it. He's got it bad. It's a sickness. I couldn't stand it. I had a boy friend once—"

"You should have one now. What's the matter with *you?*" Belle blazed at her. "No boy friend. You make *me* sick. If I didn't need somebody here, and girls weren't so hard to get, I'd let you go this minute. I won't have him talked about that way, and don't you forget it. I won't hear any more."

All right, all right, there won't be any more. She thinks I hate him. So I'm safe. I've got to watch my step, though. Can't be fired.

"There, now," said Belle, patting her arm as she passed by on the way to the cream pitchers, to make certain they were full. "I didn't mean all of that. But goodness, how you tore into him! Can you blame me for coming back at you? Nobody ever said such things before, so you shouldn't expect me not to care. What about that boy friend? 'Once,' you said, but I'll bet he's still on deck and you've had a fight. Sounds so to me. Now wasn't it more about him, what you said, than Mac? Honest, now."

Well, that can be my line.

"You're pretty smart," said Sadie. "OK, it's the boy friend that bothers me—so much on my mind, I see him everywhere. I like him, too, but that's not it. I *don't* like what he thinks about me and any other man I happen to mention—any other person, even, any other thing. Anything I say, he twists it and squeezes it till something comes out that wasn't ever there. I'd say he had a dirty mind, except that I really do like him—sometimes."

"What he thinks, or what he says? Maybe it's you again. If he doesn't say things, how do you know for sure?"

"Oh, he says things—sometimes. Often enough for me to know. Mostly, I admit, I have to figure them out myself. Let's see, I say, now what could have caused him to look the way he does? Not at me, understand, oh, no, anywhere but me. The floor, the ceiling, the back of a chair, the cracks in the plaster. If he would only look at me, then maybe I could handle him. Fact is, he's casing the inside of his own head. I can tell by the way his eyes get black—like I said—and he tightens up all over, and loses color, and sweats."

"My!"

"You think I'm putting it too strong. You think I'm crazy."

"No, but—"

"If I ever did go off my rocker, he'd be the reason. He leaves me no self-respect, no life of my own. In lots of ways, Belle, a woman thinks just like a man, like any human person, and she wants to keep on doing that, with no questions asked that men don't ask each other either, or women when they're together like me and you. You and me don't discuss love all the time. So what do I do when he sweeps dirt out of some corner that was absolutely spotless? Some gentleman holds a door open—a glass door at that—for me to go through first, and he says: 'Who's your friend?' He doesn't say this right away, so I've forgot, or else I never noticed—you know, it's ordinary, it happens every day, and yet I hope I gave the gent a pleasant eye, and thanked him. So I say, 'What friend?' 'The one,' he says, 'you looked at a certain way, the one that opened the big door down there.' We're in the mezzanine now, looking for seats where we can smoke. 'I was coming with the tickets,' he goes on to say, 'and saw you with him.' '*With* him! We just happened to be there.' 'Who's *we?*' he says, and then he's off. Well, I don't say anything at all. Which means to him I'm dreaming about this stranger I'll never see again and don't want to. Sorry I ever did—*if* I did, which I doubt. But the boy friend, he doesn't doubt. He believes everything, even when he makes it up. And he can make up the damnedest things. He's got genius that way. But they tell me it's not a soft life, living with a genius."

"He does seem to have it worse than most. Yes, I can see he gives you a tough time."

"*The* worst, and don't think I'm making *that* up. What

would you say I ought to do, Belle? Shut the gate on him for good, and lock it? Even if I do like him, there's no percentage in what I go through, having him think what he does."

"Think?"

"*And* say. You guessed it, we had a fight Sunday afternoon. I mentioned Mac."

This is dangerous, but I'll take a chance. I've got to be in the clear and *know* I am.

Belle seemed not to have heard. She was busy making a lemon pie look better.

"I mentioned Mac," said Sadie again.

"You did? How was that?" A certain strain sounded in Belle's voice, ordinarily relaxed and low. She didn't look at Sadie.

"Oh, it was natural. Why shouldn't I talk about where I work, and who I work for? I talk a lot about you."

"Yes, I suppose so."

"And Mac. At least I mentioned that there was a husband. So he asked me what his name was, and naturally I said it— 'Mac.' 'You never told me about *him*,' he said. 'No reason to,' I said. 'Maybe there's a reason not to,' he said, and I could see him get that look around the mouth. 'Maybe—' 'Oh, God,' I said, 'will you shut *up*?' Then he was really off, so I left him and walked home—too far, with those new shoes on I told you about, and I might have been sorry—changed my mind—gone back to the car—but I didn't. The idea. Me and Mac!"

Belle closed the pie-case and said nothing.

"Me and Mac! Can you imagine? I said I hardly ever had two words with him, I said you were my friend *and* boss, I said, why, Mac's gone on you if any man was ever gone on his wife, anybody can see that, I'd never think—*he'd* never think—I said—"

"You said plenty, I'm sure," said Belle at last.

"I did for a fact, and this time I believe it worked. He came around last night, and not once did he bring the subject up. He knows when I *really* mean it."

"Don't you always mean it? I thought he never had anything to go on."

"That's right, he doesn't. But I get madder sometimes than others, and this time, if I do say so, I gave him the works."

"I see."

"I mean, I convinced him."

"Then he's not hopeless. You seemed to say he was."

"He's pretty hopeless."

"So is everybody. But somebody sticks by them, and that makes a lot of difference. If you want my advice—do you?"

"Sure."

"Stick by him, and straighten him all the way out. It can be done."

Stick by who? This joker doesn't even exist. I made him up because I was in that box. And now I'm in this box. I might have known. She's worried, Belle's worried, and it's all my fault. I just wanted to talk about Mac, even if it was this way. How'll I clean it up?

The boy had finished his doughnuts, and Belle went forward to let him pay her. As he closed the door behind him she looked out of the front window to see if people were gathered at the entrance to the needle factory. They always stood there a few minutes, chatting and looking up at the sun, before some of them crossed the highway and came here. It was a little early yet—she glanced back at the clock—so she returned to Sadie.

"It can be done, what I said. I never had the problem myself—you're wrong about that—but anything can be done by a person that tries. The question is, whether he's worth it. What would you have if you did get him straightened out?"

"Oh," said Sadie all too eagerly, "he's worth it. The only thing is, can I do it? You don't know—Brick." He had to have a name. "Some days, no kidding, he comes down on me like a ton of 'em."

Both women smiled as the kitchen door swung open for Mac to pass through with a pile of heavy plates, which he distributed beneath the counter before he said a word. Then to Belle: "Empty house, I see. Never get rich that way." As usual, he didn't know Sadie was there.

"They'll be over soon," said Belle. "Don't worry, there'll be the regular rush. Everything ready with you?"

"Yes, ma'am." He blinked at her as he turned to go back. And Sadie thought: How warm, how sweet, old Stoneface. But he never sees I'm here, it's not for me, that little joke, the same one every day. Shall I say something? But what?

He started to push the door, then stopped. "Tell you one thing, ma'am."

"What's that?" said Belle.

"You look all right this morning. You look good."

Belle's eyes *were* bright, said Sadie. And his were full of something that filled her too—more than filled her, so that she felt like breaking.

"Get out of here," said Belle, not meaning it. She even blushed a little.

After the door swung to she said to Sadie: "See, dear? Mac's not the jealous type."

"No, I guess not. I never meant that anyway. Or anything I said. *Anything.*"

Does that cover it? I think so, she's so pleased. And wouldn't I be if—no, I'd rather he was jealous of me. Fat chance, for nobody ever told him I was born. But what if he did think things about me, right here behind my back, things he oughtn't to but did? Unfair things, about me and the customers—how good, how warm, would I feel then. It might be me and Brick he carried on about, as if there was anything in that, as if—as if there was any *Brick.* My God!

"Are you all right, dear?" Belle was tapping a saltcellar, to free the holes.

"Did I say anything?"

"You said 'My God!'"

"I did? You heard me?"

"It was sort of under your breath, but I heard you. I thought you might be feeling rotten."

"I do."

"See here, Sadie, maybe this place is bad for you."

"No, no, it's good."

"The work might be too hard."

"No, no! Don't I do it right?"

"Oh, yes, but—"

"Listen, I don't mean I was sick or anything. I was just talking to myself—about him."

"Who?"

"Brick."

"Oh, Brick."

"Sure. I was saying to myself I'd try it, what you said."

"Why, now that's sensible. You just give it a good try."

"I'm going to."

"And don't imagine things, dear."

"I won't." I will, though. She can't stop me doing that, as long as I remember not to talk out loud.

Honeymoon

WHOM SHOULD SHE pray to? Russell had told her everything would be all right: again and again he had told her, and hugged her to prove he was not mistaken. But all it proved was that he had confidence in their scheme. His scheme, rather, though when he insisted she agreed. And she still agreed, for she would do anything Russell wanted. She was worried, nevertheless. Somebody might see something, and write to Mr. Lord. That would be worse than Russell could ever understand.

The most Russell had said against Mr. Lord was that he was a stinker for refusing to let them live in the cottage the first week after they were married. Only a week, and they wouldn't hurt the cottage. It was closed, like the big house, while Mr. Lord enjoyed himself in Florida. And who knew more than they did about taking care of it? They had done enough work there, outside and in, to deserve this little favor. It was Russell, of course, who asked. He had written Mr. Lord to say they were getting married on St. Valentine's Day, and could they have the cottage if they left everything as they found it? They didn't have the money for a trip. They weren't even sure they had enough to live on afterward. It was a sudden idea, getting married; but it might be that he would have to go on working at Sunwise Farm, and she at Mrs. Waldron's, for months and months before they had a place together. That was why it was so important to have a honeymoon, even if it was in the cottage. A couple of mice, Russell called it, making a nest where they didn't belong. But better than nothing.

Of course he didn't write all this to Mr. Lord. He merely asked the favor. And when Mr. Lord refused it, he didn't even say he was glad they were getting married. Russell was mad about that, too; but not so mad as he would have been if he had known why. She thought she did. As a matter of fact she knew she did. All the times Mr. Lord had tried to get her to go there with him, on summer nights when there were no guests, no people at all to know—it was perfectly safe, he had said, smiling at her so horribly when he said it, stopping his car and whispering to her while she stood and hated him and wished he would die—she could never tell Russell about those times. They were the reason, of course. And they were part of the reason she was worried. If somebody saw something, and told Mr. Lord! Then *he* would be mad—mad enough, maybe, to tell Russell stories that weren't true.

Cherry shivered, waiting in her little room over Mrs. Waldron's kitchen for the sound of Russell's truck. Mrs. Waldron thought they were going away for a week—really away—and so did Gus, the foreman at the Farm. There hadn't been any trouble about that; and Mrs. Waldron had been nice enough this morning to say she was glad they were getting married, and to give her the box of handkerchiefs that now was in the suitcase with her other things. Mrs. Waldron wouldn't be here when Russell came for her. Cherry was glad of that, for she didn't think she could lie any more about where it was they were going.

They were to be married at four o'clock, by the town clerk

in Tamworth, and Russell was coming at three. By five, when it was almost dark, they would be at the cottage, and no matter how cold it was at first, Russell had said, they could begin their honeymoon. The shutters were tight enough to keep candlelight from showing through. The electricity was off, of course, so they would have only candles. And there probably wouldn't be any sparks from the fireplace chimney that people could see. Who would be passing anyway? Russell didn't have a doubt in his head.

But she did, and she wanted to pray. All day, though, she had wondered how to do it, and to whom. She didn't know about such things. God himself—she didn't dare do that, for weren't she and Russell lying and stealing? She couldn't ask God to help. Or the others they talked about at church. Not Jesus, not Mary. They wouldn't be interested in seeing to it that Mr. Lord never learned anything. She and Russell were going to cook in the fireplace, and they would sleep in front of it, on blankets he was bringing from the Farm. She couldn't ask Mary—well, to what? She hastened by the question. Perhaps there was nobody in the other world that cared what she and Russell did on St. Valentine's Day.

St. Valentine. Who was St. Valentine?

She was ignorant about the saints. That wasn't the kind of church Mrs. Waldron took her to. Maisie Sullivan would know. But she hadn't seen Maisie for months, and anyhow she couldn't ask her. Nobody in this world must know.

St. Valentine. She shut her eyes where she stood, one hand still resting on the window frame through which Russell's red truck would be visible in a few minutes, and said the name several times.

Then she found she had begun.

"St. Valentine," she was saying in a low voice, "St. Valentine, whoever and wherever you are, will you be good to Russell and me—Cherry Beckwith—will you help us tonight, will you make sure nobody sees? You don't know us, because we are not your people, but we are being married on your day, and tonight the honeymoon that Russell wanted is beginning. But where we will be is a secret from every person on

earth, including Mr. Lord. Especially Mr. Lord. Tonight, and
every other night for a week, and every day, be with us two,
St. Valentine, and bless our honeymoon. There is nobody else
who can help. I have no family, and Russell's is far away.
There is nobody to help or bless us. I have no right to ask it,
but will you be our saint? If you are listening, please understand that Russell wouldn't like to have me pray. But that is
because he has no doubts. Please include him, though. Now he
is coming, and I must go. Thank you, St. Valentine, if you
have listened. I am Cherry Beckwith, that soon will be Cherry
Hart. Good-by, good-by."

"Hello, Cherry."
Russell was calling up to her from the corner of the green-
house. He was calling loud because he hadn't turned the engine
off, and he was saying nothing but her name. He never said
things like "darling" or "sweetheart." Her name itself was an
endearment to him, and the way he said it made her like it
too.
He had to call her again before she seemed to hear. Then she
waved, picked up her suitcase, and ran down.
"What were you doing, Cherry? Changing your mind?"
They talked very little on the way to Tamworth, and on the
way back, as it grew darker and colder, even less. There was
no snow for a change, but the ground was frozen till the ruts
in the cottage lane looked like iron gouges when they got
there.
It still wasn't dark enough, Russell said, so they would drive
around for half an hour. "We should have killed time in town,
getting a soda or something," he added, self-conscious all at
once.
"No, honey, this is better." She sat closer to him.
They drove up Roberts Hill to North Tamworth, paused
there, and returned in frosty darkness which no star, no planet,
modified. Russell had planned to leave the truck in Simpson's
barn, an unused hulk of a building up the road a little way
from the cottage. As he shut the big doors behind him, Cherry
seized his free hand and clung to it. The other hand held the

bag into which their blankets and utensils were stuffed. The bag, slung over his shoulder, was awkward and heavy, and sometimes he needed the hand Cherry had in hers; but she never let it go.

"Will it be all right, are you sure?" she asked. They were almost there.

"You know it will," he said. He was not impatient with her.

Then they were in the living room, feeling their way around. It was as cold as a funeral vault, but before Russell struck a match, even, he lifted all the windows and felt the shutter slats, to convince himself that they were tight.

"Now, Cherry!" And he struck one of those long blue-headed matches he always carried. It flickered on the covered chairs, the ghostly sofa opposite the fireplace, and the litter of seeds and shells that mice had left on the hearth.

"Here!"

He hastened to fumble in the bag for a candle. When he found it he lit it with another match and set it in one of the empty holders on the mantel. Cherry stared at it as if it were the only life in the world. "That's good," she managed to get out. She was shaking.

"I didn't tell you," said Russell. "I chopped plenty of wood up at the place and brought it down here day before yesterday. It's outside. You wait, Cherry."

"No!" She went with him and helped him carry in enough for their first fire. And when it was blazing she drew him near to her, nearer even than before, and kissed him so eagerly, so desperately, that he said, for all his happiness in the excitement of her doing so: "You're still afraid. Listen, it's all right."

"I know it is." But it wasn't. There must be some crack of light showing, somewhere; and when the fire mounted in the chimney she was sure a spark or two must be shooting up into the darkness.

"Who would notice?" Russell insisted. "Who would care?"

She got her mind off it as soon as he pulled from the bag the little frying pan they had bought this afternoon at Tamworth.

"Oh!" she cried. "We didn't bring my suitcase out of the truck. The eggs are in it, and everything."

"Lord!" said Russell, and did not see how she trembled at the word. "But you can be getting the blankets out while I go for it. Back in a jiffy!"

She went with him again, however, and on the way back stopped him in the lane.

"When we opened the door," she said, "do you suppose—"

"I certainly don't," he said. "Anyway, we'd have seen a car passing. There wasn't a car, was there? We'd still know by the lights, downhill or uphill. You've got the jitters, Cherry. Wait till we're warm again."

"Russell! Isn't that a crack of light from the side window, there by the barberry bush?"

"Don't see any, and you don't either."

"But what if someone did?"

"Who? The state police?" He laughed, pulling her on.

"Oh, honey, don't say that!"

They *would* notify Mr. Lord. And worse.

"All right. I'll just do this." He put both arms around her in the pitch-dark lane and kissed every part of her cold face, over and over again.

"There! That better?"

They went in. But Cherry whirled at once to shut the door.

"Still jittery," said Russell. "You'd think the FBI was out there."

"Don't say that either."

But he was busy with the blankets. The room was warm now, at least in front of the fire, and Russell was spreading all of them out.

"I know what," he said, straightening suddenly and coming to her with his face flushed, his eyes shining. "You don't believe me because we're not really married yet. Look here, Cherry."

But she ducked away from him and got the suitcase open. "Here's everything," she said, pretending not to know what he meant. Her heart was pounding too.

He stood by her, self-conscious and uncertain, while she got the eggs out of the tin box she had packed them in, and the slices of sweet ham. He watched her without a word as she proceeded with their supper.

They ate almost in silence, sitting next to each other on the floor, facing the fire. The fire made the only noise there was, a hissing and a cracking that was good to hear, both of them thought as they looked at it and listened.

Then there was another noise. A car.

The car stopped.

It waited while they waited. When it started again, they knew it had turned into the lane.

"Oh, St. Valentine!" Cherry thought she had said it under her breath, but Russell turned from the window to which he had run and said: "What's that?"

"I didn't say anything," she whispered in her terror. "Russell, what do you suppose—"

"Listen," was all he said. "Don't move."

A man's voice, crisp and suspicious, came clearly to them from beyond the window glass and the shutter.

"I'd swear," it said, "I saw a light in there."

"I still think it was a reflection from our own lights when we came around the bend." This was another man, a quieter one, with a voice not so distinct.

"The door's locked, of course, but I remember this shutter. It's the only one you can open from outside. Lord ought to have it fixed. Lucky now, though. I'll have a look."

"St. Valentine!" Cherry knew she couldn't be heard this time, for even if she had wanted to she couldn't have cried aloud.

"St. Valentine! Now—if you ever heard me. Please!"

The trooper was having trouble with the catch, but pretty soon that would be over, Cherry said, and then—

"St. Valentine! If you heard me, help us now!"

The shutter strained, but still it didn't budge. Russell tiptoed to the door, slid the bolt noiselessly into place, and came back, this time to Cherry's side.

Why was the light in the room growing brighter? For it was, and the fire hadn't changed.

Both of them saw it at once, and involuntarily shrank as if to escape it.

But it came from no single source: not from the fire, not from the candle above the fire. It was brightening everywhere, as if the whole room were aflame. And the brightness was growing. It filled the corners, it made the slip covers luminous, it glistened on the picture glass, it lit points of fire on the empty candle sockets, it came in white waves over the floor.

Even Russell was pale. He stared everywhere, above and around him, as at something that could not be.

But the color was returning to Cherry's cheeks. She was the brave one. She thought she knew. And as the light brightened again, and again and again, she did know.

"Don't worry," she whispered.

Russell heard only the shutter as it tore open and two faces looked blankly in.

Was it because the troopers were surprised by so much light that they had this unseeing look on their broad faces? They didn't blink, either, or turn to each other and nod.

"Well, I guess I was wrong," said one.

"Come on." The other was fastening the shutter. "I told you it was our own lights. This shiny hardware—that could have done it."

The voices retreated, the car started, and soon there was nothing to hear except the hiss of the fire, and of Russell's breath as it let itself out suddenly.

"You see?" said Cherry, feeling how cold his hand was when she took it. "I told you not to worry. *I'm* not worried any more."

"This light!" He was still breathless, though the brightness was decreasing now.

"What about it?" Cherry dropped to her knees on the top blanket, forgetting their unfinished supper.

"What *about* it!" Russell followed her down. "What *about* it!"

"It's black light," she said. "St. Valentine's light. It's only for us. It wasn't for them—those troopers—or anybody else. It's—"

"Valentine! Say, I got you one and never gave it to you."

He searched the inside pocket of his coat and brought out a card whose tinsel glistened in the room like a star.

"Oh! That's pretty." She pulled his head to her and kissed it.

"But this light!" He was stubborn, and wouldn't give up. "What happened, Cherry? What do you think happened?"

"Never mind, honey. Look, it's going out anyway."

For it was. It went out by degrees, as it had come, until the fire was all there was, and the candle that both of them forgot till morning.

The Facts About the Hyacinthes

SHE READ the sign aloud: *Incorporated 1740.* "Now it's only three more miles."

"Good—for you. What if they don't like me?"

"Then they'll throw you back. But I'll go too."

He slowed the car down and kissed her wrist for the seventh time since they left the main gate of the Academy. That was early this morning. It was now ten o'clock.

They were there before he knew it. The pavement changed to a dirt road; there was a wooden bridge to cross; then this last hill, a sharp one, with loose gravel. At the top of it, on the right, a little house.

Marie had said it was little, but not this little. She had said it was new. It wasn't new. Then he remembered. It was new when she moved into it, at six. So they had always called it "the new house," to distinguish it from the one Papa came from, over the hill, and the other one, farther along this road, where Marie was born. Peter said to himself: I must fit my notions to the facts.

He looked at Marie, but she was looking up the gullied

driveway. Nobody knew they had come. He followed her eyes as they went from one object to another on the littered slope where she had spent all of her remembered life until she went away to the Academy and met him. Littered was the word. Pieces of cars, ramshackle sheds, and piles of wood for which no use could be imagined lay here and there as if the wind had dropped them. The stones by the front foundation of the house, though, he understood. They were what Marie had laughed about so many times; the terrace Papa planned, he had never built. There was not even a wall for loads of dirt to be dumped behind. The stones had weathered with the house; both looked ancient under the May sun that fell in bright fragments through the few maple and ash trees there still were where woods had been.

Peter noticed how Marie's glance lingered longer on the stones than elsewhere. She must have seen, exactly as he did, how the absence of a terrace raised the house as it were on its haunches, so that it looked like an animal, startled, staring absurdly down at the road. But there was no apology in the smile she turned and gave him. Nothing had changed because he was there. When she laughed, as at once she did, it was in the same way she always had.

"You see," she said. "He hasn't lifted up a single stone."

"Wordsworth."

"Certainly—but here comes Bouncer."

A hideous little dog, thin-legged and sharp-nosed, ran down-hill to devour them; then, recognizing Marie, went into spasms of joy that rendered him more hideous still, for his teeth showed in a queer way as he fawned.

"Hello, foolish, this is Peter." But Bouncer was interested only in her fingers, which he jumped again and again to lick.

The noise he had made now brought the children running too—all six, in the order of their size. The little boys, Freddie and Jacques, were there before the others, their round heads buried in Marie's skirt as they butted and butted, trying to get further in.

"Here!" she said. "Look at *him*, too." They didn't seem to hear. But Celeste did, and stood shyly, holding on to Pauline's hand, until Peter put out his own. Then both girls shook it, studying his face and Marie's together, as if they were one person. Roger soberly let Marie kiss both his cheeks, then retreated with Moïse to stand in the middle of the driveway, kicking the biggest of its pebbles back and forth. "How's school?" he said. "You off every Saturday?"

"Yes, but I can't come every week. Peter drove me. Where's Mama?"

It was a superfluous question, they seemed to think. They wheeled, or the younger ones did, and Marie followed them, with Peter behind and the big boys last of all, up the slope and around the corner of the house to where the back door stood half open. The door, like the corner of the house, was black where hands had clutched it. Peter, awaiting his turn, wondered how many flies went through in hot weather.

Marguerite Hyacinthe, washing glass jars at the sink, pretended not to know anyone had come. The whole company was around her before she stopped.

"Hello, Mama." Marie kissed the sallow cheeks, then kissed them again.

"You're late." Marguerite wiped her hands on her apron. "Is this Peter?"

"You know it is," said Marie. "Papa around?"

"He drove her," said Jacques.

"Papa took the truck," said Marguerite. "He'll be back in time to eat. Freddie, your face is dirty."

It was, thought Peter. Jelly and earth; and some time this morning he had cried—fallen down, probably, and rubbed his eyes with both fists. Not that the other faces were different.

Freddie did nothing about it.

"You all right?" Marguerite glanced at Marie as if she doubted it; and yet of course she didn't. She had this set look, with only the ghost of a smile about her eyes. She worked like ten women. Her back showed it, and her hair.

"I'm fine." Marie pulled her away from the sink. "Come and sit down, Mama, while I show Peter the house."

"Nothing to show," said Marguerite. But she went with them, downstairs and upstairs. She was proudest of the fireplace in the living room. Felix had built it out of stones he picked up on the hill, and it drew well. There were pictures of everybody on the unstained oak mantel; of Marie particularly, at three stages of her growth. She was the oldest, and she had gone away to school.

"Hear about King's barn burning?"

"No," said Marie. "When?"

"Last week. Wiring, they think. All the hay that was left, and they couldn't get four of the cows out. Papa and the boys were up all night. Fire department never got there."

"Poor Mr. King."

"Poor Mrs. King."

"Yes, of course. Now, Mama, Peter ought to look around outdoors."

"There'll be some things you haven't seen yourself. Wait a minute and I'll go too."

"She likes you," whispered Marie to Peter as her mother went in to take the jars out of the rinse water and stand them upside down on the drainboard.

"Why not?" He said it absently, as if he didn't think it humorous. He meant he liked Marguerite. He was thinking all the time: Everything about the place is just as Marie described it, except that to one who didn't love it, it would look—but he didn't finish the thought. Marie loved it, of course. But not as something she glorified by doing so. It was already glorious. The very fact of it was splendid. Marguerite, with her yellow cheeks and her drawn eyes that stared at things a little longer than they should—Marie worshiped her for what she was, and had been transported when she saw signs—what signs Peter didn't know—that Peter was accepted. Marie was his student, and they would be married no matter who said yes or no. But this wasn't it. Marguerite liked him, and Marie was proud of that. As proud as if Marguerite were—here he stopped, ashamed, and shut his mind to everything except the fact that the children were waiting for them in a semicircle outside the door. They knew the animals were going to be looked at. And Marguerite, having put on an old coat-sweater, was coming out of the bedroom, smoothing back her hair with one brown hand. She looked at him directly for the first time today, and said to him, not to Marie: "Come on."

Papa was driving up from the road as they rounded the house on the way to the horse barn. There was only one horse; Moïse said they had to see him first.

"Marie's here!" shouted Jacques, running toward the truck as it clattered to a stop.

Felix got out, stood looking a while, and waved—a quiet wave. Marie had prepared Peter; he would talk little. When he came up to them he kissed Marie without a word and shook hands with Peter before his name was spoken. "Have to take this feed in," he explained to Marguerite as if she were the only one who would understand him. Felix and Marguerite Hyacinthe; and her name had been Lemoire. Marie was all French, thought Peter, and looked it. Yet Felix under his frayed cap, with the bill broken in a dozen places, was very different from his black-eyed daughter, and so was Marguerite. The daughter was unaware of this. "Get through quick," she called after him. "Could Peter help?"

"No, it's not much."

Marie smiled as they trooped off to the horse barn, where Moïse opened the sagging door and led out Hector, a benevolent roan who had been waiting for this moment; or so it seemed. He advanced a few steps, stopped, and fell into the same doze he had been enjoying before they came. Their hands went over him, nose, neck, and shoulders, while he lowered his head and blinked.

"Good horse," said Peter.

"We got him cheap, from Sedgwicks. Had a bad foot, but it's all right now. Celeste, keep out from under him. Come on." Marguerite was already on her way to the next exhibit.

Moïse backed Hector into place, fastened the door with the bent nail that was there for the purpose, and came after them on a trot.

"Ever see pigs?" Marguerite asked Peter. She would soon know whether he had or not.

It was the smell she had in mind: something that staggered you at first, along with the snorting and the screaming of the beasts as they mounted the partition, their forefeet in a trough, and begged for slop.

"Good pigs," said Peter. But Marguerite smiled with more than her eyes. She could see he was appalled. "Hogs," she said, as if correcting him.

"They're getting fatter, though." Marie helped him out.

The little boys were dancing up and down. "Rabbits!" Freddie insisted. "Rabbits next!"

"How many have you got?" Peter went ahead, holding Freddie's hand.

Freddie hesitated, rolling his eyes toward his mother, who would know. When she didn't say the number, he answered importantly, "You'll see."

There were at least a dozen big hares in the filthy box which Peter had passed without seeing it on the way to Hector. They sniffed at the wire door, and tumbled over one another when Marguerite's hand went in. She brought out an enormous white one, dangling it by the ears as she turned it every way for them to see how fat. She put it back suddenly and went on.

"You show him the rest"—she addressed all of her children at once, including Marie—"Papa's hungry and I have to go in. Don't forget the geese."

Peter watched her as she went, noticing how the heels of her old shoes turned on an occasional rock or root in the path. She went rapidly, from habit, turning her head toward the chickenhouse, where Felix was unloading the bags, to see if he was coming soon. The sun was overhead now, and she made no shadow. She was a clear object, thrown suddenly into a relief of which she was unconscious. Her hands swung a little awkwardly at her sides; she was used to their being occupied. Yet she had come out to show Peter the animals. Peter and Marie. She ran a big world here: all these children, this house, this litter, these creatures in their compounds, this silent husband in the crumpled cap, and last of all, if she ever thought of it, herself. The thing she didn't know, perhaps, was that all women do not live as she did. Or, if they have seven children, that sometimes those children are without the sense these had of being proud that everything around them was as it should be: theirs as well as hers, and hers as well as theirs.

Marie was watching her too, unmindful for the moment of the geese, the chickens, the heifers, the bull-calf, and the goat she was being pulled at by several hands to see.

"Your mother," said Peter quietly, "she is—"

"I miss her all the time at school." Marie's black hair and eyes were for once indifferent to Peter's gaze, and so were the bright patches in her cheeks. "I miss her, but you mustn't say so. She worked so hard to send me. Papa, too."

They started after the children, but he stopped her before they reached the corner where the great geese were.

"Listen," he said. "A discovery. I thought I was coming to see *them*"—he waved at everything. "What I have seen is you."

"You do that every day." She was puzzled and pleased.

"I never did before, not really. The way you—"

"What?" And yet she wasn't pressing him to go on. Indeed it was almost as if she thought he had better not.

"The way you love them, and keep on loving them, without one idea in your head—"

"That's nice. No brains."

"Don't interrupt. Of anything but—well, of—"

"What?"

It was clear she didn't understand, and that was best. He could never explain; which made her perfect. The girl he had fallen in love with—how much more of her there was now! And all because she hadn't changed since ten o'clock.

Maggie at the Well

"Maggie, did you forget about the butter and the meat? And the milk? And the pickles—you know what Grandpa says— any dish with cucumbers in it has to be cool as cucumbers."

Maggie scarcely heard her mother, though in the far room—
how could she miss it?—Grandpa's grumbling went on without stopping. If it wasn't about the sweet-and-sour, it might be
about the well-rope; that had bothered him all day. Should be
a chain, he said; and when nobody paid him any mind, as usual,
he moaned about the dampness down there that would sure as
hell and high water rot the best rope in time. 'In God's good
time,' he probably said, with the same old groan to show he
was in on every one of God's secrets. The sad ones, she meant;
he took no stock in the glad ones.

Neither did Maggie tonight—or it would soon be night;
she should have gone long ago to wind the crock up out of the
well and bring its contents in for supper. Instead of this she
had stood where she still did, by the window, looking through
it for somebody that would never come again out of the
woods beyond the sheep shed; would never wave, then come
running and pull himself, panting, over the sill and into the
room beside her, and no matter who else was there watching,
stare at her like a wild man who didn't know where he was, then
suddenly say: "It's you! Ha, ha!" and kiss her. No more of
that now; it wouldn't happen again; and she knew she had
been right when she told Dave it mustn't. She was through
with him for good, and that was best.

Why did she still stand there then, hearing her mother yet
not hearing her? "Maggie, it's getting late!" Yes, yes. Well, it
wasn't because she *wanted* to see him. It would make her sick
if she did. She was merely going over in her mind what she
would call out across the clearing if he ever had the nerve to
show himself again, after what he did and what she said.
Merely practicing, she was. And her black hair—'truelove's
hair' he used to call it—grew blacker and blacker as she
thought of him and Phyllis and *her* hair, her taffy hair pulled
tight to make a knot, that he had picked at, trying to undo it,
that early morning at the dance when most of the people had
gone home but he still circled and stomped in the middle of
the floor with who but Phyllis Crooks, that no-good from
Goshen, that tow-head with the popeyes that anybody could
see was only out to steal whoever she could lay her hands on;

and she did lay hands on Dave, on his back, his shoulders, and his chest that she pretended was too close to hers when all the time she was pulling him smack up against her, never letting the poor boy go. Poor boy! Poor nothing. He liked it, and whenever Maggie caught his eye he looked at her like a stranger, and drunk at that; though he wasn't drunk.

"Maggie! Did you hear me?" Yes, yes. On the way home—it was two at least when the music stopped—she walked ahead of him as if he wasn't there, and when he stepped faster to catch up she stepped faster still, and finally ran. But she couldn't outrun Dave, so at the front gate she gave it to him with her tongue. "You—you—!" That was all she could get out at first. But then she found the words. She was listening to them now, and not to her mother. "Don't you ever come here again! No, I mean it, don't you ever! That baby-face! Keep her, keep her, for all I care! Who? *You* know—the nerve of it, asking who! The one with the doll wig and the china eyes— popeyes—oh, if I could only get my hands around her neck, I'd make 'em pop real good, I'd make 'em stand clear out. Then when I was through with her I'd drag her off and bury her under some last year's leaf pile. They'd never find her there, or if they did they wouldn't know it was a person. Two cat's eyes and a hank of artificial fuzz." She knew it wasn't artificial, it was just a color she hated, but it sounded worse that way. Dave kept letting on there wasn't anything to be excited about; and the more he did that, the more furious she felt. If he had only admitted it, and apologized. No, even then that wouldn't have helped. The two of them, so close since either could remember; so close, so sure. Oh, that was over, and it wouldn't do any good if she *could* choke somebody to death and cover them up with last year's slimy leaves. Or the year before last; the farther back the rottener, the better.

"Maggie!" So she went. The screen door slapped shut behind her as she started with her basket down the zigzag path that wound around the smokehouse toward the old well they didn't use any more except to keep things cool in summer. The last thing Daddy did before he died was to say: "This will do for an icebox" and lower himself into it to clean out the

trash—old rubber, old cans, old shingles from when the barn
was roofed—and make it smell of nothing but black water and
wet stones. Her mother thought he took a chill down there,
and that was how the pneumonia set in. While he could still
talk he denied this, but it might have been. He rigged up a
windlass at the top, a nail keg with a handle that turned it,
reeling and unreeling twenty feet of rope. The far end was
fastened to a wood frame around the big crock—ten gallons—
they kept the food in. The rope was down there now, resting
on the cover; all she had to do was wind it up; the load was
heavy, but it would come. She knew all about that. It was her
job and nobody else's. She had even developed, she thought,
some special muscles that made it easier, now that she was used
to doing it.

The evening was hot and still, and it wasn't as dark as she
had thought. The sides of the smokehouse as she went around
it gave off some of the sun's heat they had soaked in all day. In
the woods there wasn't a sound: not a snap, not a rustle. The
birds had gone to bed, the small ones anyway; and it was too
early for the big owl to start hoo-hooing farther in.

Maggie reached the well-top, the box of grey boards out of
which the iron handle, idle since morning, waited for her
capable strong fingers. She put down the basket, lifted off the
cover, looked in, and felt rather than saw the water at the
bottom: a column of coolness, ascending. The tope tightened
as she turned the keg, first with one hand then with both. Was
Grandpa right, she wondered, about the chain? Even a chain
could rust; nothing lasted forever. Like her and Dave. And she
gave all of her attention to the final turn before the crock
would appear to let itself be swung over till it rested on the
plank Daddy had nailed there for the purpose.

Here it was, steady in its frame. She guided it into place on
the plank, slid off its cover, and glanced in; she always did this,
though there wasn't the slightest need; nothing could disturb
whatever it had in it. Tonight that would be a quart jar of
sweet milk, a pint jar of buttermilk for Grandpa, a lump of
butter wrapped in silver paper, the leftover chicken, and the
pickles—forever and ever, pickles, sweet and sour.

On top, though, something else. A big tulip leaf, leathery
and green, lying there so flat, so still, so strange. How could
that be? She picked it up by the stem, dropped it at her feet,
and looked again, startled, at something it had hidden. She
squinted, to see better, and almost let go of the lid. Something
yellow, something hairy, spread above the jars. A giant
spider—ugh! Maggie shivered, remembering the cobwebs that
often stretched across the opening: millions of them, made in a
single day—by this? Yet it didn't move. If she was scared, it
wasn't.

She set the lid down carefully on the far corner of the well-
roof; then, raising it a little, let it fall—thump—and watched
for any result. None whatever; the thing didn't tremble, or
contract, or enlarge, or disappear. Nothing; not a twitch.

If there were only more light; if she only had a lantern; a
single match. She could see, though, that the object was bright
yellow. Or one end of it was, the big end. It tapered at the
middle and then got wide again, like a doll lying on its face.

Yet how could *that* be? Crazy. But then, not quite so terrible; not alive.

"Pick it up, Maggie." It was Dave saying this behind her. He
hadn't made a sound, then there he was.

Well, he could stay there. She wouldn't look around or say a
word. She was glad she hadn't jumped—given him that satisfaction. Maybe she wasn't surprised after all. Of course she
was, but—

"Maggie, pick it up. Won't bite you."

She did, but only to see what it was.

A rag doll, with yellow yarn for hair, and marbles for its
eyes, blue marbles, glass ones, that stuck out—popped out—so
far, she wondered what was keeping them in place.

Popeyes.

Then she noticed the red string around its neck, wound
tight, several times, and tied so it wouldn't loosen.

And the tulip leaf. She stooped down for it. It was gone.

"I've got it," said Dave. "Look." But she wouldn't.

"Then listen." She knew what he was doing: twirling the

stem between his fingers, making the whole thing go whush as it flopped and fluttered.

The noise stopped, and she felt something at her neck: the leaf being drawn across it. She reached up. It was gone again.

"One leaf's no pile," he said, "but big enough to bury *that*. Poor Phyllis. Who choked her till her eyes—"

"Dave Dillon!"

"Maggie Winters!"

"You fool."

"Now that's more like. Thought you'd never speak to me again."

She laid the doll beside the lid and turned around. "Thought you were smart, making this silly old thing behind somebody's back."

"I *was* smart. Somebody else was, too, that found it." He had stepped away a little and was smiling uncertainly at her: at all of her, from head to foot. "Come here to me."

"I won't."

"Why not?" He stopped smiling.

"The nerve, asking why not. That isn't so smart."

"I mean, can't you get over being mad?"

"I wasn't just mad. I was killed."

"No, you weren't." He pointed beyond her. "*She's* killed."

"She really dead?"

"She always was."

"Oh, no, she wasn't. One time she wasn't."

"Well, one time's not forever. Come here, Maggie." It was his way of asking for a kiss.

"Listen!" She turned about briskly and started lifting things out to put into her basket. "People starving, and you carry on like that."

"Let me help."

"You can lug this up to the house." She wound the rope around a cleat and slid the roof over the well.

"The house." He hesitated. "Do *they* know? Did you tell *them*—

"What?"

"Didn't they miss me all week?"

"I think so, but they didn't say. I never told anybody—how could I? Phyllis Crooks! The only one I know missed you—know for sure—"

"Was that black witch that lives there? Did *she* worry? Did *she* fret?

"Black! Who's black?"

"Well, black and red." She knew her cheeks were burning in two spots she never could keep white. "And peppery all over. Red and black pepper. You know the one I mean—the blazer. She can get too hot to hold."

"She can, can she?"

"Sometimes. Come here."

He hugged her to him like old times.

The Brown Cap

THE MAN in the pine woods wondered how many animals knew him as one who came here every day. Where none but stray hunters had walked, so far as he was aware, for twenty or thirty years, now he arrived, a white-handled ax over his shoulder, each afternoon at two o'clock and started chopping. This was the ninth afternoon—he counted carefully, glancing away among the tall black trunks behind him up the needled slope of boulders and smooth, springy ground—this was the ninth afternoon of his trimming operation, and it was almost over. The sun had ceased to play like an intermittent searchlight between the dark, feathery tops to the west of where he stood; it would be time in another hour to be going home. And he would tell his wife that the trimming was nearly done. He would also remark—he was sure of this—that he regretted the fact; for he had never enjoyed anything more. He would even like, during this minute while he rested, to let the animals know how much he would miss their invisible company.

There was no use looking for them again, to see if they knew he had paused and was considering their presence. His eyes were too poor for that. His glasses—he felt for the case in his hip pocket, but did not take it out—even his glasses had never showed him an uplifted foot, a pair of curious or fearful eyes, a shadowy beak arrested in its flight from limb to limb. He still believed that the silence about him had a telltale quality, as of acute listening, as of suspended breath. But he would have to leave the matter there, and go on to litter the forest floor, as now for nine days he had, with the dead lower branches of white pine trees which long ago should have dropped, where now under his hands they dropped, to rot with time and snow and rain.

It was pure pleasure—it was in some sense a secret pleasure—to move from tree to tree, judging each one as he approached in terms of the difficulty it would offer. He was not a woodsman; he was not even a farmer; he was—and he hesitated over the words—a quiet gentleman whom few knew much about, there being so little to know. At liberty on his own land, he was in a queer sense lost to the world, which did not note his dull brown cap among the pines, or listen when his ax came accurately down between the dead limbs and their live parents, the trunks that looked so much better because at last they stood black and alone.

He was not a woodsman and yet he had learned this art. If nobody knew he had, nevertheless there was a satisfaction in the assurance that he did what was good for the timber to be felled here some day: not by him, or for him, or for his children. Children? He had no children. The lumber would be sawed by strangers, by other men who in their turn owned the land; and they might never pause to speak of the fellow who had seen to it with his own hands that knots would be far between in the planks and boards which time already was forming inside this bark. For that was why he trimmed the trees. The lower branches, shaded till they died, were slow in falling then; and as long as they extended there, horny and dry in the continuing shade, the growing tree could not enclose them. Two years hence the wounds he now made would be

well-healed, and the cylinder of each trunk would be on its
way to a column's perfection.

But each tree offered its peculiar challenge. If the younger
and straighter ones were easy to strip—the butt of the ax,
descending, knocked them clean in perhaps ten seconds—the
grandfathers of the grove had to be attacked with strategy no
less than strength. Not only were the branches big enough to
require the heaviest of downward and upward blows; they
were in most cases twisted into fantastic shapes, crossing and
interfering with one another so that a man could scarcely
enter the thicket they made, let alone maneuver his ax. The
thing to do, he had found, was to make a clean start somewhere: to reach in, regardless of stabs and prickles, and clear
away an area of bark. Then the ax had headroom; and soon it
could land its blows where they were needed, up and down
and around until the whole trunk stood confessed in the shape
it had been destined for. The contorted branches might make
an almost impassable litter on the ground, but he knew that
time would remove it, leaving the floor of needles as smooth as
it had been when he started here weeks ago. The only difference would be that the trees would then stretch dark and clean
as far as man's attention was able to penetrate: dark, clean, and
numerous, for as the pines lost their surplus they seemed to
grow in number, exposing and preening themselves in a kind
of pride which matched his own, the maker of the procession.

He went on chopping and thought again of the animals who
must be aware that he did so. He asked himself how many of
them resented the change he was making in their habitation.
The heaps of branches on the ground would be obstacles to
fox and skunk and wildcat; and those same branches would
have ceased to be perches for certain birds he heard rather
than saw in these cool hours when the far sun seemed to listen
also to the sound their wings made within the confinement of
the grove. No matter. He must do what he was doing; and the
next generation of beasts would thank him for it, since the
woods then would be the kind of woods, ancient and clean and
dark, that fairy tales are told about. Tales, for instance, of the
woodcutter and his wife, and of the foster child who thought

to find her way back by dropping crumbs of bread for a trail. But the birds came down and ate the bread, and the foster child was lost. He smiled, in the serious way a solitary man will smile, at the absurdity of supposing that animals knew or cared about all this. These animals, anyway; here in this latter day when woodcutters still had wives, no doubt, but when—

He thought of his own wife, as solitary in the house beyond the pasture as he was here among the trees she never visited. She had come down once because he asked it—she had found her way, after crossing the brook where he told her to, by listening for his ax—but there had been little for them to talk about, and she had not waited to walk back with him when the sun went down. She was there when he came up at his usual hour, and a good supper was ready in the kitchen; but it was as if she had already forgotten her expedition, and he never asked her to repeat it.

He wished he did not bore her as he did. He knew he did, and knowing it made matters worse. He did not bore himself. He had learned how to live quietly, doing such things as now he did methodically and well; and this was enough of a life, of a retired life, for one like him. For one like her—well, he didn't know; and he doubted that she knew. She might be bored, and indeed she was; but she didn't seem to consult the distance for anything that differed from what she had in him. If she sometimes looked away, it was absently and patiently. She suffered him—that was the word, and he winced a little— with a grace peculiar to her own form of quietness. They were a solitary pair; not even a foster child interrupted the tenor of their years. Perhaps that was a mistake, but if so, both of them had made it. He was not aware that she wanted a third one in their house, and if this had ever been his desire he felt it now no more than mechanically, as something he ought to feel rather than did.

He said her name to himself, without sound and without pausing. Elizabeth. And at once he was invaded by a sense of guilt because in his thought he had exaggerated her indiffer- ence. She was not indifferent really. She would kiss him when he came home—kiss his eyes, for that was her way—and there would be pleasantries between them as they sat down to supper. He was up to his old tricks, he was unjust to her in being just to himself. Or what he believed was just. If he never came home she would miss him, naturally; but the experience would contain none of that anguish he once had been able to imagine in the heroines of tragedy. His disappearance would not be tragedy, and nothing could make it so. When he was younger there had been violent occasions and bitter words between them: bitter on his side at least. For he accused her of coldness. And she had never been able to understand. She was not cold, she said; she loved him very much. He had learned how not to torture her into further extremities of the sort. She could not love him very much, for he was not that sort of man. Just how much she did love him he had long ago ceased trying to measure. It was sufficient, and that was all. It made him happy enough. As happy as he deserved.

He moved to a new pine, the largest and toughest of them yet, and hesitated longer than usual to move in upon the barrier of gnarls and prongs it presented. It was worthy of careful study, as perhaps Elizabeth was. He *had* been unjust to her. Approached with no more desire and determination than the most formidable of these trees had asked from him and got, who knew what she might yield of—well, of whatever it was he had never known how to take from her and use? For his own good and for hers. She was always there, and he didn't know why.

He remembered now the many times he had wondered at the willingness of women to spend their lives with men. Their whole lives. To go where they went, to sit and eat in their houses, to dress and undress there, to sleep, to see friends, to be well and ill, to wake and dream. He was not sure that he had ever understood it in the case of a single man he knew. The more he contemplated it, the more amazing it became. And in his own case it made no sense at all. He and Elizabeth had been in love, which explained the beginning. Had been? He still was. But she—she couldn't have meant those words: I love you very much. Yet she had said them; and she might say them now if he would let her. Not that he forbade it. He simply doubted that she could: always and simply doubted, so that the art of their conversation was for him the art of protecting her from the thought that she must try. He knew only too well how to throw the moment away, to cool and flatten their discourse whenever it threatened to go higher than he thought she cared to go. His love was considerate, he said, and he had even been complacent as he said it.

Too complacent. He was certain now that he had been unjust. And not a little cowardly. For Elizabeth had stayed with him. This was an enormous fact, a fact that flooded him all at once with warmth, and with something else that perhaps was shame. Her love had kept her where he was. When her father died, and she spent seven weeks in the west, a train brought her back to him at last. To his house of all places on earth, and to him of all men. He recalled the wonder of it now—her stepping down at the station as if she belonged, of course, to this: to this, to this, and to him. And ever since that day, as ever before, she had sat and slept with him as if he too belonged wherever *she* was. And she had protected him from having to ask her if she loved him very much. She knew as well as he did how to prevent high words; for she remembered how once they had gone shrill—shrill to the point of ugliness. For the more emphasis he heard in her voice the more he doubted. He asked for emphasis, and when he got it, shouted it down. He could not be reassured. And so her life with him had been her way of showing that he didn't need to be.

The pine, like a great thing of bent legs and thrusting arms, was still before him, challenging his skill. He let the ax slide through his hand till it rested on the ground. The sun had still a quarter of an hour to shine, but he would start home now. He would come in that much early, just a quarter of an hour, and when she asked him why he would tell her what he had been thinking—tell her, he said almost aloud, how much he knew about her and himself. Whatever she said, and however she looked at him, he would go right on and say it all.

But he had not turned to go, and suddenly he knew why. He knew that she would look at him—yes, in a kind of terror. Not of him, for she loved him. And he said the words again.

But of the chance that this moment too might grow into one of those crises she had studied so wisely how to prevent. He was confident that it would not be so, but how could he expect her to be confident? She would not have had the preparation of this afternoon, she would be surprised and frightened. And that would spoil the moment. So he knew he must take care. The same kind of care, loving and intelligent care, that she had used these several years. She must understand as slowly as he had that all was well. That neither of them doubted, that both of them were one, in plain fact and forever.

He would not go at once, then, and have to explain his early appearance. This big one, and three or four others that stood in a cluster he could hardly see through: he would finish them, even if they kept him later than usual, in dusk that made an ax unsafe. It would be quite safe. And at home, with Elizabeth, it would be safer to be able to say something like this: "I stayed, dear, to finish down to those white birches in the ravine, so that tomorrow I could make a fresh start beyond them." This would be safer because she would think nothing of it. There was time enough for him to show her what he wanted to show her, quietly and thoroughly. There was all of time between them, just as there was all of faith and love. That being the case, there must be nothing now for her to be startled by, nothing for her to wonder at or doubt. He would be quite ordinary. An easy thing to accomplish. For once it gave him pleasure to tell himself this. It even gave him a sense of power, so that he moved in on the big pine with a blithe ax whose blade answered every turn of his rediscovered will.

As the second limb he struck at bent and fell halfway to the ground, its stiff extremities rattling on each other from the force of his blow, he heard a skirmish among the leaves at the top of the slope, where a few bare oaks interrupted the stand of evergreen. A grey squirrel, he supposed; and he glanced up to see if he could make out its bushy tail. He saw nothing, of course, and returned to the business of his ax.

As the limb severed itself and crashed he was aware of a further rustling, well over the slope, that came to his ears like an echo of the first, or like a member of some series of forest

sounds that had started on its own course, now that the sun
was going down and he was soon to be leaving. He was sure
the animals were learned in his habits. However little they
enjoyed his presence here, they probably timed some of their
movements by his own, absurd as his might seem.

Not so absurd, though, as the movements of his mind in
love. Beasts managed such things without mind at all, and perhaps that was better. Simpler and better. Without delays that
took years, without scruples that confounded success until
success, if it came at all, came only at the sunset of two lives.
The human way was the hard way. It was wonderful and
beautiful, but it was hard. And musing on the difference, he
reached for the case in which his glasses lay.

He would take them out and put them on. He would see
what he could see; and the squirrel, if that was what it was,
might laugh all he pleased at the further oddity of lenses, of
the big insect eyes that appeared without warning on human
faces and stared. Confusedly and ineffectually stared.

The final gleam of sun on delicate glass was not what the
hunter had aimed at. The brown cap, colored like a stag's head,
was the trouble. But it was through glass that the bullet entered.

The big tree in which it came to rest was never to be
finished.

Twentieth Floor

At the end of the corridor there was a window whose
curtains were always blowing. In this June weather the sash
was seldom lowered, so that a copper screen through which
the wind hummed and whined was the only barrier against
outdoors. The noise of the city, twenty stories down, was

somehow less noticeable than this music made by meshes of fine wire. Perkins regularly observed it as he left the elevator and started walking toward his room—their room, of course, for Annabelle was sure to be waiting in it, quietly and faithfully, every day when he got back.

He would come late in the afternoon, and Annabelle was rarely in his thoughts as he whistled his way along the corridor at the end of which another whistling matched his own. He whistled nothing in particular, but he was loud and brisk about it. The screen was less loud, and even less particular as to tune; yet he never failed to hear it, or to grin when he did so. Perhaps it was a reminder that in the last room on the right there would be Annabelle. Perhaps it was a signal, preparing him to grin again as he flung open the door and received his due, his daily due, of never-failing kisses. If Annabelle had been absent from his mind since morning, the restless curtains may have been what prompted him now to pretend otherwise. For that was what she liked. She wanted to think she had been missed. The restless curtains, and of course the song, monotonous, self-satisfied, that sang itself behind them—the whole thing was what Perkins noticed, coming every afternoon to the end of the long, carpeted corridor.

Today, though, it was raining, and the sash was down. So there should be no music to answer his, and the curtains should hang straight. But they didn't. They were swinging—definitely swinging—as if someone had just parted them to go through and had let them fall together again.

Perkins stopped whistling and paused in his tracks. But this was silly. There was nowhere to go between the curtains except down. Could somebody have brushed them, passing by? No, that was silly too, since the corridor was a dead end. He would have seen anyone who had been there.

He went on again, pulled the two lengths of gauze apart, and looked through the window at the grey rain that drizzled over roofs and water towers as far as he could see. There was no wind that could have forced its way in and moved the curtains. There was no wind at all.

And so, by the way, there should be nothing to hear, no whistle or hum or whine. But there was. There was *some* sound, and it wasn't those raindrops he had watched hitting the sill outside. It wasn't outside, it was around him in the corridor. Or it was back of him, between him and the elevator. It sounded more like that.

He turned quickly. But nothing was there. The car clicked somewhere in the shaft, letting somebody off or taking somebody on. Nobody, however, was visible on this floor. He realized that he had expected to see some person, not some thing. Nobody was there. And yet the noise was human. It was not singing exactly, or humming; it certainly wasn't a whistle. It was more like a voice—or two voices—that talked very fast, so that the words were indistinguishable. They might not be words, even. They seemed far away—not sad, but far away.

Far away? That couldn't be. For if there was any noise it was here, where he stared and saw nothing. He straightened his tie and faced around. He couldn't have a ringing in his head, could he? He hadn't drunk too much, had he, with Bovici? He was sure he hadn't—any more than the usual, and so far as Bovici went, the necessary.

Before he could get his hand on the knob the door opened and Annabelle stood there.

It couldn't have been somebody in the room with her, could it? Two voices. And come to think of it, if it *was* two, it was both kinds, a woman's and a man's. But—

"Hello, Harvey," she was saying. "What are you standing there for? I heard you down the hall, and then you stopped. Don't you want to come in?" She kissed him as she always did.

"Sure. I just stopped, that's all. Any objection?" He grinned and sailed his hat across the room, landing it expertly on her bed. "Take a nap this afternoon?" The spread was a little awry.

"Yes, I always do." She moved after the hat, to pick it up and hang it in the closet. "I always do," she said without looking around.

He yawned and dropped into the biggest chair, the chair by the standing lamp. "Soft life *you've* got."

She turned suddenly as if she had something to say, though she didn't say it.

He grinned again. "Come here. Any complaints?"

Still she said nothing. She was looking out of the window, to which she had gone slowly and uncertainly.

"What's the matter with you?" He raised his voice. "You don't like it here? Married a month, and you don't like it any more."

She ran one of her hands vaguely over the curtain that hung between her and the rain. "You don't take me anywhere," she said at last. "I thought—"

"You thought! I knew it was going to be that. Listen, Belle. I'm in business, and you're *not* in business. See? It makes a lot of difference."

She still watched the rain. "I don't even know what your business is," she said.

He sat up a little straighter, glaring at her pretty back, her brown hair that fell so naturally to her narrow shoulders.

"It's a good business," he answered after a while. "We're going to be all right. You don't worry—see? That's your job. You don't worry, or ask questions, or by God pass complaints." He waited until his voice lost some of its sharpness. "You don't like this, do you, Belle?"

"It's all right." She spoke softly, making the best of the truth. "We're not staying forever, though, are we?"

"Hell no!" and he laughed. "So *that* was the trouble. You thought—well, that's a good one!" But when he saw how serious she was he changed his voice again. "Not that it won't be me that says when we pick up and move to another stand. You're not packing yet. Which reminds me—how's the shoplifting? Got everything you want?"

Her eyes went to the closet door. "A few things," she said. "When you first came. Lately I haven't—"

He got up suddenly and crossed over to the closet. The door, which stood slightly ajar, swung wide open under his hand and he rummaged among the dresses that hung there in half-darkness.

"Good girl," he said. "But you can do better by yourself. You've got every morning, remember, to buy duds."

He went on into the bathroom, but came out at once. "Say," he said, "it's funny what happened just before I reached the room. The curtain in that end window did peculiar things; and I heard noises. Or thought I did. I guess I have ideas too. You're not the only one."

She smiled at him and shook her head.

"You know what I thought once?" He came closer, as if what he was about to say must be considered confidential. "I thought I heard somebody talking in this room. Two people."

She backed to the window, her smile gone, her gaze moving swiftly to the door of the closet he had left open; and after that to the bathroom where he had been.

"What's the matter?" He laughed again. "I was nuts, that's all. Nobody's here, and I didn't even think there was. It only crossed my mind. People could have been talking in the next room, or in the one across. I don't believe it was that, though. I was simply nuts. What's the matter, don't you like me to be nuts?"

She searched his grey eyes with no laughter in her own. "What kind of noises?" she insisted. "What kind of talk? Who—"

"Forget it! Listen—where do we go for dinner? You're taking me to dinner in a nice, nice place. Look here!"

His arms went around her roughly, and she made the faint protest he was used to hearing.

She lay with her eyes wide open in the dark and listened to the chimes in the insurance tower as they played their full tune and then struck twelve. Slowly and sepulchrally they struck. She counted, from one to twelve, then listened for another sound to commence. Or to resume, for it had been in her ears before the chimes took over. It had been there ever since Harvey, home with her from dinner and drinks, got back into his own bed and turned his face toward the wall. Harvey

wasn't hearing anything—anything, she said quietly, said won-
deringly, with nothing but her lips, anything like what he had
told her he heard this afternoon.

What was it Harvey heard? She almost sat up in her anxiety
to know; but she kept herself resolutely down, resolutely lifeless under the cool sheet that was her only cover this warm
night. The more lifeless she lay, the clearer those voices might
become. If she seemed to pay no attention, they might speak
out.

For she had heard them too. She had heard them before
Harvey did. She had even seen—but no! She didn't know what
she had seen, or whether she had seen anything. Seen any*body*,
of course she meant. If it was anything at all, it was a person.
And that person was here, was somehow here, right here in the
hotel, right here in the room. Her mind chanted the phrases
monotonously. Right here in this hotel, this room. That was
the way the voices went on—never stopping a sort of murmur
which seemed to please them very much. She couldn't hear
what they said, she was only aware of the eagerness with
which sound answered sound, as if two ghosts—if they were
ghosts—had met in some corner of the world to take up a
conversation death had interrupted. Interrupted, but only for
a little while, since here they were at it again, murmuring to
each other and laughing. Yes, they were very earnest, and yet
they could laugh like two old friends. The laughter didn't
mean they weren't serious. It only showed how well they were
acquainted. Or, if they were ghosts, how well they had been
acquainted in the real world.

This world wasn't the real one, though, this one in which
she lay. This wasn't Mossville, where every street would be
shaded now with the big trees she used to walk under with—
against her will she finished it—with Joe. Only a month ago,
and a little more, she had walked down Elm Street with him at
midnight, at just this hour, explaining and explaining.

It had been hard for Joe to understand why she was marry-
ing anybody but him. Hadn't both of them always taken it for
granted? Why, they had known each other their entire lives.
They had done everything together—almost been drowned

together that winter on the ice—and everybody in Mossville expected it too. Maybe, he said, he shouldn't have taken it for granted. He had been going to say something at Easter, but he hadn't been perfectly sure then about his job with Mr. Eccles. It was settled soon after, but he still hadn't spoken. He guessed it was too late now. And he tried to laugh.

Then she heard it—the easy laughter, far away and yet right here in the room too, that always mingled with the murmur of two happy and busy voices. They seemed to be the voices of two people who knew each other better than words could say. For she caught no words. It was two heads together in the night, whispering—no, not whispering, for they made a kind of music, they had body to them, like live voices—an endless series of confidences, sometimes grave, sometimes amusing, but always real in a way that only those two comprehended.

It had been hard for Joe to understand how much Harvey's money meant to her father. Or his air of having money—of making it like that, just out of nothing. Harvey hadn't been in Mossville, at the Mossville Inn, more than three months before Dr. Brewster knew what he wanted his daughter to do. Dr. Brewster. She said her father's public name, and two tears lay in her eyes. People thought he was more successful than he was. They didn't know about the money he had lost, and how desperate he was. Her father had been good to her ever since she could remember. She could be good to him, too. She never let him know how much she hesitated over Harvey. The morning he saw them off on the train—the tears in her eyes grew as she remembered how he bit his mustache and smiled. He was losing her, but he seemed to say he had done her the most good he could. He couldn't have known how Harvey would change as soon as they got to the city, to this hotel, to this room where it shamed her now to think what a prisoner she was. He told her so little, and he was so bitter when she wanted to know more. Harvey in Mossville had been handsome and free, and he still was; but it was his freedom now, not hers or theirs. It wasn't even as if she got credit with him for being the solitary wife he wanted her to be, the wife to whom he came back—from where, she wondered, and from seeing whom?—every afternoon at six or so. She wasn't sure he enjoyed it either. Not really sure. He talked so little, and said so few things that he meant.

The tears were dry in the corners of her eyes. Had Harvey meant anything by looking in the closet and the bathroom the way he did this afternoon? Of course he hadn't found anything. Any*body*. Nobody else was here. Just the two of them, herself and Harvey. The two of them forever, here or in some other room, in another city. He had made that clear. The future was clear and hard. She saw all of it at once, staring up at the white ceiling which reflected even in darkness some of the lighted city whose sounds she heard.

But she heard the voices, too. There they were again, and she thought one of them must be her own. The other one was Joe's, the deeper and obscurer one. The two of them went on without ending, without emphasis or pause. How serious that murmur was, and yet how easily it left their lips, and how often it slipped into a sort of laughter—not jokes, not things a third person would find funny, but secret things of which each knew the value without being told. It was a conversation that said nothing, it was a dialogue between two heads intent on nothing but themselves.

Should she ask Harvey in the morning what *he* had heard? Nothing was stranger than that he had heard something too. If he heard this—

The murmur died away as the big bell in the insurance tower struck one. She must try to sleep now. She turned her head gently on the pillow and looked over at Harvey's back, angular under its sheet. She wouldn't bring the subject up tomorrow. It wasn't anything at all, perhaps. There could have been someone in the next room. Or Harvey could have had too many drinks with that man he said he had to see. It wasn't fair to keep him thinking about—well, about this. It was nothing for him. It was nothing at all. Anyway, she had married Harvey. She had married Harvey, and her father saw them off at the train. She must think of Dr. Brewster, too, who couldn't have known, not really, about herself and Joe. The only one in town that didn't. The only one; and oh, so close to them both. Too close, of course. But anyhow, the only one.

She turned the other way, toward the window, and told herself the rain had stopped. There was no wind, and yet the curtains were moving. There must be a little wind, a night breeze or something. What had Harvey said about the curtains out in the corridor? But she must stop thinking about all that. Pretty soon she would be imagining things. A third person in the room with them. Not really, but as if—

Would it be Joe, wanting to talk some more?

She closed her eyes tightly, tossed several times, and slept.

But her sleep was not the deep one she had thought she wanted. It was still dark when she opened her eyes suddenly and listened.

Not that there was anything to hear. Silence had opened her eyes—silence, and no movement in the room. She looked at the curtains through which night, the city night, was a visible thing, a dim, orange thing without shape or size. They hung straight; there was no wind, and nothing inside the room disturbed them. No*body*.

She listened carefully, trying not to breathe. The voices had gone away. There was no person here, no third one. No Joe.

The name soothed her, so that she dozed again for perhaps an hour. When she awoke, it was still in an empty room. Empty except for Harvey and her. She looked over at Harvey, who had never moved, and then at the ceiling again where lights from somewhere threw the same pattern as before.

When had she first heard the sound she now missed so sorely? When had she thought—no, known——that somebody was with her? Only today. Only, in fact, this afternoon. And not so very long before Harvey came in and said something about curtains and voices. It seemed longer; she could believe she had been living thus for days, for weeks. But it had begun only this afternoon. And already it had stopped.

If it was Joe, Joe Morrill her oldest friend, her best friend, too; if it was Joe—but she shook her head and blinked, scolding herself because of the singsong into which she had relapsed. She could say it all more sensibly than that.

If it was Joe, she repeated slowly, then Joe had gone. He had come to be friends with her again, even though she was married; he had come to talk in the old way, forever and easily. And she had not answered; she had failed him when he came. With how much longing, how much effort, he must have sent himself through the miles between here and Mossville; and with how much faith that she would answer him. He had been so real that even Harvey heard him, even Harvey knew someone was here. But she had let him go. It wouldn't have hurt to keep him. To keep his ghost.

But that wasn't it. Not his ghost. He himself was now in Mossville, in the old house on Poplar Street where his mother died; he was home as always, thinking of her.

All at once she was wild to have morning come. Just as soon as breakfast was over, and Harvey had gone, and the maid was through in the room, she was going to write Joe a letter. There was no reason why she shouldn't. She had thanked him for his present, the small square leather diary she started to write in and then stopped; but there were plenty of other things to say, and she didn't have to tell him the truth either. The truth about her and Harvey. She could write about the restaurants here, and the parks. And she could close by making it clear that she knew he had been thinking of her. She had been thinking of him too. She would say that. She would say: "Especially yesterday, and last night when I couldn't sleep very well, I remembered many of the things we used to talk about." But she would write it rather casually even then. It wouldn't do to be more than casual. Simply enough to let him know.

Harvey, opening the door to admit the breakfast table, rubbed a hand over his freshly shaven chin and wondered why Annabelle was still asleep. She usually was up before he was, but here he had dressed and shaved, and she wasn't conscious yet.

When the flunkey had lifted the silver covers and was gone,

he went over to inspect his wife once more. She lay facing the window—that should have awakened her, but it hadn't—and there was a smile on her small face such as he had never seen there. Good going, he said to himself. She was dreaming of him, and she liked it. Well—

He ate his breakfast rapidly and tiptoed out.

The sash was up as usual in the corridor window, and a sunny breeze, lifting the curtains and letting them fall, was all the life he saw there. Not like yesterday, he thought. But it couldn't have been anything. He paused by the window, looking out. He was to meet Bronson downstairs in the lobby at ten, and they were to pick up Bovici at his office a few minutes later. Lunch at the Paddock—that would take a long time.

He started for the elevator, but changed his mind and opened the door of their room.

She was on her back and her eyes were wide open, but she didn't seem to know he was there.

"Say," he called in. "Dope wore off? Going now. There's nothing out here, nothing like what I told you yesterday. Everything under control? Love me?"

She sat up and took his kiss with the other sort of smile, the sort he was used to. "Good-by," she said, and he went out wondering what she had dreamed.

She tried all morning to write her letter, and failed. She scarcely saw the maid when she came; which surprised the maid, for this lady usually talked, as many of them did when they were lonesome. There she sat at the mahogany desk, with pages of hotel stationery before her, and simply looked out of the window. Or she would write a little, then crumple the sheet and drop it into the basket by her side.

She was trying to sound casual, to say it just right. The letters she began were either too excited, too intimate, or else too much the opposite. Too cold. She realized why this was. She had never talked to Joe as she talked to others. And she had almost never written to him. They hadn't been apart that much. The sort of things they said—could they be written at all? Excitement wasn't right; and intimacy—that was misleading too. It never had been what was said that mattered. It was how it was understood. Nothing very personal, oddly enough. If Joe were here she could look at him and he would understand. But he wasn't here. That of course was why she was writing him, to let him know she knew he had come and gone. Or why she was trying.

It was time at last to go down for lunch in the dining room, but she wasn't hungry. She wouldn't go down till she had a letter to take with her. She would mail it in the big brass box by the cashier's window. That was where she always put her father's letters. It was easy to write *him*. She didn't have to worry so much about untruth and truth.

She had to be satisfied in the end with something very poor and short. "Dear Joe," she wrote. "You haven't heard from me since I acknowledged your nice present. I'm not very good about using it, but I will be I think when I am better settled and have more to say. I never kept a diary, you know. I told *you* things. Well, now I must learn to tell myself. The city is fine, and so are Harvey and I. He is busier than he expected, seeing friends, but we go out pretty often and take in the sights. Also, some mornings I shop. I hope you are as happy as I am. How is Mr. Eccles? Does he still look over his glasses in that pompous way? You must think of me, Joe, as I think of you. I will never forget what a good friend you were and I hope still are. I was thinking of you particularly last night, when it was hot and I couldn't sleep. It hasn't been as hot as the papers say. At least up here on the twentieth floor it doesn't seem so. But last night it really was, and I got to remembering old times. Not so old either, are they? Well, good-by. Annabelle."

It was three o'clock when she went down with this. Too late for lunch, but it didn't matter, for she still wasn't hungry. An hour from now she could have tea in the room. That would be enough till dinnertime.

As she turned away from the box by the cashier's desk she heard her name spoken, and gasped.

"Bella!" That was what her father called her. And there he was, hurrying to her from the house phone whose receiver he had just put back on its hook.

"Bella!" He said it again as he reached her and took her into his arms. He said it with a forced smile about his mouth and eyes; and still she was too astonished to utter a word.

"I was calling your room," he said to her. "You didn't answer."

"I was down here," she explained—superfluously, but she didn't smile. What was the matter? Why had he come?

"I was mailing a letter," she said. "To Joe Morrill."

She had never seen him pale before, but he was now.

"Bella!"

"What *is* it, Dad? It's a wonderful surprise to see you, I haven't got over it yet, but what is it? What's the matter?"

"Bad news, Bella." He didn't seem able to look at her any more. But then he did so, with determination. "You'll be sorry to hear—I came to tell you—Joe is dead."

She was whiter than he was as they moved with one accord toward the elevator where a trim boy, splendid in his purple suit, stared at them, his fingers on the mechanism that would take them up.

She was so white when they got inside the room that her father used both hands to guide her to the bed, where at last she lay and looked at him—used all her strength to look at every line in his face, as if one of them must take back now what had been said down there. That terrible thing. It couldn't be true. And she tried to rise when he looked for the bathroom, found it, and went into it for cold water to restore her. She tried to rise and follow him, but for a moment she couldn't move.

"Don't," he said, coming to her side with a washcloth which he folded and unfolded. "Don't do anything, dear, or say anything."

"But *how?* The worst thing would be not to know. You mustn't wait to tell me. *How?* It's so terrible—you don't understand. I must know."

The washcloth went over her face as if it were the face of a child. "I suppose I should have waited," he said. "But you spoke of the letter—"

"It's gone! It's gone, and he'll never see it!"

"Now, dear. Don't talk." Yet he did, studying her all the while. "My darling, you never told me—oh, I should have realized. Bella, dear, don't think you have to talk. Or even listen. It was Joe Morrill—you didn't tell me, darling, it was Joe that—"

"How, how, *how?*" There were two spots of red in her cheeks, and she was struggling to sit straight up. "It doesn't matter about that. Just tell me what happened—when!"

"All right." But he said no more until he had returned the cloth to its rack in the bathroom—had wrung it slowly, slowly out and hung it there while she watched him, her eyes burning.

"All right, darling," he began in the same slow fashion, studying her again. "It was last night."

"Last night!" she repeated the two words in what seemed to him like terror. How could it be terror?

"Last night. But listen, dear, till I finish. You know that old car of Joe's." He went on more rapidly now. "He started off in it about the middle of the afternoon. He was driving here. To see you if he could. I met him on Main Street, and he told me. There was something he had to come to the city for, and while he was here, he said, he would try and see you. That's all, Bella, till some time after midnight—one o'clock, maybe—when they called me. Nobody understands how it happened. The road where he went off wasn't bad or anything. He simply went off—what are you doing?"

She was on her feet and had reached the closet door, through which she was dragging her new yellow suitcase.

"I'm going back with you," she said.

"Now, now!"

"I *am!*" she insisted, fiercely, "I *am!*" She was already taking things down from hooks, she was already slipping blouses and skirts from hangers. But some dresses she didn't touch. One end of the closet she never went near.

Her father sat down and watched her. "You mean now?" he said.

"The first train." She had the yellow suitcase half full. "It's at five, I happen to know."

"It is. But Harvey—what about him?"

"I'll leave a note for Harvey. He's never back till six."

"What will he say? What will he do?"

But she was answering no more questions. She was snapping the suitcase shut, she was taking one more look about the room.

"Maybe Harvey will come too," Dr. Brewster said. "To-morrow, maybe."

"Maybe he will." Her color had all come back as she put out a hand and led him to the door. "We've just got time," she said. Then: "The funeral—when is that?"

"Not till Thursday. You don't have to hurry for the funeral. You could come tomorrow, with Harvey."

She shut the door and locked it, then stood by the corridor window, looking out of it in a trance which the curtains, blowing gently against her waist and knees, did not disturb. Her father did not disturb it either. He waited, the suitcase in his hand, till she turned and said: "I could, but I'm going now."

As they went down the carpeted, immaculate corridor in which not even a ghost walked she said a strange thing. He was always to remember it.

"He was here all the time."

"Who? Who was here?"

But the elevator door was opening, and she put him off with her fondest smile, the faraway one he hadn't seen since she was a girl.

"Oh, nobody. What was I saying? We'll be just in time if I don't take too long with that note."

He had forgotten the note to Harvey. She scribbled it at the desk and left it to be placed in the pigeonhole where his key was, waiting for him at six.

"Come now," she said, walking ahead of her father out to the street. There was that smile again, the one he hadn't seen for years. He knew it by the way she walked. Yes—when he caught up with her—there it was. He couldn't mistake it, even though she was crying too.

Rescue

HE HAD plenty of time to think about what he was doing. He had plenty of chances to go back. And plenty of excuses, for he was risking his life. With a heart like his, who would have blamed him for giving up?

The snow would be easier to get through if he could see better—see it, the snow, and whatever lay ahead. The flakes that were driving past him had something to do with this, but less than he had supposed when he started from the house, and the porch light had so whitened the thick fall that he felt as if he were stepping into a solid of some sort: a soft solid, yet one impossible to send the senses through. Now that he was well away from electric light, there was a natural light between heaven and earth: not moonlight, for there was no moon, but whatever it is that keeps even the blackest night from being pitch. And this natural thing—the idea of light, rather than light itself—lived somehow in the flakes, communicating to each one of them a ghostly power to go driving by as if it saw just where it went, though that was only to the ground, or rather, to what covered the ground, and covered it, covered it, ever more deeply as the minutes passed. Deeply, and yet so lightly that he thought once more of soft solids in which, as in a featherbed, the mind could drown.

And yet it was dark. The flakes, once fallen, ceased to glow; the banks, the drifts, the whole body of the world was dead; and ahead of him he saw—well, said Haggard, he saw nothing at all except a desert strewn with fantastic formations, with odd shapes of hill and wood such as a painter might invent. This was his field, and he had walked here off and on for forty years, since he himself was a boy; but now he didn't know it.

Jesse should have come back two hours ago. His own boy, who had sworn he could find the place in the brook, a mile up the mountain, where the pipe crossed. The water in the house had stopped running, and Jesse knew how to turn the emergency cock up there so the air would bubble out. Haggard had watched his lantern disappear into the red pines, and had sat too long by the window waiting for it to come again. Two hours—too long. He should have started before. Helen would have, or any of the older boys. But they were in town, and here he was with his heart, that had no business out of doors on such a night. Anybody would have said that. Two hours, though; if he had been going to start, it should have been much sooner.

He hadn't known it was so cold. The only good thing was the softness of the snow. He found it astonishingly easy to get through, one deep step at a time. No crust, no pack—his galoshes, following each other through the all but impalpable white, sent clouds of it ahead of him; helped, of course, by the wind that tried to worm itself between his neck and the sheepskin collar turned up high to protect it. Occasionally the wind veered, whipping in from the west. Then his right ear filled with snow, so that he had to take a glove off and pick the cavity free, shaking his head and stamping as he did so. He probably shouldn't do this, but it bothered him if he didn't.

Why had he waited so long to start? Was it because Jesse had been so confident? He was always confident. At twelve he was just the same; it had never been knocked out of him. Everybody knew he thought himself the brightest of them all: five boys, and he the brightest. He really was.

Haggard, pulling his left foot out of an unexpectedly deep hole, and panting with the effort—feeling, furthermore, a familiar pain shoot up from the center of his chest in the direction of his left shoulder, then halfway down his arm— Haggard heard the unspoken words come back to him with the distinctness of an echo: He really was. Jesse should never have been his least favorite son. He really was the brilliant, the perfect one.

A pang, not of the body at all, made itself felt in him nevertheless. He had confessed it, hadn't he? Jesse's own father had said in so many words: My least favorite son. Haggard fought against the words as he always had, yet here they came again: My least favorite son. The other boys were not comparable with this one who couldn't help being what he was and showing it. Had he ever tried not to show it? He wouldn't have succeeded if he had, any more than a lamp can look as if no one has lit it. But he hadn't tried—oh, that was clear enough. The time he came home with his first report card. All 100's, from top to bottom. And he laughed. The older boys thought it was no joke; Reuben looked hurt, and it wasn't envy. Poor Reuben and poor Garry. They didn't understand. But their father did. It had been so easy, Jesse meant. And so ever since. Nothing came hard to Jesse. That was why he could be confident; he knew beforehand how things would go.

Haggard hated fathers who spoke of favorite children. The strictest impartiality—he had disciplined himself in that, without realizing how much discipline he needed. Now he did. He still loved Reuben, and Garry, and Guy, and Tom, whom he had protected so long against having to be measured by their little brother, the bright one. Defended, even, when the measurement was made. He always refused to praise Jesse, or to pretend that he knew why others did. This had been a sort of leaning backward; and before he knew it he had frozen into an unnatural bent.

For it was unnatural. He loved Jesse just as much. Not more, he said, not more, but just as much. Yet he had sat there in the window a full hour longer than he should have. Half an hour at the most was enough time for Jesse's lantern to show itself again among the pines. It had looked so pretty going in: half extinguished, then three-quarters, then nothing but a faint fraction of itself, bobbing among the lower branches before the solid foliage put it out. In no time at all it should have shone again. When this was over, said Haggard, and Helen was home, he would tell her how he had calculated the moment. Helen had no favorites, no unfavorites. He thought he knew this and knew she had never suspected how he felt. He would simply say: I waited so long, and then I went.

He would say this if he got back. He guessed he would get back; that one pain was nothing, and there had been no other. His breath was coming a little shorter, and there was this gone feeling, as if his diaphragm had fallen away. But he would ignore it. He wasn't very tired.

He supposed he had intended to punish Jesse just a little bit for bragging about how well he knew the place, and how thoroughly he understood the principle of the air valve. Nobody else did, not even Sturgis who installed it; but Jesse did, and his eyes had been very bright as he started off in his reefer and stocking cap, with the blue-and-white mittens Helen had knitted. Haggard tried to remember: Had he wanted Jesse to fail? To miss the crossing and have to stumble through the woods, following the stream up and down until he found the pipe under the black water? It wouldn't be frozen there; it never was, where it rippled over the rocks.

But not to wander till he got too cold. Or slip on one of the big stones and—

Haggard refused to imagine that.

His own foot, sinking through the feathery white, struck a little incline of last week's ice and slid perilously, bringing him almost to his knees.

He must be careful, he whispered. For a moment he could not get his breath. He had put forth so much strength to keep from going down.

He stood still, waiting. His chest hurt under the tightly-buttoned fleece that covered it and kept it warm. Too warm, perhaps. He felt flushed. And a star—was it Sirius?—that suddenly brightened through a gap in the overcast of cloud and snow went suddenly in lopsided circles overhead. A huge star, brilliantly white and blue, like Helen's mittens. No, Jesse's. No, Jesse himself. Such eyes! Such burning hair!

He staggered forward as he saw the yellow light of a lantern playing among the red pine trunks.

He fell shapelessly and sank half out of sight as Jesse, starting to run, called out:

"Who's that? Dad? You didn't need to come. I took care of

it—the water. But the falls were frozen. I had to drop big rocks—here! Get up! You mustn't—Dad!"

For the first time, thought Haggard as his brain ticked to a close in the cotton that ever more softly, softly wrapped it, the dear boy doesn't know what to do. Not that it matters. I love him so. And all of them—exactly the same. And Helen, who is coming home—as much as all five put together.

It was a good way, this way.

Mandy's Night

THE OTHERS couldn't find him, but she could. Big One always came when she called.

She did so now. "Bigwin, Bigwin," it sounded like. "Bigwin! Where are you? Don't go to sleep and stay asleep, or you'll never wake up. Don't go to sleep in the snow. Bigwin, say something. Mandy will hear."

She felt like lying down herself, and resting in the deep soft white. But everybody always said: No, don't do that. She had never been out alone like this before, with the whole family wondering where she was. Or did they miss her? Should she have told Mama she was going to look for Big One? He was old, and carried his head on one side, like a person that was hard of hearing. "Deaf as a turnip," said Papa Jim after supper tonight. "No use calling *him*. He'll come or else he won't. Stone deaf, that cat." But she knew he could hear *her*. Pretty soon he would, and miaow, and come walking funny in the snow the way he did yesterday when he followed her out to the barn: one foot high up and then the other, complaining every step. So why did he ever follow her? She knew. He liked her just as much as she liked him. He wasn't complaining about *her*.

"Bigwin, where are you!"

When no answer came, though she leaned and listened with all her might, for the first time she was fearful. And for the first time she felt the cold: a still cold, without any streaks of windy warm in it; far away and close about, a creepy cold that got inside of her no matter how tight she wrapped her arms around each other. This old coat that used to be Opal's—after it was Esther's, after it was May's—was thinner than it used to be, especially where the holes were that Mama couldn't mend any more. That was all right, Mama did her best, and the boys were just as bad off: Jim's sleeves not long enough, and Orville's blue pants ragged at the bottom. That was all right, everything was all right; a nice family, people said so. And look. This wasn't one of those black nights she never, never went out in. The snow, and maybe a moon—but she couldn't see any—something made it light like early in the morning, so that if Big One was there she ought to see him, poor old Big One who was somewhere, somewhere, listening for *her*.

"Bigwin!" Was he in a snow nest, a deep one he had made by turning round and round before he curled up and put his nose between his paws, was he where he couldn't hear anybody? Maybe that wasn't it at all; and she clapped her hands hard to keep the frost out of her fingers. It bit, they said; and it really did just now, before she frightened it away like a mouse that had nipped the very ends, under the nails where Opal, for a joke, put some of her polish Sunday morning; the pink stuff was still there, or some of it was, a few shiny spots. Maybe Big One wasn't sleeping anywhere at all. Maybe he was on a rock—that one, over there—watching her with his head on one side, waiting for her to come and get him. She squinted through the queer light, the half-light of snow and moon, and didn't see him. Of course he was white too, white all over, and clean for such an old cat—sometimes they stopped washing themselves, but Big One hadn't—so he might be there and not be looking any different from whatever was behind him. He wouldn't know this; he would think she saw him because he saw her, the way he did when it was dark on the stairs and he got stepped on by somebody going up, and let out a yell, not understanding how nobody ever wanted to hurt

Big One. Nobody in her family ever wanted to hurt anything or anybody. A nice family, people said so, and she knew it herself; she loved them all, and didn't blame Papa Jim because he made no extra money to buy the things they needed. They didn't really need them very much. Everything was all right. There couldn't be a happier family than the Columbines— "could there, Bigwin?" She said it aloud, suddenly; then stamped her feet because they were being bitten too. If she only had rubbers; or mittens; or a wool cap with a tassel, like the red one Doris Breen, the new girl, wore to school. It was all right, though; she didn't really need such things; or she wouldn't in a month or two, come spring and good weather, and the snow gone.

She started toward the rock where Big One might be; just started; and stepped into a place so deep and soft that she went into it over her knees, way over, so that when she tried to pull her feet up they felt heavy. She tried again, and she couldn't even tell she *had* feet, they were so far down there, and warm for once, as if they were somebody else's. She sat down, and now *she* had a nest to keep all of herself warm in, the very way she told Big One not to. Maybe people didn't understand about that. It felt so good, how could it be bad? "It's all right, Mama," she barely heard herself whispering before she settled sidewise and ceased to be aware of anything at all.

When she woke she still couldn't move her arms or legs, but it didn't matter, for she was lying on Opal's mattress by the kitchen stove. She opened her eyes wide enough to see this, then shut them again. Her head hurt, and she was cold inside; but waves of warmth were coming at her from the open oven—shouldn't they close that?—and she could hear a fire roaring. Wood! She forgot to bring it in after supper, when Mama told her to. Jim and Orville must have split some of the chunks in the back shed—all of them, it felt like; her cheeks fairly burned, and her hands, her feet, stung like needles. The reason she forgot was Big One. Big One—where was he? She thought of sitting up to look around the room, but somehow she couldn't yet, any more than she could keep her eyes open, any more than she could speak.

Where was everybody?

Then she heard Mama saying: "Oh, I do hope Doctor was home! He isn't always, but he might have been this time, just this time, this once. Esther, go look down the road."

But May must have been standing by the window, for she cried out: "That's him, I think. No, it's Papa Jim turning in. My, I hope— Oh, Mama, there's another car—that's Doctor!"

Dead silence, while they waited to make sure. Then stamping on the porch, and Papa Jim saying: "In here." Jim was opening the door to the hall, and Orville was helping; the bottom of it dragged because a hinge was off and nobody ever fixed it.

Doctor didn't say a word at first; just called for a lamp and looked at her; then, when that wasn't enough to see by, turned a little flashlight on and went all over her with it, head to foot, feeling her gently, pressing some places that hurt, so that she winced; but she must let him to this, she mustn't ask him not to, she mustn't whimper or say "Ouch!"

"What do you think, Doctor?" That was Mama, not talking very loud. "Will she—will she—Mandy, she's our youngest— will she—"

"Don't know yet." He seemed to be deciding. "You've got her too hot here: too near the stove. The circulation has to take its time about coming back. So far there isn't any. She doesn't feel my hand."

"Yes, I do." She must let him know. "Yes, I did. It hurt."

He laughed. "Well, why didn't you say so? That's fine. *Where* did it hurt?"

She opened her eyes, and all of them were standing in a ring, their own eyes large and dark in the shadow of the lamp.

And Mama—was she laughing or crying?—said: "Oh, you'll never get Mandy to complain. She never did, she never will. That's Mandy for you." Now she laughed for sure, and it seemed to do her good.

"Boys," said Doctor, "pull this over to that corner by the door." He meant the mattress. It was an old thing, and might come to pieces. But it didn't, and she rode over the rough floor so smoothly, it was like the Arabian Nights.

"Now bring me a blanket—something to throw over her chest—and a pail of snow."

"What?" said Papa Jim: the first sound out of him since they came in.

"A big one—dish pan—anything. I said snow."

The back door banged, and she knew the boys were getting it.

"You can all take turns rubbing her," said Doctor. "Cold *and* hot: that's indicated."

"Indicated." Papa Jim was impressed, and so was she. Indicated.

There was another car, and May ran to the front room to see. She came back breathless. "A lady's getting out."

"Probably Mrs. Breen," said Doctor over his shoulder. "She was calling on my wife when your dad got there. Said she might come over too."

Doris's mother. That beautiful girl's mother. What would she think when—

Mandy, Mandy! She was ashamed. She stung with something worse now than the cold, the hot. Mrs. Breen would think they were a nice family, for they *were*. She was ashamed.

Doctor took one of her hands in both of his and stroked it, steadily stroked it; if there was snow she didn't feel any. But there must be snow, for she had heard the pail put down beside her. And now Jim took her other hand, clumsily; he rubbed too hard. Mama, who had tucked the army blanket tight around her, was taking off her shoes. "Oh!" she said—she sounded scared—"poor Mandy!" But Doctor only said: "You work on those. Don't stop."

They were all around her, rubbing, all but May, whom she could hear come in with—Mrs. Breen? How could Doris's mother really be here?

She was, though, and her voice was like Doris's, only deeper in her throat.

"I hope I won't be in your way," she said. "I even thought I might help. Could I, Mrs. Columbine?"

Mama never stopped. "Thank you, ma'am. May, bring a chair for—"

"Oh, please don't bother. Can't I help?"

They ought to let her, she wanted to so much.

But Doctor only grunted, and Mrs. Breen stepped back a little. Where was Orville? Just standing there, probably; just watching her.

No, he was dragging the rocker in from the front room. Oh, dear, would it be dusty?

"Thank you, but I won't." But then she did. It was kind of her, when Orville had done that.

"I went by our house to tell Doris, and she wanted to come with me, but I said No, it would make too many. Doris is my daughter."

"I know she is," said Mama. "Mandy talks about her."

"She does? How nice." They seemed to think she couldn't hear. But she did, every word. "Mandy was the only child in the whole room, you know, when Doris went to school the first day—we're new people, we moved here just this fall—the only child, Mrs. Columbine, to come up to Doris and say things to make her welcome. She even put her arm around her; Doris came home and told me that."

"Mandy would," said Mama.

"And ever since it has been the same. Doris, you understand, feels that Mandy is her best friend."

"Maybe she is," said Mama, adding slowly: "Mandy has a lot of friends."

"I'm sure she has. I only wanted you to know—"

"Ouch!" She tried to help it, but she couldn't; Doctor hurt so.

"Good girl," he said. "Now we're in business."

If she only had kept quiet, there would have been more about her and Doris.

"You're glad she cried?" said Mrs. Breen.

"Best possible thing." Doctor stood up.

"I understand she went out to look for a cat," said Mrs. Breen. "Did she find her?"

"Him!" She was surprised by the strength of her own voice.

"Bigwin!" She hadn't forgotten him, and yet—"Where's Bigwin?"

"Up on your bed," said Orville.

"Get him," Doctor said. "Do her good to see him."

She could hardly wait while Orville went up and came down again. Then there was Big One, shivering at her side.

"Bigwin, where *were* you?"

He was busy licking himself, or trying to. He really couldn't, he was so weak. And the tips of his ears were folded over in a curious way; folded and swollen. She pulled her right hand out of Jim's and touched them with her knuckles; she still had no feeling in her finger-ends. Big One cried with pain, but didn't jerk his head away; too weak for even that.

"He will lose those," said Doctor.

"His ears? Oh, Bigwin!"

"Just the points. Otherwise I think he'll be all right. Would there be any warm milk for him?"

"He had some," said Mama. "Then he went for Mandy's bed. But couldn't make it; Orville carried him."

He was doing his best to get under the blanket, next to her. Orville noticed, and helped him in. Ah, Big One, Big One, don't shiver any more. And as if he heard, he stopped; then started purring. Such a good sound, feeble as it was. Such a good friend. Mandy had a lot of friends.

Doris, too, and all the rest at school. And all the neighbors. All the family. All the old boards of this house, that smelled so good. All days, all nights, summer and winter.

"Bigwin, where *were* you?"

"Right on that rock there," said Papa Jim. "Didn't move; we thought he was a goner. You didn't either."

"Did you think—"

"Sure thing." He laughed a little.

"What's funny?" said Mama. "Doctor, will she—"

"Yes, she will. But keep her good and warm. Don't take the cat away."

Just anybody try.

"Mrs. Columbine, I must go now. I'm glad I saw you all this

way. Is there anything you need—anything it wouldn't be convenient for you to—"

"Not a thing, thank you just the same."

"Goodnight, then."

"Goodnight, and come again."

She wanted to say, bring Doris. But all at once it was too much work. Too sleepy. And Big One there, purring so loud at last—whoever would have heard?

Plain and Fancy

A BIG LEAF, gently disengaged from the maple over their heads, came sidewise down through the summer air and settled between her hands, put up to catch it.

"Grandpa," she said, holding it out to show him, "why don't they all blow down? What makes them stay up there?" She looked high into the tree. He didn't, partly because he was thinking of an answer, partly because he was busy with the stones he was laying. The cement was ready for the last tier, and after that was in place they would go home for supper. His old car, pointed downhill, waited for them on the other side of the white gate with the bell on it that tinkled when you went through. Mrs. Knapp never took the bell in. It hung there all winter, and maybe tramps disturbed it, but nobody knew.

"What makes you think it blew down?" Only the softest of winds was playing in her hair. "Might have been a worm."

"Worm? Oh, no. It must have been the wind. Why don't they all blow off?"

Now he had his answer. The trowel went on, smoothing the wet cement around a sharp, three-cornered stone that fitted well where he had laid it, as he told her without looking up: "There was a tree once, did lose all its leaves but two. No wind either. Just fell off. I don't know where they went, but anyhow, they're gone."

"You said, all but two."

"That's right, I did. They're all that's left, those two."

She pressed the leaf she held across her small knee, making a green cap of it, with points. "A real tree, was it?"

"Yes, it was real. Still is."

She jumped up from the low canvas stool he always brought for her to sit on and ran off across the yard to see if Mrs. Knapp had any elm or oak with only two leaves on it.

Vincent watched her go and then went on with his wall. He took her with him everywhere, and answered her questions this way. He couldn't leave her home alone. He only worked on nice days, when it wouldn't hurt her to be out; and he worked by himself, at easy jobs like this one here, rebuilding the piece of wall that held up Mrs. Knapp's flower garden. He was glad the old lady hadn't come yet from the city. It was better to work alone, with only Barbara by him on her folding stool. She had no other company, and she didn't understand his stories—didn't yet—but it wasn't bad for children to have to figure such things out. They did it, sooner or later; it helped their brains to grow. Barbara remembered every tale he told her. Some day she would understand them all.

There were only two of them left out of all the Hitchcocks. Sarah died, then all the boys but Henderson went off. He didn't hear from them except at Christmas time: Howard and Claude would write him then, and maybe send him something. Harley, the oldest, never wrote; but Warren remembered his birthday every year; a card came. Of course Ted died, not more than a year after his mother. He was the only one that died; the rest just went away, as boys will, and as they should; they had their own families, but it was too far to bring them. Henderson was the last to go. He married Mildred Beal, a nice pretty girl they all knew, a close neighbor. She lived with her uncle; Henderson married her, and brought her home to live. But she died when Barbara was born, and Henderson couldn't stand it where everything reminded him of Milly. He shouldn't have run off like that, and if it hadn't been for the wreck he'd have said so himself, and come back. Henderson didn't die, he was killed. The truck he got a ride on turned over, just four miles out of town. So there were only two of them left out of all the Hitchcocks.

When Barbara didn't return at once around the corner of the house he began to worry. He knew he shouldn't, but he did. He had to have her in sight or else he couldn't go on working. He straightened up, rubbing his back where it was stiffest, and started looking for her, and calling.

"Barbara! Where'd you go? Barbara, come here!"

She appeared suddenly around the opposite corner, behind him; but she didn't tell him she was there. Instead she watched him as he rubbed his back again and peered across the lawn between two plum trees that long since had shed their blossoms. He leaned against the weatherboarding of the kitchen wing, as if he needed its support, then trotted forward, calling her with new anxiety: "Barbara, come here to Grandpa, right away!" He disappeared around the wing and she followed him, curiously; one might have thought she had never seen that bent old man before.

It was with the same curiosity, as if she wanted to try something out, that she answered him at last: "Here, Grandpa, here I am."

Vincent came running back, and she thought he would pick her up and kiss her; but for once he didn't. He merely grunted and went on past her to his wall. "Fooling me," he said. "You saw me all the time."

She studied him from her stool as he examined the wall and looked about him for the stone he had put down when he missed her. He seemed to have forgotten her already, but she knew he hadn't.

"Why do I have to be where you are? I'll come back, I always will. Why do you think I won't?"

He went on rummaging among his pile of rocks; but paused once to pull out his big watch to see if the hour had come for them to start home. It hadn't, so he whistled a few notes, rubbed his hands together, and ignored her question; or it looked as if he did.

He had no business, people said, keeping her to himself this way. Milly's uncle, John McCullough, had seemed to think *he* ought to have her after Milly died and Henderson got killed. But there wouldn't have been a woman caring for her that way either, unless John married again, and he never had. The neighbor women talked a lot, and hinted how he ought to give her up to one of them. Maybe he ought to, but he didn't think he would. There had been no little girls in his family. All boys; and if three of them had daughters of their own now, at least he never saw them, only their pictures. It wasn't easy, taking care of Barbara. Mrs. Hartshorne helped with the clothes, and whenever there was sickness it was natural he should carry the child there—just back of his own place—and leave her to be nursed. Not often, though; there hadn't been much of anything the matter with her. That wasn't the main thing anyway, Mrs. Oliver said. It was playmates, and after a while, when she grew up, it was telling her how to behave with boys, how to be modest and careful. It made him mad, thinking of that. Maybe of course he wouldn't last long enough to see it. He would be worse than a regular father.

Sarah would have been the best thing for Barbara, and she'd have been the best thing for Sarah. Their last two boys, Sarah hoped, would turn out to be girls. Henderson used to say he wouldn't have been born if his mother hadn't wanted a girl, and he was right. Nothing like a little girl. Like Barbara, anyway. It wasn't true that boys, little boys like Henderson was once, were hard customers to bring up. When they were little enough they had their soft side too, and their delicate feelings. But there was nobody like Barbara, at least now. She made all the difference to him in that house. It wouldn't be anything without her: no sun, no sound. Of course in another year and a half she would be going to school, and then she couldn't stay with him all day. It made him sad to think of it. One way or another you lost them. Still, it was a whole year and a half.

He looked at his watch again and quickly put it back in his pocket.

"Come on, you bad girl. Going home now. Bad girl, you went and left Grandpa."

"No, I didn't. Can I drive?" She meant, could she keep one hand on the wheel all the way. Around corners, too.

"We'll see," he said. He scraped the bottom of the mixing board and went to stow his tools in Mrs. Knapp's garden house, to which he carried the key. "While I'm doing this, you run on out to the car."

From the interior of the shed he heard the gate bell tinkle, and smiled. She liked coming here the best of all, because of that. She must be through now, and in the car, and sitting behind the wheel. It looked like a big wheel with her behind it.

They were on the main road in a minute, Barbara close beside him, helping with her left hand.

"Shall I hit that car?" he said. A shiny black one was coming towards them.

"I won't let you."

"Good."

Then they were home, and he was pretending he didn't know what they would have for supper. But there it was, the bread and milk, and the raspberry jam, and four cakes of Mrs. Hartshorne's sausage that he fried. The late sun streamed into the kitchen window as they sat and ate, gilding the child's head with its pale hair he had told her to comb carefully when she washed her face and hands. She wasn't good at it yet, but she did her best. Mrs. Hartshorne showed her, and kept it trimmed.

Vincent had coffee, but of course she didn't; and when he was finished with his second cup he said: "Now what?"

"Now what?" She said it the same way, mimicking him. "Now what?" They ended every meal this way, except the lunch they took with them to jobs.

"Well, a young lady might want to run over and see an old lady about something or other."

Mrs. Hartshorne wasn't old, but Barbara thought she was. Twenty years younger than Sarah would have been, with children not grown up enough to think of leaving home. Hartshorne himself was out there now in the garden, staking his tomatoes. One of the boys was helping him, and Ruthie, the youngest of the family, was swinging in the swing.

"You go swing with Ruthie."

She slipped down from her chair and was gone before he could get out one more word.

Just like she lived with them, he said. And in a way she does.

He meditated upon this as he cleared the table, brushed it free of crumbs, folded the red tablecloth and put it in a drawer of the sideboard, and went with the milk and butter to lower them into the deep hole by the back door where they kept cool all summer. In a way she does. She lives with them as much as me. For an hour every evening, anyway. For a whole hour she forgets I'm here, she goes and leaves me and is one of them. Maybe I oughtn't to keep her. Mrs. Hartshorne there— for all she's got to do, she'd take her in a minute. Maybe I've got no business with a little girl.

All of his joints hurt him at the thought, and he went to sit down on the bench he had made at the base of the ragged pear tree that would have no pears on it this year. He could see across to the other house, and hear both children's voices by the swing. Ruthie had got out and was helping Barbara in. She was half again her age.

Maybe I've got no business, he repeated to himself. But it was torture to do so; and he began to think of all the ways it was better for Barbara to live where she did. A whole house— not big, but he kept it clean—and all his love. Yes, all of it since everybody else was gone. More, even, than there was before. It was no harm to Sarah to say this. More than ever before. He only lived to wake up in the morning and go into Henderson's old room and wake Barbara up. Sometimes she was already up; sometimes she came and woke him—pulled at him, and stared at him soberly as he opened his eyes; as if she had thought, maybe, he never would again, as if he might have died in the night. But of course she never thought of people dying. Little children don't. Barbara was always serious, though, in the morning, at least until he said "Hello." Then she would laugh and run downstairs, and he would have to call her in for breakfast.

He couldn't imagine it without her.

But he ought to try, since any day it might be true. Or any

evening. This one, now. What if she didn't come back—let's
see, in half an hour? She usually didn't stay longer than that.
There was a dip in the ground between her and the Hartshornes', and it was a dear sight, her dress disappearing into it a
few seconds, then bobbing up again. And about that time she
always waved, and maybe called to him if he was sitting where
he was now, under the pear tree that would have no fruit this
summer.

The two girls, tired of swinging, had gone in by the kitchen
door. A lamp was burning there, though it hadn't quite got
dark yet. Hartshorne was inside too, and Allen, who had been
helping him with the tomatoes; and all the rest—it was a big
family, as big as his was once. Probably there was a lot of talk
around the table where the lamp was. They might be talking
about the time when Barbara would be one of them. They
might even mean tonight, and Mrs. Hartshorne, or else her
husband, might be getting ready to walk over and let him
know; without Barbara, who was busy watching the boys
work a puzzle—the two oldest were great for puzzles.

What if this was the way it was?

Vincent tried to imagine saying yes. But it was almost as
hard to hear himself say no. Plenty of times he had said it to
Mrs. Hartshorne, and she hadn't argued much; but now, if she
came tonight, it wouldn't be so easy. For some reason it wasn't
clear any more just what his answer ought to be. It couldn't be
a story, Mrs. Hartshorne was a grown woman, she wouldn't
have the patience Barbara did, she wouldn't listen like a child
to what she didn't understand.

Or did Barbara listen any more? Maybe *she* was growing up.
Maybe she only pretended, out of kindness to his mind that
wandered. She could be tired of how he talked; and tonight,
over there, she might be the gladdest of them all because Mrs.
Hartshorne was coming to tell him. His mind, it didn't wander; but she might think it did. You never knew with children,
they didn't *let* you know; until too late.

But here she was, racing up the slope as if something in the
dark had scared her. It wasn't really dark; and yet he hadn't

seen her till this minute. If the door slammed he didn't hear it. How could she have gone into the dip then out again without his noticing?

Anyway, here she was on his knee. She had jumped there, out of breath, and now was holding his head between her small hands, making him look straight at her.

"Did you have a good time?"

She nodded. "Grandpa!" She looked at him a certain way that he well knew, and it ought to have made him happy; but he was trying to imagine—

"Grandpa!"

"What now? What do you want? It's getting late, it's bedtime." He did his best to brush the question off before it came.

"That bell at Mrs. Knapp's house."

"What bell?"

"You know, on the gate."

"Oh yes, that bell."

"Does it ever ring all by itself?"

"How could it? Somebody has to push—"

"And if it ever did, and nobody was there, would anybody hear it?"

"Silly! Nobody, anybody—what kind of talk is that?"

"Would there be any *sound?*"

"Why, no, of course there wouldn't. There'd have to be a pair of ears." He put his hands over hers. "Did you wash these good this morning?" Each held the other's head: an odd sight, if anybody else had seen it.

"Grandpa." She pulled herself free and stared at him. Her eyes were all he could see in the growing dark. They were disappointed.

And because they were, he knew she hadn't wanted a plain answer. She wasn't tired of how they talked. She had run all the way home for that.

"Grandpa."

"What now?"

"Tell me."

Now he had it. "Oh, you mean about the old king and the little princess that somebody stole."

She took her hands from his cheeks, turned about, and settled comfortably against him.

"The king was so old, it was hard to believe he could have such a small daughter. But he did, and the old queen was dead, and the two of them lived by themselves in a high tower with woods and deserts all around it. Far as they could see, there was nothing but sand and trees: some places white, some places green, but all such a far way down and a long way off that you couldn't make out any animals or people. They had a good time together, those two: such a good time, they didn't need to talk. Whatever he thought, she knew before he said it; and the same way with him—whatever was in her head or heart came to him faster than the fastest word can fly. So she didn't need to say any. Once he told her it was like listening to a wire that hums or a bird that sings; it was a high, fine sound, he said, prettier even than her voice; so very high and fine it was that nobody else could have heard it at all. Of course they talked out loud sometimes, to the servants that cooked for them and made their beds and dressed the little princess in her Sunday silks and satins. But they spent most of their days together looking out over the green woods and the sand. They had names for every part of the world they saw—Hour Glass, Velvet Shoe, Tick Tock, Coffee Cup, and Doll's Eye, names like that—and pretended they heard voices coming up to them, and saw faraway people waving. They had a good time together, that old king and his small daughter.

"Then one day she wasn't there. He got up as usual and went looking for her, and started calling her name—Margaret, Margaret, that was her name—but she didn't answer, either way, out loud or like a bird song flying high and fine out of her heart. None of the servants could tell him where she was; nobody saw her go. She didn't go of course because she wanted to. A neighbor king came in the night and stole her out of the white and silver bed she slept in, an evil king who wanted her in his own castle beyond the farthest of the forests.

His idea was to keep her till she was old enough to marry his son. All of the girls in his kingdom were ugly, and so was the son. How terrible if she had gone with him all the way.

"She didn't, because the old king her father—he was leaning out of the west window, crying—suddenly heard her voice. Not her own voice, for that wouldn't have carried so far, but a high, fine sound like a song sparrow, or a wren. A thin sound it was; it could hardly get here over the deserts and through the trees. But he leaned out farther and listened, and there it was; almost like a mosquito it sounded, but more beautiful and sad. She was crying too, and she told him: 'I'm halfway between Velvet Shoe and Coffee Cup. If the horsemen hurry they can catch up with us and bring me home. There's only the ugly king and me; I am behind him on his high black horse. Send all our horsemen, hurry!'

"And so he did, and there was a fight; but in the evening they came trotting back, the horsemen he sent. The old king was still leaning out of the window, looking down across a valley where the road dipped and disappeared for miles and miles. He thought he saw white horses on the other side, but he wasn't sure. He waited a long time—it wasn't long, but so it seemed to him—and then there they were, galloping up the slope. And she was on the front horse, behind his bravest warrior, waving.

"Soon she was in the high tower, sitting on the king's knee and telling him—well, there was a lot to tell; out loud, too. Yes, there was plenty, don't you suppose?"

But Barbara was sound asleep, so that he had to carry her in to bed. She hadn't wanted a plain answer. He would never know, though, how much of this fancy one she heard. Not that it mattered. Barbara wanted to come back. The Hartshornes were good people—not evil, not ugly—but Barbara was here.

Fisk Fogle

"WHY DID Charlie have to get killed?"

"Why did we have to read the letters? The lieutenant simply said: You know where his people live. Send these home."

"We did send them, all but one. Why couldn't the lieutenant have done it himself?"

"Why did Charlie keep everything? Most of us don't."

"Quiet. The guard."

Night after night it went on like this, across the cold floor of the tent the brothers tried vainly to sleep in while the Army of Cumberland, resting from Stone River, got ready for Chickamauga.

"Lem! Are you awake?"

Sometimes he pretended not to be, just as Larry did when his turn came to be called. Then they would be at it again.

"What are you going to do? Have you said anything yet—written her anything?"

"No. Don't talk about it."

And yet they did, endlessly, without either one of them touching the quick of his own condition. Each kept it secret how he really felt; or hoped he did. Certain things, he told himself, could not, should not be said. Besides, the letter had made both of them ashamed.

Six weeks ago, judging by the date, Charlie had got it from Fisk Fogle back in Somerstown. Fisk was a loose-mouth, and nobody believed the reasons he gave for not being in the war—just yet. But one thing he wrote had nothing to do with him or the war or Charlie Nelson; except that if there had been no war it wouldn't have happened. For then a man would have been home with his wife. Two men. Two brothers,

196

married on the same day—September 2, 1861—to girls who had
been friends so long, and looked so much alike, that a stranger
might have mistaken them for sisters. Not that anybody did, in
Somerstown. There were no strangers in Somerstown.

"If you see Lem and Larry, don't tell them what a couple of
ladies you and I know are up to. Lem and Larry know them
too, mighty well; but they better not hear about this. The
ladies are even careful not to tell each other. At least I think
so—you never can be sure. Neither of them is lonesome any
more. The nights are cold for some of us; for Lem and Larry,
too, wherever they sleep; but not for a couple of farmers I
could name that come in town after dark, snow or blow, and
don't have any trouble with back doors."

It was not to be believed. Fisk was a fool who would think
anything, say anything. Yet he had said this, and Charlie kept
it. Why had he kept it? They knew why he hadn't showed it
to them, even though he called himself their friend. He wasn't.
He never got over the fact that Mary took to Lem instead of
him. With Fisk it was different. Margaret couldn't think seriously of *him*, and said so. If he hated Larry, it was his own
fault, and nobody had any sympathy with such foolishness.

It couldn't be believed. And yet it sounded true. When
Charlie was picked off in that rearguard action after Stone
River, and the lieutenant, going over his effects, found the
bundle of letters which he disposed of as he did, Lem and
Larry opened one of them out of curiosity merely. It was not
much; it was from Charlie's mother, who barely knew how to
write. Then they had gone on, feeling guilty but justifying
themselves because, as they said, any news from Somerstown
was meant for them. It belonged to them in a way. They were
about to stop, even at that, when they came across this thing.
If one of them had been reading it alone he might have kept it
from the other. But they both had it in front of them. They
read; and read again. They didn't say a word about it until it
was burned. They hardly looked at each other. And if they
talked now, night after night, they still didn't say very much.

It couldn't be true, and yet it couldn't have been made up.
That much they did say, over and over, lying in the dark and

listening to each other in the sore hope that one of them might do something, say something, to chase away the nightmare.

"Quiet. The guard." It was a relief to have silence forced upon them; or to act as if it were, for there was no rule against talking. Then it was a relief to talk again.

"Larry! Are you awake?"

Lem knew he was, but waited. At last he said: "Are you sure, now, you haven't written? Their letters last week—I don't know how to answer mine. What do you think we ought to do? We aren't doing anything; not even getting mad."

"Be still. Don't talk about it."

"Those farmers. What farmers?"

"Be still."

"He couldn't have made it up, the way it sounded."

They both believed it without wanting to. They didn't know how, even, and yet they did. It would have been easier, felt better, to be shot. This was a blow that landed again and again. There was nothing the matter with them; all day they looked like other men—no hungrier, no colder in this raw spring weather; then darkness would come down, and with it the certainty that the blow must fall again, over and over through an endless night of wondering what each other thought.

Tonight it was Larry who went to sleep first. Lem always knew when this happened by the way Larry breathed. It was not that he breathed more heavily, but that he breathed at all. While he had lain there thinking, the blows landed and took the wind out of his lungs. At least this was true in his own case. Sleep was a blessing when it came. It blotted out everything, and you could even dream that things were well: here, at home, and everywhere. Last night he had got up once and lit the oil torch they had, and held it over Larry's face. It was quite peaceful, as if Larry in his sleep had learned how to be content with whatever was, had been, or would be; yet as if one thing had not been after all. Lem was sure that Larry had forgotten, as the ground forgets those who have been buried in it long enough. And deep enough. The dead, perhaps, sink down in it as drowned men do in lakes and seas.

The flap of the tent lifted—Lem knew the sound of canvas over canvas—and the low voice of the guard said: "Who's in here?"

"McAlester." Lem sat up; and wondered if his brother heard.

"Orderly gave me a letter—just come in—for Lemuel Mc-Alester. That you?"

"Yes." He felt for the letter and took it; and felt it again in the dark.

"Why now?" But the guard had gone. A strange business, sending mail around in the middle of the night. Did the Captain know? Maybe they were moving sooner than the rumors said.

He found the oil torch; hesitated; and lit it as quietly as he could, shading it from Larry's eyes. The letter was not from Mary; he had both hoped and feared it was. Last week, when the other one came, he could hardly read the words. "Dear Lem"—but was that true? Then all the other things she wrote, about his family and hers, about the snow, about prices, about the business she was taking care of, the feed business—farmers—he was blinded as he read. He was glad this wouldn't have to happen now. But who was the letter from? There was something about the hand—

He tore it open, and at the bottom of its single page he saw: "Fisk Fogle."

The torch, trembling in his grip, set shadows dancing like monsters on the far side of the tent, over Larry's bed. He looked up at them and winced. If it had been Mary's name, what then? A sudden rush of warmth into his heart told him he wished it had been. It was love that blinded him last week when he read her words; not doubt, but love; or love in spite of doubt; and that had been hard to bear. Yet he would bear it a thousand times again if he could. *This* name—his eye wandered slowly up the page.

Dear Lem:

We heard here about Charlie's death, and his letters have come home. Mrs. Nelson had them on the table when I went over yesterday. I looked to see if one letter was there, and it wasn't. I will tell you about it. There is going to be drafting done in

this State, and before that happens I will volunteer. So I will
tell you about that letter. It was not true. If Charlie ever
showed it to you, or if you saw it when you were sending the
others back, you will know what I am talking about and will
understand. If you don't know, it won't matter. I won't say
what the letter said, except it was untrue. Charlie and I wrote a
certain way to one another. Well, I wanted to tell you this in
case I volunteered and anything happened to

Your friend,
Fisk Fogle

Lem read the lines a second time, and a third, and a fourth,
before he knew what he wanted to do. He wanted to sing out
so the whole camp would have to listen: "See here! See what
Fisk Fogle says!" The blood was hammering in his ears as he
got up to wake Larry: to shake the daylights out of him if
necessary, but anyway to get him on his feet and make him
read the letter.

He took the torch over and held it so that its light flickered
on the placid features of his brother, lost in the happiness of
sleep.

Why was he still asleep? With so much noise—but Lem,
standing there and looking down, remembered that there had
been none.

Now, motionless, the torch steady in his hand, he studied
Larry's face. The happiness of sleep? It was more than that.
Larry smiled—not as children do, but as a man might whose
most intimate faith had been confirmed. He was home with
Margaret, believing all she said. Or he had never left home; it
was a world without nightmare; even the war had not been
dreamed of yet except by orators and politicians. There was
no Tennessee, and no cold spring air with danger behind every
tree, and gunsmoke up the hills. Larry was somewhere else, in
another time. Sleep had more than blotted out his misery; it
had cured it.

Lem moved the light farther away, then blew it out
abruptly. Its rank, oily odor lingered in the air, pleasing him as
he found his way back into the place where he had lain so long

awake. He pulled the heavy blanket tight around his chin. Larry wasn't cured for good. Only the letter would do that. But it was wrong to rouse him now. The first moment he stirred: that would be the time. Meanwhile there was Mary to lie and think about; to turn over and think about again; to keep awake with, talking as sometimes they had done at home, saying as nearly as possible no words at all, yet proving everything. It was a sleepy sort of talk, however, that would prove nothing to strangers.

When Larry woke up an hour later he listened to see if Lem had gone to sleep. He could always tell by the silence in the tent; it was relaxed then, and Lem's breath came regularly.

It was that way now, and he was sorry, for there was something he wanted to say—if he remembered it. Something he had decided as he slept. Something about Fogle. They had believed Fogle and not the girls. That was it. He wanted to know if Lem had thought how contrary to reason it was to believe Fisk Fogle for the first time in their lives, and about this thing.

"Lem, are you awake?" He said it softly, and was convinced by the absolute stillness that he had not been heard. Too bad. It might make Lem feel better to have it put this way.

Lying and listening for the first sign that his brother's sleep had grown restless, and himself growing weary from no cause that he understood, he remembered that there was a difference between believing and knowing. Whatever they believed, they didn't *know*. Lem knew nothing now, however peacefully he slept. Larry envied him this peace, and wished he had his own again. Yet genuine peace would not be possible until they *knew*. Even the worst was better than nothing at all.

Or was this true? Lem would not say so if he could talk in his sleep. Sleep was the best thing as things were.

He sat up and felt for the torch. It had been moved, but he found it at last and lit it cautiously. One sight of Lem's face might send him back where he had come from when he woke. It was only an hour or two till reveille, but he needed those.

He was glad he had been so quiet. Lem's expression was like

nothing he had ever seen. A letter was crumpled in his right hand, which had come out from under the blanket in spite of the cold. Mary's letter, that he didn't know how to answer? Perhaps he did now, or thought he did.

And yet he didn't know a blessed thing.

Larry, extinguishing the torch, wondered when either of them would.

The Courage and the Power

"SHALL I go to him, my child? Shall I do what I can do? I can do anything."

Helen opened her eyes slowly, not believing that a person would be there to see; and saw an old woman with bright cheeks sitting in the chair by the window. She had thrown the stockings and slip on the floor, where they lay in a small heap, and was looking hard at Helen.

"I can do anything," she said again. "But only if you wish. You must have the courage. I have the power."

Helen sat halfway up, then changed her mind. She closed her eyes and turned lazily to the wall, luxuriating in this moment of doubt that she was yet awake. The sun poured over her, warming the wallpaper and flushing her own face by reflection. The sun! But she had pulled the shade when she lay down.

She turned back, and the ancient person was still there.

"You wonder, my beautiful child—"

"Why do you say 'child'?"

"I saw you moving in your sleep, and you were beautiful. All such are mine, or can be if they wish. All beautiful women. Even old ones."

Helen thought: Her cheeks and eyes. Her arms, even, and her hair. She *must* be old, and yet she shines.

She lay still and closed her eyes once more; but opened them instantly, knowing she was wrong.

"You wonder how I got here, and who I am? Never mind. The shade is up because the sun should see you." The window was just as Helen had left it, open eighteen inches or so. But she wouldn't have come that way. "The sun loves you as you are, I know, and is in no hurry for you to dress. But you must dress, and I shall see you do it."

"No!"

And yet it happened.

The stranger in the room, taller than she had seemed at first, got up and walked about, continuing to speak; and the effect was not only to reassure Helen but to make her glad she had consented. It was as if another mirror watched her than the one she had; a mirror that warmed her with the pleasure it took in her image, once she was up, and flattered this image until it was, thought Helen, itself a shining thing. She could say this without vanity, as if she were another person standing there. Yet it was vanity too, for she took pleasure in being seen, even by herself.

"Good! You had nothing on. Now turn that way—slowly. You *are* my child. What is your name?"

"Helen"—with surprise that it wasn't known.

The bright face lost half its age in the sudden smile that glowed. "And what is his?"

Helen, who was reaching for her white slip, seized it with a start and held it tightly to her, like a shield.

"Come, come, my child. He will see you too some day—if you have courage. What is his name?"

"Who?" Helen listened for any other sound in the whole house. There was none.

"I am not impatient, but you know I know. I mean the one you were thinking of before I came. It is why I came. I cannot be absent when such things are thought. Not dreams, either, as foolish girls would say. You are not foolish, and so you will admit that they were thoughts: firm thoughts, with flesh on them, and color. But not this color."

For Helen, sitting to draw her stockings on, her face down

and away, had turned—all of her—so deep a pink that the very
rug seemed to know it, and darkened in sympathy.

"What is his name? When you have told me you will have
your own beauty back. This is shame's color. It does not become you. My children flush with joy, and even with mod-
esty, the mother of desire; but not with shame. I would have
you look as you will look when he first knows you love him—
him, and not yourself, or your sense of what is proper, having
made certain promises. You promised yourself to the wrong
person, and these others in the house—I saw you listening—
have not learned that you know it. But you do. What is his
name? He scarcely knows either, and without your help—my
help—would do nothing. I come only to those who need me.
You are such a one, and so is he. For he would be your lover if
he knew. Was this the thought?"

The girl looked up almost in terror—not quite, for eagerness
quenched it.

"How did you know?"

"What is he called?"

"Terence."

"Good. And where?"

But the girl shook her head. She was by the window now,
looking out through the spring leaves. They were half-size,
but growing, growing. Branches rose and fell with the delicious effort.

"You will not tell me where he is? I could go now, tonight. I
could be there when he wakes up tomorrow morning. Those
leaves—there is to be one more fine morning, then stormy
darkness; a full week of that."

Helen, somehow free to laugh, did so. "In *his* room, when
he wakes up?"

The old woman smiled. "I love laughing. Go on."

Helen stared.

"I'll never tell you," she said.

"Then I must go wherever you go. It will take longer, but
no matter. Some afternoon, some evening, you will be where
he is—where both of them are, the one you don't love and the
one you do. I shall watch your eyes. This Terence—I know

already how they will look at him. They have seen him here,
and they will not be able to forget."

"Here?"

"He is the one whose hands—"

"Please!"

"But you want to hear, you want to remember. They
touched you everywhere; yet with such love, you didn't call it
touch. Nor will you ever; his hands are not heavy, nor his eyes
dull. Do they say he is good?"

Helen hesitated.

"I see. The people in this house—are you worried? No one
can hear us talking."

Helen listened a second time. Her mother must have gone
out, and neither of her sisters made as much as a mouse's noise.

"They do not hear, and you do not hear. But there is one
thing you know: he will be good for *you*. You were so happy
when he laughed, and his two hands, moving where yours
did—"

The girl put her fingers to her ears.

"There, too. Oh, everywhere."

Helen whirled about as if in anger, but she couldn't disguise
her eyes, which said: Go on.

"You will look everywhere till you see him, and then you
will shine all over as you shine now. No matter what you
wear, this will be visible to me. And to him; for I will open his
eyes. Men's eyes are always blind till we do our work. They
think they can't have us, and then discover we have them:
have had them, morning after morning, with the sun and birds.
You went to sleep this afternoon—confess—because you
couldn't bear to be without him. You could not wait till morning. Nothing is if he is not. Your life—you could not walk
about and waste it, so you slept. It is a drug you have been
taking. But now, my sweet child, you are well. I will go where
you go, and open him like a poppy, like a walnut, like a stair
door, like a—"

Helen, laughing, finished with her skirt and sat down before
the small mirror whose last word it was her custom to take
without argument or question.

There were steps in the hall, and Marian came in.

"You been having a nap? I thought everybody was gone. Dave called. The two of you are invited out tonight. A party. At the Campbells."

"Who else? Did you ask?"

"Oh, me, and the Montgomerys, and Jim and June. Bob Deacon, too, I think."

"Who else?"

"Melanie Kurtz. Why do you have to know?"

"That all?"

"Some friend of Melanie's. And Terence Hiatt."

Helen wondered why Marian hadn't noticed.

She turned, and no third person was there.

"What's the matter with you!" said Marian crossly. Helen had run to the window and was peering out.

"Nothing. The leaves—they're so pretty. This fine weather won't last long."

"How do you know?"

Helen didn't explain. She was repeating to herself: "You must have the courage. I have the power."

She was deciding: I even have the power.

I, Tobit

THE OLD MAN heard them say they were coming in, and looked up from the charcoal fire over which he had been rubbing his hands.

"Is it all right?" The fellow in the handsome overcoat stooped to walk under a scaffold that separated the unfinished building from the sidewalk and the icy avenue beyond. He stood in the opening, not as if he doubted his welcome but as if he were curious about something he saw. "My wife noticed your fire and wanted to stand by it a little bit. We're waiting for a taxi."

"There's one." The old man heard it coming.

"Never mind. We're cold now, and would rather get warm this way." The young man—yet he wasn't very young—stood still in the shadows, hesitating before he turned to call the lady in furs who was stamping her feet by the curb.

"I guess it won't matter." The old man looked down at his charcoal again. He was sitting in a small mahogany chair, with arms, that had seen better days. Plaster dust lay on its rungs, as on everything else in the enclosure. A damp smell of new bricks had by no means yielded to the little heat the fire sent forth. It was a good fire, but only in its area: the iron box it filled, and the air above it. "I'm guard here, with orders not to let anybody in. But you—"

"We won't carry the building off."

"You couldn't do that. Well, come on in."

He got up as the lady, stooping too, advanced with her hands out. Her husband didn't follow all the way. "Thank you," she said. "But I wouldn't take your chair, not for any-thing." Even her face was hard to see well in this darkness; yet her eyes gleamed as she smiled. "Please sit down, or we'll go."

The old man, who had shown how short he was when he stood up, did as she demanded. He had on a stocking cap, and mittens stuck out from one of the pockets of his reefer. The collar of some other coat, or it may have been a sweater, was visible underneath.

"This feels so good," she said. Her gloves were off, and she was holding her palms low over the coals. She had nice hands. No rings, except for one—plain gold. "You could have kept us out. We appreciate it and promise not to steal a single brick."

"It isn't that," said the old man. His small face was smooth and benevolent. "But I can't say I know, now, *what* it is. I've been guarding buildings for Hiram Hancock all these years, and nothing has happened. I sit here like this, and nobody comes in. I've heard noises, but when I went to see it was only pigeons in the window holes, or new plaster dropping, or boys. Birds and boys never did any harm. Even at that, this is a real job. They have to have somebody. Mr. Hancock himself told me so once. He came here—not to this building, of course, but

another one, years ago. He's built most of the city, it seems
sometimes. He's a great man. He gave me this chair. He said it
was out of his own house."

"He must think you're all right too," said the man in the
shadow.

"Come closer and get warm; there's room." The old man
sounded as if he had forgotten his second guest.

"No, now now. I'm out of the wind. Have you always done
this kind of work? Isn't it slow business, being night watchman, especially when nothing happens?"

"But something might. The main thing is to be ready. The
main thing is not to care about yourself. My wife always puts
up coffee for me—I heat it over this when it comes midnight—
and to be sure she thinks I'm foolish not to look for different
work. But I don't know, at my age. Anyway, it's a satisfaction
to guard solid buildings, built by a solid man. It isn't much, but
it's something, and I'm proud because I have never gone to
sleep and let anything happen. I don't know what, but I may
have accomplished more than I knew. Not that I'm proud of
anything except that I can say I have walked in the ways of
truth and wakefulness all the days of my life."

A bus went by on the avenue, groaning in low gear because
of the glaze beneath its tires. When it was out of hearing the
young man said: "I, Tobit, walked in the ways of truth and
righteousness—"

"So! You're one of the few that know. I'm glad you came in
here, you and your wife. It's remarkable, your knowing. Look,
it's almost midnight. I'll heat my coffee now, for you—both of
you; I don't need it myself. My wife just thinks I need it. I'll
keep awake all night now, thinking how you knew about
Tobit."

"Truth and righteouness, *he* said. You've changed it."

"Well, a little, just to fit the difference. Shall I heat the
coffee?"

The lady was about to protest when she felt a pressure on
her arm.

"It would taste wonderful, no doubt about that." Her
husband clapped his hands together, indicating that he was
cold. "If it will give *you* pleasure—"

"It will," said the watchman. "Here!" And he brought up a
tin pail from the dark side of the chair. It hissed as he set it on
some wires that were stretched across one corner of the coals.
"You can drink out of the same cup, I suppose. But how did
you know about Tobit? Are you a student?"

"Not now."

"A teacher?"

"Oh, no."

"Then it *is* remarkable. Are you a Jew?"

"I don't think so." The fellow forced a little laugh.

"You'd know if you were, these days. If I could have been
one, I would. Now that may sound funny, but I mean it. A
great thing, to be one of Tobit's people. He's been my man for
more years than you've probably lived. I have a son, or I
believe I have. My wife says no, he's dead in the west. She says
I killed him, sending him out there. She never lets up on me
about that. Her name's not Anna, any more than mine is
Tobit. But I did get her to name our boy Tobias. And now I
don't know where he is."

After a silence: "Where did he go? You say you sent him?"

"Oh, it's a long story. Which one of you wants this first?"
He was pouring the coffee into a battered aluminum cup. "I'd
put your gloves on, my dear. The handle's hot."

She did so, and sipped the all but boiling liquid. Then she
had to set it down.

"Tobias was Tobit's boy, you know, and he sent him a long
way off, to Media, to bring back some money that Gabael had
been keeping. An angel went with him, or it turned out that he
was one. My son had no angel, unless some stranger helped
him. But about the money: it wasn't cash, it was a house and
lot my father always told me he once owned in Denver, Colorado. I never was there and saw it, but I had no reason, after
the old man died, to doubt that it was still in Denver, Colorado. We were hard up, as usual, so I sent Tobias out. My wife
was against it, but I sent him." He sighed. "That was ten years
ago this winter, when he was nineteen, and maybe it's true he's
dead. But I'm not giving up."

"Didn't he write?"

"A little. Then he stopped. He said he wasn't having luck

with the house and lot. The authorities couldn't find any record. The last thing we heard was, he would try again. My wife is a good woman, but she bears down on me about this. To you I'll say she may be right." He sighed again, but remembered the cup and motioned toward it. It would be cool now, perhaps too cool.

"I'll try some," said the young man, stepping forward. But he retreated rapidly, carrying the coffee into darkness with him. "It's fine," they heard him say. "I'll finish it."

"There'll be another cup." The old man rubbed his hands over the fire. "It's a satisfaction to have something to divide. The only reason I'm sorry not to be rich like Hiram Hancock is that then I could share more. As it is, though, I have the best satisfaction of all. I have walked in the ways—you know the rest of it."

" 'All the days of my life, and I did many alms deeds to my brethren and my nation.' "

"That's right!" The old man peered with pathetic eagerness into the gloom. "The only trouble is, Tobit had God to walk in the ways of. Now I don't know what you people think, but I say we don't have God any more as the old Jews had him. Even the new Jews don't. It's a terrible fact: most people of this generation don't know who to walk with. The country? But that's other people. Yourself? But who are you? Who is anybody if someone out of sight, older than all the world, can't be there watching and rejoicing when you walk the ways? So I don't claim that Mr. Hancock's a substitute. Yet there he is, and I have guarded his buildings for him without making one mistake. He tells me that, and I'm satisfied. Have you heard of Mr. Hancock?"

"Sure. He's famous. What does he pay you, if it's any of my business?"

"That's between him and me. My wife says not enough. She thinks I'm a ninny to go on working for so-and-so dollars a week. Tobias, too—he used to call me Hancock's slave. That was one reason I sent him to Denver, Colorado. If he could locate the lot out there and get it sold, he might have less to say. Not that I minded; he was just a boy. One thing he didn't know. If he brought the money back, or the deed so I could make a sale, I was going to give him everything. He was the only reason I cared about it. He's the only reason I sit here now. I'd have given up long ago, like my wife, but I said to myself: I'll keep on at the job, as if nothing ever went wrong; then maybe nothing will; maybe he'll come back, that is. Not that Mr. Hancock would have it in his power to reward me as God rewarded Tobit. I never thought Mr. Hancock was God. But there might be something—there still might be—in staying on the watch. So here I am. But Tobias—"

He could not go on. He had felt all he said.

"Thank you for the coffee. You were very good to us strangers."

"Don't go. There's one more thing, and it's not serious. You remember in the story how Tobias got a wife as well as money? Sarah, the daughter of Raguel? Poor girl, she had lost seven bridegrooms on seven wedding nights; a demon strangled them. But the angel made a preparation that stopped this. So when Tobias came home he brought a woman with him: a fine thing for Tobit, who was the first to see her. I don't suppose Tobias got a wife that way, in Denver, Colorado. And if he does come, he won't have to cure his dad of blindness. Tobit couldn't have seen Sarah if the boy hadn't thrown a powder in his eyes the angel gave him. There were pigeons in those days too, and Tobit thought they had taken away his eyesight, dropping their droppings on him when he lay all night once under the walls of Nineveh. I've always doubted that that was the reason, but he thought it was, for the book says so, and he does the talking. Anyway, suddenly he could see, and he saw Sarah."

There was a long silence while the lady drew back to stand beside her husband.

"Toby!" she whispered. "Tell him!"

"What's that?" The old man had caught the name. "Toby? The other boys used to call Tobias that. We didn't—I didn't."

"I do."

"What's that?" The old man was getting out of his chair again. "Call who?"

His son stood before him, his eyes shining. "Who says you aren't blind? Talking to me all this time, not knowing who I was! Pigeons! How's Mother? How's Maggie Ransom? You don't live on Race Street any more. We went there."

"Catch him!" cried the lady. But he was not falling. He only seemed to be.

"God, boy! This could have killed me." They were kissing each other, tall and short. "And this is—"

"Sarah—really Sarah. I never thought of it before, but we're the only ones—our generation—with the right names. Thomas Ransom, you're nobody."

"My dear, my dear. *You* made him come."

"No, he decided to. But it's a long story, where he's been. I hardly know myself."

"She didn't know about the money. I got it, and I spent it. That's why I couldn't come home then. Afterward—well, I couldn't make it all at once."

"Maggie Ransom! How'll *she* know? I can't leave here." Thomas was desperate, confronted with this problem. "I'll tell you. One of you will have to go and bring her. It won't wait."

"I'll go," said Sarah.

"No, I will." Toby was firm. "She wouldn't believe you. She's hard to convince. Where is it, Dad?"

"A long way—2547 New Drive."

"Now I do want a taxi."

Thomas and Sarah stood beaming on each other.

The Sign

HE SHOULDN'T HAVE got his feet wet when he crossed the brook; one rock was slippery, and he went in up to his ankles. Not that it was cold in the woods, in spite of the black shade, but he didn't want to think about anything except what he was here for.

He wondered if they missed him yet. He didn't tell Papa he was going, or either of the girls. How could he tell them? Especially if he told them why? "You won't say what Mama was like, so I'm going up there to find out, and I'll stay as long as I need to." Papa's orders were to keep out of the pines—any and every one, keep out. They went for miles up the mountain; it was easy to get lost in them, even for a grown man, even for him.

Nin wasn't lost. He wasn't sure he cared if the directions did mix themselves up. It might be better that way; then he would have nothing to think about except what she had been. She died when he was born, and nobody talked about her enough. Papa had a picture, and the girls said Yes, they remembered, she wasn't very tall, and she was good to them if *they* were good, and even when they weren't she was sweet, she made them sorry they had hurt her feelings, she cried instead of scolded. At least Nan said that; Mayme was more likely to put him off as Papa did, leaving anyone that listened the impression that he asked too often and wanted to know too much. "How can you describe a dead person?" Mayme said this once, but he knew it could be done. If he had ever seen her he could do it, because he wouldn't have forgotten anything: the way she really sounded when she talked, the way she closed her eyes or opened them, the way her hands lay in her lap. Nobody told him things like that, as if they had never noticed.

So he stopped asking; and one day last month after a hard long rain, when the woods were wet and the pine trunks were darker than ever, and looked bigger, he decided on a plan: he would cross over and keep going till he got a sign—saw something, heard something, felt something that he could take for true. And he would stay there till it came, without anything to eat because when you are hungry your eyes and ears are sharper, and as for water, he could find that anywhere, though where he was now the needles under his feet were dry and brown as sawdust. Yet it was just as well that he had waited till dry weather.

The pines ahead of him were all about the same size, and their brittle side-branches, stuck out stiff and dead, were alike too, so he couldn't find his way back by keeping track of the trees. But who wanted to find the way back? Not yet. He had only started. He knew he wasn't lost, because he could hear one of the cows bawling back there; he could even tell which one it was—Pint Size, who maybe had had her calf, and Papa might be looking for him to help bring her in. He was going on, though, up and on, to where there wouldn't be noises he knew by heart, to where everything would be strange, and he would be too. He had to get everything he was used to out of his head, or else there might not be a sign. He was glad to feel his feet dry and warm at last. They were part of his body, and he had to be free of that. He stepped lightly, and looked straight in front of him as the mountain climbed.

In a minute, though, it fell away on the right: a deep ravine that sloped down, with probably a stream in it. But he wasn't thirsty, so he swung left and up as the main bulk of the mountain did. It was rougher where he was going; he could see ledges, and here and there big boulders with ferns on them. He would have to pick his way around these, and he supposed he could count on them as landmarks if he had to, coming back down again. That great one off there, for instance, with the flat sides and top, and not a crack in it anywhere. He would certainly recognize an object like that.

When he was quite a way past it he looked back, and it had disappeared among the pines. Well, no matter. But he was a little tired now, and he believed he would sit down. He did so, against a rock one side of which was concave so that it fitted his shoulders perfectly. He closed his eyes, marvelling at the softness of this granite, and did not open them until a jay screamed overhead, and he started up as if the scream had been a call for him.

He must have slept a full hour, though he wasn't sure. The air was now a little cooler in the woods, and what sunlight there was seemed to come from lower down. He was surrounded by a silence that was all the more noticeable after the shrill, wild, brassy voice of the jay stopped echoing among the boulders he could see above and beyond him.

Her voice could never have been like that. Mayme had said

once, impatiently: "Yes, it was nice; not loud, you know, like
Aunty Jimson's, that would scare a year's growth out of a deaf
horse. No, it was pleasant-sounding; but how can you describe
the way a person talks? Why do you have to know, Nin? You
never heard it, and you never will."

If he could learn just one thing up here: the sound of
Mama's voice. The other things were less important, and anyhow they might come to him with this, they might go with it
as a name goes with a person. He did of course have Mama's
picture; Papa let him keep it on his bureau, and he had studied
it till he could see it in the night. But Papa said it didn't do her
justice. Maybe so, and yet it told him she had large dark eyes,
soft straight hair, and the beginning of a smile: only the
beginning, for she seemed to be changing her mind about that
just as Mr. Renner clicked the camera.

The grey stone at his head was not so soft now, and his
knees felt sore from not having been bent. He got up suddenly
and stared back down at the woods through which he had
come. The trees did look alike, and so did the big rocks. He
wasn't sure what direction the house was, or the place where
he had crossed the brook. There was no sound at all, now that
the jay had stopped. A few little cracking noises, yes, where
squirrels might be busy in the highest branches, but other than
that, nothing. The woods themselves seemed to be holding
their breath and thinking about him; trying to decide, maybe,
why he was here, and wondering if he knew how to leave
when he had to.

He didn't exactly have to, and wouldn't for a long time, but
it might be sensible to *see* if he could. He would walk back a
little way, making certain he didn't go in circles as some do
when they are lost. He picked out the biggest visible pine, one
with a great side-branch that curved up and made a double
trunk, a pair of enormous dark candles, a U, an urn—U for
urn—and made for it; and reached it, and patted the rough
plates of its bark as if they were the walls of home. Yet nothing told him where home really was. The ravine was no longer
in view on his left, so he could only guess where Nan and

Mayme were at this moment, thinking perhaps of him and asking Papa where he was.

It took some resolution to start off again and shrug such thoughts away. But he did so, saying to himself it was too soon to imagine being home. Tomorrow morning, maybe, after breakfast. He would slip in then and fix himself some bread and milk while nobody was looking; then the first one that came into the kitchen would say: "Good Lord, here's Nin at last! Where on earth, boy, have you been? We've been asking all around." If it was Mayme, she might be caring more than she usually did.

He had to admit he was hungry, and the thought of cold milk made him thirsty too. The images of three people who would miss him tonight were suddenly as clear as glass; as if he looked over their shoulders while they watched themselves in a big mirror, saying in queer startled tones: "Where's Nin?" However, here he was—*he* knew—and he didn't forget what he had come for. He would shut his mind to the question of where in all these woods was the right direction down.

Yet his mind kept going off by itself, feeling its own way among the pines, touching them one after another in the faith that touch alone would guide it where it wanted to go. The only trouble was, it touched the same ones over and over. It travelled back and forth and round and round, precisely as— yes, he remembered now. Last summer, at Uncle Tom's house where he had never been till then. It was a house full of relatives, with many rooms upstairs, and the night was hot and still, so that he couldn't sleep. But then he did, and *walked* in his sleep: up the stairs, down the stairs, into this room and that, feeling, feeling the people in their beds, so gently though that he didn't wake them, then after what seemed hours of fumbling, back into those same rooms again, and the same breathing sounds, the same backs and breasts and arms, warm under the sheets, that let his hand go over them like a moth, like a moon shadow, without ever rousing up and crying out "Who's that?" When he did find his own bed at last he was exhausted, and of course slept like a dead person. He didn't tell about this the next morning. How could he? And it hadn't done anybody any harm. He had never known, for one thing, whom he was touching, just as they hadn't known that he was there.

His mind, going sleepily among the trees, was ignorant too of which ones it touched; and they were ignorant of being touched. Suddenly this seemed terrible to him, and he sat down again, for his knees were weak, at the base of a pine whose trunk was entirely encircled with moss—no side of it the north side, no hope in that. So it would be tomorrow morning, he said. His mind now, himself then: no difference, no hope of being told what way to go.

But he should be thinking of other things—one special thing: her voice. There came a twinge of guilt because he had let something else come foremost. Not yet, he said almost aloud. Patience.

Patience. He remembered how proud he was once when he used that word and Nan doubted he knew what it meant. "I know," he said. "What?" "Waiting." And Nan laughed. "That's right. You know."

It was a matter of waiting, and here was as good a place as any to do it. He stared ahead of him, his eyes lifted a little.

But then he scrambled upright again, for he saw—No! Yes!—an owl on a dead tusk of pine protruding from that giant tree, the third one from where he had sat down. A barred owl: he knew from Nan's bird book. Was it sitting or standing? Anyway, there it was, staring down at *him*, each circular eye inside another circle, as if the eyebrows went wholly around. Four silent circles, trained on him and growing larger as he looked.

Maybe, however, not on him. The bird didn't move any more than if it had been stuffed, and none of the circles changed its shape, its perfect shape. Asleep in the daytime? Yes, they did that, with their eyes open, Nan said; she wished she could see one once. Well, here was one, and he would tell her about it if he ever got home.

If he ever—stop that.

The owl never blinked, never shifted a foot, never lifted a feather. Why was it there, unless—but how could a bird tell him anything, how could a bird even know what he ached to be told? This one anyway, with its horrible voice: he knew how it wailed and hooted and stopped the hearts of mice and

rabbits it was about to swoop on in the dark; or skunks, whose
smell it didn't mind, for its feathers were full of it and the
book said it didn't even know, the filthy thing.

The circles continued to enlarge, and all at once Nin knew
he couldn't stand them any longer. He stepped back so that
the tree by which he had been rose between him and the beast,
and felt his own heart going loud and fast, nor could he stop it.
Nor did it stop itself when he saw, off to his right, great
plumy wings go with no sound whatever, without touching
any solid object on the way, on and on, curving and swerving
only a little as they missed the treetops, on and on till they
were out of sight. The owl could not endure him either. He
leaned against the trunk beside him, his heart still pounding,
his forehead damp with terror.

And now there was no doubt of it: he was thirsty. If he had
only a handful of cold water to drink—or lap, for he would do
it slowly, not wasting a drop—he wouldn't be afraid. Of
what? Of nothing, really. The owl was gone, and it hadn't
made a sound. He ought to be glad of that, whereas he merely
felt more solitary than before, more unimportant. The woods
around him were more real than he was: so much so that he
seemed to occupy no space himself. Who was he in all this
world? His mind, no longer outside of him among the trees,
seemed a small, helpless thing. Had it come back to him for
comfort? He could give it none.

The plan, though. Something still might happen if he kept
his courage up, if he only pretended not to be afraid, if he sat
down again, or lay down where the needles were especially
deep and springy, and let a little time pass—just pass, without
his doing anything about it. That way he might even manage
to stop feeling thirsty. What was it but a feeling? Days could
go by before he died of it, and he wasn't going to die.

The dark was coming down from all directions, and coming
fast. It moved on the level, too, advancing like a thing alive, an
animal, from every side. He shivered, and it took all the
strength he had to crawl in between two nearby boulders that
leaned together at the top: not a cave, exactly, but it was
something like a room, and the needles there were something
like a bed.

He lay on his back, his hands beneath his head, and wondered if he would ever go to sleep; or, assuming he did, if he would catch a cold, a serious cold, from lying still all night with nothing over him, and with shoes on that recently had been wet. They still might be; he fancied that they were. There was some dampness in these needles after all. Pressing them, he brought it to the surface; and more would come, like water from a sponge, the longer he stayed there.

This was when he first heard the bell. Not that he knew at the beginning what he heard. It was someone speaking to him, rather, it was someone singing. No words; nothing distinct; simply a voice, not strong, that came and went like someone weeping, someone sad, someone a long way off whose very thoughts were sounds, sweet sounds, that came and went in waves; died out, then came again, but never loud, never harsh, so that if you didn't listen to them—as he intently did now, sitting up—they might not be there. But they were there, and Nin dared to wonder if this were not his mother he was hearing, if this were not the sign. Or had he gone to sleep, and was he dreaming—sleepwalking, *feeling* voices that would die when he woke up?

But he was not asleep. And here the waves kept coming, kept ringing softly in his ears, as if a bell—

The bell. It was the one at home. One of the girls was pulling at the rope, or Papa was, to tell him where the house was, and the barn, and the big shade trees, and the watering trough where the rusty pipe had never failed to run a full stream as far back as he could remember. So clear, so cold—he swallowed, or tried to swallow, but it was painful, and he only listened, listened, as the melancholy notes kept on arriving.

At home, if you stood under the bell as it swung, it wasn't sweet like this. It could even hurt your ears, as if it had a crack in it. There was no crack, Papa said; you had to be away from it to know how nice it sounded. And Nin knew that. But never as he knew it now, when he knew at the same time—he was so sure, he almost ceased breathing—that this was how her voice had been. It went with the eyes that smiled yet didn't smile, that wept yet didn't weep; it went with the smooth hair,

220   MARK VAN DOREN

and the hands—but those were not in the picture—that lay so
quietly in her lap, waiting for someone else's hands to come and
touch them, take them, hold them. Someone else's. Papa's. His.

The bell stopped and didn't start again. He crawled out and
stood there, staring. No matter, he knew where it was, he
couldn't miss it. Right there. Keep going. The darkness wasn't
solid yet, he wouldn't have to feel his way.

Suddenly he was running—a mistake, for he fell over a
twisted root, and in the effort he made to straighten up before
he struck the ground he lost his sense of where the bell had
been. He went down so hard that he was dazed for minutes
and lay on his side, panting. On his feet again, he had no
notion where to resume running. No, walking; he mustn't take
any more chances.

As if they knew down there, the bell now found its voice
once more. He frowned, concentrating on the direction of the
sound, and stepped forward carefully, determined not to fall
again. This time he wouldn't go astray; the sweetness of the
bell was like a string that led him, on and on and down and
down.

He passed the great boulder with the flat sides; he could just
make it out. Good. Then the ravine was on his left, as it should
be; and the bell grew louder, louder. No longer sweet—yet
why should he say so? It was home, and nobody there knew
where he was. When they did know—

"Nin! Nin!" That was Papa calling him, from some place
not so far ahead. Papa was in the woods too, looking for him.
Which sister then was at the rope? Both of them, taking turns?

He wanted to answer, "Here I am!" but his throat was too
dry. Also, his heart was too big for where it was; it beat so
hard, he wondered if even Papa could hear it.

They almost ran into each other, it was so dark at last. "Nin!
That you?" Then Nin was holding on for dear life to the
familiar over-all jacket, and Papa, speechless himself, was
hugging him.

"You crazy boy," was all he said, "you crazy boy."

"Who's ringing the bell?"

"Both girls. Or no—Mayme now. I can tell. She swings it harder. Nan's with Mayme. They've been out of their minds. Where've you been? What possessed you?"

"Stop a minute, Papa, I want to ask you something."

"Now what? Don't you want them to know?"

"Listen. Mama's voice—it wasn't like that, was it?" Whang, whang! His ears were all but splitting.

"Lord, no! Your mother had a nice voice, a pretty voice."

"Sweet, Papa, would you say?"

"Oh, yes. When I was off a piece, in the south pasture maybe, or up in the woods—why, then the bell did sound like her. She would ring it to call me, and I would say to myself, which is it, her or—"

"Papa!"

"Now what?"

"That's what I heard."

"Where, boy?"

"Up there where I went. I heard Mama."

They started on again.

"So now I know. I *heard* her."

A silence. Then: "You heard the bell."

"Which was it, Papa?"

A longer silence. "You heard both."

"You really think I did?"

"I know you did. But come on now, we've got to tell the girls, we've got to stop that noise there, I can't stand it. Come on. And mind you, watch your step."

Birdie, Come Back

DRUNG lass night, drung the nibey fore.

This wasn't what the radio said, but it sounded like it. Studs swallowed thickly, trying to get last night out of his mouth.

Birdie was downstairs smelling the place up with breakfast, and hoping it would do him good. Or making like she hoped. Good God. It was a week this morning since he found out what he knew about her and Herman.

"Can you come down, dear? Egg and sausage getting cold."

Where did she get that "dear?" It was a new line, to fool him. A fancy line—too fancy.

"OK."

But the floor tilted as he tried to rise, and he fell back on the bed. Her bed looked so nice and cool, as if she hadn't turned over in it all night. His was just a pile of laundry. The only good thing about his bed, it was under him.

He got up again, though, and it was better. Give it time, and it got better. Good old head. Wouldn't she goggle if she knew what was in it? Her and Herman.

"Hurry, dear."

"Coming down!"

And he was—so loose in the joints, his right knee knocking every rung of the banister, that she was at the bottom when he landed, holding a hand out, helping him over the wax of the hall floor. Pretending she didn't see anything special, trotting a little ahead of him in her starched morning dress, smiling like a kitten with a bowknot at its neck.

He jerked himself free from her, and almost fell. She was too noble to notice, but both of her hands guided him through the door and into his place at the white table with its leaves out, and cornflowers in a blue vase.

He tried to imagine coffee. No good. Or marmalade. He held his head.

But she was bringing everything. So many trips from the stove, the heels of her slippers tapping in tune to the radio. Drung lass night, drung the nibey fore. Sure. Why not? You don't know Birdie like I do. He might have to go and put that bed under him again. The toast was burning, and it smelled like human sacrifice.

"There, dear."

A brown egg stood before him in a little cup: a cute cup, that swung with the table as the table swung with the icebox and the stove. The ceiling went half-way round then back again, then half-way round, then back again. He ought to get out of here.

But Birdie's hands, floating by on both sides of his head, caught the egg cup and held it down—almost held the table down, and yet not quite—no, they went back and forth with it, right and left, one of them turning the top of the egg while the other tickled it with a knife blade: tickled and teased it, finding the weak place where it would crack all the way round. He knew about that. Birdie beheaded eggs.

She finished, but the top was still on. She always left it on, like a lid. He only had to lift the lid and reach for salt and pepper.

Her hands coming away again—one of them had the knife in it. She could accidentally—she could be behind him like this and not notice—she could find the weak place in his neck—she could—

"There, dear!"

He jumped.

"Why, Studs! What—"

"Standing back there—reaching around—couldn't see—scared me."

"Here I am." She had dropped the knife on the drainboard and was bending her face down close to his. "See me now?"

She had no shape at all. She changed from thin to wide; she went curling off like smoke; she wavered, she folded and unfolded, she was like one of those funny mirrors at the beach.

But it wasn't funny, what she might have done. Maybe Herman told her to. Maybe she had tried. No nerve.

"Studs! Why don't you look at me? You said—"

"I said don't call me dear."

He did see her eyes before they went up—fast—out of sight, and she wasn't there any more. Not even in the kitchen. He heard her slippers on the stairs.

He shook his head carefully. He took it in both hands and turned it, then turned it back. Still on all right.

But the egg's head. It only seemed to be on. An uneven

crack ran around there near the top. One touch, and off it would tumble.

Even now it wasn't quiet in its place. It heaved a bit—only a bit, and then it rested. Soon, though, it was at it again, as if something inside were giving it punches from beneath. Like the lid of a teakettle, bouncing from the steam.

Studs stared. Was something doing this?

He looked wildly around him, hoping Birdie had come back. He would tell her to take everything away—everything, quick. But there was no Birdie; and when he looked at the egg again its top was doing a dance.

"Stop," he said. "Studs don't like it."

When it didn't stop, he reached for the fork at the right of his plate; missed it; tried again; studied the swing of the whole table, this way, that way, up and down the room; mastered it; and at last had the silver weapon in his palm.

He pointed at the egg, solemnly, and said: "Now stop."

His very first aim was good. The tines went forward, neatly into the crack, and the head flipped off. It fell to the plate, rocking on its round side a second or so, then was still.

Not an egg, but an eye—a bird's, a small reptile's—blinked at him out of the cup. One eye, that blinked a second time and after that stayed open, fixing his. It was a big eye for the beast it belonged to—a featherless chicken? a lizard? a little poison snake?—but it was tiny in itself, and glittered meanly, like an unlucky gem, among the moist coils that filled the shell. It was a hard eye, that wouldn't let him go; that kept him staring as it stared, until an intense voice, low and ugly like a locust's, said suddenly out of the cup:

"So you found out. You know about her. At least you think you know. Did you suppose she had a heart? She did; she does. But the heart—what is it but a stone, a little hot stone? What was it in her, what *is* it in her, but a little hot rock that loves itself? Now why should this bother a man? No stone loves another, and no heart. She may not even love anybody else. *He* thinks she does? Ha, ha! Then he's a bigger fool than you. He's sober, and he believes. You're *drung*, and you don't care."

Studs heard it—*drung*—at the same moment that he heard the radio stop and felt Birdie's arms around his neck. She was kneeling on the linoleum, crying.

"Dear! I'm sorry I left. Can't I say dear? I came down again, I wasn't mad. Studs, Studs, look at me and tell me what the matter is! I don't understand. Every morning for a week now—it's just the same, no matter what I do or say. I always did say *dear*—it's what I think—and you liked it till you changed. What happened, honey? You say such things! You don't talk like Studs at all."

He kept staring at the little reptile, whose eye never left his. And now there came the buzz, the sting, of that small voice.

"She's good at this. Listen if you want to, but remember!"

"That egg!" said Birdie, following his gaze. "It's bad! Oh, and I left you with it! Here!"

"No, no, no, no, no!" He tried to stop her, but of course he wasn't fast enough. The lid clanged on the garbage pail.

He stumbled over to take it off, but reeled and missed it altogether.

"Studs!"

He was on the floor, trying to get up.

"Studs, I can't stand it. What makes you drink so? I haven't mentioned it all week, but every morning. . . ."

"Lemme be."

She was bringing one of the cushions from the living-room sofa, and the afghan of all colors.

"Head up a little. There. Now go to sleep if you want to, but don't kick this off."

She dropped suddenly and kissed his eyes.

The cool cushion was wonderful. He lay listening to the faraway sound of Birdie's feet and wished she would come back.

He heard nothing from the grey pail under the sink. Was that why he wanted Birdie to come back? So he could tell her to give the snake some air? No. He shut his eyes tight. No, let it smother in there. It hadn't even told him he was right about—it made him think he didn't know. Now he never would. But neither would he know what to believe. That busi-

ness about the little piece of stone. How did it go? Forget it,
said Studs. She's all soft, all good. But it would be way inside,
where you couldn't feel. It might be there at that. In everybody: women, men. Even little children. They *seem* so good.
Birdie *seemed*. 'Dear.' Let her say it. 'Dear.' Let her worry about
him. Let her cry. Even if the rock was in there—well, it was in
everybody, and some showed it in their eyes, their voice.
Birdie didn't. He couldn't complain about what he saw. But
what *didn't* he see? What did Birdie think when she was—
could the letter have been a mistake? He didn't know for sure.
When would he know? He never would. If he got sober,
would he believe, like *him?* Like who? Never mind. He
couldn't believe again; not quite. But he would care; the sala-
mander was wrong about that. He would always care. The
best he could do; and the funny thing was, it didn't seem so
bad. Didn't *seem*. Inside, of course—but let that go. Smother
it, smother it.

Birdie, come back and let me feel how soft.

Skinny Melinda

MELINDA's big four-poster fairly shook each time it thundered. She had got out of it, breathless, ten minutes ago, and
still she stood on the thick red rug to which she had run to
keep her feet from getting cold; though there was little chance
of that this hot, this terribly humid night. Her thinnest nightgown was almost too much to bear. She felt it sticking to her
in the dark, and would have slipped it off except that when the
next lightning flashed he might see her and say something she
didn't want to hear.

There were only a few things she liked to have Steve say,
and that was when they were in bed together, close and sinful,
and she gave herself utterly to what she had never dreamed of

before that night he knocked on the front door and told her how he had watched her in the hemlock pool. This horrified her; he saw that it horrified her; that excited him—excited her—and it ended with his carrying her up here with all her clothes on and tearing them from her one by one, until—

And there he was now, his hair jet-black between the pillows; for he always took both of them, and tousled them and crushed them while she lay with nothing under her head except—sometimes—his arm with the blue and red tattoo on it, or his rough hands working in her hair. There he was now, although she couldn't see him in the pitch dark of the room: her room, that people thought so dainty, and her women friends exclaimed over, envying her its puffs and frills. But there he was, so silent that she knew he was asleep—yes, even now, after that savage clap of thunder, just over the house, with no interval between it and the hideous, hideous lightning. The room still seemed to be full of white fire; it wasn't, of course, but a picture was printed on her mind of how he lay there and heard, saw nothing.

If he was like that, she wouldn't wake him. He would laugh at her for being afraid. As if it were simple fear that made her tremble whenever the night sky screamed down at her, as it did oftener and oftener, so that pretty soon, she thought, the whole night would split open and swallow her up. Not him, not both of them, but her, just her, Melinda Marsh, the last one of all the Marshes, the one in whom a fine family—oh, so proud—was coming to some awful end she still couldn't clearly foresee, but she felt it was on its way.

Why hadn't she ever married? Mother wondered every time it failed to happen; and died despairing of her tall, thin daughter who turned her back on men, nice, eligible men, because she was determined to be an old maid and live alone in this house forever.

Turned her back. What if Mother had known about all the men—not eligible either, the list of them was a disgrace—from whom she twisted away only when she was tired of loving them, or having them love her, and wanted to sleep until her strength returned and she could love them more? How had it

begun? With Martin, of course, who then was twice her age
and the husband of Mother's best friend. It was in his house,
when Agnes was away—oh, she remembered. Then all the
others; they seemed to know about her even though she acted
properly at parties and looked like any other lady they might
meet. Lady. Ladies married gentlemen, more or less, but her
first taste of something different, something dark, had spoiled
her for the thought. It was always the next one, the one who
hadn't appeared yet, though she knew he would, that she
dreamed about and waited for.

And she hated it too. It was sinful, and so she hated it as
much as she loved it. In between, and after. That afternoon in
the hemlock pool—she had never done anything like it before,
and as things turned out it was probably a mistake. No, for it
was how this thing with Steve had started, and she had loved
that, unspeakable though it was, better than all the rest. Yes,
for here she was in the middle of her room, shivering with
shame, with terror.

Suddenly, that afternoon, she couldn't stand to think any
more of how dirty she was being to Beth, meeting Arthur in
motels all over the county, night after night, again and again,
and over and over, because he was wonderful, wonderful, and
she never tired or turned her back to him. Suddenly she said to
herself: No! No more of that, with him or anybody else, it's
finished. And she dressed in white clothes, and walked down
to the cool water there by the big rock, where Father had
taught her to swim, and slipped in without undressing, and
stood a full hour, not moving, in the belief that thus she might
purify herself, even punish herself, before she came out a
different woman. And it did seem to work.

She talked to herself all the way up to the house, saying she
was more like Mother than she had ever been since she was a
little girl and worshipped her, and thought evil things of
Father because he owned her. It lasted through supper and the
early evening, when she sat and read. Then tap, tap, tap on the
front door, and there was the Morrisons' handy man, Steve
Knott, whom she had scarcely ever noticed around their place.
She thought he had come over on an errand, to borrow some-

thing; but soon enough he told her. He was in the woods when she was, and watched; and it was her not taking off her clothes that set him wild. First he said to himself: Why? Then he said: Why not? Why shouldn't it be me, tonight, when nobody knows? He had understood about her too—even Steve Knott, with whom it was the worst yet to do what she found herself doing that very night, again and again and over and over. How could this be? At thirty-eight she wasn't beautiful any more, assuming she had ever been. She had too little meat on her: Steve's words, that she didn't like. But it was better that way, he said; and long before daybreak he proved it. There was nobody like Steve.

She heard him stir in the still blackness of the bed, and held her breath; but even when thunder, unannounced, jolted the very timbers of the roof, he didn't stir again. Good. Yet she must wake him before the sun came up, if it ever did. Of course nobody knew he came to her like this, and nobody must. He was the only one she had ever had at home. The others—she went away to do it, in every kind of place. Never in Mother's house.

And now the giant cracks of lightning came so close upon one another that Melinda shook like a thing pursued. Yes, that was it. The lightning was after *her*, and wouldn't rest till it had reached in and through and found her. She, Melinda Marsh, was why the storm had happened. It wasn't fear so much, it wasn't what she had felt as a child, when Father took her on his knee and explained about electricity; it was mortal danger. It was immortal danger. It was the awful end whose particulars had not been clear to her before. The whole world, that knew the truth, was after her at last. This was her punishment: not by cool water, in a place that she had chosen, but surely by fire in its most terrifying, its most final form. She wouldn't be washed clean, she would be burned to nothing at all, not even a crisp. She knew now that this was why she had left her bed, and why she had run—but of course there was no place to run. It was coming now, it was arriving, it was here. The terrible truth had found her out.

The window by her dressing-table rattled as if someone

were shaking it, trying to get in. Then there was silent lightning—for some reason, worse than if there had been noise—
that showed her in the mirror over the hairbrushes what she
looked like at this moment: Skinny Melinda (Steve's name), her
hair crazy and her eyes black as coal, as burnt-out coal.

Dark again, dead dark, and all at once she knew she couldn't
stand any more of this. It wasn't time to wake Steve, but she
would. She had to tell him; had to tell somebody; had to hear
herself cry out. It was too much to take all by herself.

Only a few steps back to the bed; then "Steve! Steve!," and
she was shaking his shoulder. "Steve! Wake up! Steve! Don't
just lie there like—"

"Who is it? Oh. What's the matter?"

She knew he was reaching for the lamp, and stopped him.

"For God's sake, Melinda." He spoke thickly, still half
asleep. "What's going on? Let me light the light."

"No!" And though she hadn't intended this, now she was
down where he was, pressing against him with all her weight,
and weeping. "Steve! Have you really been asleep?"

He didn't move; he didn't respond with his arms. "Still am, I
guess. Look here, Melinda, not *all* the time. Have a heart."

Hadn't she known he would say something like that! But she
was glad of it. It was more now as if he were her husband; as if
they had other things between them. Better things. Terrible
things, if necessary; just so they had them together. Could she
make him understand?

"Did you get up?" he said. "Wow!" For there was that
ghostly lightning again, as if the storm had lost its voice; but it
filled the room as before, and she felt him pull at the sheet,
thinking perhaps to shut out the sight. "Some weather. Is it
raining?"

"I don't think so. Just lightning—like that—and dreadful
thunder. Steve!"

"What?"

"It's a punishment."

He moved if possible less than ever. He might be making
sure he had heard right.

"We shouldn't be here—you know, I've said that before—we shouldn't ever have been here."

"Nuts. Where else? What difference does it make?"

"All the difference—there! You see?" Intermittent flashes, like a message, searched every corner of the room; still, however, without sound.

"Yeah, I see. Said the blind man. It won't hit the house. Hardly ever does."

"Oh, that's not it."

"Well then, for God's sake what is?"

"Steve." She had just remembered something.

He waited.

"Steve."

"Now what?"

"Could it be, you think, that they'll find us the way they found those two in the Fox house?" She lay away from him all at once, shuddering.

"Fox house? On the pond road? Found who? Never heard of it. Been empty a coon's age."

"You must have heard. Everybody has. No one went there all those years, and now nobody ever will, not since they found them."

"Found *who?* Listen. I don't get this."

"Yes, you do. You're just pretending you don't know about the skeletons."

She was right. He didn't say a word.

"That couple on the bed, lying there—that woman, that man—under what was once a blanket, but now it was remnants—threads—and they were too—I mean, they fell to pieces when—"

"Sure. Now you mention it, I remember."

"Oh, Steve, it may be *that's* the end."

"End? What end?"

"Of us. Of me, anyway. Steve, I can't stand it any more." A dozen fans of light, some brighter, some fainter, opened one after another so rapidly it was like a shutter working, it was like wings beating. "And yet where can we go? It would follow us. It knows."

"Hey, now. I'm not going any place. Not yet. It can't be more than midnight, can it? *Who* knows? We've got plenty of time." She heard him yawn. "Who knows?"

She couldn't tell him. They would never be like husband and wife, having other things together. There was no man now that she could be like that with. As for Steve, it was outrageous ever to have thought—

He yawned again, and the next flicker of radiance from the window showed her that he had turned over. He was almost snoring.

Flicker. Another one, just one, feeble and brief. The storm was leaving them.

Melinda got up as quietly as she could and went again to stand on the red rug. Could she leave without his hearing? He wasn't going, but she was.

Where?

It didn't matter much, just so she got away and kept on going. But could she do it quietly enough? The wardrobe doors were creaky, and where was the key to the money drawer? She would have to take all she had; she wasn't coming back. In the morning he would sit up suddenly and look around—

The light came on at the head of the bed, and she thought for a moment she would scream. Steve sat there watching her; he had only pretended; he was good at that.

"Hey! Come here."

"No."

"Skinny Melinda, come here to me!"

"No. I thought you were asleep."

"*You* ought to be."

"No. I can't sleep."

"No, no, no!" He mocked her. "Skinny Melinda, I can put you under. Remember? Old doctor, he's got ways. Look"—he twisted the alarm clock so she could see—"it's only ten to one. Come here right now."

"No." But she was going to him all the same. What difference would a few hours make? In the morning, after he had slipped off, she would have all day to—

What?

She had to admit she didn't know. Just yet. But she would stay awake and work things out. No matter what Steve said or did, she would stay awake.

The storm was over, and nothing had happened like—well, like *that*. She shuddered again, and then stopped shuddering. A breeze was moving the curtains. She did feel cold, at least a little. It was best to humor him; it was easiest, till tomorrow.

"Turn out the light," she said.

The Long Shadow

THE EIGHT HOOVES of Stephen's horses made a dull music that soothed Harriet as she travelled by her brother's side. The children, thank God, slept soundly on the back seat. She had been afraid they would cry all the way.

"Not *all* the way," Stephen said now. "It's a thousand miles to the Connecticut line; I drove down in forty days. When Father and Mother came it took them forty-seven, but the roads are dry this time of year, and there are more bridges than there were then; it's the fords that used to take time, particularly through Virginia. They couldn't cry for forty days; and anyway, they're Indians. Who ever heard—"

"They're little boys, and they are leaving home."

"I know," said Stephen. "Their mother isn't Cherokee. Or are you?" He didn't turn to see how she took this, nor did he seem surprised at her silence, which lasted two full miles. The Georgia road, yellow and winding, was not as dusty as the ones at home. At least there was that to be said for clay. A wonder anything grew in it. Yet things did. The cotton fields, brown and ragged, watched them go slowly past.

"I'm Cherokee enough," said Harriet after a while. He might have forgotten his own question, but he hadn't. Ever since they themselves were children in Connecticut it had been like this. They always understood each other. Their conversation never really stopped. "I'd like it to be all, but of course it can't. Maybe if—"

"What?"

He knew, though. She was thinking: Maybe if Elias hadn't been killed there would have been years and years in which she could study to be all Indian, and maybe succeed. Not that such a thing was possible. And yet in one sense it was true already. In ten years she had certainly changed.

The sister he remembered would have talked more about the terrible way Elias died. All she had told Stephen was how she begged the Cherokees to kill him faster. Twenty, thirty knife wounds, none of them enough to end his breathing: they wanted it that way, and wouldn't listen to her until he had been stabbed as many as fifty times, and then did die without having once cried out. To her the two hundred executioners were gentle, and in their own way kind. They said they would take care of her until her family came. Even at Elias they weren't angry. It was simply that he had taken the wrong side. He was for obeying President Jackson and moving to the Indian Territory. These were not; they would stay and fight if necessary. Now the whole tribe was gone beyond the Mississippi, and Stephen had found Harriet in an empty house, with a white woman from over the hills to help her with the children, and Negro women to help the white woman.

Harriet had never mentioned that night again, nor did she mourn for Elias. When the time came she was ready to go, and she never looked back. So here they were, with little Elias and John asleep on the back seat, riding north to what would never be for them more than half a home. Stephen tried to imagine the boys up there, and couldn't. They didn't *look* Indian, especially; but they were. What would they do when they grew up? His children's cousins—queer!

"You know, Harriet, I've always been ashamed of the way I acted."

"When?"

"You know." Naturally she must, for it had been the first

trouble between them. And now it was the last. All that was over for good, it had to be.

"Yes, I know. You mean when I gave you the letter."

"Yes. Why did it have to be a letter? If you had just told me—"

"No, Stephen, it would have been the same either way. And anyhow, I *couldn't* tell you."

"Why not?"

She looked behind her to see if the boys were all right. They didn't stir except with the motion of the carriage; their black heads rolled right and left like things that didn't belong entirely to them.

"I think," she said, "it was because Mother wouldn't tell you. She insisted that I should. 'You two,' she said, 'have never had any secrets from each other, so you mustn't have this.' Of course she was afraid. It was too much for anybody, I suppose. The feeling was so strong about the Mission boys. They could come there to school, and learn to be Christians, but they couldn't—"

For the first time she sounded bitter.

"I mean," she went on, "we couldn't be Christian to *them*. They had to be strangers among us, even the best of them, like Elias. He *was* the best. When he got sick and Mother took him into our house, I could wait on him upstairs if she was busy, I could take his meals to him, but we weren't supposed to talk. As if he were a prisoner or something. He was sick all summer, and we couldn't talk about anything except how he felt or what he needed."

"How he felt. For instance, about you."

"Oh, we never spoke of that. I knew, and he knew, but we never said so. Mother thought we must have; otherwise, how did we know we wanted to marry each other? Well, it was never mentioned."

Stephen took the whip from its socket and flicked a fly from the roan horse's rump. He seemed devoted to this task.

"You didn't believe it either," she said, "afterward, when you read the letter. That was the first you knew anything about us at all, wasn't it?" Stephen did not turn his head. "Yes,

I'm sure it was. Even Mother hadn't guessed. When Elias
should have been well, and wasn't, she asked him one morning
if he was troubled in his mind about something. He denied it,
but she pressed him over and over, and at last he said: 'I want
to marry your daughter.' 'That can't be!' she said—I can hear
it now, though I wasn't in the room. 'I know it can't,' Elias
said, 'and so I am troubled. I wouldn't have told you if you
hadn't made me.' 'But Harriet—you've told her.' 'No, she
doesn't even dream of it.' But I did; every night I dreamed of
being his wife, just as if he had asked me. Then Mother came
downstairs to me and said: 'You don't love Elias, do you?' I
looked right at her and said I did. Then she told me I must tell
you, that very evening after supper in the parlor, when we
always had an hour together: the only time we really had,
since you worked all day at the sawmill. I thought and thought
of how I would say it—how I would begin, I mean—and then
gave up; I knew I couldn't. So I wrote the letter."

"And locked the door."

"One door. I did that before supper, and folded the key in
my handkerchief. The other door I didn't lock till I saw you
opening the envelope. You were smiling; I suppose you
thought it was a joke, or one of my little poems. Then I
couldn't wait. I ran out and locked the north door behind me,
and took both keys to Mother. I said: 'I'm going up to my
room, and you mustn't let Stephen out of there till he promises
to behave.' "

"Behave." He repeated the word tonelessly.

"Because I knew. I was hardly upstairs before I heard you
screaming 'Harriet! Harriet!', like a madman. It was horrible
to hear. And yet I didn't hate it. It was what I knew would
happen. It had to, almost."

"Almost. I'm still ashamed."

"Don't be. It didn't matter even then. My mind was quite
made up."

"It didn't matter how I felt? That I was like the others? But I
wasn't like the others; I was worse. I've never told you what
came into my head as I read what you wrote. That was brief;
it came like a bullet. 'Dear Stephen: I am going to marry Elias.

I love you. Harriet.' But something else came with it, something that hurt still more. I knew you had been carrying his food to him, and making his bed."

"No. He made that."

"Well, you had been in there, again and again. And I hadn't liked it much. But before this I didn't know why. The thought that came like a second bullet, like a poisoned arrow, was of Amnon."

"Amnon?" She was puzzled for a moment.

"You know. Absalom's half-brother, in the Bible. He was sick for love of Tamar, his half-sister, and didn't know what to do about it until it was put into his mind that he should take to bed and call for Tamar to bring him good things to eat. She brought them, and while she was in there he—"

Stephen didn't know how to go on. But it wasn't necessary. She remembered.

"And then," she said, "the first minute after that was over, 'the hatred with which he hated her was greater than the love with which he had loved her.' And he sent her away like a dirty thing that he could never touch or see again. But Absalom, her own brother, took his time and killed Amnon. And King David, the father of all three— Oh, Stephen, how could you have thought of those? You knew it wasn't like that. You knew—"

"I do now," he said, "but then I was—what did you say?—a madman. Yes, I believe I was. All I could think of was you in that room, close to his bed—"

"Elias wasn't pretending to be sick. He *was* sick. And he was not your half-brother, unless all men are."

"But you were my own sister."

"Were?"

"Are." He reached to pat her hand, but she removed it. "You won't forgive me."

She waited, watching the tops of weeds where insects, dizzy with the heat, hovered uncertainly, insanely. "Yes, because you forgave *me*. You came to the wedding. And you didn't tell me then this terrible thing you thought. If you had—"

"Well?"

"I'd have died."

"Harriet!"

"Oh, I won't now. Nothing can kill me any more than I've been killed."

"Poor girl." Her hand came back to where it had been, and he touched it.

But she was thinking, and scarcely noticed. "Stephen, it was so different!"

"I'm sure it was."

"I mean, nothing happened to make him hate me. Nothing ever did. Day after day we looked at each other, and some days that was all. We said so little, we must have been afraid to talk. There was that rule, you know, about Mission boys being silent on the village street, as if they were mutes, or had had their tongues cut out. And then for one of them to be in somebody's *house*—that was hard for Elias. And yet he talked to Mother. She said he did. He told her about down here." Harriet looked far to the left, where trees along a creek dozed in the sun. "He was homesick for Georgia."

Stephen looked away too, trying to see this land—but they had left the hilly part—as Harriet had seen it.

"Will you miss it much? Will they?" He nodded backward toward the sleeping boys.

"We shall miss Elias."

Then for the first time she really wept. All at once the tears came, all at once her face, which she never lifted her hands to cover, grew ugly with grief as it stared, contorted, straight ahead over the horses' backs.

Stephen could not take his eyes from the dreadful sight. To him it was not dreadful; it was good, or it would lead to good. These tears, which she didn't wipe away—how could there be so many?—were washing something out of her, were carrying off whatever made her strange and still, like someone he had never known. The thing that made her ugly now would end by making her beautiful again. His own sister, from whom he had never had any secrets.

"I know you will," he said at last. "Tell me more about him."

She was suddenly quiet.

"I told you how he died."

"Yes, but—"

"No more now. Please, Stephen, let me just remember. He was so pleasant—you never knew how pleasant. Or how serious, how good."

Stephen winced at one thing *he* remembered. That night at home, when his mother unlocked the parlor door. He rushed by her without a word and went out to find the Fowler boys. They had said more than once that any Indian who took liberties with a town girl ought to be burned and hung and shot. He found them, the loud-mouths, and they burned an effigy of Elias right on the green. They couldn't make it look like him, so they yelled his name as they dangled it from a limb of the big locust tree beyond the flagpole. And they pretended they were shooting at it too, though they had no guns. Then Stephen came home, exhausted, and slept till noon the next day. Nobody in the family—his father, even—spoke of what had happened, or at any rate of his part in it. Harriet certainly didn't. Nor could he look at her that evening at supper. He was already beginning to feel ashamed; and to wonder if they had kept it from Elias, who wouldn't have heard anything if his window had been shut.

'You came to the wedding,' she had said. Ah, but that was months later, after both parents were reconciled, and after talk in the village had died down. Stephen wouldn't go to see Elias, who got well all at once, or claimed he did, and walked off, his back straight, his head level, his feet moving expertly through the grass, to his small hot room under the eaves; the school building wasn't half big enough for all the red, yellow, and brown boys it held. Stephen stayed out late every night—not with the Fowlers, though—and therefore saw little even of Harriet. For the first few weeks, anyhow. It was during those weeks that there was so much talk of her going to New Haven for the winter and living at Aunt Martha's. She might forget Elias that way, Mother was foolish enough to think; or she might meet some nice boy who would be better for her—better for them all. Stephen wasn't present at these conversations, yet he knew they happened. And he wasn't too much surprised to hear that Harriet had refused to go.

As if she were reading his mind, she said: "Even he wanted me to go."

"Elias? To Aunt Martha's?"

"Yes. He was afraid that all the real feeling had been on his side; that I was merely sorry for him, or merely being, as he called it, lovingkind. But I couldn't have borne it, being away from where he was. It was sad enough not seeing him every day now that he was back at school. It had got to be necessary that I should; I mean, it hurt not to. So I knew what it would be like at New Haven. I wouldn't sleep, I wouldn't eat. They would have to come and get me—what there was left. You understand now, don't you? I had to be with Elias till I died. I thought it would be me that died, I thought—"

She stopped, and Stephen, considering in silence how long a shadow Elias cast, glanced sidewise to see if tears had taken over. But she was still looking straight ahead: all the way to Mother's house, perhaps.

"You understand, don't you?" She scarcely more than whispered. "I can't be sorry I did anything I did. Other things might have been easier—might have—but I wouldn't change one hour of all that time, that time. It was hard to leave home—leave you—but I couldn't have stayed there and breathed. It was hard to be here some days; not all of his people wanted me; but then we built our house—"

"A good house," said Stephen. "It was all Mother talked about when she got back. Father, too; he seemed surprised that Indians could build a house. With corners, and with doors that banged."

"The boys banged them—oh, how could I be sorry that I have these boys? I wonder if I oughtn't to wake them. They're missing so much; they're not seeing the country."

"I wouldn't," said Stephen.

"Well, you're right."

"I was right about something else, too. I said they wouldn't cry all the way home."

"They hardly ever cry."

"I noticed that. I hope mine notice it. A perfect example."

"Perfect. 'Be ye therefore perfect.' Elias was. He never made a sound when—Stephen, I can't even be sorry he died. I mean, like that."

They were coming to a town. Harriet turned around to tell the boys, but they already knew it. Each of them was on his knees, his black hair stiff, his eyes enlarged and curious, studying the unkempt, the alien houses.

The Streamliner

THE MATTOON cut was even deeper than Amos remembered. The first snow of the year, falling thinly through this last grey hour of afternoon, kept on falling toward the tracks down there; he watched the flakes sail past him, then settle slowly, slowly, till they whitened the sunk roadbed. There was no wind, and Amos didn't think there would be much snow. But he was glad to have this much, since he wouldn't be coming home for Christmas. He had come now because he could, and the snow told him he had picked a perfect time to do it.

The Big Four train was already out of hearing toward St. Louis. From where he stood he could see both ways. Nothing but silence, west and north; nothing but signal lights burning cold and small in the distance. The Illinois Central lights, so low there in the cut, seemed to be falling with the flakes, seemed to be settling too. But of course they weren't. They were waiting for the streamliner that would take him north and home.

He started for the covered stairs—might as well go below and kill the next ten minutes near the station. When the streamliner came it would come fast.

He wondered, descending, whether anyone at home was thinking of him now; saying, perhaps, "Amos is in Mattoon."

Nobody, of course, would know he was climbing down these stairs with his big black suitcase. It would be as hard for them to know that as it was for him to guess how any of them looked now: standing where, doing what. It was still unreal, coming home. So for that matter was Baltimore, which he had left last night. His room there—he couldn't see that either, except as the place where he hadn't been homesick. He had boasted of this in letters. It was close to work, too. Very convenient. But now it was a long way off, as home still was, though he had only forty-four miles to go.

He came out onto the platform, set down his suitcases, and listened. Was that it?

A low, hoarse sound, somewhere to the south, as if a hemisphere had stirred and moaned in its sleep. Then silence again. Was that it? He stepped under a dim light and looked at his watch. It could be. But the sound had seemed so far away; as far away as Centralia, as Carbondale.

He heard it again—ugly and low down, close to the earth—yet louder now, and a little clearer, like a warning to be ready.

Then there it was, at some country crossing, in full cry. It disturbed the whole world with its honk—its honk! honk! as if great geese were flying—and now a long beam of light, lowering itself from the north star at which it had been pointed, swept the cold platform, blinding Amos.

Even then the streamliner wasn't here. Half a dozen people came out of the station door and looked where Amos looked; but the light was still to increase until it filled the cut, and the Diesel was still to bear down on them, looking bigger than all the space between these walls: bigger, said Amos, than Mattoon. For he knew. He had stood here before, excited by the threat that was, of course, no threat. It was nothing but the streamliner making sure that everybody understood how far it had been coming, and how fast. From New Orleans, from Memphis, and from Cairo. All that way, from pole to pole, like wild geese flying.

Hon-n-n-nk! The last crossing, south of town, then here it was, the whole groaning thing, on top of them, its headlight rolling one vast eye, rotating its terrible beam as if in search of dark towns to devour in unknown country under the Great Dipper low ahead.

As the long cars slid to a stop and doors, opening, poured their warm light on the snow, Amos trembled with an excitement for which nothing had prepared him.

He had done this before—waited to get on and find the seat where he would spend those minutes between here and Champaign—yet never with the sense of doom that now came down upon him. Not doom, either, if doom suggested death. But the importance of it, the power! This mighty thing, moaning through the night and snow, to take him home! He was coming on a visit—just five days—and North America knew it, and said so.

Honk! Honk! He was in his seat now, by the black window out of which he could see nothing, and the engine had picked up all the speed it lost by stopping at Mattoon. Coles County, Douglas, and then Champaign. He did not need to see the flying farms. He knew they were there. Tuscola—he watched its lights stream by, but he would have recognized them with his eyes shut. Then more darkness till Champaign. But in that darkness how many places, swimming in prairie distance, he identified with half-open lips as the streamliner under and about him, behind him and before him, sang its ponderous song.

His father would be opening the thick gold watch his own father gave him forty years ago, and saying—maybe with a glance out of the parlor window—"Amos'll be here in no time."

His mother, stooping to inspect the oven where perhaps corn bread was browning, answered without looking up: "Maybe the train is late. But I didn't want supper to be late. This bread—it'll be ready when it should be."

Constance, coming downstairs buttoning her skirt at the waist, both hands busy on her left side, laughed at what she heard. "Who knows? He might have missed connections at Mattoon. But then he would have telephoned. He knows the number; he still does." She was teasing them and him.

Arthur and Frank were parking by the station. Frank said:

"Here, this is a good close place. That grip of his—heavy as a house—I bet he brought it full. The snow—it's stopping, damn it."

"No it isn't."

Then they argued.

The snow, thought Amos, *was* thinning out. He would tell them they were both right.

But how did he know what Arthur and Frank were saying? What Constance, what his mother had just said? Why did he assume that the boys had driven over alone to meet him? Not all of them. Just these.

Assume? He knew. He was sure he did, and that he heard the car door bang. Then Frank said: "Let's stay outside till we hear the train." But Arthur: "No—through and under—the last track, the express track. Come on."

And at the same time, two miles away, Constance yawned. "When did you say big brother was arriving?"

"You're only pretending not to be excited like the rest of us," said her mother—his mother. "I know you. And me. I was that way once. Here—put the butter on, and the glasses."

He heard it all, and his heart beat as it would never have done in the old days when he was home, the old days before last June: a long time for the first one who had gone to stay away.

The Diesel, ramming through the darkness, had smelled Champaign ahead; it sent forth hoarse and hungry cries—no longer a bird now, but a bull-necked beast that nothing could stop or slow as it advanced on its belly, searching out destinations where no destinations were except as it decided.

Five minutes; four minutes; three.

Amos thought: It is wonderful, how I heard them. He couldn't any more; even the streamliner, its power cut off, was coasting in, past Green Street, past Springfield Avenue; only a minute now.

But in this drowning minute Amos saw if he did not hear: saw everything at home as it had always been, and as it still was even with him gone. For five days he would be a part of what he saw; but only for those days. His father would con-

tinue then, as he was doing now, to peer at the thermostat
above the bookcase, making sure the house was warm enough
to sit down in. After that, wiping his bifocals, he would walk
from room to room, seeing how things were; visiting the
kitchen last, to sharpen the carving knife and with its per-
fected edge to threaten whatever cat looked up at him from
the linoleum. Amos supposed there was a new cat now; but
there would be a cat, rescued from the alley by Frank or
Arthur, who complained without cause that their mother—his
mother—was indifferent to four-footed orphans. She seemed
indifferent but wasn't; it was she who fed them, and remembered to let them in. Constance would never cease to set the
table as she did tonight: with flourishes, as if to suggest a more
fashionable board, a more splendid spread of linen than was
here, yet this would do, because it was their own, and she
freely consented to be one of them as long as no one forgot
that she was who she was. Later in the evening, when the boys
had gone upstairs and she was in her room—what then? Amos
knew how quiet things became; and how in the morning noise
resumed; how it did every morning, and how when the mail-
man came his mother was always there to take the letters and
circulars before they could be put in the box. The car in the
garage, the front door mat, the telephone book hanging in the
hall corner with a green pencil attached, the sliding doors,
one of which never worked without an effort, that shut off the
downstairs guest room except when special company was
there—he saw all these as if he were home already. He saw
them as no one there could see them: close up, yet far away, as
if a stranger saw them.

But he was not a stranger.

He was, though, if a while ago these things had been unreal.

Now they were so real that he could see nothing else: no
Big Four train going east again, no Cincinnati, no Baltimore,
no lonely room where he got up each morning and made ready
for work.

He was so homesick he scarcely could stand up. Yet he
must, for the streamliner was gliding to full rest, and people
with their coats on stood at both the doors. To know what

homesickness was he had needed merely to come home. And he wasn't there yet. Tonight, tomorrow, it would be worse. And the third day, the fourth. Then the fifth. He wondered how anybody ever did it—went away the second time.

Arthur and Frank, their breaths white before them, came on a run, waving, and stopped where Amos would descend.

And beyond them came the other three, more slowly, Constance last. She wore a new bright-red beret.

They stood in a row, their faces up, till the train stopped absolutely.

"You *all* met me!" said Amos, kissing his mother first. "All of you. All five."

"Why not?" said Constance. "Big brother think it's wrong?"

He shook his head.

Wild Justice

"WILD JUSTICE? But justice is always wild. Dig Job out of his grave; ask him. God's justice—the only one there really is—it wasn't orderly for Job. There were no lawyers then; no indictment; no due process. It was a whirlwind; and it never justified itself. It looked to Job like what his lordship says revenge is. Wild justice? Well, of course!"

He didn't want to sound excited, but he knew he did. Horace was the last man who should realize how deeply he had thought about this matter. He might be giving himself away. It wasn't time for that; not quite. They were in the car and Horace was driving; exactly as he had planned; but it was twenty miles to the high curve at Pownal where he would jump and Horace wouldn't. Because he couldn't. The door on that side wouldn't open. And neither could Horace, when he saw what was happening, turn back the wheel; it would be locked tight, like the door; and like the accelerator, which would stick, or seem to stick, and take him over, over, over, six hundred and forty feet—it was enough, he guessed. Horace would have been driving his friend's new car; plainly, that would be how it was; and some might even sympathize with the owner. Three thousand dollars' worth of metal gone like that! It was a good investment, though. Nobody knew how good.

"God's justice, yes." Horace answered readily, as if he had thought about it too. You never could surprise Horace. Except that soon he was to have the surprise of his life. His life! Benny could hardly control the laughter that went racing through his lungs. "But no man knows what that is. Those who claim to are the dangerous ones. You understand—they're mad."

Why were they talking about this? They had started off quietly, like old times; and then he quoted Bacon. "Revenge is a kind of wild justice." Apropos of nothing he had said the words. He should have let Horace go on talking about his infernal family—Helen this, and Robert that—and about the silly work he did so well. It wasn't work for Horace; nothing was hard for him. Everything paid; everything turned out right. And this was the way it had been from the first, from the time they were boys; and then young men; then men. No grinding up steep grades; no grit of disappointment; no failure, even temporary. Nobody dear to him had ever died. All smooth, all smug, all willingness to help whoever was less lucky. Thank God, though, Benny Lane had never taken help; had never even let it seem he needed any. Horace believed he was happy too.

And now he really was. For who could have planned this as he had? The strip of lath that he would manage with his feet, prying and pressing the accelerator down just when they got to Pownal curve. It was the perfect length, and after the accident it wouldn't be there any more; it wouldn't stay in place. The wheel and the door—those took mechanical ability, those took some time and study. Not the door so much as the wheel. That little ratchet, he was proud of it; he wanted even now to

demonstrate how it would work. He had only to bend forward over Horace's knee and click a button on the dash.
"What's that for?"—he could hear Horace saying it now. And
then it would be time to tell him. He would already have given
the wheel a swing; and even as he did so he would begin his
speech. Not long, but clear. Decisive, those three sentences.
Then out of the car—one jump, he had practiced it, he knew
just where to place his right foot, then his left—as Horace, not
so calm for once, so knowing, or so cool, went down and
down. Six hundred and forty feet, by the contour map. That
was enough for Horace.

"Mad? Then God's mad, too." He didn't mean this, but he
had to say something. Or he did mean it, perhaps. Oh, well, it
didn't matter.

"No," said Horace. He had just lit a cigarette, but he flipped
it out of the window. "Impossible. We can't imagine it."
The "we," said Benny to himself, was most offensive. We
can't. Who can't? How did Horace decide such things for
others? He always was that way. "We just don't know," he
said sometimes. Meaning, Benny supposed, himself and all the
wise men in the world. Too bad, but we don't know. I'm
telling such as you that even we on top can't see so far. Down
there, my friend, where you live—

"Ha!" He laughed aloud, thinking how soon it would be
Horace way down there, not him.

He shouldn't have done it; for Horace, startled, suddenly
slowed the car up; suddenly stopped.

"What's wrong?" Horace was sitting there so solemnly; it
was ridiculous.

"I shouldn't have thrown that out. A dry summer, and the
signs say—listen, Benny, let's back up; it might have landed in
leaves or something. How's the road around the curve? Lean
out and see."

"I'll do nothing of the sort! And you won't either! Signs!
Don't be a sissy!" He shouldn't sound so furious, but he knew
he did.

Horace, as if he had expected this, drew off the pavement
and touched the ignition key. The motor became silent, like

the hot blue sky above them. They were on the level stretch this side of where the mountains really started to pile up. All the way to Canada they rolled, enclosing a hundred valleys where this car, or any car, if not driven well, or if defective—doctored—

"Horace! What now? You fool, keep going!" He knew it was a mistake to lose his temper. But here they were, three miles from high ground, and six more from Pownal Summit.

"I'll take care of it myself," said Horace. "Don't you bother." And he made a move to open the door beside him.

It didn't work, of course. Now what?

Horace didn't look alarmed. "It's stuck," he said, twisting the handle both ways. "Have you been having trouble with it?" He reached through and tried the outer handle; pushed the rubber button on the sill; pulled it up again; then pressed against the whole door, knocking it with his open hand. "Did you lock it? Some new way? I never know about these things."

The idiot! So noble, too, not noticing the little fact that he had been called a fool. You would think he had no ears. A wooden man. Well, that was it. That was exactly why—

"Benny," said Horace.

"What?"

"Won't you get out and see?"

"What! Here?" It was the wrong place. They were wasting time.

"Then I'll climb over you."

"Oh no, you won't! What difference does it make? You know damn well that cigarette—"

"Benny." Horace looked directly at him; he hadn't been doing so, but now he did. "Please get out. I'll be right back. It isn't far; and while I'm gone, maybe you can discover what the matter is with this." He meant the door.

"What's the matter with *you?*" Benny was yelling. He knew he shouldn't, yet there was satisfaction in it.

"Benny. Please get out."

He could have struck him, he could have strangled him. But that was not the way. He must be careful after all. He must hold on to himself. A little patience—but not like Horace's, not dead like that, not stupid, not disgusting—a little patience, just a little; then success. All right, he'd manage.

He opened his own door, suddenly, and slid out. "Come on, then."

Horace came.

There they stood facing each other.

"Well, why don't you go and see the forest fire? Do you smell smoke? I think I do. Run, don't walk, to the nearest hydrant." Sarcasm was better. He liked his own voice, delivering it this quiet way. At least he hoped it was quiet.

Horace backed away from him. A car passed, and Horace waved at the driver; but wasn't seen. He turned his head, then looked back into Benny's eyes. He was nervous now. He was even scared, thought Benny. Scared of what? This wasn't the place. Yet there could be no doubt of it. The damn fool was afraid.

Horace backed another step, twisted a foot in the gravel, and started running.

"Here!" screamed Benny. "Come back, come back!" He knew he wouldn't see Horace again; never alone, like this. "Come back! I wasn't going to kill you here!"

Now why did he say that? Had Horace heard? He was around the corner now, he was out of sight. Maybe he hadn't heard.

Even if he hadn't, though, something was clear as a bell. Horace was terrified. The cigarette? That wasn't it, and never had been. He was running away to tell somebody. Due process. Tame justice. Horace's kind.

Now what?

The sky was hot and blue. There wasn't a wisp of wind. A few cars passed, paying Benny no attention. The mountains lay off there like sleeping mice.

His legs gave way and he went down. "Fool, fool," he whispered to the weeds; they smelled of tar and sunshine. "Fool!" He didn't mean his friend.

Not Like Tom

"IT'S NICE TO TALK ENGLISH," she said. "The wise woman knows everything but English." She turned her head slowly on the pillow and smiled uncertainly, as if trying something out. Only her lips had any color in them; the wise woman had seen to that.

"Not everything," said Scoville. He sat a little distance from the bed, his raincoat over his knees, his long light hair in a tangle of which he still seemed unconscious. He had walked into the room with eyes only for her; not for the narrow white walls or the one window down which water was streaming. "I've asked a doctor to come in."

She had turned her head away, perhaps because the intensity of his brown eyes was hard to bear. But now she brought it back, alarmed. "Oh, Scoville! Not an American doctor."

"Veritably French," he said. "He doesn't know a soul outside of Paris, and he doesn't speak one word of your favorite language."

"That's good," said Linda weakly. "I'll be glad for once. But you didn't need to do it. I'm all right."

"May I see the baby?"

She closed her eyes, as if the problem were too difficult. "I think not. I don't even know where she keeps him. Do you hear anything?"

Neither of them heard anything but the rain. Madame Féger, who let him in, had disappeared down a dark passage and doubtless was beyond recall.

"Tomorrow, maybe. I'll come earlier. Or later."

She looked at him, then at the ceiling. "Scoville, dear. You musn't go to so much trouble. You've been too good to me; I think you saved my life."

251

"I know I did." Only Scoville could have said it. "But any-body would have. A valuable life; two lives, in fact. I haven't heard from Tom."

"I have. He's flying back tomorrow."

He studied her absent-mindedly. "Then I won't come."

A tear formed in her eye and rolled down on to the pillow. "Scoville, dear." She attempted a smile. "You're too good to be true."

After a while he said: "And so you never loved me."

"I do love you."

"Not like Tom."

He shouldn't be saying this again. But since he had, it was easier to say: "No, not like Tom."

He shifted the coat on his lap, carelessly, so that one sleeve drooped to the floor. He looked at the glass of water on the table by her side. He considered the extra blanket, folded at the foot of the bed. "Are you warm enough?"

"Oh, yes. Too warm if anything. But she said I must keep this on."

"The water—is it fresh?"

"I think so. I'm not thirsty. I'm all right, dear."

"And so you never loved me. I'm too good." He didn't laugh, denying it.

She decided to pretend she was asleep. He would go then, unless he thought he ought to wait for Madame Féger to come back. He might do that, of course. But she would risk it.

"Linda." She heard him say it twice, and didn't stir.

"Linda." Then he left; but when he stood up she felt him moving the extra blanket farther from her feet; and she had never known a door to close so softly.

She missed him, and felt lighter because she did. The air in the room began to move again, in currents she couldn't trace but was somehow certain of; they collided above her bed or slipped idly over one another, all but audible, all but rippling, like suspended streams. The waterfall on the window had been opaque, depressing; but now she saw through it as through a magic lantern, and made out Tom's plane tomorrow, glistening in thin blue skies above the Mediterranean. Tom was coming, and she wouldn't worry any more.

For a whole week she wouldn't worry. After that—but her thoughts, careering between these walls, failed to take her any farther. Another assignment, perhaps, and Tom would be off again. But that wasn't it. Tom himself—how unlike Scoville he was, how not to be counted on. When he knew all this—she listened for the wise woman, who might be coming with the baby—he would marry her; like a shot he would, and shower her with belated kisses. And yet that wasn't it. She simply couldn't see ahead. She didn't think she had a future. A lifetime with Tom: how was one to imagine such a thing?

How, for instance, was one to explain him back home? Scoville they knew; he had followed her here; or rather, he made her come. She pretended she had plans to study music—anything to get away from Scoville so that she could think about him. It had seemed then that all she needed to do was think about him. Missing Scoville, she would know how good for her he was. So she came; and in a month he sailed too, on the same boat from New York; and Paris had become a hard place to breathe in.

"I know I did." Yes, he had saved her life; or at least he had found Madame Féger and made all the last-minute arrangements. She would never be sure what passed through his mind when she told him what was going to happen and insisted it must be kept absolutely secret—no doctor, no record of the thing that might turn up at home; not yet, anyway, not now, not until Tom came. Scoville disagreed, of course, and argued; but then he gave in and went to work as only Scoville could. Perhaps he had expected it; for him a baby would be logical, once he was able to believe that she and Tom—oh, she remembered how that had been, how all but impossible it was to convince him. For nothing had been clear to Scoville; every other friend knew, but he didn't. She had to be very explicit; had to say things she would never say to any other man; or woman either, no matter who the woman, wise or foolish.

She made an effort to imagine taking Tom back home; not now, but sometime. With the baby it was easy; but she couldn't see Tom in the living room, she couldn't hear them saying things to him. They wouldn't trust him, for he wasn't Scoville. They might like him, but he wouldn't ever seem to be their son-in-law.

She made the effort, then desisted. There was no use in it. How did she know, even, that Tom would still be here to take? The difficulty wasn't simple, a matter of him and them. First it was him and her. How long would she have Tom? How long, how long—

She knew his ways, and the memory of them, mingling with the words how long, how long, went round and round the room, under the grey ceiling that Madame Féger should have freshly whitewashed. A wonder Scoville hadn't thought of that. Although, of course, there wasn't time.

There never would be time for anything. The baby came too soon, at least by her own calculation; she hadn't finished thinking about Scoville, the very thing she crossed the sea to do, when Tom stepped in and stopped it; and now tomorrow was so soon, so soon. She admitted for the first time that she didn't know how he would feel about all this. She listened again for Madame's heavy step, and was almost thankful she couldn't hear it. She didn't know he would be glad. She thought so, but she didn't know. There wasn't a person in the world who knew his heart that well. If anybody did, she did. But unpredictability was his one vice.

His virtue, too. His charm.

She said the word aloud, and it was *lik*e a charm. The air in the room flowed down around her, bathing her breasts and face, cooling her knees beneath the blanket she had thought of throwing off. The blanket didn't weigh an ounce; and she herself, so light upon the mattress, weighed precisely nothing. She didn't care how long. As soon as Scoville left, poor dear, she had known everything. There wasn't any more to think about except how Tom would act tomorrow. Not the next day; not next year; but just tomorrow. That was riddle enough. She saw him already, through the weeping glass, high up in blue air, flying from the south. She didn't care how long, if she could last till then.

She knew she would. She really was all right. She felt so well, in fact, that she could weep as windows do, as that one did, because the world was kind and washed it. But the wise woman wouldn't understand. Here! she was coming. Sober now, and sad. Or sound asleep. Asleep was best, with the door opening that sudden way.

How could she, for whom no day was different from another, have known it would be Tom?

Consider Courage

THE LITTLE MALAYAN at the amusement center—or was he from Amoy?—stood exactly where he had stood last week and the week before, and the week before that. Lander, crossing over from the northeast corner of the intersection, made sure of this and quietly rejoiced. Ridiculously rejoiced. He had told no one he knew, not even his wife, about these periodic visits to the amusement center where an absurdly small Oriental made his living by two birds.

Tropio Birds, the fly-specked card in the window said. "They will take a dime from your fingers and bring you a good luck message. Come in and see the Tropio Birds." He had, two months ago, and here he was again, prepared to do it for the ninth time. He could never have explained.

Except, of course, that the bird-man always failed to recognize him, or pretended to fail. His dry little face, so perfectly oval, so perfectly yellow, never changed when Lander held out his dime. The black eyes merely dropped to one of the two cages; a thumb flicked open its wire door; and out hopped the bird, ascending by steps to a perch from which its long, thin bill could seize the coin. Then, while its master resumed his stare at the street whence new customers might be coming—but none ever came while Lander was there—the black-

and-yellow creature, slenderer than a robin and more neat, made its jerky way across the arched bridge that led to the castle. Castle was what Lander called it, but it was only a box with a door. Yet it was a charming box, made of reeds set close together; and it came to a sort of peak or cupola at the top. At any rate the bird opened the door with its beak, hopped over the threshold, fished among some folded papers on the floor, seemed to find one that was satisfactory, pecked at it, held it, hopped out again, closed the door, and returned toward Lander with his message of good luck. As a matter of fact it gave the tiny paper to its master, not to the tall stranger standing there; just as it had done with the dime—dropped it between two bamboo slats of the bridge, into the cupped hand waiting for it—before it opened the door. Lander noticed this the first day, and noticed subsequently how the procedure never changed.

Nothing ever changed. The two birds took their turns with the same knowing air; their owner waited for that next customer who never came; and the din of the amusement center, not to say the traffic of Broadway, went on as if no such island of silence existed in its midst. For this was one thing that had struck Lander from the first. The pinball machines might chunk and clatter all they liked; the smack of rifles in the shooting gallery might never cease; the pingpong games downstairs, and the barkers' voices by the front door, might compete with the hooting laughter of boys who looked through peep-holes and told the whole world what they saw; but the Tropio birds worked on in a silence so perfect that it annihilated noise. While Lander's eyes were on them his ears heard nothing at all, even in this outrageous corner of New York. And so with the movements of their little master. They were made with such a grace as ignored, rather than rebuked, the blatancies about him. They were such movements as suggested rest. They matched the parchment face upon whose delicate, tired features peace had settled—was it a thousand years ago?

Two words were always murmured at the close. "Your birthday?" But Lander, who the first time had answered and been given a sheet of paper with the zodiac printed at its top, no longer acknowledged the question. He knew by now what characteristics he possessed in consequence of having been born in Gemini. He was a "remarkable individual," a "dual personality" destined to be happy and miserable "almost in one breath"—a fiend, maybe, but then quite certainly a saint. He loved change; he yearned after knowledge; and moderation had no meaning for him, he was for "one extreme or the other." He was courteous and kind, though people who did not understand him thought him selfish. He was likely to marry "someone born abroad." As for occupation, he might be a bookkeeper or a poet. His "fortunate day" was Wednesday.

He had smiled at all this. Mariana's native town was the same as his, and it was no foreign town. Yet Wednesday was the day when, walking back from his lunch with Muller, he decided to follow Fifty-Second Street across the city and suddenly had seen the birds. Wednesday, therefore, was the day he came again: the next week, and every week since then. He had even taken to lying at the office about lunch. He was never free, they thought, on Wednesday. And he never was, except to come here. He was glad nobody knew.

Only one thing was never the same. The message. What would it be today? When he unfolded the miniature document, what would he read and then fold up again? His left coat pocket was stuffed with little wads of platitude which he would have a hard time defending against Mariana if she found them. They said such things as this: "The joy of living and the good will of those near and dear to you means more to your peace of mind than the trivial things of life." Or this, which for banality beat even that: "If you are searching for the impossible, this message will not help you, but sincere and honest effort will bring results beyond your expectations." That he should walk eight blocks to consult such an oracle! It said each time the same thing after all, however foolishly the phrasing differed. Life is earnest. Stop smiling, and Providence will love you. Good old Providence.

Now he was lying to himself. For in the same pocket with the others, folded there to be felt by thumb and finger, was last week's legend from the castle. He knew it by heart, and was saying it almost aloud:

> You are in danger. But the thing to fear—
> What is it? Do you know? For it is coming,
> Coming, it is closer, it is here
> Already—oh, the humming, humming—
> Listen! It was in you all the time!
> (Another day, sir, bring another dime.)

Lander watched the little Malayan as the bird went briskly about his business. Did he know about last week? Had he been waiting for this moment as Lander had been waiting, no matter how he pretended otherwise?

Not a flicker of interest was visible in any of those features: in the black eyes, in the yellow forehead with its tracery of fine lines, in the blasted cheeks which so patiently sustained the pressure of all past time upon them, in the small hands, the perfect hands that rested in each other as their owner, unblinking, gazed out on Fifty-Second Street. Not a flicker to show that he knew how much one message stood out—cried out—among the many he had seen delivered.

The bird was coming back.

"Tell me," said Lander, shifting to the left a few inches so that the eyes could not avoid him. But they did. "Tell me, can you read those slips? Do you know what they say? Does the bird really pick them out at random? Last week—"

It was no use. The bird was here anyway, and the message was being taken from its mouth.

"Your birthday?"

Lander, feeling like a fool, turned away with as much dignity as he could and went to stand by the window where the turtles were, the painted turtles with gold monograms on their small pathetic backs.

He opened the paper halfway, then looked over to see if by any chance the Chinese eyes were upon him.

They were, he thought, for the tenth part of an instant. Then they turned back into themselves; but not until they had darted a glance toward one of the pinball machines over which a young man slouched, apparently studying the figures under

the glass. Apparently, thought Lander, only apparently. For
the young man seemed excited about something. About me,
said Lander? About this?

Absurd. He was hardly more than a boy. He was waiting for
someone to come. A girl, wouldn't it be?

Lander finished opening the slip, and—there it was. He had
not been wrong. It was for him. He stared and read the words
again:

> No outward foe is ever to be feared.
> Such things as were not with you all the while—
> Lions, and thieves, and the supposed Weird
> That walks in wind and murders with its smile—
> You are in danger, but yourself is cause.
> Consider courage. It despises those.

He read them a third time—they were difficult—then suddenly looked over, past the mute countenance by the cages,
straight into the flushed eyes of the pinball boy.

But he was not a boy; not exactly, Lander thought. He was
young, and yet—

Lander, conquering his famous reserve, walked toward the
machine.

"Look here," he said. "Do you know anything about this?"
The paper had crumpled in his hand.

Was it embarrassment or pride that answered? Were the
blue eyes under the untidy hair finding it hard to look into
his? They did so, steadily.

"I ought to. I wrote it."

"*You* did?"

"And the other one, last week."

Lander looked back, incredulous, at the booth where the
birds were; and saw that something stranger yet was happening. Two new customers stood there, two girls, and one of
them was rummaging in her handbag for a dime.

"She won't get *this*—what you did," said the boy. "There
was only one of those."

Lander smoothed the slip out, folded it carefully, and put it
in his pocket. "I don't understand," he said. "You wrote this
for *me?* And got *him*—"

"But don't blame him. He palmed both papers, as a favor to me. The bird brought him the usual thing, and he substituted the unusual—it seemed so, did it? Unusual? Better than—"

"Better? Of course. But what it said—what the two of them said—"

"You were interested in that? The same thing, then. What I meant by better."

"But who are you, and how did you know?"

"I hang around here; I like it. I saw you the first time, and thought you would come again. When you kept on coming, I knew you were my man. My public. I don't mind admitting I'm a poet. But it's a hard trade these days. Nobody cares what poems say. They aren't necessary any more; they don't tell anybody anything. I thought if I could get you to listen, really listen, I'd be doing what no other poet has done since I was born. The few things I've had in magazines—I never heard from them. And the book I printed myself—it had some sale, but I never saw one page of it being read. I printed these for just one reader—you. I suppose you noticed the type was different. I had to crowd it on the slip."

"Yes, I think I did. But the main thing"—Lander looked sharply at the lad—"was what they were about."

"That's fine! That's what I meant!"

"But—well, you know—the—well, the danger."

The poet smiled. "It wasn't personal."

Lander didn't smile. Perhaps he was not relieved.

"Everybody's in that kind of danger. The important kind. It wasn't personal. Or if so, it was Socrates talking. His favorite idea—you didn't recognize it?"

"No."

"But you were interested? Worried, even?"

"Yes."

"Then it was good. That's what I mean by good—by better."

"I'm not a judge."

"They all say that. But you are. You just proved it. You read every word, and then—"

"Have you had lunch?"

"I don't eat much in the middle of the day. But if you do—"

"Not very much."

"You will be my guest."

"No—you."

"But I'm not poor. My old man stakes me."

They started out past the girls, one of whom was giggling. The little man was not amused. "Does your father—is *he* a judge?"

"Of me, certainly."

They were an odd pair, walking down to Lindy's.

The Little Place

OLD HENRY toiled down Eden Street, counting the blocks till he should be out of the business section and headed south toward home. He did this every evening on the way from work. But tonight, just as the lights were coming on, he lost his count. Something was different. He said to himself, half-way between Polk and Van Meter streets: "I don't remember any shoe shop here. Right on the sidewalk, too."

For so it seemed to him as he veered over to investigate. He didn't understand how he could be looking down Eden Street and yet into a shop. And in fact he wasn't; for in another minute he stood in front of a tall mirror, staring at himself, and heard a man's voice saying pleasantly: "The shoe shop is behind you."

He turned, and saw what so far he had seen but in reflection. It was surely the smallest shoe shop in the world: set back and in at a curious angle from the street, and occupying no more than a niche in the wall of store fronts he had been passing. There were no machines in it, and no rows of repaired shoes waiting to be called for. There was nothing but a narrow

cobbler's bench, with six or seven leather soles piled neatly on
it beside the customary tray of nails and an assortment of
knives, needles, and hammers. There were two lasts, of course,
the big one and the little one. And behind the bench, in the
poor light of an oil lamp, there sat a young man, smiling.

"Come in," he said. "There is room for one more—just one.
I saw you up the street, and hoped—"

"In the mirror you saw me." Old Henry shifted on his tired
feet, wondering why he wasted time this way.

"How else? I see everybody. But not everybody sees me.
Most of them see only themselves: as you did finally, but then
you had to."

"Yes, but before that I saw you—this place—not me."

"The glass could have turned a trifle."

Old Henry looked around him. "Been here long? I go by
every evening. I never—"

"No, I'm new. The reason I hoped you would come in was
that—forgive me—you looked tired."

"Always I am tired."

"I believe you."

"I am old."

"I believe you. And yet a fresh pair of soles might make you
forget it. I hoped—"

Old Henry looked away. "Nothing is the matter with my
shoes. My feet, either, except that they are old. A trick, was it,
to get business? Mind you, I am not a man of money."

"Then there will be no business. Now that you are here,
though, I could look your shoes over—mend a stitch here, put
in a nail there—for nothing. If you will take them off—"

"I think I better not."

"Here is a stool. Sit down."

Old Henry sat watching the hands of the cobbler as they
went nimbly over the soles they had helped to remove.

"You are right," mused the young man. "These are in fair
condition. And yet—here, for instance, I could make them
perfect." He pointed to cracks along the edges of the soles;
and before any protest was possible, pried them still wider
with a short, thick-bladed knife.

"Now!" said Old Henry. "What have you done?"

"Wait till you see what I *will* do," said the cobbler, humming to himself as he reached for the rest of his tools. Old Henry overheard this much:

> Weary come, Weary go.
> I am old, and I am slow,
> But I shall not be tired again,
> Though I walk in cold and rain.
> I am old, and do but creep,
> Yet all my bones have gone to sleep.
> How sweet a thing it is to know:
> Weary come, Weary go.

The cobbler, before he drew tight the last stitch in either sole, slipped between the layers of leather a thin piece of paper, making sure that it went in right side up. The right side was the printed side, for the old man saw lines of black words.

"What did you put in?" he asked.

"What you just heard," said the cobbler. "Now, with my compliments, goodnight."

Before Old Henry could say thank you he was on the street again, picking his way carefully toward the next intersection.

It was true. He wasn't tired—just yet. But that was because he had taken a little rest. Another block, or two or three, or nine or ten, and it would be the same as always. Pain everywhere; his joints hot; his heart heavy.

The cobbler saw three ragged boys running down Eden Street, dodging in and out among the adult pedestrians like so many hounds on a scent. They did this every evening, and as invariably was the case, the smallest of them trailed behind the other two. He was not only the smallest, he was lame; or if not lame exactly, he was handicapped in running by a weakness that showed as well in his pointed face and his abnormally large eyes. But it didn't occur to him that the others ought to let him overtake them. They never looked around.

Then here he was, his eyes larger still as he stared about the shop into which he had been whirled.

"Your name?" The cobbler asked it quietly.

"Tonio."

"A good name. But your shoes—they are not good. You cannot run."

"It isn't my shoes." He looked down. "I don't—I can't—"

"Let me see them, Tonio. Take them off."

The boy leaned and listened as the cobbler, turning the shoes over and over in his hands, sang softly to himself:

> The best is the worst,
> The last is the first.
> Tonio, Tonio, where will you fly?
>
> Only so far
> As the other ones are—
> Not to be better, not to go by.
>
> Oh, but you could,
> And come to a wood;
> A river; a mountain; the sea; the sky.
>
> Only so fast;
> Then each will be last.
> Once I am with them, oh, I can die.

"Die?" said the boy. "What are you putting in my soles? Why did you open them that way?"

"So many questions!" The cobbler laughed. "Good-by, Tonio. Hurry along now and catch up with those two. What are their names?"

But Tonio was gone.

A man with a dark hat stood in his place. He scowled at the cobbler, demanding to know where he was and why the mirror had misled him.

"Sit down there"—pointing to the stool—"and take them off. Your shoes."

The fellow took them off.

> One step,
> And then stand still:
> An ugly monument of will—
> Yet not the power—
> To move and kill.

> One lifted foot
> And then no more:
> A stiffened statue, set before
> This turning glass,
> This fading store.

Why did they sit there, doing what he said? Even this murderer, whom the words angered so much that he stood up suddenly and raised both arms as if to strike the singer down. But all that happened was that he found the shoes in his hands and felt himself rotating toward the sidewalk whence he had come.

He took one step, and then could not take another.

Hour after hour he stood, unable to stir, until a sharp-eyed man who had been watching him from across Eden Street came over and said: "What's up? You never gave us *this* headache before—stopping traffic."

Though it was midnight, a circle of the curious had formed. It included an old man and his staring daughter. It included three small boys, one of whose faces shone with so rapt a pleasure that it was strange the sharp-eyed man missed it as he glanced about him.

"Well," he turned back and said, "if you won't talk here, I know where you will. There is plenty we want to hear. Where you been hiding, Smithie? Come along. Lieutenant's orders—bring you in."

Still the man did not move. But with great difficulty, as if his throat were sore, he whispered: "In there—that shoe place—*he* did this to me."

"What shoe place?"

The eyes of the curious followed quickly.

"Behind the mirror—a *little* place—in *there*."

"What mirror? Where?"

There was none. The shop was gone.

"Are you a policeman?" Old Henry stepped forward, his daughter holding tightly to his arm. "That is—no complaint, understand you—but I had *my* shoes fixed in there tonight—

and look! I walked all the way back—it was a pleasure—made
her come too—to tell him—well—"

"Well, what?"

The only answer was a serene, uncomprehending smile as the
woman pulled her father out of reach and went back with him
down Eden Street.

"Like me," said Tonio. "I saw him, too. I was in there—just
for a little while, then I caught up with *them*."

But the other boys, no lovers of the police, were not to be
seen now. Tonio heard their running feet halfway to the next
corner and flew suddenly after them.

Some runner, thought the sharp-eyed man. His feet don't
touch the ground, they really don't.

But what was going on here?

"Anybody else know anything?" The sarcasm got what he
wanted, silence. "Break it up, then. Keep moving, all of you."

They melted away, and he was alone with the dark hat
again.

"I'll take *you* in if I have to carry you. Do I have to?"

Ten minutes later, with help from the station house, he
did.

The Lady Over the Wall

THE GREEN LAWN was their great land—for chipmunks, all
the world there was except for the clean holes, the size of a
silver dollar, down which they could disappear. Below ground,
certainly, there were passages and rooms: another world, and
perhaps for them the real one. But up here was where they
were seen; up here was where they mattered to the huge children for whom they were the summer sun's best plaything.
Light, thought the children, amused itself with openings in
trees, bird wings, and the backs of chipmunks—most of all

with those, whether they rippled along the irregular summits of stone walls or streaked like shadows over the cut grass, their stripes no more visible at that moment than the swiftest thought is, or the trembling of a doubt. But the stripes were there: an instant's hesitation, and light laughed in them again— those intense little bands of white and black which told everything about the creature beneath. He wore them as if he knew he did; and knew that one of them ran all the way forward to his almond-shaped inquisitive eye.

This was the eye that studied you from the stone wall if you stood quietly and watched. It watched you too, the back behind it arched, the whole coat quivering with readiness to run. Then, if you no more than lifted a hand, the dive—the liquid disappearance, as if mercury had poured—back, or down, or even up into the nearest aperture the granite offered. Of course he had known about the aperture; he had come out of it, his nose twitching, to inspect you in the first place; he had his plans, as you had your size, and your way of thundering when you stepped across the green lawn.

The walls seemed to be the end of his world. He may have scampered beyond them now and then, but he was never seen to do so; he, or any of his fellows. There were too many of them, the children's mother said; they climbed the stalks of the tiger lilies and nipped off not only the black seeds but the blossoms in their prime; they dug up bulbs in the border bed; they drilled their neat holes everywhere—particularly, she complained, in the nice grass about the front door stepping-stone. They were honeycombing the very threshold of home. One hole there might not have mattered; but now there were three, and more were possible. Any morning a new one could appear, made no one knew how, nor with what unimaginable energy, nor leading whither. They were another race, she said, preparing underground to take over all the world when they got numerous enough.

How serious was she? It was hard to say. She talked to them as if she thought they understood—scolding and stamping while they sat, ready to run as usual, and took her measure with their little almond eyes. Perhaps they liked her anger

better than they did the fleeting attention of men and children.
It was a sign that somebody really saw them and was aware of
what they did; of the fact that they worked as well as played.
She worked too, as gardener, in the same element with them:
roots, rocks, dirt, and sun and rain.

She never knew which one she scolded. The children may
have supposed she did, she sounded so personal; but there is no
way of telling chipmunks apart. They are many, and they are
one. Each is all; which is why any of them is so astonishing.
This is no less true of robins and wrens, but in those cases the
fact is not so laughable; nor so wonderful, depending on how
it is regarded.

Beyond the south wall another set of eyes considered what
went on. A single pair, perhaps, but this would not have been
easy to prove. They saw so much, unseen. For who but the
animals knew they were there? The chipmunks especially
knew it; and took it so much for granted that they never
paused or shivered, meeting that glance. Were they a woman's
eyes? They seemed so in their speed and softness, in their dark
size and speechless power. They were the light by which these
creatures lived; not the white sun, which saw all things at
once, but this light alone, that shone protectively, intelligently,
out of pupils almost as ancient as the sun. As the moon, certainly. They were more like the moon, the golden moon of
early evening, that sends down love instead of fire. The chipmunks frisked and chattered in such a radiance: subdued, and
yet sufficient to their life. Or so it might have appeared to
anyone capable of seeing the goddess of their nights and days.
They loved her in a half-light which the sun enclosed, and no
one therefore saw. None of the giant children, smiling at the
painted backs that bounced from stone to stone of the south
wall, guessed in what shadow—less light within more light—
they had their little being. Diana's shadow; yet Diana never
showed herself to be seen.

It was September now, and a fourth hole had appeared by
the steppingstone. They saw it one cool morning when dew
still sparkled on the grass. But it was the chipmunk that
sparkled—paused at the lip of the hole, his stripes flashing,

then flicked out of sight as if the earth had eaten him. Rather he was eating earth, said John, who went and told the rest. Not literally eating it; pawing it, rather, and pushing it, patting it, pressing it, until the tunnel down there was perfect; till there was no earth where earth had been, but a tube of dark air, descending slantwise to some chamber where even now, perhaps, maple seeds were being stored against the winter.

Was the slope to the front door being undermined? No one really thought so, yet all of them took pleasure in pretending that they did; John less than the others, for he believed it might be true. He hadn't forgotten his mother's first words when he went to her with the news: "Now we're in for it! That corner of the house will sink, and one of us, or maybe some visitor, will go down."

He watched the hole, and the turf around it, as a terrier would do; except that terriers have no concern for the contours of a lawn. They wait, but only for the coming forth of prey. John's vigil, to begin with at least, had something else in view. He looked for signs that the surface of the earth was changing. When he saw any, he knew what would have to be done.

He kept his air gun just inside the door, by the encyclopedia case. He even practiced with it, afternoons, in the vegetable garden; hitting clods, hitting small stones, hitting the lower leaves of the staked tomato plants. Then he would put the gun back in its place, always making sure its barrel was full of shot.

The days were getting shorter. It was dark now as soon as supper was finished, so that John had to take a flashlight with him when he made his last trip of inspection. He would send its beam in a wide circle about the hole, then draw it in and in until it rested at the center where there was nothing to see; nothing but a little shaft that turned after a few inches and went off in the direction of the house. He would stick the flashlight in as far as it would go, realizing, of course, that its rays would not bend and follow the intricacies of whatever passage was there, but hoping nevertheless that somehow the chipmunk would be warned that he was watched. Threatened, rather. For the boy was serious.

Tonight—it was the first evening of fall, and crisply cold— he had no sooner trained his light on the hole than he cried out so that all indoors could hear him: "Look! Something's fallen in!"

"What! The well?" The rest of them, come running out, teased him when they saw what he had seen: a ball of dry grass, with fine roots tangled in it, and even strands of hair, wedged in the passage, a few inches down where it turned and went parallel to the sod, or a little more than parallel, for even there it must keep going down if the deep chamber was ever to be reached.

"A bird's nest," somebody said. "I wonder how it got in so far." They pulled it out and tossed it under the Andromeda bush nearby. Remarkable, if the wind did it. Nothing else could have. Well!

But the next evening, as rain began to rustle in the shrubbery, there it was again; the same ball of grass and roots and hair, in the identical position it had occupied before. And John's flashlight found nothing under the Andromeda bush. Whatever it was, it had been dragged back into place. This *was* its place, he whispered to himself; and decided not to tell another soul.

After three more experiences of finding it there, however, he couldn't keep the secret any longer.

"Every night, you say?" His father questioned him sharply. "Then it's a plug. Something to close the hole with—keep warm with. I never heard of them doing this. You're the first to know; be careful now or you'll be famous. A flashlight, too!"

"Diabolical," put in his mother. "I tell you they mean business. They'll take over. Think of the little fiends down there, planning and planning. Regular engineers!"

They took John indoors with them and told him to forget. But he couldn't sleep that night for wondering where the plug went every morning. The chipmunks took it down, no doubt; then pushed it up at nightfall, as the air grew frosty. He agreed with his mother. Maybe she hadn't been serious, but he was. Devils and engineers.

The next night he slipped out before anyone was aware. The plug was in place, but it didn't look the same. He saw something like claws at its edge, and thought the whole object looked like an animal—a chipmunk, of course—that had rolled itself into a ball and gone to sleep, sacrificing its own comfort so that others might have more.

The flashlight trembled in his hand. He wanted to reach in, and yet he didn't.

He brought a stick and gently thrust it down. The ball, prodded, did not stir. He pushed harder. Still the same result. Then it was not alive. It was not even a chipmunk. He had only thought it was—with stripes, even, though they were dull and dirty.

His finger and thumb, finding their way in, came out at last with something which immediately he threw away a little distance. There it was on the damp grass. A chipmunk, but a dead one; dead a long while, and dry. Hardly more than a pelt. But it was recognizable. They kept their dead, those fiends, and used them to keep warm. What depths, what recesses, must multiply themselves down there! Rooms with balls of grass; then, when those didn't suffice, more rooms with mummies in them—entire generations, it might be, laid away for just such purposes as this. Or other purposes, not yet to be imagined. He put the carcass back and went indoors.

It was gone in the morning, and hours passed before any chipmunk showed itself about the hole. It was rarely that one did, yet John had to wait longer than usual behind the big maple tree where he sat with his gun.

Then one was there. The sun picked an opening in the high foliage and streamed straight down as the boy shut his eyes and fired. He shut his eyes because the small back had been so beautiful when the sun found it. There was a lesser light as well, but only the little beast knew that—he, and the brown eyes that watched him over the wall. The south wall. The soft eyes that no one saw. They closed as the gun clicked, and did not open for a minute.

272 MARK VAN DOREN

John's own eyes, wide with grief, told him how good his
aim had been. The chipmunk, curled on its side, kicked at its
belly as if that ought to remove whatever was the matter
there. But as John came slowly up the kicking ceased; and
when he looked down he saw nothing but a bright ball, still
streaked as if by nothing but the sun.

He stood and looked until his mother came.

"Why, John, you didn't *kill* one of them? You didn't mean
to, anyway." She saw his face, so serious, and hastened to add
this.

"I did mean to," he said. "The lawn—the honeycomb—
those devils down there."

"Oh!" she cried. "I said too much. I didn't"—then she
stopped. He mustn't think it had been too much of a mistake.
He mustn't know how fond of them she was. She really was.
She scolded them for fun.

"Now I'm sorry," he said, and turned away. His gun still lay
where he had dropped it, there by the tree.

"Of course you are."

She wondered if such things as this were punished. Only,
she decided, by having to remember. There wasn't any law.
There wasn't any person to enforce it.

The lady over the wall was looking this way even now. Or
was she there? Had she ever been there? Those eyes—they
might be nothing but two dark places in the pear-tree shade that
filled the corner of the paddock. Two centers where the shade
withdrew into itself, contemplating old wars against the sun.

A single tear formed in the shadows, slowly, and fell. It was
pear-shaped, and fell as fruit falls, except that it was clear sweet
water. Yellow jackets were busy in the tree, for the fruit was
ripening. Now and then a drop of nectar pattered down,
touching many leaves before it reached the ground. This drop,
whatever its origin, touched nothing. It fell as tears fall, when
death has come and there is nobody to punish.

His Waterfall

THE CABIN he lived in by the waterfall was full of noises he did not make himself: birds by day, wildcats by night, wind overhead in the high hemlocks or down here where he was—up there it sang and sighed, down here it pounded and whistled—and always, of course, the plunging stream. For that was the noise that never stopped, though he stopped hearing it sometimes. Or he thought he did; and then he became aware of the under-noises. Not the full roar, the everlasting splash, the gurgle in the potholes—no, not those, but certain hidden sounds that never failed to startle him, so that he sat and listened doubly hard, waiting for them to repeat themselves, though this they refused to do, at least until he had forgotten to expect them.

He called them under-noises because he was not sure he ever really heard them. It was more like having heard them, for they were gone at once and nothing of them remained, nothing that he could recall by trying to, by listening with the same ears that received them—if they *had* been received, if they hadn't sounded inside his own head. He hated to admit this, but it seemed possible. For nothing he could think of out there would have had the wherewithal to cause them.

For instance, the bell. At least he named it that, though he had never heard any bell like it: one so small, so single-toned, so crystal-sudden, as if glass had been struck, been tapped, by some agency that scarcely knew it did so, some passing hand whose owner's mind was altogether elsewhere. The chief thing about the bell was the isolation at the center of which it sounded: a hush, a vacuum, a cessation, then there it was, concealed inside, folded away, like a diamond in a casket with

273

no exterior, but a casket nevertheless, a container, a cube or
sphere of inarticulate space, of hollowed-out extension.

"Cling" it would go, or "pling!"—he couldn't have spelled
it, any more than he could have assigned it to a given note in
the scale; it was beyond alphabets, it was superior to music—
not better, he meant, but above it, high over it: alien to its
range. Some days he fancied that a drop of water, separated
from the rest, had found its way to a small stone that was not
stone but glass, natural glass; or if stone, then semiprecious,
even precious, with tongues of emerald, of ruby, ready in it to
testify concerning their sly presence somewhere down the
slope the torrent struck. The waterfall was neither broad nor
high; it was nothing that strangers came to see, but it was
constant, winter and summer, and he lived among the many
sounds it made; they nourished him, sleeping or waking,
almost as much as the berries and meat he consumed to keep
his body strong. The many sounds: but this one of the bell was
always strange and new, like something he had never heard
before, though he knew he had. There it would be—"tling!"—
and perhaps he would rush out to identify its source. Too late,
however, for it did not call again. A kind of call it certainly
was; if not to him, then to someone or something capable of
knowing what it meant. He would never have that knowledge,
he had long ago decided; but the decision did not kill his
curiosity.

Or there was the crescendo, equally sudden, equally unannounced, of the cascade itself, as if more water all at once
came over from the pond above and dumped itself inconti-
nently, improvidently, upon the broken rocks below. There
would be a pronounced increase of the swishing sound that
had been so steadily there: the sound, he thought, of brushes
passing over other brushes, of liquid shivering into spray, of
water infinitely dividing. This was so incessant a sound that his
ears took it for granted and scarcely gave it notice, except at
these moments when something multiplied it. Yet he knew
that nothing did. He walked out many a time and proved this.
The flow was unaltering in its volume. No impediment—no
log caught on the brink, no mass of floating leaves—had held
the water back, then let it go. Nor had a gust of wind, buffet-

ing the fall, enlarged the scope of its power to reach his ears: produced, actually, more sound, regardless of who was here or not here to be aware. At first he had been certain it was that: a breeze had swept the instrument, bringing him noisier news of its existence. There was no such breeze, however, nor had the lazy wind that blew shifted its direction. No, it was not to be explained, this rise and fall of quantity, this sudden increment of music, followed instantly by just as sudden a withdrawal to the norm. On windy days of course it happened, and easily was understood. What startled him was the variation without cause, as if a waterfall, like any other living thing, had of its own nature contrived to conquer monotony. The same tone forever was intolerable even to the element that played it without knowing that it did.

Nevertheless, he told himself, there was something deep inside—deeper than the "whish-sh-sh," deeper even than the "whing!", the delicate bell—something was in there that couldn't change if it tried. The bell rang, then did not ring; the hiss of the spray increased, decreased; but this further music, since it was composed after all of inaudible sound, did not because it could not modulate. Inaudible sound: he ought to reject the thought, but instead he cherished it. For in it lay the secret by which he lived. The principle of so much sound, the soul of so much turmoil, was silence: a silence singing to itself forever and ever. In January, when the fall froze over, there was a muffled voice behind the heap of ice; some water, that is to say, continued to come over, and as it did so muttered bravely of what it would do when it was free. But that was not it exactly; indeed it was not that at all. For the sound he meant was farther down and deeper in; was so in summer too, when the heard music flourished in full cry; was eternally there, a thread of invisible silver on which the known sounds were beaded, an arc of motion whose laws the symphony obeyed. But what was there, or where it was, he couldn't have said, any more than a child can say what makes it happy, or point to where it feels good. The waterfall, his very life, spoke not so much to him as for him: spoke its own piece, sang its own song, which he was content to comprehend without benefit of brain or ear.